THE HAMPTON PASSION

Recent Titles by Julie Ellis from Severn House

THE HAMPTON SAGA

THE HAMPTON HERITAGE
THE HAMPTON WOMEN
THE HAMPTON PASSION

BEST FRIENDS
THE GENEVA RENDEZVOUS
THE HOUSE ON THE LAKE
SECOND TIME AROUND
SINGLE MOTHER
VILLA FONTAINE
WHEN THE SUMMER PEOPLE HAVE GONE

THE HAMPTON PASSION

Julie Ellis

This first world edition published in Great Britain 2001 by
SEVERN HOUSE PUBLISHERS LTD of
9–15 High Street, Sutton, Surrey SM1 1DF.
This first world edition published in the USA 2001 by
SEVERN HOUSE PUBLISHERS INC. of
595 Madison Avenue, New York, NY 10022.

British Library Cataloguing in Publication Data

Ellis, Julie
The Hampton passion
1. Romantic suspense novels
I. Title
813.5′4 [F]

ISBN 0–7278–5679–0

All situations in this publication are fictitious and
any resemblance to living persons is purely coincidental.

Typeset by Palimpsest Book Production Limited,
Polmont, Stirlingshire, Scotland.
Printed and bound in Great Britain by
MPG Books Ltd, Bodmin, Cornwall.

For all my friends in Montauk –
where much of *The Hampton Passion* was written –
and for Hero and Pirate,
who provided many happy moments

HECK-OUT RECEIPT
'ELCOME TO BUCKIE LIBRARY
ate: Saturday, August 08, 2015
me: 12:02 PM

em ID: 20270405
tle: The kilt maker
ue date: 05/09/2015 23:59

em ID: 20060464
tle: Hampton passion
ue date: 05/09/2015 23:59

otal items: 2
ank you for using the self issue terminal

One

Liz Hampton Adams lingered over coffee in the charming octangular breakfast room of her Italian-style residence, built within sight of Hampton House – where her mother and father lived with her retarded but much loved brother Francis – and tried to focus on the Atlanta *Constitution*. Mary Lou had brought her the newspaper along with the mail. The cluster of letters sat ignored beside her coffee cup. This morning her mind was haunted by an imminent confrontation with her mother.

Faint, half-moon shadows beneath her restless blue eyes emphasized her high cheekbones, the delicate oval of her face. The passionate Hampton mouth slightly parted, as though already framing the words that were certain to jolt her mother when they were voiced. Her slender shoulders hunched in tension, she read the front-page stories while she sipped the strong, chicory-laced coffee.

This morning the usual tales of terrorism across the nation were supplanted by reports of Calvin Coolidge's inauguration yesterday. In accordance with the President's wishes the ceremony had been unprecedentedly brief, the parade short and drab. Aware of the austerity of the occasion, more than a score of governors had either declined invitations or had not shown up. Color had been added to the day by the new Vice-President, "cussing" Brigadier General Dawes, who had shocked and angered many senators in his address attacking the rule that allowed almost unlimited debate. He had gone on to swear in the twenty-four new senators in a body instead of in the conventional groups of three.

Mama had been too embroiled in business at the mill to join Papa in Washington for this inauguration, as was her custom. But this morning Mama would have to make time to hear her say that she was preparing to divorce Victor. Tonight – if he was home, she thought bitterly – she would tell Victor.

For her mother her life had been for ever settled once she was married. Marriage was a comfortable, safe pigeonhole. Mama didn't have to worry about her anymore. But people were not designed to live in pigeonholes.

"More coffee, Miss Liz?" Mary Lou's warm, cheerful voice jarred Liz from her introspection. Mary Lou stood at her side with the coffee pot poised to pour.

"Please, Mary Lou."

Another cup of coffee would delay the meeting with her mother.

Liz returned her attention to the *Constitution*. The newspapers were always full of terrible stories. Marshal Foch reported the Germans were arming for another world war. Ramsay MacDonald predicted another war before 1950 unless the League of Nations grew strong enough to maintain the peace. In the United States, Harry Sinclair of Sinclair Oil warned that crude oil reserves would be exhausted by the close of 1926.

Liz abandoned the paper. This morning her personal crisis took precedence over the troubles of the world. To her mother, divorce bordered on scandal. A senator's family must be above reproach. Particularly a senator with presidential aspirations.

She knew about Papa's determination to fulfill the General's dream of a Hampton in the White House. Ever since the General – her great-grandfather – had died, Papa had plotted his life to reach that goal. Both he and Jim Russell, partners in this dream, had read law under Judge Mason until they were eligible to practice law. An important part of Papa's climb to the White House.

But the family had survived scandal before, Liz recalled. What about Papa's first wife, who had killed her lover and raced off to Paris to die in a fire only a few months later? Tina's disgrace had not kept Papa from climbing the political ladder.

Divorce was not a scandal these days. Lots of people were divorcing. This was 1925. Even some of the girls she had known at Washington Seminary were divorced. Adrienne, from her class. Margaret Mitchell, who had been a grade behind them, divorced her husband, Berrien Upshaw, last year. Berrien left Margaret and Atlanta a few months after their wedding in 1922. Gossip said – with varied conjectures as to the reason – that Margaret now slept with a loaded pistol beside her bed. Adrienne told her Margaret was seeing a lot of John Marsh, who had been best man at her wedding.

Mama was so wrapped up in the mill she didn't realize her daughter's marriage was falling apart. Victor wasn't married to her; he was married to his patients and to Grady Hospital and to the children's clinic. He came home to sleep and change clothes.

Too many nights she ate alone. After dinner she sat alone in the library. She read detective stories. She did crossword puzzles. She listened to the radio. She was sick to death of all their broken social engagements because at the last moment Victor was called to the hospital or to a patient's bedside. Even when they entertained, she could never be sure he'd be home. How many times had he been called away from a dinner party before the first course was served?

She was bored with bridge parties and teas and Junior League luncheons. She flinched, hearing in her mind the repetitious conversations:

"Did you see John Barrymore in Beau Brummel*? Wasn't he just fascinating?"*

"You must come over and play mah-jong some evening. It's the cat's meow!"

"Did you hear about the girl who died in that dance marathon up in Chicago?" Or New York or San Francisco or Boston. "Wasn't it awful?"

When was the last time Vic made love to her? Sometimes

she suspected he looked on that as an obligation. How could a man who had been so passionate the first year of their marriage let weeks go by without touching his wife? So he was eleven years older than she. At thirty-five he wasn't an old man.

At intervals errant suspicions crept into her mind. Was there another woman in Victor's life? Sometimes she looked at his office nurse – young and pretty Irene McDougall – and wondered if Irene was taking her place.

Women had always been attracted to Victor. They were drawn to his quiet good looks and his inner intensity that lent drama to even casual remarks. And he was a doctor. Lots of women fell in love with their doctors. How many doctors fell in love with their patients?

Was Victor having an affair with a patient? Someone she knew? The possibility was unnerving and humiliating. This was a suspicion she always sought to banish from her mind. But traitorously it returned.

The phone rang in the library. Liz heard Mary Lou walk into the room and pick up the receiver.

"Jes' a minute, Miss Adrienne." Mary Lou's voice filtered down the hall from the library. In a minute she appeared at the doorway. "Miss Adrienne wants to talk to you. She's over at her grandmama's."

"Tell her I just drove away," Liz instructed. She must not allow herself to delay the confrontation with Mama.

Adrienne had dropped her son Tommy off at her grandmother's house on the way to Terminal Station, Liz surmised. *She* should be going to Palm Beach with Adrienne. But Victor disapproved. He said Adrienne was terribly fast. Was Victor afraid his wife would go to Palm Beach and have an affair? Because he was having an affair?

She had been delighted when Adrienne built a house right next door to theirs. Most folks preferred to be closer to town. They built their houses away from the mill. Adrienne said she liked the privacy out here. Victor was blunt; he said Adrienne built out here after her divorce because she could have her noisy parties without anybody around to complain.

Adrienne was always running off to Palm Beach or New York or Europe. She said she could take just so much of Atlanta. Her husband settled a fortune on her after the divorce, when Tommy was only two months old.

Liz's eyes focused on the cluster of letters beside her place setting. She might as well go through the mail. Another stalling device, her mind taunted. But when she had scanned the mail, she left the breakfast room and went out through the rear of the house to the garage. Matthew was polishing the chrome on the new Packard. He was disappointed when she told him she would drive herself this morning. He loved being behind the wheel of the car.

Liz pulled out of the garage and drove away from the house, designed to provide a side view of the family mansion yet to be spared the sight of the Hampton Mill. It was absurd, Liz thought, to take the car for what was the equivalent of two city blocks. She could walk to the mill in five minutes. It was habit to drive.

Everybody drove these days. The downtown stores were complaining that cars were ruining their business. Instead of going to town in the evenings and on Sundays, the way they did when she was a little girl, folks climbed into their cars and drove away from town, looking for "curb service" when they wanted a "dope" – Southerners' pet name for Coca-Cola, or ice cream or a chocolate milk. At night Five Points – once the place where people used to congregate – was deserted.

Liz parked in front of the mill. She frowned at the clatter that came from the red-brick, sprawling structure with its endless opaque windowpanes. She hated the mill. The sight of the pallid men, women and children humped over the machines saturated her with guilt.

She got out of the car and stood motionless for a moment in the balmy March breeze. Gearing herself to endure the hot, moist air that spewed forth from the building. She had come to the mill to talk to her mother because here she was sure of privacy. At Hampton House there always seemed to be a servant hovering nearby. Why did she feel it so urgent to make Mama understand that she had to divorce Victor?

Liz walked into the mill, bracing herself for the noise that would assault her ears. At the end of the corridor she saw her mother, wearing one of the classically simple dresses that cost more than any worker could earn in a month, silhouetted in the doorway of her office while she talked with one of the foremen.

Liz viewed her mother with momentary detachment. Approaching forty-six Caroline Hampton was still a beautiful woman. A towering success in a man's world. But Liz's pride in her mother was tainted by a sense of her own inadequacy in comparison. Her mother, she jibed at herself, was never haunted by self-doubts or indecision.

Mama and Papa had been disappointed when she refused to go on to college, unlike many of the other students at Washington Seminary. But Margaret Mitchell had stayed at Smith for only a year, and other girls – like Adrienne – just made their debuts with the Debutante Club and joined the Junior League.

She envied Margaret – over all the girls she had known at Washington Seminary – for having a fascinating job on the *Atlanta Journal Sunday Magazine*. Margaret had been on the newspaper for almost two and a half years now. Being a debutante had not stopped her from going out to work, though some catty old dowagers whispered that she had to leave college and go to work right after her mother died because her father's business was doing so badly. She must remember, Liz exhorted herself, that Margaret called herself Peggy now that she had a byline on the newspaper.

Why couldn't *she* have done something like that? Margaret was always involved in something exciting. Her mind shot back two years ago, when Rudolph Valentino had been in town on a personal-appearance tour. Margaret trailed him to the Georgian

Terrace Hotel for an interview. She had to climb out on to the roof to talk to him. Afterwards the Sheik picked her up in his arms and lifted her back through the window. Every flapper in Atlanta had just about swooned over that.

Margaret had driven all over town in a Rolls-Royce with Harry Thaw – the millionaire playboy who years ago murdered famous architect Stanford White and managed to be acquitted. She did a story on Rebecca Latimar Felton, the first woman US Senator. She even had herself swung from a tall building in the kind of harness that Gutson Borglum was using while he was carving the Stone Mountain Memorial, to see how Mr Borglum felt out there.

Everybody in this family – except for Francis and herself – had something to make their lives special, Liz thought with sudden clarity. Mama was the head of a cotton-mill empire. Papa was one of the most powerful senators in the country. A leading pacifist. Her older brother Josh had been brilliant all through school; everybody expected him to make a name for himself in medicine once he was out of medical school. No doctor in the state had a practice that surpassed Victor's. But she was nobody. Caroline and Eric Hampton's daughter. Victor Adams' wife. Kathy's mother.

Francis was happy in his limited life as long as Mama could smooth the path for him. They must pretend all the time that Francis was just like any normal boy his age. But Francis could not go to college, Liz acknowledged. He could never have a profession. Mama would have to create another world for him when he graduated from his special school up in Washington, where the teachers were aware of his limitations and dealt with them. Only because of Victor's heroic efforts had Francis come this far. She remembered Francis' early years, when he made their lives miserable with his bizarre behavior.

"Liz, honey –" Caroline's face lit up as she spied her daughter, then became solicitous. "Is something wrong? Is Kathy all right?" Her mother adored her only grandchild.

"Kathy's fine." Liz struggled against self-consciousness. "I – I need to talk to you."

"Come on into the office." Caroline Hampton's eyes betrayed her anxiety. She knew Liz had not come to the mill to pass the time of day. "I had a letter this morning from Josh," she reported, settling herself behind her correspondence-laden desk.

"What did he have to say?" Liz sat in a chair and crossed her legs, sending her knee-high skirt above her gartered silk stockings. She ran one tense hand through her auburn-touched blonde bobbed hair.

"He's working hard, as usual. I worry about Josh," her mother admitted. "Going to college up in New York, in the midst of all that crime. Speakeasies everywhere you turn, Josh says."

Liz laughed.

"Mama, there're plenty of speakeasies right here in Atlanta." Adrienne made a point of knowing the addresses of the best ones.

"How's Victor?"

"I don't see enough of him to know," Liz shot back. "We missed the Mischa Elman concert Tuesday night. Vic was called to a patient." *Was it a patient?* "He missed Adrienne's dinner Wednesday night. I went alone." Adrienne had insisted she come without Victor. Normally she stayed at home when he was unable to go with her, but one extra woman at the dinner table didn't upset Adrienne.

"I understand Adrienne's parties are inclined to be –" Caroline searched for a diplomatic description. "I hear they're apt to be – different."

"Adrienne always rustles up some fascinating guest." The fascinating guest at Wednesday's dinner had been a bootlegger who brought rum up from the Caribbean. Sitting next to him at dinner she had recalled the article in the *Literary Digest* about the poisoned rum that had invaded New York and Washington just before Christmas, and that caused blindness or death for so many. But the bootlegger insisted his rum was the real thing – brought straight from Jamaica. "Mama, I want you to know first," she plunged in. *Don't weaken.* "Even before I tell Vic. I'm going to divorce him."

Caroline was very still. Only her eyes betrayed her distress.

"Liz, you mustn't act in haste," she reproached.

"Mama, I've thought about this for months. It isn't an impulsive decision." Months of lying in bed alone, waiting for Victor to come home.

"I know you love Victor—" her mother began, but Liz brushed this aside.

"We have no marriage. Vic is married to his profession. His patients see more of him than I do." Liz paused. "Irene sees more of him."

"There's no other woman in his life."

"I'm not saying he's unfaithful," Liz hedged. *I don't know.* "But I don't mean anything to him. I've become a fixture in his life."

"That's not true!" Caroline was indignant.

"Then let's say I don't mean enough," Liz amended, her color high, "I'm too far down on the totem pole." Already she felt her strength ebbing away. *Why do I let Mama do that to me? It's time I learned to stand on my own feet. I've always been dependent on somebody.* "I don't know what I'll do with my life—"

"Liz, you can't throw it away like this!"

"I can't go on like this, Mama." She had no real money of her own, just the income from the small trust Mama had set up when she was eighteen. She had no training. She had worked with the children in the clinic up until the time that Kathy was born. Victor had humored her, she jibed at herself; she had not been truly helpful. But women today were learning to earn their own way in life. It was no disgrace for a woman to work.

"I realize how much you're alone, Liz." Her mother chose her words with care. "It's one of the penalties of being married to a doctor."

"It isn't just Vic's practice that comes between us. The children's clinic demands every free hour. There's no time for me."

"Ask any doctor's wife if she doesn't face the same situation." Her mother's eyes were compassionate. "Talk to Victor."

"I've tried," Liz told her. "He doesn't hear me. It's over between us. I'll learn to live without him."

"Adrienne put this into your mind," Caroline accused. "Divorce means nothing to her."

"Adrienne has nothing to do with my decision."

"Adrienne has no respect for anything. If her parents hadn't died in that terrible accident, they would be heart broken by the way she lives. But let's not talk about Adrienne." Caroline leaned forward, her hands clasped on her desk. "It's your welfare that concerns me. Even in these crazy times divorce is a desperate step. You mustn't subject Victor and yourself, and Kathy, to anything so devastating." The distended vein in Caroline's throat betrayed her agitation. "It would be terrible for Kathy if Victor and you divorced. How could you deprive her of her father?"

"Kathy will see him." Liz's smile was strained. She was visualizing the scene in Adrienne's living room last Sunday when Adrienne's former husband returned after taking Tommy to Piedmont Park. Tommy had cried to stay with his father.

"Liz, you're showing a total lack of responsibility," her mother said impatiently. "Victor and you have a good marriage. You can't discard it like the balloons from last year's New Year's Eve party."

"Maybe it's good for Vic and Kathy." Liz's eyes were turbulent. "It's bad for me."

"Liz, this is ridiculous. Victor adores you. You love him—"

"He treats me like a figurine on the shelf of a display cabinet. To be brought out and admired at intervals. That's not enough for marriage." *Of course I love Victor. But how can I go on living with him? I have to divorce him and find a new life for myself. I can't survive this way.*

"I am so sick of the selfishness of today's young people!" Caroline's diplomacy fled. "Nothing means anything to any of you except enjoying yourselves. All this cynicism and discontent. The past was terrible, to listen to you all – and the future offers nothing," she mimicked. "You're all indulging yourselves."

"The world was ruined by the time we grew up." Color stained Liz's high cheekbones. "Every time we pick up a newspaper we're reminded of it. How can you expect us to be enthusiastic about the future?"

Caroline stared at her beautiful, pampered daughter.

"Liz, can't you see how lucky you are? You have everything you need to make your life complete. A husband who loves you. A precious little daughter. Every luxury available. What else do you expect?"

"Mama, sometimes I'm so miserable I wish I was dead," Liz said with a chilling detachment. "I wake up in the morning, and I wonder how I'm going to survive another long, empty day."

Mama never knew loneliness. Mama never knew the inanity of sitting at endless women's parties, saying all the expected things. Smiling and laughing as though the world was absolutely beautiful, because that was the facade Southern women were taught to present. They must have been sweet and charming while Atlanta burned, she thought bitterly.

"I knew from the time you were a little girl that you'd never be content with playing the young society matron who flits from one party to another," Caroline conceded. "God knows, I couldn't do it. Devote yourself to some worthwhile charities. Become involved. There's so much that needs—"

"No, Mama," Liz interrupted. "Don't lecture me about playing Lady Bountiful. Keeping myself busy with 'worthy causes' won't add anything to my life."

Caroline flinched.

"Since when is it in bad taste to do good?"

"I'm twenty-four years old, and right now I'm concerned about finding some meaning in my own life." Liz fumbled in her purse for a cigarette. Her mother frowned. Mama detested seeing her smoke. "I don't expect you to understand. You're obsessed with the mill and the workers. You don't need anything else."

"The mill is an important part of my life. But my husband and my children have always had first call. Don't ever forget that, Liz. Even now that you're married, you come before the mill. You must know that?" Caroline searched Liz's face for reassurance.

She had loathed the mill as a child; it demanded so much of her mother's time. When Kathy was born, she had stopped helping Victor in the children's clinic. She swore to herself that Kathy would have a full-time mother. It still amazed her that Josh had never resented the time their mother devoted to the mill. Mama's kingdom, she had thought in bereft moments.

"I'm telling Vic tonight that I'm divorcing him." Liz forced herself back to the present. "If he comes home while I'm still awake. I long ago gave up waiting up for him."

"Think about this before you talk to him," Caroline pleaded. "Wait six months," she said more forcefully. Liz knew her mother sensed her ambivalence. "You need to be away from him for a little while."

"I'm away from him constantly. He hasn't been home for dinner in over a week."

"I mean completely away," Caroline elaborated. "For a couple of weeks, at least. As it happens, I need you to handle a situation for me. I meant to call you at the house tonight to discuss it." Mama was fabricating, Liz told herself. Fighting for time. "I'd like you to go down to Miami for two or three weeks. I can't leave the mill right now – business is too chaotic. I've been negotiating on a tract of land down there with a broker named Pulaski. The deal sounds fine, but you know about the phoney promotions in Miami. I worry about buying without actually inspecting the property. I'd like you to go down to

Miami and talk with this broker. Have him show you the property. Go over the whole tract on foot. If it doesn't appear promising, ask him to show you other tracts. I don't have to tell you how Miami is booming."

Liz knew that people flocked to Miami from all over the nation. The Dixie Highway was clogged with Miami-bound cars. Atlanta businessmen were disturbed about the exodus from the city to Florida. This wasn't the winter-season trek of the rich to Palm Beach or Daytona. This was a "get-rich-quick" hysteria that seized people in alarming numbers.

In Atlanta the banks were losing accounts because of the migration to Miami. The stores were losing business. Real estate sales dropped to a new low. Everybody was greedy for land in Miami, where money was to be made in dizzying amounts.

"Mama, I won't be manipulated," Liz said after a moment.

"I'm not manipulating you," Caroline declared. "Everybody knows that money is to be made in Florida." She hesitated. "I don't often talk to you about business. Everybody says that Atlanta is a boom city itself. The 'Atlanta spirit' is supposed to personify the post war growth of the South. The city is tall with skyscrapers, rich with railroad lines. Conventions pour into town. But the textile industry – the life blood of the South – is sick."

"I don't understand." Liz was bewildered. Her mother's anxiety was obviously deep.

"All the mills are in bad shape. Not just the Hampton Mill. We're lucky – we're managing to break even. Some mills are going under. Not just in Georgia. All through the country. And the farm land I own isn't paying its way. With the price of cotton dropping, the farmers can't meet their obligations. Wall Street may boast about the nation's prosperity," Caroline said grimly, "but the textile industry and the farmers tell another story."

"Are we in serious trouble?" The Hampton fortune was one of the most substantial in the South. Some day it was to be shared by Josh, Francis and herself. It seemed inconceivable that the Hampton empire could be in jeopardy.

"I believe we can weather the storm," Caroline said. Mama was being dramatic, Liz thought with relief. So profits were dropping; they were still one of the richest families in the South. "Still, we have to face reality. The South is not sharing the prosperity of the rest of the country. You can't live in the state of Georgia without knowing what the boll weevil has been doing to us." Liz could hear her father talking in pain on this subject:

"The boll weevil hasn't only brought disaster to the farmer. The merchants are suffering. Banks are failing. Farmers who've lived on their land since the beginning of this country are being foreclosed. Their children are running to the north for jobs. The older ones come to the towns to work in the mills or the overall plants, or at whatever odd jobs they can pick up."

"I know what the boll weevil has done to us," Liz said. But families like the Hamptons were untouched. Weren't they?

"There are fortunes to be made in Miami through smart investing." Liz remembered the colorful newspaper articles about the land deals in Florida. A lot bought for $800 ten years ago was worth $150,000 today. Promoters with a thousand dollars as their sole asset were making deposits on a "proposition" and selling their options within a week for $50,000. "Like this large tract of land that Pulaski has written me about." Caroline's voice vibrated with enthusiasm. "The price has gone up twice since we began discussions. If Pulaski's facts and figures are accurate, it's fine for developing. But I don't trust long-distance deals. I want to be sure I'm not buying land that's two feet under water or ten miles from roads. I have to be sure of a clear title."

"I don't know anything about land," Liz objected.

"You're bright," her mother said with confidence. "I'll draw up a list of points you're to check out for me. The closeness of roads to the property. The availability of water. That sort of information. You'll know what to do."

"I'm not sure I can handle it." Yet the prospect of spending a couple of weeks in Miami was appealing. It would delay the agony of telling Victor she meant to divorce him. How could she love Victor and hate him at the same time? "Where would we stay?" She would take Kathy with her, of course. "Hotels are jammed. People live in tents. Men are paying twenty-five dollars a week to sleep on part of a porch."

"I have the best contacts in Miami. I'll arrange for comfortable accommodations. I'd like you to leave immediately." Caroline radiated charm. "You'll have a wonderful time."

"Mama, you're manipulating me again," Liz reiterated.

"I'm asking for your help," Caroline insisted. "You'll be in touch with my lawyer down there, Mr Gateson. He'll follow through on the legal end. Florida is beautiful this time of year. It isn't the hot season yet. There are hibiscus, orange blossoms, palm trees. Kathy and you can be in the water every day. Invite Janet to go with you," she encouraged on impulse. "Janet and Wendy – Kathy will love that. I'll cover all their expenses."

"Janet's too proud to accept that." She didn't see as much of Janet – her closest friend since they were six and Janet's widowed mother Ellen became Mama's secretary – as she would have liked since Janet had begun to work at Rich's, the popular department store. Janet's husband Kevin never seemed able to make enough to keep them, even in the modest fashion Janet accepted as their lifestyle. "You know how Janet is about money. Besides, she couldn't take time off from her job."

"Come to the house for dinner tonight. Afterwards we'll work out plans for your trip," Caroline said as someone knocked at the office door. Business was intruding, Liz was familiar with that. "Bring Victor along."

"If he's available."

Liz's face tightened. She had come here convinced she was divorcing Victor. She would wait a while, she rationalized defensively. *Nothing has changed. I'm divorcing Victor.*

Two

The temperature in Atlanta had dropped to an unseasonable low in a cold spell that swept in from the north-west. The morning was gray and dismal. Liz drew the fur collar of her coat snugly about her throat as she emerged from the car in the parking area at Terminal Station, and pulled the matching cloche over her ears.

Miami warmth would be delicious, she told herself while Victor and she walked into the cavernous station. Victor had left the house this morning at 6 a.m. to make hospital rounds before the departure of the train at 8.25 a.m.

Right behind her parents Kathy was plying her nursemaid Patience with questions about the Florida trip.

"I never saw the ocean," Kathy effervesced. Her blue eyes, so like her mother's, were luminous with excitement, her silken blonde hair a burnished mantle about her shoulders. "Is it bigger than a pond?"

"It was a miracle you were able to get rooms at the Royal Palm on a few days' notice," Victor remarked, an arm closing about Liz's waist. "Their guest list is impressive. International statesmen, financiers, royalty traveling incognito."

Liz smiled slightly.

"Mama has a way of managing things."

Liz's mind darted over the minutiae of travel. Kathy's teddy bear was packed. The medical remedies for colds and coughs, hardly likely to be required in Miami. Her trunk – sent on ahead to the hotel – was crammed with the new bright-colored pajamas that were the latest resort fashion, with slip-on sweaters and wrap-round skirts and golf dresses because sportswear dominated the Miami scene.

"I hope I packed everything," Liz said in last-minute nervousness.

"You can shop for whatever you've forgotten. Miami's quite civilized," Victor said humorously.

Liz inspected the long pullman waiting on the track.

"That's our train, isn't it?"

"That's it." His dark eyes lingered on her face. "I'll miss you."

"You'll hardly know I'm gone." A flicker of hostility glowed in her eyes when they met his. "You'll be too busy."

"I'll come down to Miami for a few days," Victor told her in sudden decision. "I'll wire you when I'll arrive. No, I'll phone."

"That's what you think now," Liz said. "But some emergency will come up at the hospital – or somebody will be terribly sick. You won't come down to Miami," she prophesied. "It'll be like all the other times."

"I'll come," he vowed. Mama had talked to him, Liz thought, and was irritated. "I'll phone you when I'm about to leave. I'm tired. I could use a few days of sun and sand."

He did look tired. The best-looking physician in Atlanta – which prompted so many unnecessary house calls from women patients.

"Vic, do you know the last time we went away together?"

"Asheville," he said after a moment with a sheepish grin.

"I don't count those two days in Asheville when Kathy was five months old," Liz said. They had been supposed to remain three weeks but an outbreak of scarlet fever had him rushing back to Atlanta. "The last time was our honeymoon." On the ship across the Atlantic, in hotel rooms in England and France and Italy they had made love every night. Victor had rejoiced that she was passionate. "We've never had a real vacation together." Even weekends at Hampton Court, the family plantation, were interrupted.

"Miss Liz, folks is boardin' the train," Patience worried. "We don't want to miss it." Patience was looking forward to seeing the ocean for the first time – with the depth of pleasure experienced only by an inlander.

Victor herded them to the train, saw them settled in their drawing room. He kissed Liz goodbye with an unexpected show of ardor.

"You need a haircut," Liz remarked to mask her surprise. Who would remind him to have his haircut if they were divorced?

"I'll go to the barber tomorrow," he promised.

Victor stopped for a brief conference with the conductor before he left the train. Asking the conductor to keep a protective eye on them, Liz surmised. She held Kathy at their drawing room window for a farewell wave to her father before the train pulled out of the shed.

She could almost believe that Victor would come down to Miami. If he did, their marriage might have a chance.

Victor dashed from the station with an awareness that he would arrive at his clinic for troubled children at least fifteen minutes late this morning. He liked to be there when the parents brought in his small patients for the day's activities. He hated losing fifteen minutes of the hour and a half he cut from his practice each morning for this, the project closest to his heart.

Later in the day he would salvage as much time as possible from office visits and house calls. Three evenings a week he spent in conferences with individual parents. He had to fight against skepticism even on the part of the desperate parents who brought their children to him. But he had the gratitude of those who stayed for the long pull and saw their children helped.

Victor was convinced his method could be useful in treating many of the world's troubled children. "Unnatural children," some people still insisted on labeling them. Look how he had brought Francis along. He had been his first case in Atlanta. It was frustrating that he could not give more time to the children's clinic. It was distressing that he could find no time for the book that begged to be written. He had set down a rough draft of the first three chapters eight years ago. Since then, nothing.

Caro had rebuked him for leaving Liz alone so much. But surely Liz understood the demands on him? His practice was enormous. It had to be, to meet their financial needs.

Some day Liz would inherit a third of the Hampton estate. He would share the Adams fortune with his two sisters. But until that time arrived – and he prayed it was distant – it was his responsibility to provide for the expensive needs of his family.

Caro and Eric had been more than generous in building the house for them when Liz and he were married six years ago. His parents had given the fine furnishings for the house. But a house that size required a large staff to maintain it. Sometimes the waste in running that household shocked his New England soul. Liz wore exquisite, expensive clothes: She shopped extravagantly for the house. Entertained lavishly. It was his responsibility to provide for her and Kathy in the fashion in which Liz had been reared. His practice was the means of fulfilling that responsibility. The children's clinic operated at a loss.

Arriving at the clinic Victor threw himself into the early morning routine, soothed a discouraged parent, coped with a staff member ill-suited for the tasks required of him – but trained personnel was a luxury he could not afford. For half an hour he worked with a seven-year-old girl who was showing progress after almost a year of stubborn resistance. Moments like this made all the efforts worthwhile.

At ten sharp Victor left the clinic and hurried to his office knowing he'd find a line-up of patients in his waiting room. He made a mental note that this was his evening at the Hamptonville Clinic, where he saw mill patients without charge. At regular intervals Caro made an effort to have the mill pay him for these services, but it was a source of pride for him to contribute his time.

He opened the door to his reception room and strode inside, with no awareness of the flutter his appearance created. A cluster of women, fashionably frocked and coifed, looked up from their magazines with welcoming smiles. He acknowledged their presence with an answering smile that included all and hurried into his examining room, followed by Irene.

"Mrs Jackson doesn't have an appointment," Irene sighed, "but she insisted it was an emergency. I figured it would be easier to squeeze her in today than have her drag you out on a house call tonight."

"Irene, you're a jewel," Victor said, and the pretty little nurse colored with pleasure.

"You're to call this number in New York right away." She pointed to a message slip on his desk. Her eyes twinkled with the knowledge that he would be pleased. "They want you to lecture at some meeting up there. About your work with the children."

Victor lifted one eyebrow in astonishment.

"Get them for me. Then you can send in the first patient."

By March 1925 Miami had been transformed from a drowsy small town on Biscayne Bay into a crowded metropolis. The land where Morgan and Lafitte and their private hordes had preyed on the helpless and the unwary was host now to a new brand of pirates. Miami was the happy hunting ground for real-estate swindlers. Even an astute millionaire – New Yorker Jacob Goodman – had bought 400,000 acres, sight unseen, and discovered he owned a swamp. This was repeated on a smaller scale endless times each week.

At the crowded but dreary Miami railroad station, where the southbound train disgorged passengers eager for their first sight of Magic City, Liz felt herself caught up in the excitement that Miami generated.

She knew Palm Beach, long the haunt of the very rich and social. At intervals she had gone there with Adrienne, before Victor rejected such trips, to endure endless rounds of cocktail parties, dinners and visits to the casinos. She loved the sun and the stretches of hard white beach, though she disliked the hysterical display of fashionable attire and ostentatiously expensive jewelry. Most visitors to Palm Beach had little taste for the water or sports.

Miami was new and adventurous. It had moved far beyond being the playground of the rich. Adverts boasted of the pleasures of golfing, swimming, playing tennis under the Miami sun. Everybody talked of the fortunes being made each day by the venturesome speculators. A $600 investment could be elevated to a $60,000 fortune in a week's time. Miami was the Klondike of the 1920s.

With the help of a porter Liz settled Kathy, Patience and herself in a taxi and headed for the Royal Palm Hotel. While Patience helped Kathy out of her coat, Liz slid off her own. Her coral, two-piece knit traveling frock was all that was required in this summer weather.

Liz focused on the surging humanity that jammed the street. It swiftly became obvious that Miami was full of Americans of meager means. Avid, Liz sensed, to change this status. She suspected the absence of the depressing apathy that inflicted the mill workers and the tenant farmers of Georgia. It must have been like this in the Klondike, where every prospector was convinced he would make a strike at any moment.

"We got traffic lights now." The driver pointed with pride. "And some downtown streets are gonna be converted to one-way startin' next month." He chuckled. "Boy, did that make folks mad." He was silent for a moment as a car just ahead, with South Dakota license plates, moved on at a signal from a traffic officer shaded by a huge umbrella. "These roads ain't wide enough for the traffic we gotta handle," he continued amiably. "We don't have just a winter season now. Folks keep comin' all the time. All the hotels except for the Royal Palm and a couple of others stay open all summer."

Liz sensed some contribution was required of her, though she would have preferred to sightsee.

"The roads are quite modern," she said. It seemed to her that here the sun was brighter, the grass was greener, the hibiscus redder than in Atlanta.

"These here roads was made for horses and mules. But they're all macadamized now," he said with pride. "Did you know, this whole city was built round the hotel you're goin' to? Henry Flagler built the Royal Palm back in 1896. He put it at the mouth of the Miami River, where it flows into Biscayne Bay, and the city just spread out all around it. Mr Flagler, he had the city laid out for about eight thousand people. We got over a hundred thousand now."

At last the taxi swung away from the mass of cars, buses and jitneys, and drove along the shorefront of Biscayne Bay, lined with royal palms and ornamental lights.

"Mama, look!" Kathy chortled.

The water of the Bay was an iridescent medley of various shades of blue.

"It's lots prettier than the muddy Chattahoochee." Liz laughed.

The driver maintained a running commentary as they drove towards the hotel past endless stuccoed mansions. The architecture paid tribute to Florida's Spanish heritage. And everywhere grew tall, regal coconut palms and Australian pines.

"We got sixteen skyscrapin' hotels and office buildings all along the bayfront," he boasted, "and fourteen goin' up this year. Ain't a city in the country that can match this one!"

They approached their destination, picturesque against a backdrop of yachts, cabin cruisers and fishing boats on the blue water that entranced the three from Atlanta.

"That's her. The Royal Palm," the driver said with proprietary pride. "She can put up six hundred people."

An imposing colonial structure, painted yellow with white trim, sprawling in decorous opulence in the midst of a magnificent garden area, with a long, narrow porch extending along its width. A parade of rockers was occupied by chatting guests. Other guests – the women in golf frocks, skirts and sweaters, the men in colorful knickers – were bound for the golf course or tennis courts.

Liz emerged from the taxi with Kathy and Patience, to be engulfed instantly in the lavish hospitality accorded every guest at the Royal Palm. *I'm glad I allowed Mama to persuade me to come to Miami.*

At nine o'clock the next morning, when Patience had taken Kathy off to the beach, Liz telephoned Rick Pulaski's office. The line was busy. For forty minutes the line continued to be busy. In exasperation Liz ordered a taxi to take her to his office at an address just off Flagler Street.

Traffic was as heavy as yesterday, with the drivers' tempers erupting at delays. Streets were piled high with assorted building materials. Trucks blocked the flow of traffic while their crews made deliveries. Flagler Street, Liz guessed, was Miami's major thoroughfare.

She was nervous at the prospect of introducing herself to Mr Pulaski. In her mind she ran down the list of questions she was to ask him when he showed her the tract of land. She was still astonished that her mother was serious about her handling this assignment. She knew the initial suggestion had been triggered as a diversion from divorce, yet her mother was carrying it through. Was Mama recognizing – at last – that she was a grown woman?

The taxi pulled to a stop before a long, low structure of white stucco enclosed by a tall, black, wrought-iron fence. Semi-tropical flowers bloomed in lush display. Once this must have been a fine residence. Now a sign proclaimed that it was the Pulaski Realty Company.

Liz left the taxi and walked inside the gate, left open in welcome. She followed the palm-lined path to the heavy oak door. People were being ushered into the half dozen Cadillac touring cars that sat in the courtyard by self-assured young men dressed in knickers and wearing rakish caps. Prospective buyers, Liz surmised.

She opened the door and walked into a large marble-floored reception hall brilliantly lit by a crystal chandelier. An oriental rug covered a segment of the floor. An imposing grey-haired woman sat behind an antique Spanish writing table. She was speaking with someone on a telephone. The receivers of three other phones had been removed from their hooks. Liz assumed these were tentatively interrupted calls.

"I'm sorry," the woman said firmly. "Mr Pulaski can't see you today. I can schedule you an afternoon appointment a week tomorrow." She consulted an appointment pad. "At four o'clock."

Liz waited for the conversation to be completed. The room to her left, furnished with antique velvet chairs, was occupied by a cluster of men and one woman. All waiting to see Mr Pulaski, she thought with misgivings. The aroma of expensive Cuban cigars filtered out into the reception hall.

"Yes?" The woman at the writing table at last turned to Liz. Her smile indicated that this attention was to be valued.

"I tried to reach the office by phone," Liz explained, self-conscious in this role, "but your line was busy. My mother, Caroline Hampton, has been in correspondence with Mr Pulaski about a tract of land. She would like Mr Pulaski to show me the property." Liz paused. The woman appeared affronted.

"Mr Pulaski sees no one without an appointment."

"Then I'd like an appointment," Liz said. They were talking about a sale valued at a quarter of a million dollars. Was Mr Pulaski too important to follow through on that?

"Mr Pulaski will be able to show it to you two weeks from today," the woman said after brief consultation with her appointment pad. "At nine sharp."

"I may not be here in two weeks," Liz shot back. The woman's arrogance was beginning to irritate her. "I came to Miami specifically to see this piece of property. If I can't see it, then I'll return to Atlanta."

The woman's mouth set in annoyance, but she rose to her feet.

"I'll talk to Mr Pulaski."

Bristling with disapproval she crossed to the room at Liz's right and knocked briefly. Without waiting for a reply she walked inside and closed the door behind her. A few moments later she emerged and held the door open in invitation.

"You may see Mr Pulaski now." The arrangement infuriated her, Liz thought in amusement. Her power had been questioned.

"Mrs Rambeau, have Ramon bring us coffee," a deep male voice called from inside.

Liz walked into the room that served as Rick Pulaski's office. The room was furnished in the grand Spanish manner of two centuries ago, with a grouping of ornate baroque chairs at one side. The rug on the highly polished floor was of Spanish design. Beside a window covered with a lacy iron grille that spilled sunlight into the room Rick Pulaski sat at an elaborate Spanish desk, a *vargueno*, inlaid with silver, its drawer fronts adorned with painted plaques of ivory. The writing leaf was littered with official papers.

Pulaski rose and walked towards her. Liz was startled to realize that he was scarcely more than five years her senior. Tall, broad-shouldered, strikingly handsome. His name belied his appearance, Liz thought involuntarily. He might have been a young Spanish or Italian nobleman – except for the glint in his eyes and a tilt to his smile – that hinted of a reined-in ruthlessness that was more peasant than prince. She suspected that Rick Pulaski lived in a world far removed from any she had ever known.

"I'm Rick Pulaski." He extended a hand in welcome.

"Liz Adams," she introduced herself. "Mrs Hampton's daughter." Mrs Rambeau had told him, of course, that she was here on her mother's behalf, she rebuked herself. She sounded so unsophisticated.

"Please –" He gestured towards a pair of chairs. "Sit down, Mrs Adams." He had taken note of her wedding band.

"Mr Pulaski, I came to Miami to inspect the property you've

been discussing with my mother." He wasn't taking this seriously, she fumed. She was just a young, attractive woman who had wandered into his office. Her married status meant nothing. He was asking himself what he would have to do to take her to bed. Even with today's new freedoms he was being obvious. "My mother is familiar with the swindles that take place in Miami," she said with deliberate bluntness. "She's prepared to buy *if* I approve." She recognized the fresh respect this elicited.

"That property was sold an hour ago."

"Oh." Liz was startled. And disappointed. She was reluctant to sever this acquaintanceship so swiftly.

"But wait, Mrs Adams." He leaned back in his chair, apparently in thought. "I shouldn't discuss it yet, but I'll be able to offer another tract in a few days. I'm sure it's the kind of investment that would interest your mother. The land is perfect for development." Liz refrained from telling him that her mother planned on holding the property for six months to a year and then re-selling at a substantial profit. "I can't show it until it's mine," he said with a slow smile. It was the kind of a smile that would intrigue almost any woman, Liz evaluated. Yet there was a roughness about Rick Pulaski, an air of a man afraid of little in this world and willing to gamble high stakes for what he considered important that would also appeal to men. Little wonder that he was supposed to be one of the sharpest real-estate operators in Florida. "I can't show you the property," he reiterated, "but we can talk about it. I can show you figures. May I take Mr Adams and you out to dinner tonight and fill you in on the pertinent details?"

"My husband – Dr Adams – is in Atlanta," Liz explained. "He'll be in Miami next week."

"Then may I take you to dinner tonight?" he pursued. "To discuss the property."

Liz hesitated. What could be wrong about having dinner in a restaurant with Rick Pulaski? She was here in Miami to conduct business. Rick Pulaski was selling property. Why not have dinner with him? The evening alone in her hotel suite would be a bore.

"I'm at the Royal Palm Hotel," Liz told him. "What time shall I expect you?"

Liz dressed for dinner with a sense of anticipation that was flecked with guilt. She knew, of course, that many men were drawn to her. This was a cause of recurrent astonishment to her, enjoyed in fleeting spurts and then discarded as a tawdry attribute. But Rick Pulaski had been more obvious than most men. And devastatingly attractive.

Liz frowned, impatient with herself. Why was she feeling guilty? Nothing would happen between Rick Pulaski and her. She suspected he was accustomed to having his way with women. This time he would be disappointed. She was in control.

Liz inspected her reflection in the mirror. Her black georgette evening frock, fringed with a multitude of narrow beaded strips of the same fabric, was short, graceful, beautifully chic, displayed much of her milk-white back. She wore a single red rose on her shoulder, pearls at her throat. An instinct for smart attire was her one success. Even Adrienne asked her advice about clothes.

Tonight her eyes had a special glow. This evening would be spent with a man who was blatant in his admiration. With Victor – with Mama and Papa and Josh – she always felt herself in the shadows. They were all so strong, so confident of themselves. Sitting with Rick Pulaski this morning she knew she had commanded all of his attention. Nothing intruded.

This was the first time since she married Victor that she had gone out alone with another man. But this would be business.

She touched the stopper of the bottle of Houbigant to her wrist, then was immobile in concentration at the sound of someone at the door of the suite. Patience came into the bedroom.

"The gen'men here fo' you, Miss Liz."

"I think I'd better take a light wrap," Liz decided in a flurry of self-consciousness. Was Patience surprised that she was going out to dinner with a handsome young man? "Don't sit up waiting for us, Patience," she exhorted, reaching into a closet for a black velvet jacket. "Kathy gets you up so early in the morning." Now misgivings pricked at her. Was it foolish to see Rick Pulaski outside the office?

"Kathy's so excited about seein' the ocean." Patience chuckled affectionately. "All that water! She jes' loves it."

"Don't let her go out alone," Liz cautioned in sudden alarm.

"Miss Liz, you know I ain't lettin' her away from my hand," Patience scolded. "Her no bigger'n a minute."

Liz walked into the sitting room. Rick Pulaski stood at a window, gazing out at the twilight view of the river and bay. In Atlanta it was already fully night by this hour.

Rick turned about at the sound of her greeting.

"I thought the view from your sitting room was magnificent," he said, his eyes sweeping over her with the admiration she had encountered this morning. "Then I see you, and it's eclipsed."

"Thank you." Her smile acknowledged the compliment. Her eyes discounted its sincerity.

"Do you mind if I smoke?" He held up his expensive Havana cigar in ingratiating apology.

"I dislike it over dinner." Normally she loathed cigars. In Rick Pulaski's hand it appeared a charming, masculine touch.

"There's a time and a place for everything." Rick crossed to help her on with her jacket. "Cigars don't belong at the dinner table."

"You've brought along the documents you told me about?" she asked because the accidental brushing of his hand against her shoulder had elicited an unexpected, erotic response. "The facts about that tract of land," she added when he seemed blank for a moment.

"Of course," he said smoothly. A hand reached inside his jacket to verify the presence of the required papers. "We'll talk about business after dinner." His eyes carried on an amorous conversation that both alerted and aroused her. She had spent too many evenings alone, Liz admonished herself. "I hope you like seafood."

"I adore seafood," she told him. Adrienne and she "adored" everything, Liz rebuked herself. They adored seafood, dresses by Coco Chanel, houses decorated by Elsie de Wolfe, the tango, the foxtrot and the Charleston. She must stop using that over-worked word. "Patience, be sure to lock the door," she instructed. Her self-appointed chaperone, Patience hovered close by. Her presence was reassuring. It would be so easy, Liz thought, for a lonely woman to lose her head over Rick Pulaski.

They drove in Rick's pearl-gray Cadillac to a restaurant situated directly on the bay. Rick was a favored patron. The manager himself came forward to greet them, to express his delight at their presence. The waiters were obsequious in their eagerness to please. Their table provided a picture-book view of the water, where a brilliantly lit yacht hinted at exclusive conviviality.

The seafood was superb. A mushroom and clam bisque, lobster Thermidor, tomatoes stuffed with crab-meat salad, garnished asparagus spears. And while they ate, Rick talked.

"I've lived in Florida for nineteen months," he confided. "I love Miami: the city, the people, the weather. Up in New York right now people are tramping through slush, shivering. Here there's constant sunshine and warmth."

"I left Atlanta in a cold spell," Liz said. "Though it won't last at this time of year."

"I come from a coal-mining family in Pennsylvania. It'll be cold there for a spell yet. Oh, my father didn't go down in the mines." He chuckled. Rick's smile conveyed a richness of humor, an awareness that their part of the world was an infinitesimal fragment of the whole. "My father owned a mine. I worked in it the summer of my eighteenth birthday." His gold-flecked eyes darkened to near black, hinting at a long-nurtured vendetta. "My father insisted," Rick explained.

"He ruled the family with the same iron hand he used with the miners. I hated the bastard." Rick made no effort to apologize for his slip into profanity.

"My mother runs a cotton mill. I suppose you could say she runs it with an iron hand. But I don't hate her," she said defensively. Sometimes she loved Mama with an intensity that astonished her, but there were the times when she almost hated her.

"You never worked in the cotton mill," Rick challenged.

"No." Liz laughed.

"Is your father Senator Hampton?" His eyes were appraising.

"Yes." She felt self-conscious beneath his scrutiny. "The peace advocate." She was proud of Papa's dedication to the peace movement.

"Poor little rich girl," Rick mocked.

"Poor little rich boy," she flashed back. "You didn't have to work in the mine for a living."

"Two years after my summer in the mine my younger brother went down." Again Liz felt the anger in him. "He died in a cave-in. My mother had pleaded with my father not to send Jerry down into the mines, but he wouldn't listen. 'You've got to know about the mine. You'll have to run it someday.'" He mimicked harshly. "I never did. I never will." He forced himself into a less recriminating mood. "I've had a lot of jobs through the years. I've worked on the docks, spent a year as a newspaperman, sold insurance. At one low period I was a bouncer in a New York speakeasy. Before all that, back in 1917, I went to England and flew with the Royal Air Force."

All at once Liz was cold. She was hurtling back through the years to the period when David was fighting in France. It had been so long since she had thought about David.

"Someone close to me fought with the Canadian Corps," she told him. "He died in France."

"Someone you loved," he said with a gentleness she had not expected of Rick Pulaski.

"I thought my life was over," Liz admitted.

"I was supposed to go back to college after my brother died in the mine cave-in. After that to law school. My father wanted a lawyer in the family. I took off for London and the air force instead. I've never seen my father since my brother's funeral. I see my mother occasionally. I have three sisters who mean nothing to me. They're hypocritical little bitches, coddling my father in anticipation of their inheritance," he said with contempt.

"You don't need that." Mama said Rick Pulaski was one of the wealthiest real-estate operators in Florida. Not bad, considering he was only twenty-eight or twenty-nine, Liz reckoned. "You're your own man." How would she have survived without her parents' money? Liz had seen Janet's desperate struggle to get through college, her struggle to survive in her marriage. *She* had refused to go to college. She married Victor, whose father was a former congressman, and now a judge and a wealthy man by virtue of inheritance. She had great respect for people like Janet and Rick Pulaski, who could carry their own weight in the world.

"How long will you be in Miami?" Rick asked.

"About two weeks." The return reservations were made for two weeks from today – but they could be changed.

"I'll be tied up with clients all day tomorrow, but the next day let me give you the Cook's tour of Miami, After two, when the banks close," he stipulated humorously. "Everybody in Miami is busy working until the banks close for the day. Let's make it three o'clock," he suggested.

"First I'd like to see the property." Had that grazing of her knee beneath the table been accidental? Let Rick Pulaski remember she was here on business. That she was a married woman.

"I can't show it to you yet. Not until the deal is settled. But I can show you the city."

"What about the figures? We ought to discuss them." Liz hid behind a facade of business because Rick was evoking emotions in her that belonged in the bedroom. With her husband.

"After dessert arrives," Rick promised. "We have all evening to discuss figures."

It was almost midnight when Liz returned to her hotel suite. Hearing her arrive, Patience tiptoed out of the bedroom she shared with Kathy.

"Dr Victor telephoned. He say to call him when you gets into the hotel."

Liz's face was incandescent. He was calling to tell her when he was arriving. This time he wouldn't disappoint her.

"But it's late to call now –" Liz hesitated in indecision.

"He say it don't matter what time you come in," Patience told her.

"All right, Patience," Liz capitulated.

Victor would assume she had stayed downstairs for the evening's entertainment, she told herself. Everybody knew about the night-time diversion in Florida's hotels. Big name acts performed at the hotels: Gilda Grey, Grace Key White and Ralph Wonders, Ben Bernie and the "Lads", Jan Garber and his orchestra. Why did she feel uncomfortable about telling him she had gone out to dinner with a real-estate operator?

Victor answered the phone on the first ring. He was sitting in the library reading medical journals, she suspected.

"I was anxious to know that you had arrived safely," he said. "I expected to hear from you yesterday."

"I should have sent a telegram." Liz was contrite. He had been worried. "I'm sorry."

"Something unexpected has come up. Something pleasant," he added hastily. "I've been invited to talk to a medical group in New York. About my work with the children."

"Victor, how marvelous!" She knew how much this kind of recognition meant to him.

"I'll have to leave for New York tomorrow."

"Why didn't they give you notice? But you'll enjoy it."

"Someone canceled out," Victor explained wryly. "I'm a

substitute. But it's an important meeting, Liz. All the New York newspapers will cover it."

"When will you be back in Atlanta? Or will you come directly down here?"

Victor cleared his throat. Liz tensed. That small sound was a portent of trouble.

"I'll be up there for three days plus traveling time both ways," Victor pointed out. "I don't see how I can come down to Miami. Not when I've been away from the office for almost a week."

"Victor, you promised!"

"Liz, I can't throw away this chance to talk about my work. I must go to New York." He sounded upset.

"Of course," she said after a moment. It was like all the other times: something was always more urgent than being with her. "But why can't you take another three days off?" Defiance surfaced in her. "You're not the only doctor in Atlanta!"

"There's just too much involved. It'll be rough to be away almost a week – I can't make it worse."

"Victor, three days," Liz pleaded. "You can take another three days."

"Liz, I can't." He was firm. "I have obligations to—"

"What about your obligations to your wife?" Liz interrupted.

"Honey, be reasonable—"

"I'm tired of being reasonable. Goodbye, Victor." Trembling with fury she slammed down the receiver.

Victor ought to understand how important this is to me.

Liz lay sleepless until dawn. Over and over her mind replayed the brief telephone conversation with Victor. Mama was always being called to the mill, Victor to the hospital or to a patient's bedside, Papa was always rushing back to the capital on some emergency. She was first with nobody.

When she returned to Atlanta, she would tell Victor she was filing for divorce. No more delays. She would not spend the rest of her life existing in a vacuum. Adrienne was right in living the way she did. "Sugar, you live for today. Not for yesterday, not for tomorrow. You squeeze out every drop of fun you can," Adrienne said.

Adrienne had fallen madly in love at seventeen with a boy who had died in the war. Three months later she had married his best friend Neil. But now Adrienne complained that all Neil had cared about was how many houses he was building.

After David's death and the soldiers who filled the nights after that, she had turned to Victor. Adrienne and she, both running from tragedy to men who were too busy for marriage.

Aunt Sophie, Mama's right hand at the mill as she had been the General's in earlier years, was forever complaining about the morals of the younger generation. They were no different from previous generations; they were just more honest. They brushed aside pretense. Before *she* was born, dignified, righteous Aunt Sophie – no blood relation but long in residence at Hampton House and accepted as a member of the family, had been her great-grandfather's mistress. Mama and Papa knew about Aunt Sophie and the General; they just didn't talk about it.

They didn't talk about that ugly year after David's death in the war when she ran from one soldier to another – searching for David. They didn't talk about the time Papa and Mama made love in a rainstorm while Papa was still married to Tina. That was the trouble with earlier generations. They didn't know how to talk.

When I return to Atlanta, I'll divorce Victor. Neither Victor nor Mama can stop me. This is the last time Victor has brushed aside my needs.

Three

Liz remained in her sun-splashed suite the next day, emerging only for gourmet meals in the grand dining room of the hotel. She even declined an invitation to attend the afternoon concert. Wrapped in misery she lay across her bed and flipped through the pages of *Vogue* and *Vanity Fair*, then tried to read Michael Arlen's new novel, *The Green Hat*, which everybody was talking about.

She had reconciled herself to divorcing Victor, Liz analyzed her unhappiness. Then, for a pitifully brief period, she had harbored a hope that her marriage could be salvaged. That Victor could find room in his life for her. But instead of joining her in Miami he was on his way to New York City to deliver a speech.

She fell asleep early, to the background music of the entertainment being offered downstairs in the Royal Palm's fine theater. Her last conscious thought was that tomorrow at three Rick Pulaski would be picking her up for what he called the "Cook's tour" of Miami.

Liz entered the elegant rotunda where guests circulated in convivial leisureliness. She tensed at the sight of a stately woman who clutched a tiny Pekinese in her arms while carrying on an animated conversation with her monacled male companion. The Italian Countess – whose dinner party Victor and she had attended at her magnificent palazzo in Rome when they were there on honeymoon. Fortunately she was unaware of Liz's presence. It would have been awkward to introduce

Rick to her, though Europeans were far less puritanical than Americans.

Liz frowned. Why was she making such a big thing of seeing Rick Pulaski? They were not having an affair. Yet she was uncomfortable at this socializing. Why was Rick late? It was ten minutes past three. She felt conspicuous standing waiting for him.

Then she spied him sauntering across the rotunda towards her. He walked with the erectness of a man fully aware of his potential and confident of fulfilling himself. Feminine eyes focused on him in admiration.

"Sorry I'm late," he apologized. "Trouble with the car." He took her arm with an aura of pleased possessiveness. Smiling faintly he leaned close to whisper in her ear. "The women here hate you. You're far too beautiful for their comfort."

Why doesn't Victor ever say things like that?

They left the hotel and climbed into a gray Rolls-Royce that waited outside.

"You did tell me this is your first trip to Miami?" Rick said.

"I know Palm Beach and Daytona, but I've never been here before."

"After today," he promised, "you'll know Miami."

While they drove, Rick talked about the city.

"See all these palm trees? They're props to sell the land, sometimes their main duty is to hold up signs. Land is king down here, but not to build homes or raise crops or start a business. The fever here is to subdivide. Orange and grapefruit groves are cut up, pineapple plantations turned into developments, swamp land filled in. And people are making money like they've never made it before."

Rick did not share his generation's disillusionment with materialism.

"Those figures you showed me last night sounded impressive." Liz strived to sound knowledgeable.

"Your mother will appreciate them," he said with confidence. "You sent her the sheets I gave you?"

"Not yet," Liz said. Rick's eyes abandoned the road for an instant to rest on her in astonishment. "I thought I should wait until the land is available," Liz explained.

"Right," Rick agreed. "Another few days and I'll have it sewn up."

"Then you'll show the property to me?" It was important, Liz told herself, to make Rick understand this was a business situation.

"I'll show it to you," he said with the indulgence he might have displayed in talking to Kathy. He thought this sale to her mother was a *fait accompli*, she decided in faint rebellion. He wasn't taking her seriously, although he *was* taking her seriously as a woman. She knew he would like nothing better at this moment than to be in bed with her. The atmosphere in the Rolls was heavy with restrained passion.

Rick drove her through downtown Miami. They parked the Rolls and walked along the bustling streets, the sidewalks seemed inadequate to handle the hordes intent on shopping. Liz noticed the preponderance of beggers at every corner and the vendors of cheap wares. Here and there she spied groups of Indians in native costume.

"The Indians work as caddies on the golf courses," Rick told her, "in native costume. They float around town hoping to attract tourists out to their villages to buy souvenirs. Did you know that Miami is a Seminole Indian word?"

"What does it mean?" Liz smiled at a gaudily dressed Indian woman who gazed at her dress in shy admiration.

"It means sweet water. The Seminoles gave the name to the river that flows through the city, so the city, too, became Miami." Rick was introspective for a moment. "Actually the Indians around here are still receiving a bad deal from the white man. With the Everglades in the process of being drained and white hunters pushing in, they're being deprived of their heritage and the game that used to provide them with food."

"But isn't the government encouraging them to move to the Western reservations?" Liz asked.

"Would you want the government to tell you where to live?" Rick challenged. "Would you want to leave Atlanta and go live out west?"

"No," Liz conceded. "I guess I never thought much about that." In a way the Indians were like women: both were fighting for their freedom.

Rick pointed out the Ponce de Leon hotel, headquarters of the "binder boys". Liz listened avidly to Rick's explanation of this new phenomenon in Miami.

"They've been pouring into the city for the past few weeks. Men and women. They're 'bird dogs', hanging around the railway stations and the docks, trying to sell options on land where the first payment won't be due for a month. These binders are sold over and over again, running to unbelievable prices. Everybody in Miami is out to make a killing. Even William Jennings Bryan is a real-estate broker in Miami. And on Sundays," Rick chuckled, "he runs the largest Sunday school class in the world practically in your front yard." Liz stared blankly. "At Royal Palm Park. The man-made ten-block stretch of green grass and Royal palm trees. Tonight," he said, changing the subject, "we'll drive over and have dinner at the Coral Gables Country Club and listen to Jan Garber and his orchestra."

"I'm not dressed for dinner," Liz protested.

Why shouldn't I have dinner again with Rick? Victor isn't coming down here.

"I'll drive you back to the hotel so you can change, then I'll go home and change myself. I can't go to the Coral Gables Country Club in white buckskin shoes and a Palm Beach suit," he pointed out.

The afternoon and evening were swept away in an aura of make-believe. Movie-star handsome in evening dress Rick held her in his arms indecorously tight, while they did a slow foxtrot to Jan Garber's orchestra. His knee brushed hers under the table while Garber sang "When the Moon Comes Over Coral Gables", and she laughed at the distortion of the popular lyrics. She knew that Rick was determined to have an affair with her. She promised herself it wouldn't happen although his interest was a sweet balm after Victor's neglect.

Much later that night Liz lifted a thinly arched eyebrow in question when Rick by-passed the Royal Palm Hotel to park before an adjacent building.

"This is where the depraved tourists go in the evenings," Rick mocked. "It's out of bounds to the local residents, but the Royal Palm was smart enough to provide this diversion. The Seminole Club. A casino," he explained because Liz didn't immediately comprehend the activity provided behind the sedate exterior of what was once the old officer's quarters of Fort Dallas.

The atmosphere inside the Seminole Club was convivial, and many of the women strikingly gowned. Liz suppressed a giggle at the sight of two women of a certain age in sequined gowns – resembling a pair of over-sized trout.

Rick led Liz to the roulette table. She watched while he dropped twelve thousand dollars at roulette and blackjack in an hour.

"I'll earn it back tomorrow." He shrugged.

Before he escorted her from the car to the Royal Palm entrance, he kissed her goodnight with indecent passion. But it would be unsophisticated to reject him, Liz thought.

"I'll pick you up at four tomorrow," Rick told her. "Bring your bathing suit. We'll have dinner at my house. Later we'll drive to Hialeah for the greyhound races or, if you prefer, we'll go over to the Floridian. Eddie Cantor, Jack Benny, and Sophie Tucker are appearing in the new show, and a great dance team. Caesar Romero and a woman whose name I forget." His eyes made love to her. "How can I remember the names of other women in your presence?"

"When are you going to show me the property?" Her voice was uneven, her heart thumping. She knew Rick's plans for tomorrow evening.

"Tomorrow I'll show you my house. You'll see your mother's property in a few days. As soon as I sew up the deal." Again she rebelled before his assumption that her mother was buying.

Liz lay sleepless until the sun rose over the Bay. She was playing a dangerous game with Rick, her mind warned. Her body reacted to each touch of his hand, each brush of knees under the table. When his arms had closed round her as he had held her jacket for her, she had envisioned the excitement of making love with Rick Pulaski. She ought to have told him she would be busy tomorrow.

They were going swimming at the Roman Pools. Were her Annette Kellerman bathing suits too daring? Aunt Sophie had been shocked when she saw the new one-piece costumes she had bought at Chamberlin-Johnson-DuBose.

"I don't know why you bother taking a trunk," Aunt Sophie had grumbled. "With the little cloth that goes into women's clothes today, you ought to be able to travel with an overnight bag."

Arriving at the Roman Pools next day Liz felt comforted. Most of the women present wore the new one-piece suits. When she emerged from the bath-house, she saw the heated approval in Rick's eyes.

"There isn't a woman in Miami who can fill a bathing suit as well as you do," he murmured. His eyes lingered on her bosom. All at once Liz imagined Rick fondling her breasts. She visualized herself prone on a silken couch while his mouth nuzzled a nipple.

Oh God, I'm out of my mind.

"Let's try the water." A faint smile acknowledged his compliment. Rick was bold as brass; but that was the times. Their generation spoke their minds.

They stayed briefly at the Roman Pools, then left for Rick's rented house, where he promised his houseman would be waiting with cocktails. One drink, she cautioned herself. Inhibitions fled too easily after two drinks. Maybe that was why Adrienne drank so much at parties. Sometimes Adrienne made her uneasy.

She had expected Rick to live in an expensive house but was unprepared for the palatial edifice that had been his home for the past four month.

"The house belongs to a big-time bootlegger who's wintering in your territory."

"Oh?" Liz lifted her eyebrows in enquiry.

"Atlanta." Rick grinned. "He's serving time in the Federal pen. He traveled to prison in a private club car, with its own kitchen and a staff of waiters. His cell isn't quite like home, but he has maid service, and fresh flowers are brought in every day."

"I don't believe this is Miami." Liz stared in amazement at the tall, gray castle sitting incongruously in the midst of a riotous display of flowering shrubs behind a vast stretch of private beach.

Rick was amused. "There's a gold piano in the music room and an indoor swimming pool that cost $100,000." Rick opened the door that led into a huge entrance foyer adorned with massive statuary. "All mine," he said, "until my landlord gets sprung."

Rick showed her through the lower floor of the house, then led her out to a patio enclosed by a tall, black, wrought-iron fence. A smiling houseman in a white jacket brought them cocktails. At least she wasn't alone here with Rick, Liz thought guiltily. A house this size required a half-dozen full-time servants.

In a short space of time the phone had rung three times. Each time the houseman came out to announce the caller's name to Rick. "No calls," he finally decreed with impatience. "Just say I won't be home until late this evening." He turned to Liz and re-filled her glass. "Drink up and let's go for a walk on the beach."

Barefoot, shoes in hand, they walked along the warm, white sand, then collapsed into chairs shaded by an enormous umbrella. Liz was content to sit back and listen to Rick talk. This was a fairy-tale world that allowed no intrusion. Time ceased to be.

She started at the sound of a bell ringing close by.

"That means we're to return to the house for dinner." Rick rose to his feet. "We can't afford to miss one of Lulie's gourmet spreads." He grinned. "The staff came with the house."

Before they sat down in the ornate dining room, Liz telephoned her hotel suite to say goodnight to Kathy. Her daughter didn't miss her, she reassured herself. Kathy had discovered the biggest sandpile in the world and was ecstatic.

While they lingered over dessert, Rick laid out possible evening diversions. All the while Liz read the passion in his eyes. In his mind he was in bed with her. He was pushing himself into her. With a shock she realized the extent of her own arousal. Her thighs tensed in involuntary desire.

Now there was a stillness about the house. Liz surmised that the servants were leaving the main house for their private quarters. Only the houseman remained to clear the table. Soon he, too, would withdraw.

"You haven't seen the upper floor," Rick said with a show of spontaneity when they had finished dessert and coffee. "I should show you the rest of the house before we leave."

At the head of the stairs Rick threw open a door and flipped on the light switch. Only a small bedside lamp provided illumination.

"This is the favored guest room. All done up in Louis sixteenth." He reached for her hand.

She should not allow Rick to pull her into the bedroom, Liz told herself. *Where is my will?* From the phonograph downstairs music filtered upwards: Beethoven's Fifth. She wouldn't have expected that of Rick. How many women had been brought up to this guest room in the four months Rick had been in residence?

His mouth was demanding as it settled on hers and his hands pulled her against his hard, lean length. His tongue prodded between her teeth – finding no resistance, while his body moved with hers. She had no will, she thought, first in panic, then in defiance. For the first time since she married Victor, she wanted another man to make love to her. Adrienne talked all the time about her erotic fantasies. It had always been enough for Liz to wait for Victor to make love to her, until he grew too busy with his practice even for that.

Rick moved her to the edge of the bed. She sat motionless while he stripped, dropping his clothes across a chair. His eyes never left her face.

"You see what you do to me?" he scolded, standing before her in flagrant passion.

"Let's don't waste that," she said with shaky bravado. For six years no man except Victor had touched her. But right this minute Victor was making a speech before a medical convention. He could have been here with her. He chose not to be. Now she was going to go to bed with a man she'd known for only three days. She shivered for an instant.

"Cold?" Rick was solicitous as he helped her out of her chic yellow handkerchief linen frock.

"Hot," she said with candor, standing before him in a pale-pink lace-trimmed teddy.

He reached to remove her Deuville sandals and stockings, while impatience cascaded in her. She slid the straps of her teddy away from her shoulders. With one swift motion Rick freed her and lifted her on to the bed. His eyes sweeping over her in appreciation, he lifted himself above her.

"I've wanted to do this since the moment you walked into my office," he told her, his hands fondling her breasts. His legs thrust hers apart. A low sound of passion escaped her when he probed. Her arms tightened around him while they moved together. She whimpered softly, drawing him deeper within her, moving with him in increasing frenzy until they arrived together at the ultimate moment of their passion.

Adrienne was right: "Sugar, you live for today. Not for yesterday, not for tomorrow. You squeeze out every drop of fun you can."

Liz abandoned herself to sensual pleasures. She slept each morning until Kathy came into her bedroom to kiss her goodbye before being whisked away to the beach by Patience. She remained in her suite until the time arrived to descend to the grand dining room for luncheon. Every waking moment Rick monopolized her thoughts.

Promptly at three every afternoon, with his business completed for the day, Rick would arrive and her day would begin. They kept to themselves, eschewing socializing though opportunities were rife. Liz put out of her mind the reluctant knowledge that her days in Miami were numbered.

In daylight hours they visited the Roman Pools or drove out to Musa Isle to roam about the Indian villages. They visited the new Miami Jockey Club, where a crowd of 17,000 had packed the clubhouse and grandstand at the January opening, and danced at the fashionable tea gardens, where booze was more favored than tea. In the midst of a rare torrential rain Rick took her on a tour of the Hialeah movie studio.

Their evenings were occupied with dining, moonlight dancing, and gambling. They visited the very exclusive Beach and Tennis Club – where nobody swam or played tennis – to dine, gamble and listen to Helen Morgan sing "Manhattan Serenade". They gambled at the Embassy Club and the Floridian Hotel, and enjoyed the floor show featuring Earl Carroll's showgirls at the Palm Island Club. The days and nights were studded with laughter. An almost forgotten quality in Liz's life.

On this afternoon Rick apologized because their diversion must be interrupted by business. She sat beside Rick while he negotiated a million-dollar land deal. She felt rather than understood his ruthless determination to acquire his price, his terms.

"Let's go to the house for a while," he said when they

emerged from the business conference. The expression in his eyes told her he was impatient to leave the bargaining table for bed.

"Now?" Her eyebrows lifted in a characteristic gesture of astonishment.

"Do you object to making love in broad daylight?"

She flung her head back in laughter.

"Honey, I'm always ready to make love. But I thought you were driving me out today to see the land you want to sell to my mother." She saw the flicker of annoyance this elicited from him. Was it because he thought she'd leave Miami as soon as the sale was arranged? *I should.*

"You'll see it today," he promised. "I closed the deal this morning, like I told you. The price is up," he warned her, "but your mother will quadruple her money in six months. She can afford to let it sit." His faint smile told her he knew her mother planned to hold the land until prices escalated. Caroline Hampton had no desire to build a development herself, not with the mill on her hands. And, sharp as he was, Rick knew that the textile mills were not making money at this point.

At his house they went directly upstairs. Liz was surprised when Rick led her to another bedroom this afternoon.

"My digs," he said with a conspiratorial smile. "Usually private property."

Rick showed her into his bathroom, which was nearly as large as the adjoining bedroom. In the center sat a huge black marble tub.

"Did your landlord bathe there or make gin in it?" Liz joshed.

"Take off your clothes and run us a tub. I'm going downstairs for a bottle of champagne. You'll find bath salts on the shelf there." He pointed to the display of glass shelves laden with ornate bottles and containers.

Rick knew she would be leaving Miami in three days, Liz thought. He meant to make these last days special. *I don't want to think about leaving Miami.*

"Your landlord's favorites?" Liz flipped, inspecting the lavish array.

"My favorites." Rick was momentarily irritated. "Run the tub."

There was something intriguingly decadent about sharing a tub with Rick, she decided. Something to talk about with Adrienne. She shed her clothes while tepid water flowed from solid gold faucets to fill the square, black marble tub. She chose bath salts, sprinkled the crystals into the water, then settled herself in the tub amidst the rising scent of pungent roses. This was like a Cecil B. DeMille movie starring Gloria Swanson.

The door opened and Rick walked in – champagne bottle under one arm and two exquisite goblets in his hands. He had changed into a wine-colored silk robe. He was naked beneath.

"The bottle's uncorked. Pour for us," he said, setting the bottle and glasses on the green-veined white marble floor. He crossed to a Chinese commode. Liz watched while he withdrew a large leather-bound book from the commode and brought it to her.

"Here's some artwork you may find amusing." His smile was jaunty. His eyes passionate.

Liz guessed that Rick was presenting her with a collection of erotic photographs. Adrienne would find this amusing.

"In the tub?" she chided while Rick shed his robe. "You don't want your artwork to get wet."

"We'll put it away in a few moments," he promised. "It's just an introduction." He lowered himself, facing Liz, into the tepid water, at the same time reaching for a glass of champagne. She was conscious of his eyes moving over her wet nudity while she inspected the color photographs of erotic love-making. *A deux, a trois, a quatre*, she observed with a start. She had never seen anything like this before, though Adrienne had talked about books she had seen in Paris.

"Is this supposed to be art?" she mocked after a few minutes. She closed the book and deposited it on the low-backed chair beside the tub.

"Drink up your champagne and I'll show you art. I'm an old master."

Normally Liz cared little for champagne. Today the pale liquid seemed to infuse her with a hedonistic attitude more native to Adrienne than herself. Rick took the glass from her hand and placed it beside the tub again, lifted himself above her.

"Rick, could we drown in here?" she asked with an odd feeling of detachment.

"Don't worry," he soothed.

She wasn't truly worrying, she told herself. The champagne just made her a little lightheaded. Don't think about anything, she commanded herself. Just lie here in the rose-scented water and let Rick make love to you.

Liz and Rick drove along the Bay, breathtakingly beautiful at sunset. Muted shades of orange and red cast their shadows on the deep blue water. Rick had decided to take one of the four cars in the garage with which she was unfamiliar. She was amused by the shift from the gray Rolls-Royce to a beat-up flivver.

They turned off familiar roads and drove for what seemed like almost an hour into the edge of twilight. Now Liz understood why Rick had taken the flivver. They were traveling on a treacherous dirt road.

"Rick, it'll be too dark if we're not there soon," Liz complained.

They had left behind them the palm trees and flowers and shrubs that seemed to be everywhere in Miami. The land here was flat and arid. A sign indicated that a mile beyond was the property of Pulaski Realty Company. Rick had wasted no time in having it posted. The deal had been closed only this morning.

Rick pulled to a stop.

"We'll have to walk from here."

"No road?" Liz asked in consternation. Her mother had

warned her against land with no accessible roads. For the last six miles the road had been like backwoods Georgia roads. What was Rick trying to sell her mother?

"Come on, sugar. I'll show you a 100,000-acre tract that'll be part of Greater Miami in less than a year." With a confident smile Rick leaned across Liz to thrust open the door for her.

Liz emerged from the car with a sense of unease. Six miles of dirt road and now no road at all. And Rick was talking about the purchase price going over a quarter of a million.

"About nine miles in from here," Rick said, dropping an arm about her waist as they followed a narrow footpath, "there's a sixty-acre lake that'll provide water for an entire development. Plus it'll be simple to drill wells when water's so close to the surface."

"A hundred thousand acres seems an awful lot of land," Liz said slowly, her eyes roving over the vast stretch of emptiness before them. "Why aren't there any trees here, Rick?" The barrenness was depressing.

"That's an asset," Rick pointed out. "No need to clear trees and brush. With minor irrigation the land will grow palms, tropical shrubbery, everything to make this a gorgeous tract of land. Of course, we couldn't walk this land if we tried," he said humorously. "Not in a month. Does your mother have a lawyer down here?" he asked. "She'll have to be represented by a lawyer at the closing."

"She has a lawyer. George Gateson." Liz hesitated. She wasn't sure that her mother would approve of this tract. She hadn't *seen* the lake. There was that six-mile stretch of dirt road, no road for a mile to the property. "Rick, I don't know if this is what my mother is looking for."

"Liz, I'll tell you something in confidence. You can't even tell Gateson because I'd be in a bad spot if the word got around. I have it direct from Mayor Snedigan. A four-lane boulevard is going to be built by the city, coming right out to this property. If I wasn't so tied up with other deals, I would hang on to this myself. But I'm a promoter," he acknowledged with a wry grin, "I enjoy fast turnovers."

"I'll phone my mother tomorrow and tell her about the property." Liz still held the figures Rick had given her earlier. "Should I mail her the figures or give them to Mr Gateson?" She had talked to the attorney briefly on the phone the day after her arrival. They had not met.

"Mail them to your mother," Rick instructed. "I'll see that Gateson receives another set. But let's don't allow this deal to stall," Rick warned her. "It's a hot property. It could be picked right off."

"I'll call my mother tomorrow," Liz reiterated. Rick would be upset if her mother didn't buy. He was taking it for granted that it was a sale. "Rick, is there some way we can get out to the lake?" By the time they walked even to the beginning of the property, it would be dark. Already the first star glimmered high in the sky. Romantic but hardly practical for viewing property. "And I should see the land –"

"Liz, a hundred thousand acres is a lot of territory." His voice betrayed his annoyance. "It's a full day's hike out to the lake. I suppose we could take along a tent, a water bottle and a picnic basket and stay the night," he said with an effort at humor.

"My mother will be unhappy about the lack of roads."

"Liz, I told you. The mayor guarantees that road is going in. The money was appropriated at a secret meeting of the town board. A four-lane boulevard," he repeated.

"But you said I couldn't tell my mother." Liz halted. It was absurd to walk any further. They couldn't inspect the land tonight.

"Liz, we know the road's going in. There's no problem about that. You have my word, honey. The best way to handle it is to assume there's an acceptable road already in, right up to the edge of the property. You won't be lying to your mother – it'll be built. I guarantee that. And I've seen the lake. I camped out there with a surveyor for four days. It's a hell of a lot deeper than Biscayne Bay." He chuckled. "Did you know the Bay is only shoulder deep, except in the channel – and loaded with three-foot-long barracuda?"

"I didn't know," Liz admitted, but the Bay held no interest for her at this moment.

"All right." Rick took her by the hand and headed back for the car. "Phone your mother tomorrow and explain you've seen the land. Tell her there's a sixty-acre lake. I'll have a copy of the deed made up so you can give it to Gateson. My lawyer will contact Gateson and make the arrangements."

"Rick, first I have to talk to my mother," Liz reminded.

"Baby, of course you have to talk to her. But this is a twenty percent larger tract than the original one we discussed. And the price is only a hundred thousand higher. Each day that passes prices rise in this town. You've been in Miami long enough to know what's going on." He reached to pull her to him, kissed her hotly in the enveloping darkness and released her. "Let's go have dinner and try my luck at the roulette table."

Liz lay sleepless much of the night. Rick expected her to tell her mother a decent road led to the property. He seemed convinced the road would be built. Why should it be a secret? A political necessity for the next two months, Rick said. He seemed to think that because she had grown up in a politically oriented household, she would understand. She didn't.

Rick meant for her to say she had seen the lake. How could she lie to Mama and say she'd seen it?

At last she fell into troubled sleep. She awoke with a jarring, heart-stopping sense of plummeting through space. A glance at the clock confirmed her suspicion that it was early. She left her bed and crossed to a window to look out on to the perpetual summer of Miami. She would call Mr Gateson, she decided. Before she phoned Mama.

Mr Gateson seemed astonished to receive a phone call from her at 8.30 in the morning.

"Mr Gateson, I went out with Mr Pulaski to look at a tract of land he acquired just yesterday," she began.

"You mean that 100,000 acres about ten miles beyond Coral Gables?" he asked indulgently.

"Yes." Warning signals popped up in her mind.

"Oh, Pulaski has owned that for the last ten weeks. I warned your mother against it," Gateson said.

How stupid of me to have thought Mama was sincere in having me check out the land.

The minute the Miami trip had been mentioned she had known Mama was trying to provide a cooling-off period before she talked to Vic about the divorce.

"There's no access to the land, and—"

"Could it be that roads will be built soon?" Liz interrupted.

"Not in the next ten years," Gateson said emphatically. "And at your mother's instructions I had a pilot fly over the land to check on the lake Pulaski claims is dead center. All the pilot saw was a small swamp. At any rate I advised your mother against buying anything in Miami at this time. The smart investors are sure the boom has crested. Prices will start to drop within a matter of weeks. They'll fall right down to the bottom."

"Thank you, Mr Gateson." The attorney knew she was playing at inspecting the land. It was a diversion for a rich young matron, she told herself in derision. Rick had waged an expensive campaign and lost.

She put down the phone, paused in bitter reflection, then lifted the receiver again. If she could arrange for reservations on today's train to Atlanta, they would leave.

A few minutes later, with train accommodations available, Liz invaded Kathy's bedroom.

"No trip to the beach this morning, my darling," she apologized, reaching to scoop Kathy into her arms with synthetic gaiety. "I've decided it's time we headed home. Let's start packing, Patience."

Rick would expect to meet her in the main rotunda at three as usual. She would not be there. He would ask at the desk, and they would tell her that Mrs Adams had checked out of the hotel. The party was over.

Four

The pullman chugged in a drowsy rhythm over the tracks that led north to Atlanta. Liz laid aside Edna Ferber's new novel, *So Big*, and stared out of the drawing-room window at the monotonous parade of red clay earth, where farm families worked to prepare their fields for another cotton crop. The familiar sight comforted her. In less than an hour they would arrive at Terminal Station in Atlanta. The days and nights with Rick would be buried in the attic of her mind.

How could she have allowed herself to be fooled by Rick? He looked at her and counted the profits he'd make on that worthless tract of land. Take her to bed and she'd tell her mother anything he asked, she jeered at herself. Right from the beginning Rick was sure of a sale. The egotistical bastard!

Yet it would be a long time before she could forget the laughter Rick and she had shared. The passion. That was real, she vindicated herself, no matter what its motivation.

All thoughts of divorce had been scraped from her mind. She was running home to Victor. To safety. She felt sick, remembering the hours in Rick's arms. She wasn't in love with Rick. She was obsessed by him.

It was despicable of Rick to have tried to use her to sell that barren, worthless parcel of land. Contemptible of Mama to have convinced her she was on an assignment in Miami, when in truth Mr Gateson was handling the situation.

But for twelve days she'd had a marvelous time, she reminded herself. Nobody could take that away from her.

Perhaps she would go to Europe with Adrienne this summer. She had given up on Victor going with her.

In a burst of impatience, while Kathy slept with her head in Patience's lap, Liz reached for a magazine to read. Von Hindenburg was opposed to pomp at his coming inauguration as president of Germany. There would be no military display and he'd wear civilian dress. She turned to national news. In a mid-air crash of two planes over Kelly Field, Texas, two army cadets – C. D. McAllister and Charles A. Lindberg – had parachuted to safety. A first in aviation history.

Victor prophesied that in ten years people would be flying all over the country. Even to Europe. She felt bathed in shame when she thought of him. But if he had responded to her needs, she wouldn't have turned to Rick. If he had come to Miami, as he'd promised, nothing would have happened between Rick and her. He had as much an obligation to his wife as he had to his patients.

The train arrived in Atlanta on schedule. She had cherished a faint hope that Victor would be there to meet them. He wasn't. Matthew was waiting with the new, long low-slung Franklin. This year all new cars had an enormous wheelbase.

"Miss Caroline sent a note over to the house with Jason," Matthew reported while he settled their hand luggage in the car. The trunk would be delivered tomorrow. "I got it right here." He pulled it out of his jacket pocket and gave it to Liz.

"Thank you, Matthew."

Matthew picked Kathy up and tossed her into the air while she gurgled in delight. "We all sho' missed you and Miss Kathy," Matthew said with warmth.

"Thank you, Matthew."

Liz scanned the note. Papa was home from Washington. Mama expected Victor and her for dinner tonight. She sighed in exasperation. Mama didn't ask if she had other plans.

* * *

In their large, square bedroom, cheerful with flowered wallpaper and the chintz fabric so popular for the past two decades, Liz sat at her dressing table – clad only in lace-trimmed white satin teddy and white slippers – and concentrated on applying her make-up.

"Liz?" The door swung wide open and Victor strode into the room. "How was the train trip?" He smiled eagerly as she came forward to greet him.

"Boring," she said.

He kissed her with disconcerting fervor. She felt nothing, she reproached herself. Rick had spoiled her. But Rick was out of her life. It would be a long time before he was out of her mind.

"You look well," Victor said with satisfaction while his dark eyes scrutinized her face. "That touch of color is becoming." His gaze moved over her with unexpected arousal. Her high, full breasts spilled over the lace of her teddy in inviting provocation. Her long, slim legs, on full display, were faintly gold from the Miami sun. "Liz –" He reached out to draw her close again.

"Vic, you have to change," Liz told him briskly. "Mama expects us at Hampton House for dinner in twenty minutes."

"A fresh shirt and tie and I'll be ready." His wry smile telegraphed his disappointment.

Victor crossed to the eighteenth-century chest-on-chest to select a shirt and tie, then disappeared into the bathroom. Liz reached for the wine-colored silk dress that lay in readiness across the bed. She felt guilty at disappointing Victor, yet she was relieved to have an excuse to avoid making love. Not yet. Not so soon after Rick.

Liz and Victor went to Kathy's room to kiss her goodnight, then drove the short distance to Hampton House. In the car, Victor told her about his brief visit with Josh in New York. They'd had dinner together at Luchow's and talked till midnight. Hardly aware of what Victor said, Liz fought against a feeling of entrapment. She had abandoned the prospect of divorcing Victor, yet she knew her life must change. *How* would it change?

Her parents and Sophie were in the library – arguing good-humoredly about how the current crime wave in Atlanta could be curbed.

"Liz!" Her father strode forward to embrace her.

It seemed to her that he held her with special warmth. Had Mama told him that she had thought about divorcing Victor? No, she decided, Mama always kept anything unpleasant from Papa until it had to be faced.

"Papa, you are still the most handsome senator in Washington," she teased. She was aware of questions in her mother's eyes. "And Vic's the most handsome doctor in Atlanta. We're two lucky ladies, Mama." She saw her mother relax. The divorce scare was over, Mama interpreted.

"This lady's hungry," Sophie remarked as Jason appeared in the doorway to announce dinner.

Sitting at the resplendent dinner table, Liz was relieved that the table conversation required little of her. Mama and Sophie were talking avidly about Nellie Taylor Ross, Governor of Wyoming since January 1st – the first woman governor in American history.

Papa swung the conversation to international affairs. Victor and Papa would talk all evening about the situation in Europe, she suspected. Victor – with his mother's family in disfavor in Italy – was upset that Mussolini was muzzling all Italian newspapers unfriendly towards the Fascist regime. Papa, as usual, was concerned about a lasting peace in Europe. He was fighting in the Senate for the United States to become a member of the World Court.

"For over three thousand years military men have been insisting the way to peace lies in preparation for war." Her father's voice reflected the passion with which he regarded this subject. "This is fundamentally wrong. The way for the world to acquire peace is to *prepare* for peace." His eyes swept the table. "Do you all realize that there are more men under arms in Europe right now than there were in 1914?" He shook his head in sadness. "Not one nation trusts another. Each one feels insecure including this country."

"I liked what Carrie Chapman Catt said when she spoke in Atlanta early last month," Caroline reminisced. "She said women have every right to meddle in the affairs of war. In the first place women have ceased to be non-combatants. And in the second place women pay a large percentage of federal tax, eighty-six percent of which goes to support the army and navy."

"We have a right to decide how that money is spent," Sophie said vigorously. "You can be sure few women want to see it go on guns and bullets."

"Mrs Catt reminded us that men are more war-like in spirit," Caroline continued, "so it's up to us to stand up and say, 'War is barbarian. It must be – *will be* – eliminated!'"

This family was so concerned with the welfare of the world, and she sat here huddled in her own personal unhappiness, Liz upbraided herself. Yet her life mattered, too. Mama believed that as long as she had the physical comforts nothing else counted. If all the poor people in the world were suddenly rich, Mama was sure this world would be paradise.

Liz's mind hurtled backward to her high-school years. She had gone to an expensive private school while her closest friend Janet had attended a public school. Even then Janet used to tease her about her family's wealth. She closed her eyes and heard Janet's laughter. "Sugar, you and your silken problems!"

"What do you hear from Josh?" Liz forced herself to join the conversation.

"I had a letter last week. He's definitely decided to intern at Bellevue in New York," Caroline reported with a trace of wistfulness. More years away from home. Josh was Mama's great white hope. Only Josh could give her a Hampton grandson to carry on at the mill. As proud as their mother was that Josh was dedicated to medicine, she regretted not having a son to follow in her footsteps. Now she hoped for a Hampton grandson to do that.

"Josh isn't coming to Grady?" Victor asked in astonishment. He had become more of an Atlantan than anybody born here, Liz thought.

"He feels he'll learn more at Bellevue than at any hospital in the country," Caroline explained. "It's such an enormous place."

Only half an hour after Victor had left to look in on a patient at Grady, Liz asked that Jason be summoned to drive her home.

"I'm exhausted from the trip," she apologized. She had fled Miami to safety, but safety was a vacuum.

"Did you enjoy Miami?" her mother questioned. All through the evening Liz had felt her mother's eyes on her at intervals. Mama sought reassurance that the divorce had been forgotten and the Hampton name was safe from scandal. They had to consider Papa's precious political blueprint: the White House in 1933.

"I loved Miami. That wonderful warmth even in March and the beautiful beaches." Liz managed a radiant smile. "I remember reading that Mark Twain once said that this country doesn't have any climate – only samples. He couldn't have known Miami's perpetual summer."

Her mother had manipulated her into the trip to Miami. Mama had shipped her right into Rick's arms.

How was she going to survive without Rick? She frowned at the thought. How could she feel this way about a man who had used her? Where was her pride? Yet she found solace in the conviction that making love to her had been a compulsion with Rick. Even if she had not appeared to be the route to a profitable real-estate sale, Rick would have been eager to sleep with her.

At the house Liz looked in for a moment on Kathy. Her tiny replica slept soundly. She leaned forward and kissed Kathy with a surge of maternal love. As was her habit when Liz was away in the evening, Patience slept on a cot in Kathy's room rather than in the servants' quarters over the garage. Liz tiptoed from the room, intent on not disturbing either of them.

In her own bedroom she prepared for the night – happy for the comfort of her own house yet nostalgic for the Royal Palm Hotel, where life had seemed to hold such richness.

Too restless to read, too wakeful to sleep she considered her future. Perhaps she ought to think about looking for a job. But she was trained for nothing. Victor would be upset if she became a salesgirl at Chamberlin-Johnson or at Rich's. His fellow doctors would be shocked that Dr Adams' wife worked. Mama would say she was depriving some girl of a job. Someone like Janet, whose job at Rich's was necessary for her physical survival.

Liz started at the sound of a car pulling into the garage. Victor home so early? She hesitated, then darted to the bed. She switched off the bedside lamp plunging the room into darkness, slid between the sheets, and pulled the covers about her shoulders.

Eyes closed in simulated slumber she heard Victor let himself into the house. He was climbing the carpeted staircase. In a few moments the bedroom door was opened and quickly shut.

"Liz?" he called tentatively in the dark. Her heart pounding, she pretended not to hear.

She heard him at the chest-on-chest. In search of pajamas, she surmised. En route to the bathroom he stumbled against the slipper chair in the dark, then disappeared behind the bathroom door, closing it to avoid disturbing her with light. In a few minutes he was back in the bedroom and moving beneath the covers.

Liz felt the warmth of his body against her own.

"Liz?" he tried again.

"Hmm?" She feigned sleepiness. She didn't want Victor to touch her. Not yet. The memory of Rick was painfully fresh. *Please, let me sleep.*

"Honey?" Tonight Victor was determined. She felt a leg thrown across her thighs. His hand moved to her breasts. "Missed you like the devil."

She murmured incoherently, allowed herself to be maneuvered on to her back. Why couldn't Victor leave her alone? So many nights she had prayed he would want to make love, and he hadn't. Why couldn't he have been detained at the hospital?

"The house seemed empty with Kathy and you away," he murmured, his mouth at her throat, his hands tugging at the slender straps of her nightgown. "I'm glad you decided to come home two days early."

"Kathy was getting restless," she fabricated. It was futile to pretend she was asleep.

"I wish you could have been in New York with me," he said. "It was a great experience."

Before she could respond, his mouth was on hers. She didn't want Victor to make love to her tonight. Yet despite herself her body was responding.

Later Victor talked about his trip to New York. He had spoken before a group enthusiastic about his work with children in Atlanta. He told her about the reactions to his speech, the eager questions.

"All my doubts, all my misgivings disappeared," Victor told her with a conviction that had been missing in him of late. "I know what I'm accomplishing has value. I'm contributing, Liz."

And that, she told herself again, meant more to Victor than his wife or his child. He lived in a rarefied atmosphere that held no space for her.

Liz fought to erase Miami from her memory. Each morning she awoke with the anguished realization that Rick would not be arriving at three, that the trees outside the house were dogwoods in glorious bloom, not avenues of royal palms. This was her world. Atlanta.

When she had been back in Atlanta a week, she awoke to the blare of a phonograph record. Bright morning sunlight, thrusting its way through the drapes, laid a swathe of gold across the bed. The air wore the scent of early roses. The music – Dixieland jazz – seemed a harsh intrusion. Then comprehension brought a smile to Liz's face. Adrienne was home. Only Adrienne played jazz at ten o'clock in the morning.

Liz rushed through her morning ritual, barely touching breakfast when she went downstairs. The sounds from the phonograph still ricocheted through the spring morning when she hurried across the lawn to Adrienne's house. Without bothering to ring Liz thrust open the door and hurried down the hall to what Adrienne referred to as the morning room.

"Adrienne!" Liz called in a burst of exuberance.

Adrienne was sprawled along the length of the chintz-covered sofa, propped against a mass of colorful cushions. While not a conventional beauty, she was strikingly attractive. Her black bobbed hair framed a piquant face dramatized by mascara, brilliant lipstick and rouge.

"Darling, you took long enough to come over." Adrienne pretended to pout. She reached for a water tumbler on the floor beside the sofa. "What would you like to drink?"

"Not gin at this hour of the morning." Liz shuddered and sat in a club chair that flanked the sofa. Adrienne had gin before her morning coffee.

"Carrie!" Adrienne yelled. "Bring coffee for Miss Liz."

Adrienne spilled over with Palm Beach gossip. Everything was madly expensive, she complained, though Liz doubted that this in any way curtailed Adrienne's activities. She consistently lost when she visited the "inner room" at her favorite casino – the big-stake room, Adrienne reported, and vowed to limit herself to the roulette wheel. She'd had a three-night affair with a Bulgarian prince.

"He showed me dirty movies in one bedroom," Adrienne giggled, "while his wife slept in another bedroom. I never thought dirty movies could make me so horny."

Over Carrie's strong, black coffee Liz provided a candid re-play for Adrienne of her Miami trip. Only with Adrienne could she bring herself to talk about Rick. Earlier in the week she had met Janet during her brief lunch hour from her job at Rich's but, despite their closeness, she could not talk about those tumultuous twelve days.

"Was he good in bed?" Adrienne demanded.

"He was wonderful," Liz confessed. "But I didn't trust myself to stay. I might have walked out on Vic and Kathy. I might have persuaded my mother to buy some worthless piece of land just to please him. But it's over," she said vigorously. "I can't handle Rick."

"I like a fellow I can't handle." Adrienne's eyes were brilliant. "I don't care if he pushes me around a little."

"That can be dangerous," Liz warned. Sometimes she worried about Adrienne.

"I wonder what's wrong with me." Adrienne abandoned her semi-prone position. "I'm so bloody tired of everything. I mean, what's there left to do?"

"Plenty of things."

"More trips? More booze? More men?" Adrienne challenged. Her eyes narrowed speculatively. "I'm beginning to be crazy about jazz. Jazz and the Charleston. I was talking to Johnny about it this morning." Johnny was a middle-aged local banker, married but intrigued by Adrienne. "He's taking me to a speakeasy tonight where they've got this marvelous jazz pianist. The rest of the band is *comme ci comme ça*, but the pianist is terrific. Come with us."

"Don't be silly," Liz said.

"Johnny would love it. Two good-looking broads is better than one. We'll take you home before the party gets rough," she promised. "I'm enough for any fellow. Besides, at Johnny's age he might have a heart attack trying to take us both on at once."

"Adrienne!" Liz admonished. It was stupid to be embarrassed when Adrienne talked like that. She was supposed to be sophisticated.

"Let's both wear black," Adrienne planned. "And necklaces

down to our crotch." She drained the tumbler of gin. "If Vic happens to be around, bring him along."

Victor came home for dinner but left before coffee to make a hospital call. Liz managed a strained smile when he kissed her apologetically before dashing off to his patient. She would go with Adrienne and Johnny to hear the jazz pianist. Why sit at home and do crossword puzzles? She couldn't even play the piano this late because the music might wake Kathy.

In the black georgette that Rick had liked so much Liz went with Adrienne and Johnny to Atlanta's newest speakeasy, crowded with the bored and restless eager for fresh diversion. The pianist, fresh from triumphs in Chicago, won Liz's instant respect. He was young. Probably not over twenty. He had a lean, narrow face and dark, intense eyes. He played in a style that mesmerized her.

She and Adrienne were wide-eyed in amazement when Johnny sauntered off and returned to the table, grinning in triumph, with the jazz pianist in tow. While the pianist joined them for a drink, Adrienne talked about the popularity of jazz in Europe. She revealed a knowledgeability that impressed Liz.

"Honey," she told the Chicago-born pianist, "they've been crazy about jazz in Europe since the Original Dixieland Jazz Band arrived in London at the end of the war. They take their jazz real serious over there."

"All I know about jazz," Liz confessed, "is George Gershwin. I adore his *Rhapsody in Blue*."

"Don't call that jazz." The pianist winced. His eyes were scornful. "It's pretentious."

"How can you say that?" Liz protested. "Fifty years from now people will love *Rhapsody in Blue*!"

"Don't take my word for it." The pianist spoke with a religious fervor. "Virgil Thomson wrote in *Vanity Fair* that Gershwin is a composer for the theater, but that the *Rhapsody* is 'at best a piece of aesthetic snobbery.'"

Liz and the pianist argued good-humoredly about the merits

of Gershwin. Ever since the *Rhapsody* was introduced last year she'd been fascinated by the music. To her Gershwin was holy. All at once the pianist rose to his feet and extended a hand to Liz.

"Come over to the piano and play that piece," he taunted. "Nobody here will stop talking to listen. They want Chicago jazz."

"I can't." Liz was shocked.

"Go on, sugar," Adrienne trilled. "She's good enough to play professionally," she assured the pianist.

"Yeah, go on," Johnny urged, beckoning the waiter to refresh their drinks. "Show them what Atlanta can do."

Caught up in a need to convince the Chicago pianist that Gershwin would be appreciated, Liz allowed herself to be propelled to the piano. She recognized, without vanity, that her playing skills were professional. At regular intervals she was drafted to perform at local events where she usually played the classics. She was always received with great enthusiasm.

At the piano, her hands rippling over the keys to produce the music she loved, Liz forgot her surroundings. She was alone with the haunting Gershwin music until the last sound evaporated and the patrons in the speakeasy bombarded her with applause. Now she was self-conscious, anxious to be out of the spotlight.

"Liz, they loved you," Adrienne whispered in triumph when she returned to their table. "You should be playing professionally."

Not quite knowing how the routine had come about, Liz found herself practicing at the piano for five or six hours every day. She was learning to play a new conception of jazz that a trumpeter named Louis Armstrong was spreading through the jazz world. Here was music from the heart blending with a musical technique that Liz respected.

The jazz pianist from Chicago had moved on; but he had left behind with Liz a half-dozen records made in Chicago by King

Oliver's Creole Jazz Band, with Armstrong part of the group. Liz lost herself in music. This was a way to push Rick into the locked-away past. And constantly Adrienne hovered over her, urging her to turn professional.

On a hot May afternoon Adrienne invaded the music room to insist Liz interrupt her practicing for a tall, cool drink.

"This weather is just awful," Adrienne complained. "All the fans do is blow hot air around. I told Patience, when I crossed the lawn, to turn the watering hose on Tommy and Kathy." She giggled. "Maybe we ought to join them."

"At least the evenings cool off out here," Liz consoled.

"When are you going to stop all this practicing and think about a career?" Adrienne prodded.

"Honey, I'm just having fun." Liz hedged. But she knew, in the back of her mind, that the heavy practicing was motivated by that brief appearance at the speakeasy, when the patrons had responded so gratifyingly to her playing.

"Liz, you could turn this town on its ear!" Adrienne chortled. "Johnny has contacts in a lot of speakeasies. They'd hire you on the strength of your looks," she said.

"I'm not ready." How could she play jazz piano in a speakeasy? Her family would be outraged. How would it look for Victor? For her father, the senator? Yet Adrienne's depiction of the exciting new life that performing could bring was an intoxicant to her.

"You could become professional in Paris," Adrienne plotted, sensitive to Liz's doubts about Atlanta appearances. "Nobody here has to know. Come with me to Paris. They love Americans there. I'll introduce you to everybody. I went to Gertrude Stein's salon at 27 Rue de Fleurs and met so many exciting people. F. Scott Fitzgerald," she said in triumph. "He wrote that marvelous book, *The Great Gatsby*. We'll go to the Dingo Bar, and—"

"Maybe Vic wouldn't be upset if I went to Paris for a month," Liz broke in, tense with anticipation. "But I'll have to work up to it."

"I'm leaving for Paris in July," Adrienne reminded. "Work on it fast."

Maybe in Paris she could erase Rick from her mind. Despite all his rottenness, she lay awake too many nights remembering what it was like with Rick. He was a constant dull ache in her psyche.

As Victor and she sat down to dinner that evening, Liz mentioned that Adrienne was planning to go to Paris in July.

"She's renting an apartment just off the Quai d'Orsay with a view of the Eiffel Tower. She says you can see Les Invalides and the place de la Concorde from the windows. You know, Paris has that restriction about the heights of buildings in the city –" She paused, faintly breathless. Victor was frowning. Why did he always become irritated when she talked about Adrienne?

"Have you talked to Maureen about when the two of you would like to go up to Hampton Court?" Victor asked. For the past few years they usually went to the family plantation for several of the hot weeks with Liz's cousin Andrew, who helped her mother and Sophie run the mill, and his wife Maureen. Victor and Andrew came up for the weekends.

"No." Liz was cold. Victor was going to be difficult about her going to Paris with Adrienne.

"Did you read in the morning's *Constitution* about that teacher who was arrested down in Tennessee for teaching evolution in his classroom? I think his name is Scopes."

"I didn't read it." *Why do I have to ask Victor's permission to go to Paris? He didn't ask my permission to go to New York to talk at that meeting.*

After dinner Victor and she settled themselves in the library. She focused on reading the new book by Theodore Dreiser, *An American Tragedy*, that most people thought quite daring. It had been banned in Boston. Victor listened to the radio. He claimed this relieved his tension after a day of coping with patients.

She was relieved when he was called to a patient's house.

"I won't be long," he promised. "All Mrs Anderson wants is a little hand holding." His smile was whimsical. "At ninety-three she deserves that."

Liz discarded her book to fiddle with the radio dials. She was not in the mood for the symphony to which Victor had been listening.

"Show me the way to go home . . ." A sultry voice wailed the familiar lyrics.

Liz returned to her chair. The music was irreverent and relaxing.

After a longer visit than he had anticipated, Victor left the Anderson house. His mind dwelt on his wife. Liz was still angry that he had not gone down to join her in Miami. Caro had urged him to go. She said Liz was alone too much, that their marriage needed bolstering. Why? Liz knew he loved her. She knew she was the only woman in his life.

Damn it, he couldn't have turned down the invitation to speak in New York. It was important. More than anybody else Liz knew the potential of his work with children. She was a witness to what he had done for Francis.

Liz knew what was involved when she married a doctor, he thought defensively. Masterson on the surgical service grumbled and said all doctors should take a vow of celibacy. That or wrest a guarantee from God that no patient fell sick between seven p.m. and seven a.m.

When he arrived at the house, Victor was startled to discover the lights off except for those in the foyer and on the stairs. Liz had gone to sleep already. She was angry because he had not been receptive to talk about Adrienne's trip to Paris. He would not approve of her going to Paris with Adrienne and that was what she had been leading up to.

He had never been happy when she went off to Palm Beach with Adrienne. But if he tried to explain his reasons, Liz would tell him he was ridiculous. He believed in much of the new freedom for women, but Adrienne flaunted common decency.

He moved quietly about the bedroom changing into pajamas. Not a breath of air came in through the four open windows. A fan, whirring from the top of the mantel, offered meager relief. Liz lay huddled at one side of the bed, the sheet discarded in slumber.

Faster than he had anticipated, he fell asleep. He awoke with a start. The phone was a raucous intrusion in the night. He reached for the receiver.

"Hello." He was aware that Liz was awake, too. He felt the shift of her body beside him.

"Vic, Tommy's sick." Adrienne sounded distraught. "He's been throwing up, and I think he's running a high fever."

"Did you take his temperature?" Victor struggled into a semi-sitting position.

"Well, no, I haven't. But Vic, he's been so sick."

"It's probably just a stomach upset." He sighed. "I'll be right over." He slammed down the phone. "Damn."

"Is Tommy sick?" Liz asked anxiously. "Is there anything going around?" She was worrying about Kathy. Tommy and Kathy played together every day.

"There's always something going around," Victor said drily. "There's probably nothing wrong with Tommy except that Adrienne's grandmother stuffed him with too much candy." He paused at the edge of the bed, steeling himself to go next door. Every time Tommy sneezed, Adrienne called him. Admittedly, never in the middle of the night until now.

"You're going over there?" Liz asked. Her face said she couldn't believe Victor would consider otherwise.

"I'm going," he conceded. He glanced at the clock. It was almost two. He left the house at six thirty to make his morning hospital rounds. Another night with little sleep.

"Vic, you're not bothering to dress to go next door?" Liz demanded when he reached into the closet and brought out a pair of trousers. "Wear your robe."

"Sure," he said, stifling the remark that hovered on his

tongue. Liz would think it was a big joke if he told her Adrienne had an unnerving way of throwing herself at him every time they were alone. Liz would never believe her dear friend wanted to sleep with her husband.

In robe and slippers, bag in hand, Victor hurried from the house and crossed the wide expanse of lawn that divided the two houses. Two of the upstairs rooms were brilliantly lit: Tommy's and Adrienne's bedrooms. He walked up the stairs and crossed the porch of the half-timbered Jacobethan-revival house and rang the doorbell.

The door flew open in instant response.

"Vic, I'm so worried." Adrienne hovered before him in a revealing black georgette robe. "He's been so sick."

"Was he at your grandmother's today?" Vic asked, striding across the foyer to mount the stairs.

"Well, yes," Adrienne acknowledged, trying to keep pace with him in her high-heeled black satin slippers.

"Then there's the answer," Victor said brusquely. "I told you not to let her stuff Tommy with cake and cookies every time he goes visiting."

Clarabelle, Tommy's nurse, stood beside his bed. She looked up at Victor with an apologetic smile.

"He jes' about goin' off to sleep now, Dr Victor. I cleaned him up and all—"

"Clarabelle, you can go back to your room now," Adrienne said. Her voice was edged with sharpness.

Victor pulled up a chair and sat beside the bed. Tommy was hardly aware of his presence. Victor did a cursory examination, which confirmed his suspicions.

"There's nothing wrong with Tommy except an over-indulgence in sweets," Victor told her.

"You didn't take his temperature," Adrienne reproached. "I'm sure he's running a fever."

"He's not running a fever." Victor quelled a temptation to yell at Adrienne. "I don't need to take his temperature to know that. Let him sleep. He'll be fine in the morning." His face softened as his eyes rested on the tiny form beneath the light coverlet.

Adrienne bent to turn off the lamp beside Tommy's bed.

"Let me fix you a drink." She dropped a hand on his arm, leaning forward slightly so that the black georgette robe parted to display the Palm Beach gold of her small, high breasts.

"I'm going home to bed," he told her abruptly.

"Tarry a while in my bed," she invited, moving in to him in the darkness of the room. Her breasts grazed his chest. "Vic, you're always avoiding me."

"I'm going home to my bed. To my wife."

"You're such a prude," Adrienne scolded. "You don't know the fun you're missing." Her arms slid about his shoulders. "I could show you—"

Victor reached to remove her hands as they closed in about his neck and her hips pushed against his.

"I'll forgo that pleasure. Goodnight, Adrienne. I'll show myself out." Didn't Adrienne know a man preferred to be the pursuer? And, for God's sake, she was Liz's close friend.

Victor left Tommy's room, hurried down the stairs and out of the house. Did Adrienne find something romantic about making love to a doctor? Or was it any man? He was inclined to suspect that any presentable man was fair game for Adrienne Lee.

He had never been unfaithful to Liz. He didn't plan to start that now. But the brief heated interlude with Adrienne had aroused him. He was going home to make love to his wife.

He thought about Tommy, sleeping peacefully now after his bout of sickness. Liz would be less restless, less susceptible to Adrienne's influence if she had another child.

In his own bedroom again Victor was astonished at the passion that gripped him. He tossed aside his robe and settled himself in bed. Liz appeared to be asleep.

"Honey –" He dropped one hand to her breast, knowing this was an erotic area. "Tommy's fine—"

"Oh, I'm glad," she mumbled in semi-sleep.

He lifted himself above her, sure that in a few moments she would be responsive. Liz was always most passionate when love-making was unexpected. His legs maneuvered a path for him. With luck he would give his wife a son.

Five

In mid-June Atlanta was imprisoned by a heat wave. Sounding like massive armies of mosquitos, fans droned night and day. Many an Atlantan forsook morning coffee for ice-cold Coca-Cola. Everybody prayed for rain.

It seemed to Liz that more Atlanta girls were marrying this June than in any June before. She sat through a succession of trousseau showers and bride-elect parties, forced herself into the mold of light-hearted young Southern society matron.

"I hear Peggy Mitchell is marrying John Marsh on July the fourth," Adrienne commented as they sat at a party table for another bride-elect. Like Liz, Adrienne was intrigued by Peggy's activities.

"I hope she has better luck this time," Eleanor Hobson, a slightly older Washington Seminary alumna, said with a saccharine smile. Eleanor Hobson was jealous because Margaret was so pretty and witty, Liz surmised. "I suppose now she'll stop playing at being a newspaper reporter."

"She's not playing at it," Liz defended Peggy. From her father's law partner and sometime newspaper publisher, Jim Russell, Liz knew what the job entailed. "All newspaper people put in a six-day, sixty-hour week."

"You can always depend on Margaret to do something crazy," Eleanor went on. "Remember when she performed that awful apache dance at the Micarême Ball given by the Debutante Club four years ago? Everybody was shocked to death."

"Both the *Journal* and the *Constitution* wrote it up," Adrienne said maliciously. On several occasions she had been the butt of Eleanor Hobson's criticism. "The *Journal* society reporter said it was the best act at the ball. And remember the time the *Journal* ran her picture in the Sunday rotogravure section? There she was, wearing a trainman's hat and sitting on the cowcatcher of a locomotive."

"That apache dance kept her from being invited to join the Junior League," Eleanor pointed out in triumph, "and you know everybody who makes a debut is invited to join. It was a terrible snub."

"Aren't these Brittany lace mats the prettiest things?" said another guest. "And wasn't it smart to tie them with sprays of orange blossoms?"

Liz curtailed her practice at the piano to one hour in the morning and one hour before dinner in deference to the heat. Adrienne prodded her towards a showdown with Victor about the Paris trip but the propitious moment never seemed to arrive. Already Adrienne had reserved a stateroom for herself aboard the French Line's new *Paris*, favored by American artists, writers, and musicians.

For the third consecutive morning Liz awoke to struggle against nausea. It was this awful heat, she told herself. And then her mind snapped into action. With unwary swiftness she darted from the bed to consult the calendar on her dressing table. Her eyes clung to the date, then edged backward to the earlier warning date encircled in red. She was ten days late.

Slowly Liz moved back to the bed. Her heart pounded as she considered her suspicion. Ensconced against the pillows she pinpointed her symptoms. She was not just late. She was pregnant.

Unaccountably she felt a surge of relief. No need now to confront Victor about the trip to Paris. No need to pursue a career as a pianist. She had a fair amount of musical talent, but that was not enough. She didn't possess the drive, the dedication to become a professional musician. Without that drive talent was nothing.

She had allowed Adrienne to drug her with visions of a

new life that meant escape. It had made her feel important. It had bolstered her shaky ego to imagine herself playing before hordes of enthralled listeners, hearing their applause. But she would never push herself beyond practicing. She would always unearth an excuse to avoid exposing herself to failure.

Liz dismissed the proposed career with no compunction. She felt encased in tenderness in the protective shell of pregnancy. A little brother for Kathy. She envisioned Victor's face when she told him. He would be delighted. Mama would be out of her mind with pleasure. These last insane weeks would be washed away. Victor and she would have a normal marriage again.

Victor would be home more often now because he would be concerned about her. That was natural. He had been so sweet, so attentive when she was carrying Kathy. It would be that way again.

She must tell Adrienne, she thought guiltily. Adrienne would be disappointed. Was she awake yet? Liz left the bed again to go to a window. The moment Adrienne woke up, she turned on the radio or put a record on the phonograph.

Liz leaned out the window with care, conscious of the baby growing within her. She could hear Adrienne singing along with a phonograph record. "Don't Bring Lulu . . ." Down below Kathy and Tommy played in the sandbox with Patience and Clarabelle in attendance.

Liz telephoned Adrienne and arranged to have breakfast with her in the garden. She dressed swiftly, anxious to be there by the time the herb omelets Adrienne had ordered for them would be ready. Twenty minutes later she sat across the table from Adrienne, willing herself to finish the succulent omelet despite her queasy stomach and debating about how to break her news.

"I'm not buying a thing in the way of clothes," Adrienne declared. "I'll wait till we're in Paris." Like Rick, Liz thought involuntarily, Adrienne was making assumptions. "Darling, buy your wardrobe in Paris. Coco Chanel, Lanvin, Poiret."

"I don't think so," Liz said and Adrienne looked at her in reproach. "Lane Bryant," she said softly.

For a moment Adrienne stared in shock.

"You're pregnant?" she screeched.

"I'm sure of it," Liz confirmed, "though I'm only two weeks late. But I've got the classic symptoms. I'm constantly sleepy, I've taken up permanent residence in the bathroom, and I doubt that I can finish this sumptuous omelet so early in the day." Liz felt enveloped in a comforting sense of peace.

"Liz, you're not going to have a baby," Adrienne said ominously.

"I don't have any choice." Her actions were now beyond her control. Dictated by what used to be called her "delicate condition".

"I know a doctor." Adrienne tilted her head in a gesture of triumph. "He's as expensive as hell, but he'll get rid of it for you. It'll be safe, and you won't feel a thing. You'll just stay overnight in his private sanitarium." Adrienne giggled reminiscently. "He does a thriving business."

"Adrienne, I'm not having an abortion." Liz's throat tightened in recall. She remembered the traumatic experience of her first pregnancy, by one of a parade of faceless soldiers she had slept with after David died. She remembered hysterically haranguing Victor because he refused to abort the baby, whom she lost that same night after being beaten by another soldier. "No, Adrienne," she said forcefully.

"You're going to let Vic spoil your chances at an exciting career?" Adrienne demanded. "Liz, don't be a sentimental slob!"

"No abortion." She should not have confided in Adrienne. She should have waited until after she had told Victor.

"I think you're crazy," Adrienne snapped. She stared at Liz as though she had never truly seen her before. "I plan on staying in Paris for at least six months." Her tone was cold. "I'm renting the house to a writer who's coming down from New York to work on a book. He said Florida is too depressing, now that the boom's collapsed. The roads north are jammed with people running back to where they came from."

How did Rick fare when the Miami bubble burst, Liz wondered involuntarily. But he was smart; he would have got out in time.

"I'll miss you," Liz said, forcing Rick from her mind.

"No, you won't. You're one of those women who gets so wrapped up in pregnancy she thinks nothing exists except herself and her swollen belly. Pity," Adrienne drawled, "you would have had such fun in Paris."

"Adrienne, don't be angry," Liz coaxed.

"I think it's awful." Adrienne was characteristically outspoken. "You're always talking about how wonderful Margaret Mitchell is because she's gone out and made a career for herself; but when the chance comes, you toss it away. Oh, did I tell you? Margaret may be a married lady since July the fourth, but the door on her apartment on Crescent Avenue has two calling cards. 'Mr John R. Marsh' and 'Miss Margaret Mitchell'. Now that's a girl with sense. Nobody's taking away her independence!"

Victor was unable to get home for dinner. He called to explain that a patient had suffered a massive stroke. He would have to remain at the hospital until the crisis was past.

It was almost midnight when he arrived home, exhausted and apologetic. Wearing one of the filmy nightgowns Victor admired, Liz was sitting up in bed reading Ernest Hemingway's new book, *The Torrents of Spring*, while the whirr of the small oscillating fan on the dresser blended with the romantic Jerome Kern music provided by the radio.

"You look tired," Liz said sympathetically.

"It was a rough night. But he'll make it," Victor said with satisfaction.

"I'm glad."

She listened with a new serenity while Victor told her about the case while he prepared for bed. He had not talked to her like this in a long time.

"Vic –" Liz dropped a hand on his chest when he slid into bed beside her. Her face was radiant. "I'm pregnant."

Liz was relieved when Adrienne left for Paris. She was seeing as much as possible of Janet. In critical periods of her life, she was conscious of the special relationship between Janet and herself. She never felt entirely comfortable with Janet's husband. Kevin was too aware of the difference in their financial situations.

She had been disappointed when Janet married Kevin Michaels – a transplanted New Yorker – a week after she graduated from Agnes Scott. He was a supervisor at one of the Atlanta mills. Though Janet was three years older than her brother Josh, Liz had harbored a sentimental hope that Janet and Josh would marry some day. At sixteen Josh had already been in love with Janet. Sometimes Liz was convinced Josh went to Columbia College up in New York because he couldn't bear to stay in Atlanta and see Janet married to somebody else.

At regular intervals she sent Patience and Kathy over to Janet's house, with Matthew driving them, to bring Janet's young daughter Wendy over to spend the day with Kathy. With Tommy staying with his great-grandmother in Adrienne's absence Kathy was eager for Wendy's companionship.

The months of her pregnancy were precious to Liz. She felt loved and cherished. And safe. Adrienne wrote irregularly, always with amusing stories of her escapades. She had gone off to Vienna for two weeks with a hypnotist she picked up at Deux Magots in Paris. The hypnotist had taken her to a psychoanalytic meeting, where she had met the great Sigmund Freud. "The man who freed us sexually," Adrienne eulogized, though she knew Liz viewed the Freudian cult in the United States with an inchoate suspicion.

Then Adrienne had a tempestuous affair with a marquis, and had moved on from him to a Hollywood producer twice her age.

"He says I could do as well in pictures as Clara Bow," Adrienne wrote, "but I could never bear getting up at five in the morning to be on a movie set."

Early in April Liz went into labor. Victor and the attending obstetrician were watchful; they knew she carried a large baby. Dr Paul had talked to Victor about the possibility of performing a Caesarian, but she had pleaded to be allowed to have the baby normally.

"No anaesthetic," she had reiterated throughout the last month. "I want to be awake when my son is born."

Liz went into hard labor almost upon arrival in the hospital, but progress was slow. In an agony that divided mind from body she fought to deliver this large child that was equally determined not to come into the world.

"Liz, you must let Dr Paul order an anaesthetic," Victor pleaded, his face drained of color. "You can't take any more of this."

"No anaesthetic," she insisted. "No!"

In a burst of anguish she bore down with fresh strength, of which no one in the delivery room believed her capable. With a tortured cry she pushed the baby from her. Seconds later she heard a welcome small echo.

"He's a big boy," she gasped weakly while Victor leaned over to kiss her.

"A big girl," Victor corrected her tenderly. "A beautiful daughter."

Liz's eyes widened in disbelief.

"Oh, Vic –" Tears spilled over without her being aware of them, "I've disappointed you."

"Honey, I'm not disappointed," he said in astonishment. "She's beautiful and healthy – that's all that matters."

Liz turned her face away from Victor and closed her eyes. She knew how much he wanted a son. She could see it in his eyes each time he looked at Tommy. She knew how much Mama looked forward to a grandson. She had failed them.

Her father rushed home from Washington to see his second

granddaughter. Her mother sent flowers daily, came to visit every evening. She appeared elated at being a grandmother a second time, yet Liz tormented herself with the conviction that she had disappointed Victor and her parents.

Janet and her mother – Caroline's close friend Ellen – came to the hospital to visit with Liz and rhapsodize over the new baby. Aglow with pride Victor was in and out of her hospital room at every possible moment. Liz knew he was determined to prove that this new child was precious to him.

When Liz came home with their daughter, Debbie, she spent hours each day beside her crib. With a cap of heavy dark hair and the blue eyes of the newborn, her features minute, delicate replicas of Victor's, Debbie was a beguiling infant.

"She so good, Miz Liz," Patience crooned with pride. "She ain't no trouble a'tall."

Victor exhorted Liz to remember she had another daughter; Kathy must not feel she had been supplanted, though both Sophie and Maureen were careful to lavish her with attention when they came to visit. Mindful of her own childhood, when she had so often felt herself over-shadowed by Francis, Liz displayed demonstrative affection towards Kathy. Her life was complete, she exulted. Miami might never have happened.

Liz avoided the Atlanta social whirl – feigning a slow convalescence after a difficult birth. She cherished the tight little world of children and family. Regularly, however, she invited Janet and Kevin to dinner. If Victor was tied up at the hospital, they understood. And she was beginning to appreciate the qualities in Kevin that Janet found magnetic.

In an era when it was fashionable to be cynical about serving mankind, Kevin was possessed by a yearning to be helpful. He talked with passionate eloquence about the need to unionize the textile mills.

"Every human being must find a way to contribute to society," Kevin argued, "or he's not a whole person. You've seen the apathy of the mill workers. They don't know they're contributing.

They feel they're nothing. But without the workers, there would be no textile industry!"

On a succession of evenings Liz sat with Janet and Kevin in the library and listened while Kevin spoke with an intensity that sent shivers through her. Even as a small child she had been conscious of the difference between the lives of the mill workers and her own, and had been disturbed. She felt disloyal to her mother at feeling this way.

"What happens in the Southern cotton mills isn't just a sectional problem," Kevin insisted. "The low standards the workers put up with here in the South are causing havoc in the northern and western mills. It's destroying the slight gains that labor has made in this past generation."

"Kevin says the Southern workers think that every labor union organizer is a Bolshevik," Janet pointed out somberly.

"It's incomprehensible that in 1926 – with Henry Ford's auto workers putting in an eight-hour five-day week, with New England textile workers on an eight-hour day – the cotton-mill workers down here are working an eleven-hour day and a twelve-hour night. A cotton-mill worker gets up at five thirty and rushes to reach the mill before the last whistle blows at six. He stands up all day before a machine, with an hour off for lunch, and doesn't leave till the whistle blows at six in the evening. If he's on the night shift, he's there from six in the evening to six fifteen in the morning, with fifteen minutes off around midnight to eat. It's the same for women and children over fourteen."

"My mother has always been against children under fourteen working in the mills. Even before it became the law," Liz said defensively. "But at fourteen they want to work. They're bobbin boys, they don't work more than eight hours. When they're not working, they go out and sit in the sun."

"Maybe at the Hampton Mill they're bobbin boys," Kevin conceded. "But I know mills where fourteen-year-olds – both boys and girls – spend eleven hours a day at a spinning frame. Sometimes they even work the night shift. Even in this state they can legally work eleven hours, but I say that's too much for a growing body."

"Enough talk about the mills," Janet ordered, knowing it disturbed Liz. "Isn't it awful that Aimee Semple McPherson was kidnapped like that? She's been missing almost three weeks."

"I'll bet she's off somewhere with a boyfriend," Kevin said cynically. "She'll show up any day now with some weird story that the public will swallow whole."

Victor arrived home in time to join the others in a final cup of coffee. As was his habit Victor switched on the radio to listen to what news account was available. Immediately Kevin and he were swept up in talk about Mussolini's growing power in Italy.

"He'll be in absolute control of the country within two years," Victor gloomily predicted.

"That's the man who said, during the war, that 'Italy must help the democratic powers with the war so that more liberty will exist in Europe, and the proletariat will have better opportunities to develop its class capacities.'" Kevin's voice throbbed with scorn. "It was the rich – scared to death of a Bolshevik revolution – who put Mussolini in power."

Janet frowned. She was remembering, Liz thought, that Victor's mother belonged to a rich Italian family. His mother had been a countess before her marriage to his father, a Massachusetts congressman.

"Kevin, it's late," Janet intervened, "we have to be up early. Victor, too," she reminded with a smile.

After Janet and Kevin's departure Victor told Liz they had an invitation for dinner later in the week to the house of a colleague.

"It's the Conrads' twenty-seventh anniversary," Victor said sentimentally. "We can't turn down this invitation."

"I don't really feel up to socializing yet," Liz hedged.

"Honey, Debbie is almost three months old. She'll be fine with Patience. We'll go to the Conrads' dinner," he decreed.

"It's unhealthy for you to stay cloistered in the house the way you do."

Two days before the Conrads' dinner Patience was rushed to the hospital for an emergency appendectomy. Liz and Caroline sat together in the hospital waiting room until the surgeon emerged from the operating room to tell them Patience was out of danger.

Caroline sent Mattie's young granddaughter Gussie, now a maid at Hampton House, to look after Kathy and Debbie until Patience was able to take on their care again. While she dressed on Friday evening, Liz struggled to conceal her reluctance to leave for the Conrads' dinner.

"Liz, we're running short on time." Victor's eyes told her he understood her feelings and was sympathetic. "Stop worrying about the children," he scolded gently. "Debbie sleeps straight through the night now. There'll be no problems."

"Gussie's so young." Liz was ambivalent. She was only fourteen.

"Liz, we're going to the dinner." Victor was firm. "We can't call up and make excuses now. Besides," he teased, "Gussie probably has more experience than you have in caring for children. She's helped bring up half a dozen younger sisters and brothers."

"I'll be ready in five minutes." Liz capitulated.

They left the house and drove to the Conrads' charming mock-Tudor home. The air was heavy with the pungent scent of honeysuckle and magnolias. Fireflies blinked on and off as they crossed the lawn from the car to the entrance of the house. They heard festive sounds emerge from within. Most of the guests had already arrived.

Despite her reluctance to attend the dinner Liz found herself enjoying the evening. She was grateful for the admiring tributes of the male guests, the covert, approving inspection of the women. As always she was comforted by the knowledge that she was the best-dressed woman at the party.

Conversation was lively and varied. Dr Lamartine Hardman

of Commerce, Georgia, who complained that the state had been run too long by lawyer-politicians, was campaigning for Governor. Chief Justice Russell was running against Senator George and he censured the senator for his support of the World Court. A young matron who had attended Washington Seminary with Liz reported that alumna Margaret Mitchell had just left the *Atlanta Journal Sunday Magazine* and was writing anecdotes for them as a freelance.

"Somebody said she's sure Margaret's writing an historical novel," the pretty brunette confided to Liz. "Margaret's always at the library looking for history books. She hasn't said a word about a novel. Personally, I don't think she's the type to ever write a book. She's always doing those short articles for the newspapers."

"I think it's just awful," the wife of a young surgeon at Grady Hospital declared, "the way the Atlanta Board of Education has banned the teaching of evolution in our schools. I know that Mr Bryan won the case against John Scopes last July, but the whole world – except for Tennessee – is laughing at the way Clarence Darrow cut him down." Her face acquired a zealous glow as she quoted the chief defense attorney. "'We have the purpose of preventing bigots and ignoramuses from controlling the education of the United States.'"

"Did you hear what Sinclair Lewis said when he rejected the Pulitzer Prize for *Arrowsmith*?" a colleague of Victor's asked Liz while he lighted her tenth cigarette of the evening.

"No." She smiled in interested enquiry.

"He said that all such prizes tend to make writers 'safe, polite, obedient, and sterile'." The physician chuckled. "I should have thought he would appreciate the recognition."

As Liz had expected, the conversation became general when the problems of the cotton mills were introduced. While the Southern mills were not facing the endless bankruptcies of their New England counterparts, less than half would pay regular dividends on common stock this quarter.

"Our cotton mills are taking a bad beating," Victor said

seriously. Liz remembered the long evening of conversation between Victor and her father on his last trip home from Washington. Her mother had gone with Sophie and Andrew to an emergency meeting of mill operators. Both Papa and Victor worried that Mama had over-expanded and Liz had been shocked that they feared the Hampton Mills – the Hampton empire – could be in jeopardy. Yet Mama, too, over a year ago, had told her bluntly that she was concerned. "Our mills are plagued by terrible competition and over-production," Victor summed up.

"We'll come out of it," a local mill operator insisted. "The mills have become one of the most important industries in the nation. We make a big contribution to this country."

Liz remembered Kevin's point that the mill workers were making a major contribution to the nation. But to be a Southern mill worker was to be at the lowest possible social level among the white population. A "linthead". "Poor white trash". The epithets played a raucous symphony in Liz's brain. "And of course," the mill operator continued, "the Southern mills are at an advantage. Our overhead is lower." His smile was smug.

Was Kevin right? Were the wages paid in the mills, even by Mama, who paid the highest in the state, unconscionably low?

"Our manufacturers know the importance of working their spindles around the clock," Dr Conrad contributed.

"Oh yes," the mill operator replied. "Most of us run our spindles all day and all night, while the New England mills expect to show a profit on an eight-hour day – with antiquated equipment."

Liz remembered Kevin's indictment of the Southern mills' work week, where sixty hours was legal.

"Of course, the New England mills do a better job than our mills on 'fine goods', another guest with considerable cotton mill holdings acknowledged, "but we're catching up."

"We're fortunate in having no labor shortage," someone else said. "We've got white farm tenants learning they can't survive on farming cotton. They're glad to come into the mills."

"I tell you, the South is going into a great period," the mill operator said. "This is the new frontier. You can feel the coming bigness in the air. Everywhere we look we see it: stretches of new roads; more automobiles; radio stores and restaurants and movie palaces opening up everywhere. The South," he said reverently, "is the land of promise."

But what did it promise the mill workers? Liz asked herself, conscious that her own luxurious way of life was sustained by their labor.

Driving home with Victor, Liz was haunted by a kaleidoscope of mill images. The pale faces and stooped shoulders of the workers. The rows and rows of machines where they stood to rigid attention all day amidst the clamor of machinery too noisy to allow even occasional exchanges of conversation. The tired eyes that must watch constantly for breaking threads.

"Tired?" Victor asked gently, letting a hand leave the wheel to rest on hers.

"Not a bit. I'm glad you persuaded me to go to the dinner." But she squinted uneasily as Victor swung on to the road that led to the house. "Vic, do you smell something burning?"

"Somebody's burning wood in a fireplace."

"In this weather?" Alarm made her voice harsh. Ever since the fire years ago in Andrew's cottage, when Maureen had almost died, she had been terrified of fires. "Vic, drive faster."

"You can't expect to do over twenty-five on this road," he protested, but his foot pressed down harder on the gas pedal.

"Oh, my God!" Liz's voice soared shrilly as the house came into view. "Oh, my God!"

Flames leapt from a second-story window. A fire truck in front of the house. Firemen shouted orders. A feminine voice cried hysterically.

"The baby! It's the baby's room!"

Before Victor could bring the car to a stop, Liz threw open

the door on her side and leapt from the running board. Her eyes swept the cluster of figures that huddled before the burning house. It was Gussie who was hysterical. Beside her, tears streaming down her face, Hannah stood holding Kathy – frightened into silence – in her arms.

Where is Debbie?

"Gussie! Where's the baby? Where's Debbie?" Liz shook the terrified girl by the shoulders, then slapped her hard across one cheek. Gussie subsided into sobs. "*Gussie, where's Debbie?*"

"Miss Liz, her in there –" Gussie pointed to the burning house. "I couldn't git to her!"

"Dr Adams, you can't go in!" Two firemen clutched at Victor. "The heat's too much."

"Debbie! Debbie!" Liz hurled herself towards the house. A fireman blocked her path while another grabbed at her. "Let me go! My baby's in there!" She fought frenziedly to free herself. "My baby! My baby!"

"Back, everybody!" a fireman yelled, and seconds later the nursery roof collapsed, spreading lengths of burning timber on the ground about the house. "Everybody back!"

A car pulled up and Caroline, white with shock, jumped from the running board on the driver's side while Sophie laboriously emerged from the other.

"Is everybody out?" Caroline demanded.

"The baby's in there." Liz sobbed. "Oh, my God, why did we go out tonight? We killed the baby! We killed Debbie!"

The morning was sticky and overcast, the air heavy with the scent of the masses of flowers – white roses, white carnations, lilies-of-the-valley – sent by the shocked residents of Atlanta. Victor had decreed that the burial at Hampton Court would be private, attended only by family: Liz's parents, Sophie, cousin Andrew and his wife Maureen. The only exceptions were Janet and her mother. Liz was in no condition to face the sympathy of well-meaning friends.

Ashen-faced but erect Victor stood with an arm around Liz

at the freshly dug grave in the Hampton Court cemetery, where General Josiah Hampton, his wife Louisa and his three sons who had died in the War Between the States lay buried. Only a few years ago the body of Caroline's father, Francis, had been brought from England to lie beside that of the General. At one side of the cemetery was a marker identifying the stillborn son of Tina, Eric's first wife – though not Eric's child. "Baby Hampton", the marker read. Eric had given Tina's child his name.

Debbie would lie in rest beside her great-grandmother Louisa. Victor was grateful that Caro had made this decision for him. There was space between Louisa Hampton's grave and those of her two younger sons, who died in the battle of Atlanta, to receive the tiny white casket. It seemed right that Debbie should be there.

Liz stood to stiff attention while the minister spoke words of comfort. Her eyes were shut, as though she sought to escape from life. She had been drained of tears. The other women at the graveside fought to retain their composure.

Victor was tormented by the realization that Liz blamed him for Debbie's death. If he had not insisted they go to the Conrads' dinner, Liz was convinced that Debbie would be alive. A shiver shot through him as one of the servants of the two families, huddled together along the white picket fence, emitted a piercing shriek of anguish.

"That po' lil' baby. That precious little life," she wailed.

Gussie, who had rescued Kathy but had been unable to enter the inferno that Debbie's room had so quickly become, was at home under sedation. Patience did not know that her "new baby" was dead. She would learn of the tragedy when she was well enough to be discharged from the hospital.

Before the tiny white casket was lowered into the red clay earth, Henry Roberts – the Hamptonville minister who had long been like a part of the Hampton family – stepped forward to say a few words from a little-known poet:

"Only a baby small,
Dropt from the skies;
Small, but how dear to us.
God knoweth best."

Six

Caroline awoke to the monotonous drone of the electric fan that had sat for a parade of nights atop the mantel in the bedroom she shared with Eric. Her batiste nightgown clung wetly across her shoulder blades. She was conscious of tiredness: she was sleeping poorly this summer. The memory of Debbie's death was an imprisoning nightmare.

Eyes shut, Caroline turned on one side, reached for comfort across the width of the bed and was startled for an instant that Eric's side of the bed was empty. She had forgotten in this first awakening that Eric had returned to the capital yesterday. Poor Eric. Washington at the end of August was as hot as Atlanta, and with little diversion.

Reluctant to face another sultry day just yet she reached for Eric's pillow and thrust it behind her head along with her own. What were they going to do about Liz? Her grief was devastating. She was fighting to withdraw from the world. She would see no one except the immediate family and Janet. Victor, too, worried about her.

When was Adrienne returning from Europe? Much as she disliked Adrienne, Caroline wished she were back home. For all her craziness Adrienne might be the one who could pull Liz out of this mire of despair. They all grieved for that precious little life that had been taken away, but Liz must learn to live again.

Caroline tensed guiltily at the sound of Sophie's voice in the hall. She must stop lounging in bed this way and get to the mill. Sophie looked so tired in all this heat. It was impossible to convince her that it was time she set a less hectic pace for herself. Sophie refused to face the calendar.

While she dressed, Caroline made up her mind to talk to Victor about Liz. It hurt her to see Liz's painful thinness; her clothes were loose on her; her face drawn and devoid of color. She had the fragile appearance of someone who had endured a critical illness.

Victor had been able to bring Liz out of her depression after David's death, Caroline remembered. He must pull Liz out of that solitary confinement she had sentenced herself to since they lost Debbie. Only at dinner, Victor confided, did Liz come downstairs.

At the mill Caroline phoned Victor's office and set up an appointment through Irene McDougall, the pretty little nurse who had come to work for him two years ago.

"I'll make sure he's here, Mrs Hampton," Irene promised.

Precisely at the arranged time Caroline walked into the reception room of Victor's surgery. Several patients were already waiting for him.

"You're the doctor's first appointment, Mrs Hampton," Irene said loudly – she was alerting the others in the reception room. "Why don't you go on inside Dr Adams' office and wait for him there?"

"Thank you, Irene." Caroline's smile was gentle. She suspected that Victor's nurse was in love with him.

No more than ten minutes late, Victor charged into the reception room. He exchanged brief greetings with the waiting patients, then joined Caroline in his office.

"You're worrying about Liz." Victor had guessed the reason for her call. He dropped into the chair behind his desk.

"I'm frantic. We have to pull Liz out of this depression."

"I think about it constantly. She keeps herself on an island too small to admit anyone else."

"It's devastating to lose a child." Caroline tried not to think about her grandmother, who had lost her reason when her two sons died at the Battle of Atlanta. "But women survive, Victor."

"Liz will come out of this," Victor comforted, but his eyes were pained. "We have to give her time." He hesitated, involved in some inner struggle. "Debbie was my child, too."

"Victor, I know how bad it's been for you. For us, too. You know how we loved Debbie – the way we love Kathy," she added pointedly. "Liz must be made to realize she has another daughter."

"I've tried to talk to her about going away for a few weeks. I'm sure a change of scenery would help. But she won't listen." Abruptly he arose from his chair and crossed to a window. Caroline saw his despair in the slump of his shoulders, the droop of his head. He stared out the window while they talked. "Liz blames me for the baby's death. I insisted we go to the dinner at the Conrads. If we'd been home, she's sure we could have saved Debbie, that she'd still be alive."

"Victor, it's not your fault." Caroline had suspected Liz felt this way. "Make her understand."

Victor swung about to face her. His smile was wry.

"Do you know any way to do that?"

"Maybe Liz needs to put distance between herself and all of us," Caroline said candidly. "Insist she go away."

"A colleague at the hospital – Dr Edwards – offered me the use of his mother's house down at Miami Beach for a few weeks. She's out in California. He felt it might be helpful if Liz and I went down there together." But he appeared doubtful, Caroline sensed, that his presence would be therapeutic.

"Talk to Liz about going down there," Caroline urged. She was impatient with Liz. Didn't she know that Victor grieved, too?

"I could go down there for three or four days towards the end of her stay and come home with her. I can't take weeks off from my practice. I don't think it would be good for Liz, anyway. As you said, she needs to get away from all of us, away from all the familiar things that remind her of the baby." He sighed. "Patience tells me that Liz goes into Debbie's room every day and just sits beside the crib for hours. She insisted the room be replaced exactly as it was: the same wallpaper; the same furniture; even that toy lamb you brought for the window seat. It's as though the fire never happened. Except the crib is empty –"

"Make her go to Miami. She has fond memories of the place. And insist that she take Kathy with her. Let them be alone together. And while she's away—" Caroline prodded herself to continue – "while Liz is away, have the nursery re-done. Perhaps as a home office for yourself. Victor, it was you who brought her back to reality when David died. You can do it again."

Liz sat at the dinner table and stared at Victor in consternation.

"I don't want to go to Florida!"

"Honey, you need to get away from the house." He could not allow himself to back down. "And Kathy loves the beach. How did you describe it?" He squinted in recall. "Kathy found the biggest sandpile in the world, and she adored it."

"No," Liz protested, "I can't."

"You're going to Florida. Doctor's orders." He braced himself against the genuine terror he felt in her. "Ask Janet if you may take Wendy along, too, so Kathy'll have a playmate. I understand there are two servants in the house, so you won't have to worry about anything. I'll be down on Sunday, September nineteenth. We'll come back together the following Friday. I'll make arrangements for a doctor to cover for me. I promise you nothing will stand in the way this time. I'll join you in Miami."

Looking at Liz – knowing her pain – he wanted nothing so much as to take her in his arms and make love to her. The only time since Debbie's death that he made love to his wife, she had been unresponsive. He knew she lay in his arms and blamed him for their baby's death.

"It'll be so hot in Miami," Liz hedged, but Victor knew she would go.

"It's hot in Atlanta in September," he said. "And at the

beach house you'll have cool nights. I'm looking forward to it."

"You won't come," Liz prophesied. The flare of hostility was encouraging.

"I'll come," Victor assured her. "Phone Janet tonight and ask if she'll let Wendy go along with Kathy and you." He was glad Caro had come to the office this afternoon. Caro was right; they had to bring Liz out of herself. Maybe then Liz could look at him without blaming him for Debbie's death. Maybe then he would stop blaming himself.

Four days later, fighting a sense of panic, Liz allowed Victor to see her, along with the two little girls and Patience, into the drawing room on the Ponce de Leon. The same train – new then – that had taken her to Miami a year and a half ago, before Debbie had been conceived. Janet had not accompanied them to the station lest Wendy have last-minute misgivings at seeing her mother leave the train.

"When does the train pull out?" Liz reached to close the drawing-room door, though she knew Victor must depart momentarily.

"It won't leave until eight twenty-five," Victor told her. "You have eight minutes yet. Tomorrow morning this time," he said with an air of levity, "you'll be less than an hour from Miami."

"We'll have all our meals here in the drawing room." Liz clutched at this escape. She couldn't bear the prospect of facing all those people in the dining car. "It's too hot to move any more than we have to."

"Go into the dining car," Victor insisted. "Patience, make sure Miss Liz goes into the dining car. The children can have their meals here."

"Yessuh." Patience was solemn. She knows the reason for this trip, Liz thought.

"I won't be able to eat a bite," Liz said. She felt sick at the prospect of walking into the dining car. Already her hands were clammy.

"You have to start facing people." Victor's eyes held hers. Commanding. He was right, she acknowledged unwarily. But how could she go on living as though Debbie had never existed? Why? Why had it happened? That sweet, darling baby dead, when so many miserable people dragged on through endless years. "Nothing terrible is going to happen." Victor snapped her back to the present. "Maybe you'll be in a cold sweat for a few minutes, but then it'll be all right. Trust me, sweetheart."

Liz started. Victor seldom used endearments except when they were making love. But they had only made love once since her baby had died. Did Victor expect her to have another child? Never, she thought violently. Every minute she was pregnant she'd remember Debbie. No more children. Victor would have to live without the hope of a son. No grandson for Mama.

"I have to rush to the hospital." Victor kissed Kathy and Wendy – both wide-eyed with anticipation at the approaching holiday – squeezed Patience's hand in a gesture of affection, then reached for Liz. "I'll see you on Sunday the nineteenth," he promised.

Victor's smile was convivial, but his eyes were serious. Was he relieved to be away from her for a little over two weeks? He was tender with her, yet she sensed his discomfort. Did he expect the world ever to be the same when their baby had died because they had gone off to a dinner party?

"Goodbye, Vic." She felt nothing when he kissed her. *Why doesn't he leave?*

"I'll miss you," he said softly. And then he strode from the drawing room and down the narrow corridor to the exit from the train.

Liz tried to focus on the Atlanta *Constitution*, which she had brought with her. Articles were still appearing about the death of Rudolph Valentino in New York a week ago. Adrienne liked to quote what Mencken said about him, Liz recalled – "catnip to women". Now Rudolph Valentino was dead and women around the world were in hysteria.

Liz put aside the newspaper to stare out the window as the train chugged southward, past farms where whole families were in the red-clay fields picking cotton. They had been there since sun-up. With a heavy crop again this year cotton prices were plummeting. Why didn't the farmers stop planting so much cotton? Ever since she could remember, Papa had been pleading with the tenant farmers at Hampton Court to raise other crops. It was like that all over the South: thinking people begging the farmers to diversify their crops.

Why was she going to Miami? She shouldn't have listened to Vic. A house with strange servants to cope with, she thought fearfully. And always the memory of her last visit to Miami, before Debbie was born. Before she was haunted by visions of the blaze in the baby's room. Knowing Debbie was up there.

"Mama, did you bring my bathing suit?" Kathy asked anxiously.

"I brought it, darling." Liz forced herself to smile in reassurance. Victor kept telling her, in those first awful days, that she had to live for Kathy. Poor little Kathy, she thought in self-recrimination. She had not been much of a mother these last three months. "And we brought the beach ball and the shovels and the pails." She compelled herself to become involved with the two little girls. Patience was pleased.

Her first venture into the dining car at lunch time left her in a cold sweat, as Victor had predicted. She knew it was absurd to feel such terror at being out among strangers. She must overcome this, she exhorted herself. At dinner she forced herself to go into the dining car again, and managed to exchange casual conversation with the woman who shared her table.

At an early hour Kathy and Wendy were put to bed. Shortly afterwards Liz and Patience retired to their berths. They would wake in the morning for an early breakfast on the train.

As usual now at night Liz found sleep elusive. She awoke from a period of restless slumber to discover a downpour had arrived with the dawn. She pushed up the shade to gaze out at the display of lightning that darted about the grey sky.

The train moved beyond the fields into a town. It paused in a near-deserted railway station. Liz froze as she saw a woman in black, supported by a man at her side, following a small coffin about to be brought aboard the train. She knew that woman's pain.

Liz turned her head away and cried for the child whose body lay in the coffin outside her window. It was the first time she had cried since the sticky, overcast morning when they had laid Debbie to rest at Hampton Court.

Riding in a taxi along Biscayne Bay, en route to the house where they were to stay, Liz recalled her last trip to Miami. For a little while she had been madly happy with Rick. Was that why she lost Debbie? Punishment for having an affair with Rick?

No. I won't think that.

She didn't have to worry about running into Rick on this visit. He must have left Miami when the real-estate market collapsed. She didn't want to see him. He'd used her to try to make a quarter-million-dollar sale to Mama. But traitorously memories of the days and nights she had spent with Rick seeped into her being. She had felt special with him. She had laughed with Rick. Would she ever laugh again?

As on her first trip to Miami Liz rode with a garrulous taxi driver. Kathy and Wendy giggled infectiously while they gazed at the passing sights.

"Take a look at that causeway," the driver said with pride. "Them's man-made islands crossin' the Bay. Used to be a wooden bridge there. See the new island goin' up?" He gestured with pride.

"It's quite impressive."

"We got a four-lane thoroughfare goin' from the Royal Palm Hotel," he rambled on and Liz tensed. All at once she was visualizing Rick's arriving at the Royal Palm that day she left Miami. Had he been furious when he discovered she had checked out? "It's gonna extend all the way north-west to the city limits. It'll be called Biscayne Boulevard."

At last they arrived at the charming Spanish-style house that sat no more than a hundred feet from the beach at high tide. The couple that cared for Mrs Edwards' residence and prepared the meals were effusive in their welcome. With relief, Liz realized that little would be required of her.

Patience, she resolved, would be her liaison with the servants. She would spend her days lounging on a chaise on the beach, gazing at the ocean. On the 19th Victor would come down to stay with them until they returned to Atlanta.

By the end of the following day Liz grew restless despite her determination to isolate herself in the privacy afforded by the beach house. She would go downtown tomorrow to shop, she decided over a dinner of seafood delicacies superbly prepared and served at a table set up at the edge of the water to allow her to enjoy the orange-gold sunset. She would buy something pretty to take back to Janet, and toys for Kathy and Wendy. There was a Packard Runabout at her disposal.

With an anticipation that she had never expected to feel again, Liz drove away from the house next morning behind the wheel of the beige and brown Packard, its top down to give access to the golden Florida sun. Leaning against the brown handcrushed leather upholstery she was able to thrust aside both past and future. While she was here, she would live for each day. It was a way to survive.

She shopped extravagantly for Janet and the children. Janet was always there in moments of trouble, she thought with a surge of love. She had clung to Janet even when she had pushed Mama and Maureen aside.

She carried her parcels to the car and hesitated in indecision. She had barely touched breakfast. Now she was hungry. She would have lunch downtown, she decided. She locked away the parcels in the Packard's "luggage well", awkwardly placed between the front seat and the rumble seat, and strode off in search of a restaurant.

She had finished her solitary lunch and was lingering over a second cup of coffee when she glanced up and encountered a familiar figure at a table across the room. *Rick Pulaski.* He was talking with a waitress and had not seen her. Her heart thumping, she gazed about the room in search of the waitress who had served her.

I must get out of here before Rick sees me.

It was too late. She pretended to be looking for something in her purse. Where was the waitress? She couldn't leave without her check. Rick was on his feet, crossing the room to her table.

"Liz!" Rick hovered above her. The same insouciant charm, the same mocking smile. When she knew he was so rotten, why did she react this way?

"Hello, Rick."

Be cool. Don't let him know I'm a shambles inside.

Already his eyes made passionate love to her. No more, she warned herself. She knew Rick now.

"You ran away from me," he accused, sitting across the table from her.

"You lied to me," she reproached. "You were using me to sell a tract of worthless land to my mother." She strived to sound detached. "Gateson told me."

"Liz, that was business." His smile was absurdly ingratiating. "That had nothing to do with us." But she sensed that he would be more cautious now in his overtures. "You were the most fascinating woman I'd ever met. You're still the most fascinating woman I've ever met."

"I thought you'd have fled Miami by now." Again, she glanced about the room in an effort to locate the waitress who had served her. "I thought you'd have moved on to better pickings."

Rick shrugged.

"I took a beating. I live in a less palatial house." He grinned. "My landlord was sprung from the Atlanta pen – I would have been forced to move anyhow." He reached to cover her hand with his. Her own remained immobile. She was devoid of the will to withdraw it. All at once this was eighteen months ago, when she was infatuated with Rick.

"You look beautiful. Thinner. Are you on one of those stupid diets?"

"No diet," she said, her voice taut. "I had another child. A little girl. She died in June."

"Liz, I'm sorry." His distress appeared genuine. Then she saw the question that had formed in his mind. He hesitated. "How old was she?"

"She wasn't your child, Rick." If they had not been careful, she might have borne Rick's child. "Debbie was only three months old when – when we lost her."

"That's rough." Compassion deepened his voice. She remembered his younger brother, who had died in a mine cave-in. Rick, too, had been brushed by tragedy.

"Victor insisted I come down here for a couple of weeks. He thought a change of scenery would be good for me."

"We'll go out to dinner tonight," Rick said. His voice was now a caress. "Somewhere quiet and relaxing. Maybe the Florida boom is a bust, but this is still one of the most beautiful spots in the world. We'll have dinner at a new seafood restaurant that hangs right over the ocean." He remembered her passion for seafood.

"I'm mourning for my baby," she objected. "I'm not accepting social engagements."

"You have to eat," he insisted. He exuded a sympathy, a tenderness that almost unnerved her. "I'll pick you up for dinner at seven. Are you at the Royal Palm?"

"No." *Where's my will? How dare I go out to dinner with Rick tonight!* "I'm staying at a borrowed house."

They talked briefly. Then Rick walked with her to where she had parked the Packard. He lifted her hand to his mouth before she slid behind the wheel of the car.

"I've missed you like the devil, Liz."

Seven

Liz's hands were trembling as she pulled the turquoise georgette dress above her head and settled it about her slender frame. All afternoon she had sat at the water's edge and gazed at the waves, as though she might find a solution to the fresh question that haunted her. *Why am I allowing myself to be drawn into Rick's web again?*

Was Patience shocked that she was going out to dinner tonight with Rick? It wasn't a party, she soothed herself. She was having dinner with someone she used to know before her world fell into splinters.

She touched a lipstick to her mouth, frowned at her reflection. She disliked the new hollows beneath her cheekbones that had arrived with the loss of weight. Yet she looked more sophisticated. Adrienne would approve this look. It had been a long time since she had thought about Adrienne.

She left her room to go in to say goodnight to Kathy and Wendy. They were in their nightgowns sitting up in bed while Patience told them a story.

"Mama, you look so pretty," Kathy effervesced and reached out her arms.

"Pretty," Wendy shyly reiterated.

Liz kissed them both and self-consciously told Patience she would be out for the evening.

"Yes'm," Patience said. Her smile was placid.

"Goodnight, you-all," Liz strived for an air of casualness. She needed tonight, she thought defiantly. She had to escape, for a little while, from the anguish that was a stifling strait-jacket. Rick and she would have dinner and talk, and then he would drive her home.

Rick arrived promptly at seven. The gray Rolls had been replaced by a low-slung, two-passenger Stutz which, Rick confided, had cost over seven thousand dollars.

"I'm taking care of it for a friend," Rick explained. "He's off in Europe for a few weeks."

"My father keeps a Stutz in Washington," Liz told him. "He thinks it's one of the safest cars on the market."

They kept their conversation impersonal on the drive to the restaurant. Over dinner – with a magnificent Florida sunset as a backdrop – Liz began to unwind. Time had swung backward eighteen months; it was March 1925 again. She was abandoning herself to Rick's charm, Miami's charm. Obliterating everything except the present.

After dinner they walked along the hard-packed white beach. Rick's jacket about her shoulders in the pleasant coolness of the evening. Liz welcomed this relief after the sub-tropic heat of the day. With moonlight dripping on the beach Rick paused and pulled her to him.

"I missed you like the devil," he told her again, waiting tentatively for acquiescence before he kissed her. Strangely this touched her. She remembered other moments when Rick had displayed a sensitivity that surprised her.

Liz lifted her face to his. Her arms tightened about his shoulders when his mouth clung to hers. It had been so long since she felt passion. Regret stabbed her when Rick pulled away.

"Let's go to my cottage," he said.

Rick was staying in a cottage borrowed from the owner of the Stutz. It was small, attractive, nestling on a slight incline on the beachfront. Liz surmised from the night-darkness of the house that there would be no servants about to disturb their privacy.

As Rick unlocked the door, they heard the imperious meowing of a cat.

"That's Cleopatra," Rick explained. "I acquired custody

of the house on the stipulation I keep her happy," he said humorously.

Rick pushed the door wide. A beige and brown fur figurine with china-blue eyes inspected them from atop a Chinese table.

"Cleopatra," Liz murmured and reached to draw the exquisite Siamese into her arms.

"She's a talkative character." Rick laughed. "Complaining because I'm out with another woman." But already Cleopatra was purring beneath Liz's stroking fingers. "Let me show you the house. It's a tiny masterpiece," he said with respect, "though I'm one to favor lots of space. Still, I can't complain about the arrangement. I got caught in the squeeze when land prices dropped to the bottom so fast. I won't be caught like that again." For a moment his face tightened into a harsh mask that reminded her of the ruthlessness she had sensed in him in the past.

Rick led her on a tour of the house, arriving at last at his host's overly ornate bedroom. Without bothering to switch on the lights he crossed to the windows and pulled wide the expanse of drapes so that the moonlight fell across the floor and the ocean lay like a lovely seascape before them.

"It's a private stretch of beach," Rick said, beginning to undress. "Nobody walks there except the gulls. We can feed them at breakfast."

"I can't stay," Liz said. The atmosphere was electric. She reached for the hem of her dress, pulled it above her head.

She stood before him in only her white silk teddy, shoes kicked aside, stockings flung across the seat of a chair. Stripped to skin, Rick pulled her against his hard, lean body.

"I was furious when I went to the Royal Palm and found you'd walked out." His hands pulled away the straps of her teddy and thrust the fragile softness to her waist. "You left such a hole in my life."

"I was furious at you," she said with fresh indignation. "How could you have lied to me like that?"

"I told you. That was business. But you belong in my life."

He prodded the white silk that huddled about her waist over her hips, down her slender thighs to the floor. "Did you miss me?" he challenged.

"I couldn't sleep for weeks," she confessed.

"Like me." Desire lent a lynx-like quality to his eyes. "I screwed up on business deals because I was thinking of you. Then all hell broke loose here and I had to concentrate on business. Honey, you never saw people leave a place so fast. They poured out of Miami as though the town had been hit by the bubonic plague."

He lifted her off her feet and dropped her on the bed. While the waves washed on to the shore in an erotic symphony, he lowered himself above her. Her hands caught at his shoulders while he thrust himself within her. Her eyes closed. She heard the faint sounds of her passion blending with those of Rick and of the waves hitting the beach . . .

Liz spent every waking moment with Rick. They made love with a frequency – with an abandon – that made her feel deliciously desirable. In the midst of a luncheon on the beach Rick pulled her from the table and into the cottage to make love. He cut short a sightseeing tour so that he could take her to bed. At intervals she was conscious of her earlier assessment of Rick. Yet as the days sped past, she felt a growing panic at having to return to that other life that was reality.

She awoke Friday morning at sunrise, dressed and went out to walk along the beach. The morning was unfamiliarly gray. The wind sharp. Yet already swimmers were in the ocean. She walked with her shoulders hunched, body tense, her mind racing. Victor would arrive in Miami on Sunday. She was convinced he would arrive. She would not be able to see Rick once he was here.

Patience was upset that she spent so much time away from the house, with a man other than her husband. Patience had been her nurse, as she was Kathy's nurse now. The three

Hampton children were her children. Patience – more than her own parents – knew the fragility of her marriage.

Rick said nothing of marriage. It was too soon, she told herself. Yet even if Victor refused her a divorce, she would spend her life with Rick, she thought in new rebellion. She would have to go back to Atlanta with Victor. Talk to him about a divorce. If he refused, she'd still return to Miami with Kathy. She'd build a life for herself here – with Rick.

Their parents had handed them a world that was a wreck. An ugly, empty thing, ready to blow up at any minute. How could they be expected to be enthusiastic about life? Adrienne had been right all these years. Live for today. For whatever pleasure there was to find in this rotten world.

Defiant in her decision Liz swung about on the beach and headed for the house. The wind had picked up force. Blasts of sand stung her face. She lowered her head and narrowed her eyes as she walked.

She waited impatiently for Rick to arrive. Whatever business he was conducting these days seemed to require no more than an hour or two each morning. The day assumed a new urgency for her because of Victor's impending arrival.

This morning Patience devised indoor diversion for Kathy and Wendy. Jenny served lunch in the dining room rather than on the terrace. Rick arrived while Jenny was still clearing away the table.

"The surf is wild," he announced with relish. "Let's go for a walk."

Striding against the wind with Rick seemed an adventure. It was another pocket of time removed from reality. But then they tired of nature's challenge and went to Rick's cottage.

Lying in Rick's arms during what he liked to call the "mid-game break", Liz asked herself what it was about Rick that so excited her, that made her feel special, and realized what the answer was: his unpredictability.

In all the years she had been married to Victor – almost seven of them – he had never pulled her into bed in the early afternoon because he couldn't live another minute without making love to her. Rick made her understand that nothing intruded when they were together. With Victor, she always felt that he was listening for the phone to summon him to some dire medical emergency.

At last they left the bedroom to dig out their host's cache of liquor.

"No bathtub gin for my friend Skip," Rick said with satisfaction, producing a bottle of vintage champagne.

Liz remembered the black-marble tub in the magnificent house of the jailed bootlegger, where Rick and she had lolled in the water, sipped champagne, and then made love. All she had to do was reach out and touch him, and Rick would be ready to make love again. She had always waited for Victor to make the overture. She had never taken the first step with him.

"To us," Rick said, handing her a goblet of the fine, pale liquid.

"To us." Liz's eyes were luminous. Rick meant for them to have a future. Tonight, she promised herself, Rick and she would talk. She must force herself to be open with him.

Despite the weather – because they enjoyed the raging surf – Rick and Liz insisted that they be served dinner on the wide porch of the restaurant that seemed in imminent danger of being inundated by the waves. They were alone in dining outdoors tonight.

Liz tried to prod herself into serious conversation with Rick about their future. Each time the words died in her throat.

Why am I afraid of being open with Rick?

Rick was avoiding the gambling casinos. If he couldn't play for high stakes, he preferred to play not at all. After dinner, when both were damp from the salt spray that lashed the dining porch, they returned to the cottage.

"The wind must be up to fifty miles an hour," Rick surmised

while they hurried from the car into the house. "There was a bulletin on the radio this morning about a hurricane blowing up into the Caribbean. We're getting the edge of it."

While Rick went out into the kitchen to bring out the bottle of champagne they had started earlier, Liz put a record on the phonograph. Skip, she noted, was partial to tangos. Before Rick drove her home, Liz promised herself, they would talk about how they would handle their lives.

They were in the midst of a tango when Liz froze in Rick's arms as they heard a high, shrill shriek outdoors. A second later the music stopped, as though a hand had rudely lifted the needle from the record. Simultaneously the house was blanketed in darkness.

"The power's out. We're in for a storm." Rick's voice belonged to a character in a radio play, Liz thought with irrational amusement. And what was that eerie rumbling outside? Like the background sounds of a weird radio mystery. "Stay where you are, Liz." He moved away from her in the ominous blackness.

"Do you have a candle, Rick?" All at once Liz was uneasy. Would Patience be alarmed, alone in a strange house with the children? At least, Kathy and Wendy were asleep.

"There should be a flashlight in the breakfront," Rick said and cursed as he crashed into furniture.

A moment later a weak ray of light moved across the room. Rick had found the flashlight.

"The battery's going," Liz noted.

"The power will probably be on soon," Rick soothed her. "Let's light the candles in the dining room." With an arm about Liz, he ushered her into the dining room where ivory tapers stood tall in a pair of Victorian silver four-light candelabra. "Isn't that romantic?" he mocked when candlelight spilled across the room.

"Spooky," Liz amended. "Listen to that wind."

"Stay back from the windows." Rick put a detaining hand on her arm when she made a move in their direction.

"I ought to get home to the children." Alarm gripped Liz. "Rick, I have to go –"

"Liz, we can't drive in this," Rick objected. "Listen to what's happening out there!"

The wind had picked up velocity. They heard a tree crash to the ground close by. The clatter of broken glass told them window panes were being blown into the house. Lightning gave the room weird illumination for an instant.

"Maybe we ought to go into the cellar," Liz said.

"These houses have no cellars," Rick said tersely.

This morning the raging surf had been exciting. Now it was terrifying. The waves were rushing right up to the house. Liz heard an angry meow. Cleopatra was darting through a shattered window.

"We have to get out of here," Rick said. "The house isn't built to take this kind of punishment."

"Rick! Oh, my God!"

A wall of water burst through the windows, through the door into the house, bringing seaweed and debris in its rampage. Rick swept Liz off her feet and on to the top of the massive oak dining table and leapt up beside her. In moments the room was a murky dark pool lit by candlelight.

"We've got to move to the car and drive inland," Rick said. "We'll wait until this rush of water is over—"

Another wall of water swept into the house. In a momentary lull Rick jumped down and reached to help Liz from the table. In salt water to her waist, she clung to Rick while they struggled to a rear window and climbed out into the night. Clutching each other in the wild wind they inched towards the car, parked on higher ground behind the house. Already its wheels were half-submerged in water. With agonizing slowness they managed to pull up the top of the car for what meager protection it could afford.

"Rick, look!" Liz stared in disbelief as the roof of a house flew by as though a toy flung by a gleeful child.

"Hang on to me," Rick ordered while he struggled to start

the car. "The wind must be over a hundred miles an hour now."

Slowly they moved to higher ground. The waves relentlessly followed. Close by they heard a woman scream. A flash of lightning revealed a man struggling to nail a blanket over the shattered window of a second-floor room, where candlelight glowed weakly. As the lightning subsided, a crack of a telephone pole just ahead rent the air.

"Get out of the car!" Rick yelled and shoved the door wide on his side, pulling Liz with him. They had barely cleared the car when the pole splintered the side where Liz had sat moments ago.

"That house," Liz sputtered. "Let's make a try for it!"

Where were the children and Patience? The Edwards' house – like Rick's – was right on the beach. Were they all right?

Fighting against the wind, gaining a few inches, only to be driven backward again, they struggled towards the two-story house set on an incline. In the blackness they tumbled over branches, scattered beach furniture, a door blown from the house. They stumbled inside. From the floor above came an anguished shriek.

Hand in hand Liz and Rick moved to the stairway.

"Can we help?" Rick called upstairs tentatively.

A flashlight beamed a path down the stairs.

"It's my wife." A man's voice called to them. Betraying his terror. "I'll hold the flashlight so you can see your way up."

Liz and Rick hurried up the stairs. She suspected that in minutes the lower floor of the house would be invaded by a wall of water.

"You're staying at Skip Mayner's house." The man recognized Rick. "It's almost under water now." Liz shivered. Rick and she might have been under water with it.

"Bill!" the woman cried out. "Bill, stay with me!"

"It's my wife," the young man said. His voice was hoarse with fear. "She wasn't due for two months."

"She's having a baby now?" Rick asked in shock.

Liz turned cold with horror. In the midst of this nightmare to be giving birth.

"I'll go to her." In the darkness, not waiting for the assistance of the flashlight, Liz felt her way into the bedroom.

A young woman lay writhing on a rumpled bed. Her face was etched with pain and terror. Subconsciously Liz grasped her own stomach. She remembered the intolerable anguish of Debbie's birth. The pain of the young woman on the bed was her pain.

"How often are the contractions coming?" Liz asked, leaning over the bed. The woman in labor – no more than twenty, Liz thought – grimaced as she battled another pain.

"One on top of another," Bill answered for his wife. "All of a sudden she was in labor. There was no way we could leave the house in this weather. No way for the doctor to come here."

"No! No!" the woman – a girl, Liz thought with compassion – screamed again. "No, baby! No!"

"She should be in the hospital," Bill said in despair. "It's a first baby. We didn't think it would happen so fast."

"We'll manage," Liz said. The young mother and she would have to escort this baby into the world with no outside help. "Bring some blankets. Do you have any liquor in the house?"

"Downstairs," Bill stammered. "But should she have it now?"

"I don't know," Liz said honestly. "But we don't have any anaesthesia. It might help dull the pain." She remembered her own labor with Debbie, when Victor pleaded with her to accept anaesthesia. She felt the wrenching fire that ripped at her as Debbie sought to push her way into the world.

"I'll get the liquor," Bill said, and Rick went with him.

Liz pushed aside the sheet and touched the swollen belly, knotted hard now with a fresh contraction. The girl on the bed was narrow. Liz suspected the baby was large, despite its being two months early. This was she, Liz thought, laboring with Debbie.

She tried to remember what must be done. Scissors to cut

the cord when, mercifully, the baby left its nesting place and entered the raging, outside world. Towels. Fresh sheets.

"How much longer?" the girl gasped between contractions. "How much longer?"

"Not long," Liz soothed. She lifted the white dimity nightgown with rosebuds embroidered about the neck and prodded the slender thighs apart. The girl was dilated, but there was no sign yet of the baby's head. "Soon," Liz promised. Knowing nothing.

Bill returned with a bottle of Scotch and a glass. Rick hovered in the doorway.

"Towels," Liz ordered. "Lots of them. And a pair of scissors. Rick, come over to the bed." Her voice was faintly shrill with anxiety. "Hold her down."

"She ought to have anaesthesia." The words were ripped from Bill. "The doctor warned Daisy she'd have a hard time."

"Go for the towels and scissors," Rick told him. "She's going to be all right." He took one of Daisy's hands in his and with his free arm pinned her against the pillows.

Liz poured Scotch into the glass, brought it to the bed.

"Daisy, drink this. It'll help," she urged.

While the storm raged, the three about the bed waited for Daisy to deliver her baby. With each contraction, each accompanying shriek, Liz felt herself striving to give birth to Debbie. For a little while Debbie was alive again.

"The head's coming," Liz said, flinching as she visualized Daisy's agony when the shoulders must follow. At least, the baby was coming in the proper position.

"I can't see her in pain like that," Bill gasped and stumbled from the room.

"Rick, don't leave! Hold her down!" She leaned over Daisy from the other side of the bed. "Honey, push. Push hard!"

For what seemed an eternity Daisy fought to thrust the baby from her while Liz pleaded for further effort.

"Daisy, again!" Liz ordered. "Again!" She was reliving the final anguish that had shoved Debbie into the world. Women always said you couldn't relive the pain of labor, but *I'm reliving it.*

"Bill!" Daisy suddenly shrieked. "Bill!"

"Go get him," Liz told Rick. For a moment she froze at the horrendous sound of a crash nearby. "Rick, tell Bill to come in here. His wife needs him."

The head emerged. The shoulders were wriggling into view. She waited to receive the tiny body. A little boy, she saw. Bill would be pleased.

"Daisy, it's a boy," she said with a strange exultation. "You have a son." Tenderly she placed the baby on Daisy's stomach and braced herself to take care of the cord. For a moment she remembered that she had cried when Victor told her she had borne a second daughter. How terrible of her.

How is Patience managing with Kathy and Wendy in this madness? Are they all right? I should be with them.

A few minutes later, when the cord was cut and she had cleaned the infant the best she could without water, Rick appeared in the doorway. Why was he carrying the flashlight? Where was Bill? Why does he look so odd?

"Rick?" Alarm tied a knot in her throat. Instinctively she swung her eyes to Daisy, drugged by exhaustion.

"The side of the house caved in," Rick whispered. "I reached Bill, but it was useless. He must have been killed instantly."

"Oh, Rick." She buried her face against his chest while Bill's son wailed. A tiny voice that seemed to rise above the storm.

By dawn the storm had subsided. The sun rose in the sky. A steamy heat lay over the atmosphere. Liz and Rick allowed Daisy to believe that Bill had gone for help. While Daisy and the baby slept, they went downstairs in hope of being able to signal for help.

The lower floor was inundated with seaweed and dead crabs, but the water had receded. Hand in hand Liz and Rick rushed outside. In the light of day they saw the havoc caused by the hurricane. They saw other dazed residents like themselves emerging from their sanctuaries.

Again she was tormented by fears for the three she had left behind at the house. How selfish of her to run off on her own.

Are they all right? They must be so frightened.

At a house a hundred feet from where she stood – shorn of its roof – a couple struggled to move a piano back indoors from its new home at the water's edge. A car close by lay upside down. Debris littered the beach.

"Rick, look!" Liz spied an ambulance.

"Over here!" Rick yelled. "We need help! Over here!"

The ambulance crew was en route to an emergency hospital. The ambulance filled beyond capacity. They promised to return as soon as they had delivered their patients. Daisy would start to ask questions soon about Bill, Liz thought sadly. At the hospital they would tell her. Later.

Within twenty minutes Daisy and the baby had been transported to one of the emergency hospitals that had been set up. There were hundreds of people with broken backs, broken limbs, critical injuries, the hastily assembled ambulance crew reported. Hotels, schools, churches, private apartments were being opened up to give refuge to the injured and the homeless. Morgues were being set up at the police stations to receive the casualties.

"I have to get to the house." She told herself it was a solid structure – the children and Patience were safe there.

"We'll walk along the beach. That's the fastest route," Rick said, a hand at her waist.

On every side was desolation. Trees felled, cottages flattened, cars overturned. Liz shivered when Rick pointed to Skip's house. Thank God, Rick had realized they couldn't stay there. The roof of the house was gone, one wing demolished. If they had remained, they might have been killed.

Except for the devastation of the hurricane, this might be a typical September day in Miami. The sun shone strongly. The weather was uncomfortably warm.

People were gathering on the beach, rejoicing that the storm was over. Some even splashed in the still rough surf. An elderly man, seeming in shock, wandered over the sand, exhorting everybody to leave the beach.

"The hurricane ain't over yet," he said, over and over again. "It's comin' back! It's comin' back!" At last, knowing his warnings were having no effect, he cast an apprehensive glance at the sunny sky and hurried away.

Liz and Rick walked along the beach conscious of the relief efforts already in full swing. While they walked, they felt a sudden wind come up. All at once the hurricane was bearing down on them again. The old man had been right. They clung together to battle this fresh onslaught.

"Rick, can we make it to that hotel?" Liz gasped, pointing to a building just ahead.

As she spoke, they saw the hotel sway from side to side beneath the force of the wind. They gaped in disbelief as it collapsed into a mountain of debris.

"Lie down in the gutter!" Rick shoved Liz to the ground and covered her body with his own. "Stay down!"

Eight

The Ponce de Leon was pulling into a station. Stifling a yawn Victor leaned over in his berth to lift the shade. The train was arriving at West Palm Beach. There was an early-Sunday-morning atmosphere about the station. No passengers appeared to be boarding.

Victor spied the conductor in agitated conversation with what appeared to be an official of the local railroad station. The train wasn't going to be late in arriving, was it? He had written Liz not to worry about picking him up at the station. He would take a cab to the beach house. But any delay would be frustrating. It always astonished him that he felt such a wrench at being separated from Liz for more than a day or two.

He thrust aside the covers and dressed swiftly. Though it was only six thirty, breakfast would be available in the dining car. When he walked into the car, he saw a cluster of train personnel in somber conversation. He was the sole passenger seeking to be served.

"Will we be arriving in Miami on schedule?" Victor asked the genial, white-jacketed waiter who approached him with a menu.

"That's what they's tryin' to figure out, suh. If we can git as far as Miami." The waiter's voice was sorrowful. "They don't know how much track was torn up by the hurricane."

"What hurricane?" A coldness shot through Victor.

"The one that hit Florida. Miami got hit real bad," the waiter reported. "Then it kinda swung west along the Gulf Coast and—"

"There was nothing in the newspapers about a hurricane." Victor was terse in his alarm. "No news on the radio." The waiter was having hallucinations.

"Word jes' came through real late last night. After most folks was asleep," the waiter explained. "It's on the front page of this mornin' 's newspaper. What'll you be havin', suh?" The waiter returned himself to his duties.

"Just scrambled eggs and coffee." Victor struggled to cope with the news.

Where are Liz and the children and Patience? Are they all right?

"You like toast with that, suh?" The waiter's tone was cajoling. His eyes commiserated; he sensed Victor's distress.

"Please." Victor slid from behind the table and strode to the cluster of men. "Excuse me," he interrupted. "Is it true about a hurricane hitting Miami?"

"A bad one," the conductor confirmed. "The city was completely isolated until word got through on makeshift radio late last night. Cities all around are rushing doctors and food and water down there."

"What about the tracks? Will we be able to reach Miami?" Victor demanded.

"The way we hear it, some stretches of track were pulled right up. We'll come in as close as we can. I was just talking to the West Palm Beach office. We'll have a bus to take the passengers all the way in to the city if they still want to go."

"I want to go." Victor was grim. "My wife and child are there. I'm a doctor," he added. "I can help."

At a gap in the tracks a bus waited to receive the displaced train passengers. Only a few chose to continue the journey. The others would be transported north again by train.

While the bus speeded towards Miami, Victor read about the horrors of the hurricane which were spread across the front pages of the West Palm Beach newspaper. When the sun had come out Saturday morning, most people believed the hurricane of the night before was over. They had not realized this was the menacing eye of the hurricane, that it was turning around to sweep fresh devastation through an already devastated city.

Sick within, Victor read every word of the newspaper account. *He* had insisted Liz go to Florida with the children and Patience. It would be his fault if anything happened to them. Fresh guilt choked him.

Those on the Miami-bound bus gaped in shock at the destruction that met their eyes: cottages sprawled upside down; a cabin cruiser sat at the side of a highway, a mile from water; everywhere there was debris, fallen trees, torn-up telephone poles; some streets were blocked to cars. It seemed to Victor that every window in the city was shattered.

The bus deposited its passengers and left. Victor stood in uncertainty among the frenzied activity about him. Hand-made signs indicated where improvised kitchens had been set up, gave the location of temporary hospitals. Victor blanched as a parade of stretchers passed him. Biscayne Bay was giving up its dead.

Already Miami was fighting to pull itself together. Crews worked at clearing impassable streets, where displaced clams swarmed in search of water. Other crews labored towards the restoration of electric power and the telephone service.

Caroline and Eric must be out of their minds with worry, Victor thought unhappily. And Janet. Yet there was no way, thus far, that he could get in touch with them. No reason to until he found his family.

Victor tried to remember the address of the Edwards' house. Dr Edwards had been lyrical about the closeness of the house to the water. Victor winced, sick at the implication of this. Silently he prayed: Let the four of them be safe.

"Rick, I have to keep looking," Liz said desperately. "I have to find the children!" She would not allow herself to think that harm might have come to the children or Patience. It couldn't happen again.

"We'll take time out to eat," Rick insisted. "Then we'll look again. We'll find them, Liz. They couldn't have stayed in the house." Rick spoke with deliberate calm. The Edwards' house was a heap of rubble, half of which had been washed into the ocean.

"You'd think people would have noticed two little girls with a nurse." Liz took refuge in anger. Again disaster had arrived and, again, she had not been with her child.

"We'll have coffee, and then we'll retrace our steps. We'll find them," Rick predicted.

Liz and Rick lined up in the hotel restaurant where food was being dispensed to the homeless. Last night they had slept on the floor of a church. Most of the night Liz had prayed. Now she allowed Rick to persuade her to eat because she realized she was close to collapse. Food would sustain her.

After eating they went out into the summer warmth and headed back towards the beach, stopped at each house, each hotel to make enquiries. She was conscious of others in the same frantic search. Everywhere the reminder that death had stalked the area, leaving heavy casualties.

At a table set up in a hotel lobby expressly to help those seeking lost relatives, Liz approached the sad-faced woman on duty.

"Have you seen two little girls with a nurse?" Liz began.

"Mama! Mama!" an ecstatic small voice rose above the din in the lobby. "Mama, you were lost so long!"

"Kathy! My baby. Oh, my baby!" Liz swept Kathy into her arms while tears spilled over. "Wendy, honey –" She reached to embrace Janet's daughter. Patience stood by, beaming in relief.

"Miss Liz, we was so worried about you," Patience said. "When the storm came up like that, I brung Kathy and Wendy here. I knowed that house, wasn't gonna stand up in that kinda blowin'. I figured the hotel was the best place to be."

"We slept in the ballroom last night," Kathy reported, "with lots of other people."

"We sang songs," Wendy added, "and a lady played the piano."

"Patience, thank God." Liz hugged her in gratitude.

"I was jes' takin' the children over to eat," Patience explained. Now uncertainty clouded her face. "Their clothes is all gone. There ain't nothin' left. We was back at the house this mornin'."

"Don't worry, Patience. We can buy more clothes. As soon as the trains are moving again, we'll go back to Atlanta." Liz dropped to her haunches to bring Kathy and Wendy into her arms again for reassurance. "Everything's going to be fine. I'm proud of you for being so brave." Janet must be sick with worry. "Rick, there's no chance of phoning Atlanta?" She lifted her face to his.

"No chance yet." Rick extended a hand to draw her upright again. "Let Patience take the children in to eat. We know where to find them now." Their eyes met in fresh serenity.

"We'll go back to the house," Liz told Patience before she took Kathy and Wendy to the food line. "Maybe there's something we can save. We'll come back here."

Hand in hand Liz and Rick left the hotel and headed along the beach towards the remnants of the Edwards' house.

"I told you they'd be all right," Rick reminded. "You're such a worrier."

Liz laughed. Never had the world seemed so beautiful. They stood, bedraggled and unwashed, in a passionate embrace on the beach. At their feet lay tangles of seaweed and hordes of fish left to die when the water receded.

"Let's get to the house. See if we can salvage anything," Liz said, and they walked with fresh impetus.

As they approached the house Liz gasped with rage. Who was that man pushing through the rubble? Looting at a time like this! Then she recognized him. "Vic! Vic!" she called.

Victor turned towards her – clutching Kathy's teddy bear. She saw the relief that shone from his face.

"Liz!" He swept her to him. "I was so worried." He paused, searching her face. "The children and Patience?"

"They're fine." Her throat was constricted. In the horror of the hurricane she had forgotten that he was due to arrive this morning. With an effort she prodded herself to merge two different worlds. "Vic, I'd like you to meet Rick Pulaski –" Her mind, her emotions, were in chaos. "This is my husband, Victor Adams." *Why did Rick and I come back to the house? I'm not prepared for a confrontation so soon.* "Rick saved my life." She strived to retain her tenuous hold on composure. "He helped me find the children and Patience. We discovered them at a hotel only an hour ago." Did Victor wonder that she had not been at home with them? But his face displayed only relief.

The two men shook hands.

"You have my eternal gratitude," Victor told Rick. "We'd heard nothing in Atlanta about the hurricane. The train crew spread the news when we stopped at West Palm Beach."

"The city was cut off from the world from Friday midnight until radio transmission of sorts was set up late last night," Rick explained. How could he be so casual, Liz railed inwardly. They must have time to talk. To make plans.

"You must have had a grim experience." Victor's compassionate gaze encompassed both Liz and Rick.

"I wouldn't care to go through it again," Rick acknowledged. "We were lying in a gutter for three hours waiting for the hurricane to let up. Scared to move until it did. There've been a lot of lives lost. We won't know the full extent for days. Bodies are still being washed ashore."

"I would have been killed if Rick hadn't pulled me from the car seconds before a telephone pole smashed it." Liz shuddered in recall. "It hit right where I had been sitting."

"Any time you care to visit Atlanta, please consider our house as yours," Victor told Rick.

"Thank you." Rick was not looking at her. "I'd better be shoving off." His smile was pleasant but impersonal. *What does he mean? He can't just walk away. How will I know where to find him?* "I want to see if there's anything I can salvage at my place," he continued. "You're in good hands now, Liz." Rick's eyes managed to graze hers without communication.

"Thanks again," Victor said. Gratitude made him sound almost effusive. *Doesn't he wonder how I met Rick? Doesn't he know this was more than a casual acquaintance?* "Remember, if you're ever in Atlanta, please look us up."

"I'll remember," Rick promised. The air of camaraderie between the two men unnerved her.

Liz stood in a cold sweat. Immobile. Rick was walking out of her life. This was the moment when he could take her from Victor for ever. Didn't he know that? Didn't he care? Humiliated she watched him stride away. Without a word he had relinquished her. She had only been a casual interlude.

"At least we saved this," Victor said, holding up the teddy bear. "Kathy'll be pleased to have old teddy safe and sound."

"She would be crushed if he was lost." Liz struggled to sound natural. "When can we go home?" Suddenly it was urgent to leave Miami.

"The trains won't be running for a few days, I suspect. And I can be useful here. They must need doctors desperately. I'll present myself at a hospital and offer my services."

"Yes." She was on a deserted island again. Alone. Victor couldn't see how urgent it was for her to leave Miami. He was a physician first, a husband when it was convenient. She reached to take the teddy bear from him. "Yes, Vic. Go to one of the hospitals. I'm sure you'll be needed."

Why can't Victor understand my needs?

Nine

Back in Atlanta Liz refused to become involved in social activities. She rejected well-meant invitations with the reminder that she was still in mourning. She hated herself for having forgotten Debbie's death in Rick's arms and was hounded by self-recrimination.

Kathy and Wendy had suffered the horrors of the hurricane without her comforting presence. She should have been at the house with them. Though the two little girls now regarded the hurricane as a great adventure, she reviled herself for being a failure as a mother.

She tried to wash from her memory the towering humiliation of Rick's defection. He had walked out of her life as though they were casual acquaintances. Within twenty-four hours Rick and she had shared birth and death and passion. She had felt bound to him for ever. She had been prepared to leave Victor for him. Even if Victor refused her a divorce, she would have stayed with Rick.

God, she had been naive! A stupid little schoolgirl. How could she have allowed herself to become obsessed by Rick again?

Victor was puzzled by her lack of response to him in bed. It had been one of the wonderful things about their marriage – that making love was so good for them. Didn't he realize that now she couldn't bear to have him touch her?

Perhaps she was no longer capable of feeling passion. No, her mind discarded this supposition. If Rick walked into her bedroom and did no more than touch her hand, she would be passionate.

The days blended one into another. She dreaded the approach of Christmas. A Christmas Debbie would not see. She lashed out at Victor when he talked about a Christmas tree for Kathy. Not in this house of mourning, she rebuked him. She had not yet forgiven him for taking over Debbie's nursery as an office for himself.

At her mother's insistence Victor, Kathy and Liz went to stay at Hampton Court for Christmas Eve and Christmas Day. A festive tree was set up with myriad presents for Kathy. Mama was determined that Kathy enjoy the holiday.

On Christmas Day there was a family dinner. Caroline's friend Ellen and her husband Charlie, who was doing astonishingly well in his business, Ellen's daughter Janet and her family, as well as Andrew, Maureen and their son Andy were invited to dinner. And, as always, Jim Russell, so important to Papa's political career.

"It's not a party," her mother emphasized to Liz. "Ellen and Janet and Jim are like family."

Miraculously Victor was not called to a patient's bedside during the long Christmas dinner. Josh was home from his duties as an intern at Bellevue Hospital in New York. Francis was home from his school in Washington. The faces about the table were familiar and reassuring to Liz, yet at intervals she remembered Debbie, who would never see a Christmas. The Christmas season should be a time of joy. Would she ever feel joyous at Christmas again?

After dinner they transferred themselves to the comfort of the library, gathering about the fragrant birch fire laid in the grate and coaxed into a blaze while they dined. Lily and Jason served coffee. The conversation focused on conditions in the South. Caroline was concerned about the plight of the farmers.

"Science has given them better seed, improved breeds of livestock, more efficient fertilizers, and ways to control pests, but still they live such hard lives."

"They're hit by high costs yet receive low prices for their products," Jim said. "During wartime, when they were making money, they invested their profits in more land and better equipment and they're still paying that off."

"The worst of it is the high interest rate they're charged," Eric summed up.

"Do you know how many small Southern farmers are losing their land?" Kevin asked with painful intensity. "Foreclosures are growing every year. The sharecroppers live on pork fat, corn and molasses. Is it any wonder so many of them suffer from malnutrition?"

"That's not solely a Southern problem," Josh pointed out. "We see malnutrition aplenty in the North. I see it every day at Bellevue."

"And Secretary of the Treasury Mellon is concerned about lowering income tax for the rich." Kevin's tone was scathing. Janet was upset that Kevin was on his soapbox again; Liz sympathized. But Kevin was dedicating his life to helping the poor. "So the rich will have money to spend and thus improve the economy. Doesn't that stupid old man realize that purchasing power is already too unevenly distributed?"

"Josh, do you go to the theater often in New York?" Janet tried to divert the conversation. She always worried that people might interpret what Kevin said as being communistic.

"I don't have the time," Josh said. There was a glow about him because Janet had addressed him personally. It astonished Liz that Janet remained unaware that Josh was in love with her. She knew it was bittersweet agony for Josh to be in the same room with Janet. "But I'm hoping to see Sidney Howard's *The Silver Cord* when I go back to New York after the holidays. It's supposed to be awfully good."

"Do you like living in New York?" Janet pursued. Mama seemed somber all at once, Liz thought. Mama *knew* Josh was in love with Janet. She preferred to ignore it.

"New York is a fascinating city. I've learned about people in a way I could never have learned here at home. But I think

I love New York because I know that in two years I'll be back home in practice with Vic," he said with candor.

"Senator, do you think the McNary-Haugen bill will go through Congress when it's introduced again?" Kevin asked Eric. "It's essential for the farmers."

"I've fought for it," Eric told him. "But all indications are that Coolidge will veto it." His smile was ironic. "We're not doing too well with Presidents of late. Harding had a taste for women, liquor, poker and golf – in that order. Coolidge does nothing. He naps each afternoon in the White House."

"The President naps while the coal mines and the cotton mills are laying off thousands." Victor brought up the subject that Liz knew disturbed her mother. The Hampton Mill had just gone on a four-day week. "My mother writes that the mills in Massachusetts are in bad shape."

"We have problems in our own mills," Andrew admitted. "Exports are way off on cotton goods with all the new mills opening up in Japan, India, China and South America. They don't need us."

"Blame the drop in orders on fashion," Sophie said drily. "Dresses are so short and petticoats so few. And now there's so much interest in silk and rayon."

"Did you read the article in the *Journal* about the new dresses?" Ellen's gaze moved from Sophie to Caroline. "They're supposed to be worn even shorter next year."

"Peggy Mitchell isn't writing for the *Sunday Magazine* any more, is she?" Janet asked curiously.

"I hear she's doing her column from home. She's had an awful time with the ankle she sprained back in September. She was in a cast, then in traction. The last I heard she was on crutches." Liz's eyes lighted up affectionately. "Before she hurt her ankle, I used to run into Margaret every now and then at the library." She had known her as Margaret too long to switch to the current "Peggy". "You know how tiny she is – but she's always carrying a stack of books past her head. We usually meet at the mystery section," Liz reminisced.

Jim leaned forward, a grin creasing his craggy face.

"One of the fellows at the *Journal* told me how the city editor Mr Branch barred Peggy from the city room. She used to pop in there to look up words in the big dictionary that sits on a stand near the city desk. Little as she is, she has to stand on tiptoes to look into the dictionary. Branch wondered why all the typewriters stopped every time Peggy looked up a word, so he did some checking. Every time Peggy leaned over the dictionary, her skirt would rise about an inch above the tops of her stockings, and those dastardly young reporters stopped to stare at one inch of white skin between stocking tops and skirt. And that's the story of why Peggy Mitchell is banned from the city room." Jim chuckled.

"Was there anything in today's newspapers about Sacco and Vanzetti?" Kevin enquired of the table at large. "I didn't have a chance to read the papers this morning."

"It's not good," Eric sighed. "Despite all the fine people committed to their aid." Justice Frankfurter, Edna St Vincent Millay and John Dos Passos among them, Liz recalled. "There appears to be a little hope that they can be saved."

"They're being railroaded to their deaths. The courts have no real evidence against them!" Kevin burst out while Janet looked distressed. She needn't, Liz thought; everybody at the table except for Ellen's husband was sympathetic to Sacco and Vanzetti. But Janet was afraid Kevin might say something about his new job. To most Southerners all labor organizers were communists. "What is the matter with this country? When the 'Teapot Dome' scandal broke, senators like yourself –" Kevin turned to Eric, "were accused of being 'scandalmongers' and 'mudgunners' and 'character assassins' when they dared to investigate. The religion in this country is the pursuit of profits, and the devil with responsibility."

"Caroline, I must ask Annie Mae for her recipe for wild rice stuffing," Ellen said, determined to change the conversation. "It was the best I've ever eaten."

"Could we have another round of those pralines with more

coffee?" Eric asked his wife and grinned. "If my son, the doctor, doesn't object?"

"Papa, I was counting on you to ask." Josh laughed. "We don't have pralines up in New York. Great cheese danish, but no pralines."

On an early April morning Liz awoke to the sound of phonograph music. Unfamiliar jazz exploded into the morning air from the house next door. Adrienne had finally returned from Europe, Liz realized with a surge of anticipation.

Within half an hour Liz was walking into the house next door – not bothering to ring.

"Adrienne?"

"Liz, darling –" In one of the sheer black negligées that, she said, made her feel like Pola Negri, Adrienne trailed down the hall with outstretched arms. "I didn't write, Liz," she said, her face pressed to Liz's, "because I knew there was nothing I could say about the baby that would make any sense."

"You look marvelous." Liz deliberately skirted her grief. "I thought you'd deserted Atlanta for ever."

"Sugar, I'm like the swallows and Capistrano. I bitch, but I always come back to Atlanta. Carrie!" Adrienne yelled. "Bring coffee for two out in the garden."

"What? No gin?" Liz asked indulgently.

"I'm on the wagon. Do you know how much weight you can gain from gin?" Adrienne shuddered.

"I went down to Florida for a couple of weeks," Liz said offhandedly while they strolled out into the garden, saturated with the heady scent of hyacinths. "We were caught in the hurricane."

"My God, how awful!" Adrienne paused in a melodramatic pose. "How did you survive?"

"You do your best." Liz shrugged. "But tell me about Paris." She would say nothing of Rick, she vowed. Not even to Adrienne.

"I was beginning to be bored with Europe," Adrienne admitted. "I came home on the *Leviathan*. We boarded at Cherbourg, and it was dreadful. We were held up for hours while Queen Marie of Romania came on with her entourage. Liz, you wouldn't believe it. We sat there in the rain – on our luggage – waiting for the tender to take us out to the ship. First, Queen Marie and her party had to be taken out. Then all her luggage. She travels with more luggage than Pola Negri. We were supposed to board at four o'clock. We didn't get on the ship until past nine, and it was almost ten when we were served supper."

"Did you stay long in New York?" Liz remembered she owed Josh a letter.

"Just long enough to go to the Warner Theater to see a 'talking movie'. *Don Juan*, with John Barrymore. Why don't I meet men like that?"

Almost in defiance – because she knew Victor's distaste for Adrienne – Liz began to spend a lot of time with her. Adrienne was amusing. The days dragged less in her company. Back in Atlanta Adrienne had immediately sought out a psychoanalyst. She reported each session in detail to Liz – always eliciting laughter.

Victor was making a conscientious effort to be home more often, Liz conceded – yet many nights she sat alone at the dinner table. Alone in the library after dinner, she read endless mysteries: Agatha Christie, Mary Roberts Rinehart, the new mystery writers who were cropping up. Whenever she tried to talk to Victor about where their marriage was headed, he managed to escape.

"You're punishing Vic," Adrienne said, feeling an expert since she was involved in analysis. "Your subconscious is furious with him."

Liz stared at her. Adrienne meant she was still accusing Victor of being responsible for Debbie's death. No, she wouldn't think about that.

"Let's talk about something else." Liz reached for a cigarette. Maureen kept telling her she ought to stop smoking.

"Why don't you call and ask if Dr Arnold has any time open to see you?" Adrienne asked. "He's marvelous. Except that he's so ethical." She sighed. "He refuses to have an affair with me until I'm out of analysis."

"I couldn't bear going through that." Liz rejected the idea. She wouldn't let Adrienne push her in that direction. "Have you finished reading the latest Hemingway?"

"You mean *The Sun Also Rises*?" Adrienne grimaced. "You can have it. It's too depressing for me."

The days and nights passed in a benumbing sameness. Liz felt herself captured in a vacuum. She read the newspapers and listened to the radio, allowed Adrienne to drag her to a procession of movies, which Adrienne professed to adore.

"Mencken says that Hollywood has 'the morals of Port Said'," Adrienne laughed. "But isn't it fun?"

She listened to Adrienne expound on her theory of life, and was disturbed.

"All I give a damn about," Adrienne declared, "is me – me and a few people close to me. Like you. The rest of the world could die. It wouldn't bother me."

People dedicated to justice still fought to save Sacco and Vanzetti, reiterating that the two men were being convicted because they were aliens and radicals rather than for a proven crime. Everybody speculated on the stock market, buying "on margin", convinced a killing was just ahead.

Josh wrote humorous letters about the activities of such New York gangsters as Dutch Schultz and "Legs" Diamond, though Liz knew he was convinced that gangsterism would diminish if ever prohibition was repealed. Adrienne maintained that Al Capone, Schultz and the others were no worse than the big financiers, or the robber barons of the past.

In May the country was electrified when Charles Lindbergh took off on a rainy Friday morning from Roosevelt Field in New York in a monoplane called Spirit of St Louis and headed alone for Paris. He landed at Le Bourget Field, Paris, thirty-three and a half hours later, to be greeted by 100,000 enthusiastic

Frenchman, ecstatic that the young American had completed the first non-stop flight across the Atlantic, at a speed of about 108 miles an hour. The world welcomed a new hero.

A month later the Hampton family experienced a personal triumph. Francis graduated from his special school in Washington. Back in Atlanta he was given a job in the law firm of Hampton & Russell. Liz was touched by Jim's gentleness in supervising Francis in the simple office job provided for him. Francis was a beautiful testimony to Victor's genius, Liz thought in a surge of sentiment.

Less than two months later, on August 2nd, 1927, exactly four years after he took the midnight oath of office at Harding's death, President Coolidge startled the nation with the announcement that he did not choose to run for president in 1918. Two evenings later Liz sat on the veranda at Hampton House with her father while they waited for her mother and Sophie to arrive home from the mill for dinner, and talked about the President's startling news.

"These are strange times, Liz." Tonight Papa seemed tired, she thought. It was this awful heat. He insisted on staying in Atlanta instead of going up to Hampton Court because Mama was tied up at the mill.

Liz had come back to Atlanta with Kathy because she was bored at the plantation. She knew Victor hoped, at first, that it was because she missed him.

"Only death saved Harding from disgrace," the Senator pursued. "The 'Teapot Dome' mess is on his head. This country has never seen such high level graft and corruption. We've had a government chasing after all the prizes of power, but willing to accept none of its responsibilities."

"Coolidge looked good after Harding." Liz was whimsical. "Papa, I wish you were running for the presidency next year."

"I doubt that a Democrat can win next year," Eric said with candor. "We'll stick to the old blueprints."

The Pierce-Arrow pulled up before the house. Caroline and

Sophie emerged. They were late coming home from the mill, Liz realized. Jason had come out twice to see if Mattie could serve dinner.

"You're late," Eric joshed gently. "And on a night when Mattie has red snapper waiting to come to the table."

"We were waiting to hear word of the strike up in Henderson, North Carolina," Caroline explained, dropping into one of the rockers that lined the veranda.

"We can talk over dinner," Sophie clucked. "We don't want to hold up Mattie's red snapper."

"You said nothing about a strike." Eric straightened to attention.

"It wasn't planned," Caroline said. "This morning three hundred workers walked out, demanding that the wage cuts of three years ago be reversed. Organizers had infiltrated as workers." Liz tensed. Mama had not yet discovered that Kevin was planning a drive to organize Atlanta cotton mill workers. It would be traitorous to Janet for her to tell Mama. "They expect the militia to be brought out."

In Henderson the state militia stayed on the scene for two days, then withdrew because there was no violence. The strike collapsed when nine families were evicted from company houses.

"But Alfred Hoffman signed up five hundred members for the United Textile Workers," Kevin pointed out with triumph. He was involved in another new union.

Later in the month Kevin was distraught, as were many Americans, when Sacco and Vanzetti were executed. Again, justice had been dealt a severe blow. Liz sat beside the radio, listening to the account of the last hours of the two men, and remembered another August twelve years ago, when a Georgia mob lynched Leo Frank.

Atlantans were jubilant when it was announced that October 11th would be "Lindbergh Day" in their city. Work was rushed ahead on improvements at Candler Field. All through the summer committees worked to ensure the success of Lindbergh's visit.

Everything went according to schedule despite occasional showers on the highly anticipated day. Lindbergh landed The Spirit of St Louis at Candler Field to be welcomed by thousands. Whistles blew all over Atlanta and surrounding towns, alerting the people to the hero's arrival.

A week after Lindbergh Day Sophie suffered a mild stroke. She would make a full recovery, Victor assured the distraught family three days later, but she must remain away from the mill for six weeks. When she returned, Victor cautioned them, she must limit her hours at her desk. At seventy-six Sophie must capitulate to age.

"Thank God, she's all right." Caroline exchanged relieved smiles with Eric and Liz. "I'll make sure she cuts down on work." Then Liz saw her mother's face tighten in consternation. "Eric, I won't be able to go back to Washington with you tomorrow. I can't leave the mill now."

"We'll have to cancel the dinners you've scheduled for the next four weeks." Eric strived to sound matter-of-fact. Liz knew the strategic political planning her parents invested in those dinners. Her father was laying the groundwork for a projected 1940 race for the presidency. His whole political career had been structured with that objective in mind.

"I feel terrible about letting you down, Eric." Caroline was aghast. "I've always been able to handle the mill and our social obligations."

"Mama, I could go to Washington for a month," Liz offered on impulse. "I could be Papa's hostess." It would be a blessing to lie alone in bed at night. Knowing Victor would not reach out in the dark, to be baffled by her passive acceptance of him. "Don't you think that would be practical?"

Victor was startled.

"You'd have to take Kathy out of school," he objected.

"It's only kindergarten," Liz reasoned. All at once it was

imperative to have the month in Washington. *Why do I feel I must have Victor's consent? Why shouldn't I make this decision myself?* "I'm sure I could find a school up in Washington that would accept Kathy for the month we'd be there." She appealed to her mother. Fighting to secure this Washington respite. "The parties are all scheduled within the next month, aren't they? When you're in Washington, you always come home a week before Thanksgiving." Liz strived to sound casual.

"A month covers it," Caroline confirmed. Her eyes moved to Victor. Liz felt her mother's ambivalence. Mama knew Victor was annoyed.

"It would be an interesting experience for Liz." Eric punctured the awkward silence that overlaid the tensions between Liz and Victor.

"I suppose it would," Victor capitulated, but Liz felt his inner rage.

Victor drove home with Liz in silence. She expected that at any moment he would rebuke her for cornering him into agreement about the trip to Washington. It would be better for them if he would. Why must Victor always hoard his anger? They left too much unsaid.

"I have to drop by the hospital," Victor told her as he pulled up before the house. "I may be late in getting home."

Three days after her father's departure for the Capital Liz set off with Kathy and Patience to join him. Her father was delighted with her presence. Papa was often lonely in Washington, she commiserated – with special understanding born of her own loneliness.

Was there ever a time when her parents' marriage had been in trouble? It wasn't a conventional marriage, with Mama dividing her life between the role of mill executive and politician's wife. Did Papa resent Mama's absences the way she resented Victor's? Yet her parents' marriage was solid. Once, in irritation, Mama had complained that she refused to compromise:

"Everything has to be your way, Liz." The accusation lingered in her mind. Did Victor think that?

Each morning at seven her father left the elegant row house on R Street bought at the conclusion of his first term in Congress. Liz considered the hour ridiculously early, but Eric was a conscientious public servant. He returned in time for a fashionably late dinner.

Each day Patience took Kathy to the nearby private school where she would spend the morning hours while in Washington. Kathy was enthralled with her new friends. Each afternoon she played in the park or at a classmate's home or entertained at the Hampton house. Liz resolved that once each week she would take Kathy and a chosen friend on an outing.

While her two brothers had gone to school in Washington, Liz knew little of the city. Her longest stay had been for a period of four days, when her mother had taken her there to hear her father make a special speech on the Senate floor.

Now Liz explored the Mall, visited the Washington Monument, the Jefferson Memorial and the Lincoln Memorial – completed just five years ago. She went sightseeing on Meridian Hill, where many of the foreign embassies were located. One morning, with the proper ticket in hand, she joined other tourists lining up for admission to the Senate gallery. When Senator Hampton rose to speak, she subdued an impulse to say, "That's my father."

In her attractively wallpapered, colonial bedroom Liz dressed for the first dinner at the Washington house with unexpected trepidation. Their guests were due to arrive within half an hour. She was almost overwhelmed at the prospect of being hostess to three senators, four representatives and a Supreme Court judge among other Washington luminaries, none of whom she knew.

Was everything all right in the kitchen? Had Caleb brought the right wines up from the cellar? Would anyone remark that a United States Senator dared to serve wines at his table in this era of Prohibition?

Liz started at the knock on her bedroom door.

"Come in."

Her father opened the door and walked into the room. Papa was still a handsome man. The touch of gray in his hair added distinction.

"Liz, you look beautiful." Eric leaned forward to kiss her cheek. "I can't believe you're old enough to be my hostess."

"I suppose we should go downstairs." She had felt this nervousness before the performance of a school play.

"May I, Mrs Adams?" With a debonair smile her father offered her his arm.

"Senator, I'm delighted." Liz smiled brilliantly.

Liz sat at the foot of the resplendent table, remembering her mother's exhortations about the guests seated on each side of her. The elderly judge at her left had a hearing difficulty but was a marvelous lip reader. She must enunciate carefully. The ambassador on her right was a womanizer. For an instant she panicked. Was she supposed to have placed the judge on her right and the ambassador on her left? Protocol was so important.

While Caleb and Annabel served the perfect dinner, Liz was increasingly conscious of the efforts of the new young congressman, Lawrence Burke, to draw her into the animated conversation between his dinner partner, an elderly dowager with a sharp mind and a matching tongue, and himself. Congressman Burke was a ruggedly handsome man in his early thirties. From the midwest, Liz remembered from her father's briefing. His wife was back home awaiting the birth of their third child.

"Nobody can tell me that the Sacred Rota of the Catholic Church would have given Consuelo Vanderbilt an annulment of her marriage to the Duke of Marlborough if she wasn't one of the richest women in the country," the dowager proclaimed.

"The story I've heard," a woman across the table contributed, "was that Rome granted the divorce because Consuelo's mother forced her to marry the Duke, when she was only seventeen, though she was truly in love with a man named Rutherfurd."

"Winthrop Rutherfurd," the dowager elucidated with a hint of malice. "He's married to Lucy Mercer. That pretty piece our wartime Assistant Secretary of the Navy, Franklin Roosevelt, found so delectable."

"I so admire Mrs Roosevelt," Liz intervened. God, she hated the Washington gossiping. It was worse than back home. "My mother has told me about the wonderful volunteer work she did during the war. Did you know that her food-saving plan was adopted by the Food Administration?" Liz was conscious of Lawrence Burke's rapt attention.

After dinner her father made a point of bringing her together with the new congressman.

"Larry speaks my language, Liz," Eric said, his smile expansive. "Another convert to pacifism."

"After seven months with the infantry in France I swore I'd never fight again unless the United States was personally attacked." His eyes were an icy blue in recall. A tough man in a fight, Liz guessed; and Rick's face flashed across her mind. Those who fought a war belonged to a special club. "Are you glad to be in Washington?" Congressman Burke asked Liz.

"I hardly know the city," Liz confessed.

When Eric was called away, Congressman Burke immediately offered his services as a tour guide to Liz.

"I'm standing in for my wife," he said with disarming charm. Liz was conscious of his disconcerting resemblance to Rick. It was in attitude and physique more than face, she decided. "Normally Dorothy would be showing you around Washington."

"What about the House?" Liz lifted an eyebrow in surprise. "Isn't your presence required there?"

"Do you doubt my dedication?" He clucked. "There are few days when every congressman makes a point of being in the House. Have you visited the Smithsonian?"

"Not yet." Liz realized she was flirting with Larry Burke.

That came as natural as breathing to any well brought up Southern woman.

"I'll collect you at ten tomorrow morning. You have to visit the Smithsonian. That's a civic obligation." All at once he was smiling at someone beside them. "Judge Lindsay, my wife told me to be sure and give you her regards the next time we met. She so enjoyed the dinner at your house last month."

Liz found it easier than she had anticipated to fill her mother's role at the dinner. She had grown up amidst political dinners at Hampton House; it had rubbed off on her, she decided in amusement.

While she circulated among her guests – listening more than talking – Liz worried over the encounter with Larry Burke. She knew he was physically attracted to her. Did she appear the kind of woman a man could pick up on such short acquaintance? He knew she was married. Or was it just that the young congressman was out to impress her father? Papa carried a lot of weight in Washington. A new congressman would do well to be in his favor.

Lying sleepless in bed Liz debated about going to the Smithsonian with Larry Burke. Perhaps in Washington it would be considered no more than a polite reciprocation for his having been invited to dinner tonight. She was making too much of it, Liz chided herself. Going to a museum in broad daylight was hardly a compromising situation.

Promptly at ten the next morning Congressman Burke presented himself at the house. Liz and he drove to the Mall and parked before the red sandstone pseudo-Norman edifice that is the Castle on the Mall, home of the Smithsonian Institution.

For almost three hours they devoted themselves to sightseeing. Liz was astonished to find herself relaxing in Larry's company. Afterwards he took her off to luncheon at a secluded restaurant, where, Liz realized, they would encounter none of the congressional crowd. She admired the landmark restaurant. Larry told her it had been established in 1904. Gilt-framed paintings hung about the walls. The chandeliers were of turn-of-the-century vintage. The food sumptuous.

Larry Burke was making every effort to be charming. He beguiled her with inside stories of Washington. As one of the Capital's youngest and most handsome congressmen, he was a favorite among hostesses. His repertoire was impressive.

Over dessert and coffee the conversation became more personal. He was disarmingly honest about his political ambitions. Liz showed him photographs of Kathy and Larry brought forth snapshots of his two boys.

"Dorothy is hoping for a girl," Larry told Liz. "Though she was furious at first when she realized she was off to the races again. She went back home for the duration. Six months." His tone was acerbic.

"You'll be going home for visits."

"I doubt it." Larry's lopsided smile conveyed no amusement.

"It's about time for Kathy to be coming home from kindergarten." Liz grasped at an excuse to conclude their luncheon. All at once she was afraid of the unvoiced communication between them.

"I'll see you at the Harmons' dinner tomorrow night," he said complacently. "You'll be there, of course." He laughed at her start of astonishment.

"Yes," she confirmed. In Washington she could not decline invitations. Not when she was serving as her father's hostess. The message from Larry Burke was unmistakable. He was enamored and in pursuit.

"As an unattached man I'm being invited everywhere." His eyes told her this situation especially pleased him now that she was in Washington. "The Harmons' parties are always interesting, and they're important." He lifted a hand to signal the waiter that they were preparing to leave. Only now did Liz realize that most of the diners had departed.

At the Harmons' dinner the following evening Liz found herself seated beside Larry Burke, who whispered his approval of this arrangement.

"Smart lady, Mrs Harmon."

"I'm glad to see it's not going to be a 'dry' dinner," Liz murmured, noting that the place settings included wine glasses.

"The Harmons keep a small still in the cellar," Larry said humorously. "Like Alice and Nick Longworth. I hear both products are commendable."

Before the guests disbanded, Larry slipped a piece of paper into Liz's hand. His eyes told her this was a personal message. The glint in his eyes was so reminiscent of Rick that she felt cold for an instant. Not until she was alone in her room did she read the words neatly printed across a strip of his office stationery.

"Tomorrow at ten. Show you Arlington."

Tomorrow was Saturday, but Papa would go to the office. He would be gone long before Larry drove up to the house. No one would gossip about her being shown the Washington sights in broad daylight. Still, she would not mention to her father that she was driving to Arlington with Larry Burke.

Sharply at ten, as Liz walked down the stairs to the foyer, the doorbell rang.

"It's someone for me, Caleb," she called, forestalling his appearance in the foyer. "Please tell Annabel I won't be here for lunch."

"You're looking beautiful this morning," Larry greeted her and reached for her elbow. He was like Rick, yet without Rick's arrogance, Liz thought. Rick with finesse. If Larry was ruthless, and she didn't doubt that he could be to further his career, his ruthlessness would be executed with an air of charming apology. Adrienne would go mad about him, she thought in a corner of her mind.

While they drove, Larry gave her a commentary on Arlington Cemetery. The nation's largest shrine, Arlington covered more than 500 acres. The Tomb of the Unknown Soldier was an unembellished fifty-ton block of marble, dramatic in its simplicity. Below Arlington House was the Custis-Lee Mansion.

"That'll be special for you as a Southerner," Larry teased. "The estate that belonged to General Robert E. Lee through his marriage to the great-granddaughter of Martha Washington. Mary Randolph Custis."

"Union soldiers took the house," Liz recalled, "and troops were buried there."

She was pensive as they arrived at Arlington and left the car to walk to the Tomb of the Unknown Soldier, which soldiers guarded day and night. They paused to watch the elaborate changing of the guard, which Larry told Liz occurred every half hour. She read the words inscribed there: "Here rests in honored glory an American soldier . . . known but to God."

Though the morning was pleasantly warm, she felt shrouded in ice. Who was the soldier whose remains lay there? It could be David. Though he had fought with the Canadian Corps, he was an American.

"Let's hope no other American is brought here from a battlefield," Larry said with unfamiliar solemnity. "Let the only dead brought here be old soldiers."

"I don't want to stay." It had been so long since she thought of David, but standing here the hurt was fresh.

They left the Tomb of the Unknown Soldier to visit the Custis-Lee Mansion that looks out over Arlington Cemetery. In this classic Greek revival mansion lived the man who rejected a request to take command of the Union army saying, "Though opposed to secession and deprecating war, I could take no part in an invasion of the Southern states", but who went on to command the army of the Confederacy.

"I have an errand to do while we're out this way," Larry said casually over luncheon. "I have to check on the house of a friend who's away in Europe. You don't mind, do you?" His smile was solicitous.

"No, I don't mind." She managed an impersonal smile while warning signals flashed in her mind. She would wait in the car.

"The friend who lives there comes from my home state," Larry explained. "He was supportive in my first political campaigns." He paused. "He was the only one among family and friends who warned me I was making a mistake when I married Dorothy."

"When did you discover this?" She would have expected something more original from a man supposedly as brilliant as Larry Burke.

"The first year. I couldn't consider a divorce if I was to go anywhere in politics." His smile was wry. "It was the old story. I worked for her father's law firm. He was eager for a congressman in the family. I had no money to speak of, and he was rich. He threw Dorothy and me together at every opportunity. She's a good-looking woman and fairly bright. I ignored the fact that we had nothing in common. That she was a spoiled only child. She throws temper tantrums when she can't get her own way. She does me a favor when she sleeps with me. She hates Washington. The minute she knew she was pregnant, she took off."

"I suspect you haven't gone without consolation," Liz challenged.

"Washington is full of women eager to console," he conceded. "But I have one problem." His eyes held hers. "I'm very selective."

Despite Liz's intention to sit in the car while Larry checked his friend's house, she was keenly conscious of the covert designs she was sure he harbored. Annoyance mingled with gratification in her. It was flattering to be desired by a man as dashing as Larry Burke. And he wasn't the kind to go chasing after any women who happened to be available.

Larry's friend maintained a Washington residence in a well-kept row house on N Street, just above the fashionable Mayflower Hotel. Larry parked and, apparently as an afterthought, invited Liz to go into the house with him.

"I'm fond of Chuck and terribly grateful to him; but if you want to see a truly ugly Washington house, this is it."

"That's hardly an exciting invitation." She laughed. But Larry opened the car door on her side, and she stepped out. It was like being with Rick. She had no will.

The staff of servants had been shipped back home, Larry explained while he opened the heavy oak front door. At intervals he checked to see that no intruder had made their way inside. That faucets were turned off and windows locked. The slightly strained quality of his voice told Liz he was intent on seduction.

"It's cool in the house," she said, hunching her shoulders in discomfort. The heat had been turned down to an "empty house" degree.

"The upstairs rooms will be warm from the sun," he encouraged, opening the sliding doors to show her the box-like rooms on the first floor, all of them overloaded with ornate walnut furniture, each room with a tiled fireplace.

"Ugly," Liz agreed. Why had she come into this house with Larry? She knew their destination. Her body knew.

Taking her hand in his Larry led her up the narrow, dark staircase. A door at the top of the stairs was flung wide, spilling sunlight on the landing.

"There's a patch of garden in the back," Larry told her, drawing her into the sunlit room and to a window. Masses of yellow chrysanthemums were on display below.

"They're lovely," Liz said unsteadily.

"You're lovely," Larry cradled her face between his hands and kissed her. Slowly at first. Then with passion.

All at once she was responding. Passion was not dead in her after all. Her hands closed on his shoulders. This was Miami. Rick was kissing her with a tempestuousness that reached every cell in her body.

"I've wanted to do this since the moment I saw you," Larry told her. Rick had said that. "It was pure hell to sit through dinner and not touch you." With one hand he reached to draw the shade to the windowsill.

"We're out of our minds," Liz objected. But she made no

effort to stop him when he began to unbutton the jacket of her suit. It had been so long since she had felt this way. She had been afraid it might never happen again.

She stood before him, head back, eyes closed, while he pulled away her jacket. It had been like this with Rick, she remembered. She had no will. But when he began to undo the tiny buttons of her blouse, she put up a hand to stop him.

"Let me –" With deft swiftness she freed herself of the blouse and hung it across the back of a chair while Larry pulled off his tie and jacket and dropped them on a dresser. His shoulders were broad, his waist slender and his stomach flat: a man in condition. His own gaze was pinned to the high rise of her breasts above the white lace of her teddy.

"You are the most exciting woman I've ever encountered," he murmured and lifted her off her feet and carried her to the four-poster walnut bed.

They made love with an urgency that betrayed a mutual hunger. Afterwards Liz lay in his arms – suffused with a sense of well-being. They were two people alone in a private world. Today had been inevitable. She had known that the first evening she had met Larry.

"Larry," she said in sudden alarm. "Don't fall asleep."

"I'm not," he soothed without bothering to open his eyes. "Just relaxing."

"We should be leaving." She was nervous. Suppose someone else had a key to the house? The prospect of being the subject of Washington gossip repelled her.

"In a little while," he promised, "I have a deep thirst."

Ten

Liz knew that Larry and she were being indiscreet in seeing each other daily. Although they avoided places favored by congressmen and their wives, she worried that they might be seen going into the house on N Street. She worried, but continued to see Larry at every possible opportunity. Many evenings they were dinner partners in the heavy autumn social whirl.

At the conclusion of her third week in Washington, with only one week of her visit remaining, Liz told her father that she would stay longer.

"Let's go home together for Thanksgiving," she proposed.

"Have you discussed it with Victor?" Her father seemed disturbed. She had expected him to be pleased.

"I'll phone him tonight and tell him," Liz promised.

All through the embassy reception, where she avoided spending much time in Larry's company, Liz was conscious of her father's somberness. When they arrived home, he asked her to have coffee with him in the library.

Liz went out to the kitchen to prepare the coffee. Annabel and Caleb had both retired for the night. She was conscious of a feeling of unease. Papa had been strangely formal since they left the embassy.

Liz carried the coffee tray into the library and placed it on the table that sat between the two wing chairs flanking the marble-faced fireplace. Her father was paying desultory attention to a radio newscast.

"Papa, would you like some cake with the coffee?" Liz asked belatedly.

"No cake." He brushed this aside and leaned forward to switch off the radio. "Liz, we have to talk," he said brusquely.

"About what?" All at once she felt like a little girl again. Papa was angry with her.

"About Larry Burke and you." Eric rose to his feet in a gesture of unrest. Liz forced herself to pour the coffee as though she was unaware of what he meant.

"What about Larry?" She contrived to sound politely curious. Despite her determination to be casual she filled one cup too full. Never mind. She would take hers black.

"All of Washington is gossiping about the two of you." Her father's face flushed with color. This conversation was painful to him. "Liz, it has to stop."

Liz handed one white porcelain cup and saucer to her father. Fighting against panic.

"I think it's outrageous," she said coolly. "When Larry is kind enough to offer to be my tour guide on a couple of occasions, whose business is it? Larry is very grateful to you. He said that since Dorothy was not in town, he was fulfilling her obligations."

"Nothing is secret in this town, Liz." He was remembering the days after David was killed in France, when she ran from one soldier to another. He was remembering those ugly days she thought had been finally put to rest. Unfair! "We live in the proverbial fishbowl."

"Larry took me to see the Smithsonian Institution. He drove me to Arlington Cemetery to see the Tomb of the Unknown Soldier and the Custis-Lee Mansion. What every Washington tourist goes to see." She enunciated carefully to conceal the tremor in her voice. "How dare people talk about that!"

"That's all?" Eric asked after a moment.

"That's all," she lied. Ashamed but determined. "Of course, everybody seems to seat Larry and me together at dinners. I suppose because his wife is away, and we're both young."

"The gossiping in this town is endless," Eric said in

exasperation. "But I think you should return to Atlanta on schedule. Let's not give those women more to feed on."

"All right, Papa."

He didn't believe she was having an affair with Larry. Liz clung to this. What was the matter with her? Was it impossible for her to remain faithful to any man? She felt sick that Larry and she had been the subject of Washington gossip, and that it had reached her father.

Liz dreaded the approach of another Christmas. The two most terrible times of the year were Debbie's birthday and Christmas, which Debbie had never seen. She was irritable; she snapped at Victor at the slightest provocation; she was impatient with Kathy. Always ashamed after each incident. Guilt was piling atop guilt.

She was relieved when Adrienne took off for Palm Beach a few days before Christmas. She was impatient with Adrienne's brittle conviviality, with Adrienne's involvement with her analyst. At times like this Janet was her salvation. She talked endlessly to Janet on the phone because on so many evenings now Kevin was away on business. Or she drove to Janet's house to sit and talk with her in the box-like sitting room that was shabby no matter how desperately Janet tried to make it appear fashionable.

The weather had been cold and blustery for the past two days. Tonight Liz settled herself in the sitting room before the fireplace, where Matthew had laid a fire. While Victor touched a match to strategic areas of the grate, Liz reached for the crossword puzzle book that was her nightly companion. On the evenings when he was home, Victor listened to the radio or read and she worked over a crossword puzzle. It eliminated the necessity for conversation.

For a little while Victor listened to the radio. Then he rose to his feet and strode to the door in a burst of energy.

"I'm going up to do a little work," he explained to Liz. "I'm behind in writing up my reports."

"Look in and make sure Kathy hasn't thrown off her blanket," Liz called after him.

Alone Liz abandoned the crossword puzzle. Restlessness tugged at her. She would call Janet, she decided. Kevin was up in North Carolina on business. Wendy would be asleep. But with a hand at the phone she changed her mind. She would drive over to Janet's house.

Liz went out to the kitchen to pile a plate high with the petit fours Mary Lou had made today. Like Papa, Janet loved sweets. She left the plate, covered with a tea towel, on the table and hurried upstairs for her coat.

The door to Victor's office was ajar. Involuntarily she glanced inside as she walked past. Victor sat behind the desk, his head in his hands, eyes shut. His face was etched with a private torment. She knew the snapshots spread across his desk were of Debbie.

Her hands were trembling when she pulled a coat from the closet. She had been so saturated with her own unhappiness that she had ignored Victor's grief. So full of anger, of recriminations because they had senselessly lost their precious baby. Blaming Victor. Did Victor blame himself?

She paused before the office door. She made a point of never walking into the room that had been Debbie's nursery. She forced herself to knock.

"Yes?" Victor's voice was guarded.

Liz pushed the door open further, allowing him a moment to mask his anguish.

"I'm driving over to Janet's," she told him. "Kevin's away for a few days. I won't be late."

"Drive carefully," he said.

Later, sitting in Janet's kitchen over steaming cups of coffee while Janet talked with such earnestness about Kevin's dedication to the mill workers, Liz asked herself how she could mend her marriage. Before it was too late.

She had gone to Rick out of a frightening loneliness. Rick had showered her with compliments; "Liz, you gorgeous bitch."

"Liz, you are the most exciting woman alive." "Liz, you could drive any warm-blooded man right up the wall."

Victor had told her to "drive carefully." Those few prosaic words were backed by the kind of love that could help her through this painful, growing time of her life. If only Victor and she could break down the wall between themselves and communicate.

Adrienne talked her selfish, childish prattle about grabbing all the fun possible out of life. That was the cry of their generation. The disenchanted generation. And all the while their lives were empty.

"I should get back to the house," Liz said with sudden urgency. "I told Vic I'd be gone only a little while. He's nervous when I drive at night."

"Aren't men crazy?" Janet sighed. "A breed apart. Kevin's the same way. I resent the inference that we can't drive as well as men, but it's sweet that they worry."

Driving back home, conscious of the Christmas decorations on the avenues of houses where Christmas would be greeted with pleasure, Liz thought about what Janet had confided to her over coffee. To his wife Kevin was candid about his communist ties, though his union tried to mask this. The Party was the answer to the deprivation that infected so much of the country, Kevin insisted. Not that he preached revolution, Janet had rushed to clarify. But Kevin was convinced that communist support was essential in unionizing the Southern mills. It was a frightening realization.

Kevin and Victor were both dedicated men. Her family was rich with dedication. Only Francis and she bumbled along, not sure where they were going with their lives. She felt so ineffectual. So purposeless.

Yet even with his dedication Victor was frustrated. He would like to put all of himself into his work with troubled children but his practice had taken over, grown far beyond his expectations. It had become a monster that kept him from the children. She suspected he churned inside, awaiting the day when Josh would join him in practice and to some extent free him.

It would be another year and a half before Josh finished his residency and returned to Atlanta. And Victor was disheartened that professionals were skeptical of his efforts at the clinic. He had so much to give, she thought with a tenderness towards him that was rare these days. When would this be recognized?

When he delivered his paper at that New York medical meeting, he had been encouraged. But that had been one small group who realized what his methods could accomplish. The family knew. Look what he had done for Francis.

When she approached the house, she saw that the library was still lit. Victor would hear her put the car in the garage and know she was home. He had a habit of going to bed late, though he left the house before seven to make his hospital rounds. He went to bed late, she thought with fresh comprehension, because sleep was elusive.

She walked into the night-dark house and upstairs to the bedroom she shared with Victor. Any minute now Matthew would check the doors to be sure they were all locked for the night and only the hall night lights left on. In her room she prepared for bed. She chose the white chiffon nightgown that had been bought in Paris on her honeymoon and which she hadn't worn since Kathy was an infant.

She settled herself in bed with the latest Agatha Christie novel, searched for a radio program that offered the classical music Victor enjoyed. She flinched when Beethoven's Fifth invaded the room. The first time Rick made love to her, they could hear Beethoven's Fifth on the phonograph downstairs.

She settled for the score from the new Jerome Kern musical, *Show Boat*. Josh wrote that he had seen it on a night off from Bellevue and loved the music. The strains of "Why Do I Love You?" filtered into the room. She *knew* why she loved Victor.

She struggled to concentrate on the Christie novel, while every moment she listened for Victor's steps in the hall outside the bedroom. She had been so blind. So blind. Strange, how a few words "Drive carefully" had shown her with such clarity the depth of Victor's love. That and those few moments when she and Janet had talked about Victor and Kevin.

Victor stopped short when he walked into the master bedroom. Usually the lamps were switched off, Liz apparently asleep when he came in for the night.

"How's Janet?" he asked, walking towards the bathroom. Assessing the situation.

"She's lonely with Kevin away so much." *That's my theme song*. "At least, her job keeps her busy during the day."

Should she go to work herself? What could she do? She had no training. No profession. Selling dresses at Rich's would not appeal to her. For a little while she had played a game about becoming a professional pianist. She had envied Margaret Mitchell, now Margaret Marsh, for having an exciting job on the *Journal*.

What a shame that Janet was unable to find a teaching job. She had worked so hard to earn her degree. Or did Janet avoid a teaching job because Kevin would consider that too high a social level for a labor organizer's wife? He accepted the Hamptons because his mother-in-law had been Mama's friend for many years and Janet and she were so close.

In pajamas, Victor returned to the bedroom. Liz switched off the lamps. "Only Make Believe" provided a romantic background for the reconciliation Liz was plotting. A thread of moonlight provided a silver path to the bed.

Victor's side of the bed creaked slightly as he slid beneath the blanket. He cleared his throat in uncertainty. He was afraid he might have misread her signal.

"Liz?"

"Hmm?" She turned to him in the darkness.

"You're cold," he said, drawing her to him. He knew he would not be rebuffed tonight.

"You're warm," she said.

Victor chuckled.

"Honey, that's the understatement of the year."

His mouth sought hers in the darkness. His arms pulled her to him.

"I've missed you," he whispered, his face against hers.

"I've missed you, too." She felt a soaring surge of joy. "Oh, Vic, love me! Please love me."

It seemed to Liz that Victor and she were reliving their honeymoon. Each night he reached for her in the darkness. Each night she met his passion with matching passion. Even Christmas seemed less painful now that Victor and she were reunited.

She, Victor and Kathy spent New Year's Eve at Hampton Court. There was the usual family dinner with Josh home for the holidays. Andrew, Maureen and their son Andy were there. At midnight the familiar New Year's Eve sounds filled the night. After toasting the new year with the traditional Dom Perignon, Liz and Victor returned to their own house.

Tonight Victor wanted to talk after their lovemaking. He was experiencing a breakthrough with one of the children, and this exhilarated him. From the days when she had helped in the children's clinic Liz remembered his excitement at each minor accomplishment.

"Liz, I was thinking all day –" His words were tumbling over one another now. "It's time we thought about having another child." He was too involved in the subject to recognize the shock he had administered to her. "You're still young, but I'm—"

"No!" The word was ripped from her throat. Was that why he was eager to make love so often? "I won't have another child! I told you that. I told you that long ago." When Debbie died, she warned him she would never carry another child. How could she put herself through that? Fearful every instant that she might lose the new baby, the way she lost Debbie. "How can you even think about it?" Her voice trembled with recrimination.

"Honey, I'm sorry," Victor stammered. But Liz was already

leaving the bed to rush into the bathroom. Victor might be careless. She wasn't.

The magic of their reconciliation was shattered. How could Victor be so callous as to expect her to give him another child? Nothing had changed. Her marriage was empty, and now she lacked even the incentive to leave Victor.

Victor lay sleepless far into the night. He'd thought Liz and he were breaking down the wall that had existed between them for so long. Why couldn't they return to those wonderful first years of their marriage? Why had Liz been so distraught when he talked about their having another child? What was wrong in that?

What can I do to heal our marriage? I've never stopped loving Liz. I'll love her until the day I die.

Eleven

Politics was a major source of conversation in this election year of 1928. Eric was nervous that Governor Al Smith, the Democratic candidate for president, would lose the election.

"The country's not ready yet for a Catholic president."

True to Eric's predictions Herbert Hoover won the election on November 6, 1928. It was a landslide victory for the Republicans.

For most of 1928 Liz worked in secret with Kevin and his union organizers, ever assailed by guilt that she was fighting against her mother's interests. The men and women who moved in and out of Atlanta struggling to organize the always skeptical mill workers were Northerners. None of them knew she was a Hampton. That was the condition she'd insisted upon when she offered to help with the labor movement. No one must know she was Caroline Hampton's daughter. She was Liz Adams, who happened to be concerned about the tortured lives of the mill workers.

Liz spent hours each day in the Michaels household, which had become union headquarters, engrossed in routine office work. As Kevin's union poured more funds into the campaign, he had insisted that Janet give up her job at Rich's. Liz and Janet comprised the office staff. Liz was alleviating the guilt that had been part of her growing up in the shadows of the drab mill village, knowing the Hamptons prospered on the sweat of the workers.

Kevin had convinced her that his union was to be preferred over the United Textile Workers.

"Our union *cares* about the workers. We'll allow no violence."

But labor unrest in the South had been horrendous this past year. Mama was proud that she had managed to avoid a strike thus far, Liz thought. Mama didn't know that the workers of the Hampton Mill – in spite of its reputation as one of the most progressive in the South – were being pursued by Kevin and his cohorts with an aggressiveness not yet seen in Georgia.

Then in April of 1929 news came through about the action of labor union organizers in the Loray Mill in Gastonia, North Carolina. All young men, some fresh out of college, demanded a forty-hour week, equal pay for women and children, abolition of piecework, houses with screens and bathtubs, and a minimum wage of twenty dollars a week. They were working sixty-six-hour weeks for nine dollars. Children were paid five dollars a week. Workers signed up, but the mill owners refused to recognize the union.

Active on the picket line when the workers struck was Ella Mae Wiggins, a twenty-nine-year-old mother who'd had to quit her job when the foreman refused to allow her time off to care for her children sick with whooping cough. Four of her nine children died because, without work, she had no money for medicine. But with the arrival of the state militia, the strikers retreated.

On May 7th the mill evicted sixty-two families from company houses. The union, not Kevin's, set up a tent colony in a field close to the mill. A month later a parade, meant to signal another walkout, was disrupted by recently sworn-in deputies. Late that night local police officers went to the tent colony when reports of troubles were received. One unionist and four police officers were shot; the Chief of Police died.

Sixteen strikers and organizers went on trial for murder. When one of the jurors went emotionally berserk, the judge declared a mistrial. A new trial was scheduled for September.

In the Michaels' summer-hot kitchen in early September

Kevin huddled at the table with a half-dozen men. Liz washed dishes in the sink while Janet made sandwiches.

"Janet, more ice-tea," Kevin ordered.

"I'll get it," Liz said and crossed to bring the pitcher from the ice-box.

"When are those sons-of-bitches workers going to learn that we're here to help them?" a burly bearded man of about twenty-five demanded. "The Chamber of Commerce keeps writing the Northern textile operators about the garden of Eden they'll find down here. Cheap, unorganized labor, a seventy-two-hour work week – despite the sixty-hour law – with women and children working nights. Special tax exemptions. The new mills coming down from New England are as bad for the workers as the ones already here."

The doorbell rang. Liz hurried to answer it. A young woman organizer, her face taut and eyes blazing, shoved past Liz without a word and stalked back to the kitchen.

"More trouble up in Gastonia!" she said without preliminaries. "A mob is milling around the Mecklenburg County jail. A mass meeting has been called for tonight." She paused as though to catch her breath. "A truckload of workers was on the way from Bessemer City in an open truck. A car came along and forced a collision. The car behind started shooting. The workers jumped out and headed across the fields. One of them didn't make it. Ella Mae Wiggins."

"Oh, my God." Kevin's face was ashen. "Joe –" he turned to the man at his right, "we'll drive up there tonight."

Liz turned to Janet, white with alarm. Janet put the tray of sandwiches on the table and turned to her husband.

"Kevin, be careful."

Kevin kept vowing there would be no violence in the Atlanta mills, Liz remembered. But people were dying in strikes. What would happen when the union organizers went into the Hampton Mill? Mama on one side, she on the other.

But months went past with no such invasion.

*   *   *

Josh left the emergency room at Bellevue in New York City – where he had been on duty for two shifts back to back – and went to the cafeteria for coffee before heading across First Avenue to his apartment. His back ached. His feet cried out in rebellion. A dozen hammers pounded in his head.

He should be down in Atlanta now, in practice with Victor. He had allowed himself to be pushed into extra months of duty to cover for a resident laid up with a broken leg. But he would go home in less than two months – a few days before Christmas. And on the first day of 1930, he would be an Atlanta physician.

Though he enjoyed the excitement of the city and grew as a doctor in the drama of serving at Bellevue, he was impatient to return to Atlanta and his family. At Columbia College and in medical school he had been coddled, unaware of the desperate lives endured by so many New Yorkers. He had lived the sheltered campus life. Suddenly, within the chaotic, ever frantic walls of Bellevue, he had been brought face to face with reality. He saw poverty, deprivation, desperation.

He spied an empty table in the busy cafeteria and sat down with his cup of coffee. He leaned back in his chair, relishing the relief of being off his feet.

"God, what a day!" Tim Reiss, a surgical resident, collapsed into a chair opposite him. His face was devoid of color. His shoulders sagged. "This is a Thursday that'll go down in history."

"Heavy schedule?" Josh sympathized.

Tim stared at him.

"Don't you know what's going on downtown on Wall Street?"

"I've been on a double shift." On duty he had a one-track mind. "We've been so rushed I've eaten in the emergency room."

"It's a panic, man!" Tim exploded. "I came out of surgery at noon, and there's a message from my broker's office. Come up with five thousand immediately or I'll be sold out. Christ,

I can't raise five bucks right now. I called my old man. He couldn't help. He's been covering his own shares. He's down to nothing. He's petrified."

"Anybody is crazy to buy on margin." For weeks Josh had heard the complaints of doctors in the hospital about the downward trend of the market. He had paid no attention. But he remembered his mother's constant warning that to buy on margin was dangerous. It wasn't likely that the panic on Wall Street would be devastating to the Hampton fortune. Not with Mama in control.

"Everybody buys on margin," Tim protested. "Seventeen million people play the market. Even the hospital orderlies give me tips. That's the economy we live in."

"We had a would-be suicide just before I went off duty," Josh recalled somberly. He had been aware only of the medical emergency. The psychiatrists would probe for the cause of the attempted suicide. Now he felt guilty that he had offered no compassion. But there had been no time. "He went out a third-story window. He was cursing because he broke both legs and an arm but was still alive. He kept moaning, 'no margin, no margin'. I didn't understand –"

"We'll see more," Tim warned. "Dr Rogers walked out of the hospital two hours ago. He looked like a ghost. He said he'd been wiped out."

"The speakeasies will be packed," Josh predicted.

"You still hanging around here?" The soft, feminine voice belonged to Gina Corelli, a second-year nurse on the emergency service.

"I'm building up strength to get across the street to my apartment," Josh said with a glint in his eyes despite his exhaustion. At regular intervals Gina shared his bed in that apartment.

"I need a drink." Tim stared in distaste at the remains of his coffee, pallid and ineffectual in the current circumstances. "Feel like going with me?" His gaze included Gina as he pulled himself to his feet. Gina shook her head.

"I'm going home to sleep," Josh said.

"I'll walk you home," Gina murmured with seductive promise. Tim shrugged and left the table.

"Let me finish my coffee," Josh said, reluctant to move at the moment. His eyes rested approvingly on dark-haired, dark-eyed Gina. He knew he was not the only resident whom she had taken into her bed. Passionate and beautiful, Gina was eager to marry a young doctor. He knew he was a prime candidate but he had made it clear he was a bad bet.

"If you behave yourself, I'll make dinner for you," Gina offered.

"Behave?" He lifted one eyebrow in mocking disbelief.

"Perform," she corrected. "Josh, you make me horny as hell."

"Let's go home." With sudden anticipation he was on his feet.

"You're not too tired?" she teased him.

"Sugar, you won't complain," he promised.

In his small, maple-furnished apartment, that had harbored a generation of Bellevue residents, Josh wasted no time. The door was barely closed behind them when he reached for Gina. She was warm and soft and beautifully fashioned. His hands knew every curve.

"Wait," she said after a minute.

In the shadows of the late October afternoon with the blinds discreetly closed, Josh and Gina made undressing a competition.

"You're so damn neat." She laughed, settling herself on the bed while he draped his hospital jacket across the back of a chair.

"You're so damn gorgeous." He lay down beside her.

"You're not too tired," she said in satisfaction after a few moments.

Afterwards they lay entangled in smug release. Josh was fully awake now. Over-stimulated, he jeered at himself.

"I feel awful when I think about your going back down to

Atlanta in December," she whispered reproachfully. "For good. I could try for a job in the hospital down there –"

"That would not be a good idea," Josh rejected.

"Your family would object to a nurse from the city chasing after the handsome young doctor?" she mocked. Josh knew Gina's background – a hard-working Italian family, whose children were first-generation Americans. Her father had at last acquired his own shoe repair shop.

"I think you'd be happier in New York," he hedged because Gina was waiting for an answer.

"Are you in love with some girl back home?"

"Yes," he acknowledged and felt her stiffen beside him. He had always made it clear he had no intention of marrying her. "Ever since high school." Even while he longed to see Janet again, he could taste the pain of knowing she belonged to somebody else.

"Are you going to marry her?"

"She's already married. And I'd never settle for second best," he said with candor.

"What about a divorce? People do divorce these days."

"She doesn't even know I'm in love with her," Josh confessed. "And she's probably in love with her husband."

"Oh, Josh –" Gina's laughter was indulgent. "When are you going to stop being the knight in shining armor and discover you have to fight for what you want in this world? You've always had life too easy. A problem of the rich."

"Shut up," he ordered, reaching for her again. "I can't make love to you when you're yapping."

Liz had left the Michaels' house early in the afternoon today. Janet was stuck doing a heavy mailing on her own, she thought guiltily. But the small dinner party she was giving tonight in honor of Victor's birthday was, in truth, union business. Janet and she were plotting to bring her mother and Kevin together on a social basis.

Home from Washington for three working days, Caroline

had refused to talk with Kevin about his budding labor union. Already he had involved a cluster of Hampton workers. Not enough to be effective in a strike, he conceded. Mama was furious. But this was Ellen's son-in-law and, therefore, she avoided a confrontation.

In her bedroom Liz laid out the Lanvin dinner dress that was Victor's favorite. A delicate blue, with the flounces on the skirt set on a slant, the dress left one shoulder bare. From habit she dressed to please Victor.

Their marriage survived, she often thought, because both Victor and she were fearful of change. Victor worked excessive hours; and she busied herself, surreptitiously, with Kevin's labor union. It was almost as though they lived separate lives.

She was dressed and going downstairs to check on kitchen preparations when Victor arrived. He headed directly for the library.

"You have to dress for dinner," she trailed after him.

"In a few minutes," he stipulated, striding to the radio. "I want to hear the news."

"Has something happened?"

"All hell's broke loose in New York," he said. "What happened last Thursday was only the preview of the disaster on Wall Street today. But President Hoover says our economy is on a sound basis." Victor's voice was vitriolic as he fiddled with the radio, seeking a news program.

". . . worst day in the history of the New York stock exchange," a radio announcer entoned. "Sixteen million four hundred and ten thousand and thirty shares were traded today. ATT has fallen from two hundred and sixty-six to two hundred and four, General Motors from fifty-four to forty, U.S. Steel from two hundred and three to one hundred and seventy-four. One thousand traders milled about the floor of the stock exchange."

In an aura of unreality Liz and Victor listened to the announcer's report until she exhorted him to go upstairs and dress for dinner.

"The world isn't ending, Victor."

"For many people it is." Victor was grim. "I dread to think about the impact this is going to have on the country."

Victor went upstairs to dress. Liz went out to the kitchen to consult with Mary Lou and to dispatch Matthew to the cellar for wine. Georgia might be a dry state, but few dinner parties dispensed with this amenity.

Caroline and Sophie were the first guests to arrive. Eric had remained in Washington. Caroline confirmed that she had suspected for months that Wall Street was in a dangerous condition and had sold out her stocks. Ellen was the next to arrive. Alone.

"Charlie has a bad headache," Ellen apologized for his absence. "I keep telling him he works too hard." Liz knew Janet's mother was proud of her husband's business success. He had prospered far beyond their expectations. "I should have called earlier, Liz, but I didn't know he was feeling so poorly."

"No problem," Liz soothed.

The other guests arrived in swift succession. Despite everyone's effort to create a convivial atmosphere the spirit of the party was tainted by concern over the Wall Street crisis.

Liz was conscious of her mother's resolution to avoid any conversation with Kevin. She exchanged frustrated glances with Janet. Her mother was a bright, compassionate woman. If she opened her mind to Kevin, she would understand the need for labor unions in the mills. A union would guarantee them a long denied self-respect.

Liz marshaled her guests into the dining room. Mary Lou had prepared a sumptuous dinner, though the fashion of late – with women determined to be thin and flat – was to cut down the number of courses. The table conversation grew lively over the roast beef. Maureen and Andrew had taken a much delayed trip to Europe last month, taking young Andy along with them. There was much reminiscing among the guests about trips abroad.

Then talk veered into an uneasy analysis of the panic that

gripped the stock market. Andrew admitted to having been hurt, though he quickly reassured Maureen that their losses were not sufficient to change their style of living. In a desperate effort to divert the conversation, Liz told an amusing story of Adrienne's camping trip in the Blue Ridge mountains. Everybody at the table knew her taste for the unconventional.

"After that Adrienne decided to recuperate at the Greenbrier," Liz laughed. "She's still up there."

"Amidst all that beauty in the Blue Ridge country, we find such ugliness," Kevin pounced and Liz swore at herself for giving him this lead. "Do you wonder that the workers in the Baldwin and Clinchfield mill villages want a union?" Liz saw the high color that stained her mother's cheekbones. Kevin should have waited until after dinner, when he might have cornered Mama alone. "Houses without running water. Wages under ten dollars a week. Women working without pay until they learn to handle the machines. Teenage girls working twelve hours a day for five dollars a week."

"We don't have conditions like that at the Hampton Mill," Caroline said quietly, but her eyes betrayed her rage.

"At the Baldwin Mill," Kevin pursued, as though he had not heard Caroline, "Sheriff Adkins fired tear gas at the workers, and his eleven deputies shot workers in the back. Six of them are not expected to live. Twenty-five are badly wounded."

"Matthew, what is it?" Liz asked because Matthew hung in the doorway with an air of uncertainty.

"Beggin' yo' pardon, ma'am, but they's a phone call for Miz Hammond." He turned to Janet's mother. "Yo' maid is on the lib'ary phone, Miz Hammond. I think yo' bes' talk to her."

Ellen rose to her feet.

"Please excuse me." She hurried from the dining room into the library across the hall.

"I'm sure it's nothing serious," Caroline soothed Janet. "Some crisis in the kitchen." But Janet was nervous, Liz realized.

"Miranda, calm down. I can't understand a word you're

saying." Ellen's voice, strident now, filtered into the dining room. There was a faint pause. Then Ellen's voice soared into near-hysteria. "Oh, my God!"

"Excuse me." Janet rose to her feet and fled across the hall. In the dining room the guests were silent in apprehension. Instinctively Liz turned to Victor. He was already crossing to the library.

"Mama, what's happened?" Janet's voice carried to those in the dining room.

"Charlie's shot himself!" Ellen tried to talk again to Miranda. "Stay with him, Miranda. I'm calling for an ambulance, then I'll come right home. Miranda," she shrieked, "get hold of yourself!"

"I'll drive you home," Victor said. "Liz, phone for an ambulance," he ordered from across the hall. "It's to go to the Hammonds."

Victor hurried Ellen and Janet from the house. Liz went to the phone to call the hospital. Dinner was forgotten. Immersed in shock, the others moved into the library. The two-tiered birthday cake sat on a deserted dinner table.

"Why would Charlie do a crazy thing like that?" Kevin demanded while Liz relayed instructions to the Grady Hospital telephone operator.

Kevin had not gone along with Janet, Liz realized, because of the hostility between Charlie and him. To Charlie any union organizer was a "dirty Bolshevik". Up North, Josh had written, few people took the communists seriously any longer. The Red scare had vanished. Not so in the South.

"He must have been hard hit by the stock crash," Andrew said somberly. "I fear he's not the only one who'll look for such a tragic way out."

"I should go over there," Caroline said. "Liz –"

"I'll go with you, Mama." Liz willed herself to stop trembling. "We'll be needed. Maureen, will you please ask Matthew to bring coffee and dessert into the library?"

Twelve

In a near-deserted waiting room at Grady Hospital Liz sat on a hard, straight-backed bench with her mother and Ellen Hammond. Janet had gone for coffee for them. For the past hour a heavy slanting downpour had pummeled the building, bringing an unseasonable chill into the hospital.

Liz glanced at the wall clock. In five minutes it would be three a.m. Victor and a team of doctors had been working on Charlie through the night.

"You're cold," Caroline said solicitously when Ellen shivered.

"No," Ellen said. "Scared." She left the bench to cross to a window and stared out at the sheet of rain.

"Charlie's going to be all right," Caroline said soothingly, but Liz knew her mother was anxious.

Janet returned with paper containers of coffee. She had called home to tell Kevin they were still waiting for the doctors to emerge from surgery. Kevin had come to Grady and stayed until it was necessary to relieve the woman organizer who was watching over Wendy for the evening.

Sitting here in the waiting room, close to the room where Victor and the other doctors fought for Charlie's life, Liz felt closer to Victor than at any time in years. She was proud of his skills, his dedication to his profession, his compassion. It was as though the years had rolled away, and she was twenty again and deeply in love with her husband.

"Here comes Victor –" Ellen rose to her feet as Victor walked into view. When she saw his face, Liz knew the doctors had lost the battle.

"I'm sorry," Victor said, reaching for Ellen's hand. Liz saw the pain in his eyes. "We couldn't save him."

"You'll come to Hampton House," Caroline said, an arm about Ellen's waist. Ellen was in shock. "You need to rest."

How could Ellen ever go back to that house? Liz shuddered. It would be a long time before she could wash from her brain the image of Charlie Hammond lying on the kitchen floor in a bathrobe soaked in blood, Miranda praying aloud while she tried futilely to stop the flow from the hole in his chest.

When he had driven Janet home and delivered Caroline and Ellen to Hampton House, Victor moved from behind the wheel and told Liz to drive the short distance to their own house.

"I'm bushed," he apologized. "Drive carefully. The roads are wet and slippery." He was thinking of her not himself, Liz thought.

"Vic, why did Charlie do it?"

"You saw the note." He stifled a yawn. "Poor Charlie had been wiped out. He couldn't face starting all over again at his age. Honey, this must be happening all over the country. Nobody believed the bubble could burst."

Americans were slow in relinquishing optimism about the financial state of the nation. Business leaders sought to demonstrate their faith. Julius Rosenwald, board chairman of Sears Roebuck, guaranteed the margin accounts of all his employees. Andrew Mellon assured the nation that business would recover swiftly. John D. Rockefeller said, "My son and I have for some days past been purchasing common stock."

But Christmas 1929 was not a happy period. Too many families had been wiped out by the stock crash. Too many men had jumped out of windows, put bullets through their heads, or succumbed to the gas pipe. Men in every walk of life. Bankers, brokers, shoemakers, salesmen, office clerks.

Shocked by the drop in her income, Adrienne announced she was renting out her house and heading for Europe. "I'll be wherever the dollar is strongest," she announced with a touch of bravado.

Josh came home from New York to talk about the black humor arising from the panic.

"Eddie Cantor – badly hurt by the stock crash – joked that when he heard about Mr Rosenwald's offer, he had wired to ask for a job as office boy. Hotel room clerks ask each new guest if he wants a room for sleeping or jumping."

When Eric came home from Washington, he confessed he was afraid the nation was in desperate trouble. Others, too, were deeply worried. The stock market was refusing to rally. As months passed, sales fell off. Unemployment soared. Wages were cut. In the midst of this horror elections came and went. In November 1930 Eric Hampton was re-elected to the Senate.

The farmers felt the pinch. Cotton began a downward plunge. Tobacco prices dropped. In the summer the worst drought in history had parched the fields of twenty-three states, devastated the Southwest and the lower Mississippi Valley.

By the spring of 1931 strikes swept the Southern cotton mills. The mill operators fought against the union leaders. Now some Southern newspapers were calling for reform in the mills. They demanded the elimination of night work for women, pensions for the elderly, a shorter working week. The mill owners, dogged not only by labor problems but by a sharp curtailment of orders, warned that all union leaders were communists. They played on their workers' fear of communism as a threat to God and country

On a summer-hot May afternoon Liz and Janet sat on the back porch of the Michaels' house addressing envelopes to the mill workers which, Kevin mourned, too many mill workers would have to ask their children to read for them. Matthew had driven Patience and the two little girls to Piedmont Park earlier in the afternoon.

"I think Mama's going back to work in the mill," Janet confided. Before her marriage Ellen had been Caroline's secretary. "Your mother's asked her to help out in the office now that

Miss Sophie has to take things easier. After Mama paid for the funeral, she didn't have much left from the insurance. She's selling the house to pay off the mortgage, as soon as she can find a buyer. It's not worth anywhere near what Uncle Charlie paid for it." Janet called her stepfather "Uncle Charlie". "She won't have much left over, but she can't keep up the payments and the taxes much longer."

"Josh came over to dinner last night. When Vic and he get together, they sound like the world is collapsing."

"The Hamptons aren't hurting." Janet smiled.

"No," Liz acknowledged. Sometimes it piqued her when Janet talked in that indulgent fashion, even though she knew Janet was devoid of malice. Today she knew it was a gentle reassurance. "But Vic worries about his patients."

Josh was still in love with Janet. Mama kept throwing Atlanta girls at him, but he wasn't having any of that. Mama kept hoping for a grandson. She's given up on me, Liz thought – she knows I'll never have another baby.

"Janet?" Kevin's voice echoed through the house.

"We're on the back porch," Janet called.

Kevin hurried through the tiny house to join them. His face was flushed, his eyes agitated.

"I just got word that six union members have been arrested here in Atlanta," he reported.

"On what charges?" Janet was pale. She was afraid for Kevin, Liz thought.

"Insurrection. Trying to organize a union comes under the heading of insurrection now," he said bitterly.

"Maybe it would be smart to become involved with the United Textile Workers." Janet's voice was troubled.

"No." Kevin brushed this aside. "They have no teeth. And when the AFL started a drive in January, what did *they* accomplish? The mill owners just showed them the door. We're the hope of the mill workers; they must have organizers who aren't afraid to fight. Up in Virginia the Dan River and Riverside Mills are handing out ten percent wage cuts."

"How awful." Liz sympathized. But Mama wasn't cutting wages, she thought defensively.

"The word's around that a lot of Georgia mills are starting to work a three-day week." Kevin's eyes focused on Liz. "Have you heard your mother say anything about another cut in hours?"

"No." Liz balked at direct questions about the Hampton Mill.

"We'll see riots in the mills if wages are cut," Kevin warned. "The workers barely survive when they're working full-time."

"Mama! Mama, can we have cookies and lemonade?" Wendy's voice came from the front. Kathy and she were running around the side of the small, frame house.

"Don't you chillun run in this hot weather," Patience scolded. "You'll git your cookies and lemonade a minute later."

Liz was grateful that Patience had arrived with the children. She would be able to leave shortly. Kevin had a way of disturbing her. He was always conscious that the Hamptons had so much, while the mill families had so little.

Janet brought out a plate of cookies and a pitcher of lemonade. She poured a glass of the cooling liquid for Patience to take out to Matthew, sitting in the car.

"Liz, talk to your mother," Kevin coaxed. "If she'd let the union into the Hampton Mill, it would be a big step forward. Other mills would follow her lead."

"I've tried to talk to her." Kevin knew her mother was one of the most liberal mill operators in the country. But the idea of a union telling Mama how to run her business was repugnant to her. She said the unions were unrealistic. The industry could not survive a forty-hour week and a hundred percent raise in wages. The mills would be forced to close down. "I'll try to talk to her again," Liz promised.

Riding home with Patience and Kathy, Liz tried to gear herself to talk to her mother about meeting with Kevin. Janet had been upset about the arrest of the six organizers. She was afraid Kevin might be next. The potential for violence was frightening.

Liz envied Kevin his dedication. He looked at her and thought she had no reason in the world not to be happy. Kevin and Mama were alike in one way: both thought that financial security guaranteed happiness. Did Kevin think money could make up for losing Debbie? Did having a beautiful house and servants assure a worthwhile marriage? But like everybody else Kevin never suspected her marriage was a farce. In public Victor and she appeared a devoted couple. They had been – for a while.

Didn't Kevin know that life was a scavenger hunt for everybody? Happiness came in small packets. They all lived – rich and poor alike – from one elusive high moment to the next.

Janet lay sleepless on the hot May night, hearing the first mosquitos of the year buzzing in the small back bedroom. The screens never seemed to keep them out. Kevin said it was because Wendy was always running in and out and letting them into the house.

"Janet?" Kevin said softly.

"I'm awake." She turned to face him in the spill of moonlight.

"You can't sleep, either?"

"I worry about you," Janet told him. "You could be arrested. You could be hurt –"

"The six that were arrested will get out," Kevin assured her, pulling her to him. "I won't be hurt."

"I keep remembering Ella Mae Wiggins, the six people who died at the Baldwin Mill, and the organizers who've been beaten up. You could be next."

"Not me," Kevin boasted. "I know how to handle myself. Honey, I have a mission on this earth. I'll live to make life better for the mill workers. Even though they act sometimes as though I was something lower than their bosses."

For a few minutes Kevin was silent, content to fondle his wife. At least this didn't cost, Janet thought. Kevin said the mill workers' wives were cheated; their men were too tired to make love. She was proud of Kevin's dedication. Why couldn't the workers understand he was fighting to free them from their slavery?

"I'll close the door," Kevin whispered.

She waited for him to return, welcomed the weight of him when he lifted himself above her. The poor mill women, she thought while Kevin brought himself to her. So tired, so apathetic, so colorless.

There was nothing apathetic about her response to her husband. Theirs was always a mutually desired coupling. Her arms tightened about his back while they moved together.

Dear God, let Kevin be all right. Let nothing happen to him.

After dinner at Hampton House in early October Liz tried, futilely, to persuade her mother to sit down with Kevin and his committee to discuss a union in Hampton Mill. Her mother was unfamiliarly brusque.

"I know you mean well," Caroline said, "but there's no place for a union in a cotton mill. Not in mine." She was emphatic. "I do whatever I can to make life better for my workers."

"More than you can." Sophie was blunt. "We ought to be cutting wages, like other mills are doing. Our workers are lucky to have jobs in these times. Liz, the economy is in dreadful shape. We're praying to break even."

Liz mustered a wry smile.

"President Hoover announced today that 'we have now passed the worst.' I don't think anybody believes that."

"Your father says the only good coming out of the bad times is that we'll vote in a Democratic Congress next election," Caroline said.

Liz and Josh had been brought up in an atmosphere of strong liberalism and pacifism. It upset Liz – and she suspected that

Josh shared her feelings – that her mother had developed conservative leanings. Kevin was right. It was time the mill workers shared in the fruits of their labor.

Despite Hoover's optimism conditions grew worse in 1932. Banks continued to close. Businesses failed. Unemployment soared. Farmers worried about losing their land. Some farming families were without food. In the Kentucky mountain area, where coal mines had shut down and drought had added additional hardship, relief workers discovered that families had sold their meager furniture to junk dealers to buy food. Now they slept on the floor.

Many cities rushed to enact relief measures to help their destitute residents. President Hoover insisted, to the exasperation of Eric and similar-minded senators and representatives, that help for the needy must be met by the cities, along with private charities.

"I've had a letter from a doctor I worked with up in Bellevue, Tim Reiss," Josh said, sitting in the Adams' living room with his sister, Janet and Kevin late one Sunday evening. He had stopped by on his way home from a house call. He had spied the Michaels' beat-up flivver out front and knew Janet was here, Liz thought. "Tim says that relief measures in New York are terribly inadequate. A family gets two dollars thirty-nine cents a week."

"It's less in Atlanta," Kevin pounced. "In St Louis half the needy families have been dropped from the relief rolls for lack of funds. The children hunt through the city dumps for food."

"Oh, Kevin –" Liz shuddered. "How can the Federal Government stand by and not help?"

"Two cities in Texas," Kevin told them, "have refused to give relief to Negroes. And the way I hear it, Atlanta – and some other cities – are warning the government that relief funds will run out in a few months."

"I feel guilty every time I sit down to eat," Liz confessed. "Papa said that he'll fight in Congress for federal aid, though the President will probably reject anything that's passed."

"In January, after last summer's drought killed off cattle, Hoover was quick enough to arrange for appropriations to allow farmers to borrow money for seed and cattle feed and fertilizer. But he's against giving surplus wheat to the unemployed," Janet said with contempt. "It was all right to feed starving cattle, but not starving women and children."

Liz pushed aside her distaste for volunteer work and devoted time to charity drives. She felt sick when she saw the deprivation that fanned across Atlanta, knowing it was duplicated throughout the nation. She could feel the broken pride of Southerners forced to accept charity but she knew there were those with pride so strong they preferred to go hungry.

Liz was shaken when her mother told her that the shopkeeper Noah Kahn – prone to extend credit to customers without funds – had lost his store in Marietta and was fighting to hold his head above water in the Decatur store. Caroline told Liz she had offered to loan Noah money, but he had refused. It was enough, Noah insisted, that the General had helped him with this first store all those years ago.

Liz was also upset when Janet admitted that the union headquarters in New York had cut Kevin's salary. Janet talked about going back to work, but where was there a job in these times? Liz saw the neat darns in Janet's stockings, the hole in one shoe that was covered by folded-over newspaper. Janet's dresses were faded by too many washings. Any help had to be camouflaged. Liz pretended that clothes had shrunk and no longer fit Kathy, who was slightly taller and more rounded than Wendy. She complained that the fine cashmere sweaters Victor's mother had sent during a trip to London made her itch because she knew Janet's sweaters had been worn threadbare.

For the first time in its history the Hampton Mill was operating at a loss. Sophie and Andrew thought they should close down for an indefinite period. Caroline refused, capitulating only to the extent of cutting down to a three-day week. The workers were sullen and angry. Kevin saw this as a propitious time for his union to move into the Atlanta mills, yet most of the workers seemed to fear unions more than starvation.

Then the Kensington Mill on the outskirts of the city, brought down from New England and fighting to establish a brand name, slashed wages. Kevin was determined to take action. Janet watched with a sick fear.

On a hot May morning, with the Hampton Mill closed that day, Janet sat on the porch with her mother while Kevin and his cohorts gathered together in the kitchen to block out plans for a strike at the Kensington Mills. She felt her mother's intensifying resentment of Kevin's activities.

"Janet, this is no time to strike," Ellen said sharply. "Kensington may even welcome a shut-down if they have no orders on their books. No mill in the country is operating without a loss. I see the figures that come into the Hampton office. I know."

"The mill owners have been living off the sweat of the workers too long." Janet zealously quoted Kevin. "A union is their only road to protection."

"The communists are using people like Kevin for their own ends." Ellen was contemptuous. "They don't care about the mill workers! They're just out to foment trouble in this country."

"That's not true," Janet protested. "The party is helping out with money and leaders because they see the need."

"They come in here with their newspapers – the *Daily Worker* and the *Young Pioneers*," Ellen said, grimacing in distaste, "and they preach that our government is the enemy of the people. I don't like that, Janet. This is the finest country in the world."

"Millions of people go to bed hungry every night. That has to be changed!"

"It will be! But not by a bunch of communists pushing their way into this country, bent on revolution! But you won't believe anything I say. You've built Kevin up into some kind of god in your mind. Sure, I know how bad it is for mill folks. It's bad for other people, too. But this Depression won't go on for ever. Things will change."

"They won't change for the mill workers until they have a union fighting for them." Janet tugged at the neckline of her dress. This first heat wave of the summer was into its third day. "Their power is in the union."

Janet looked up with a start when the screen door swung wide. Kevin and the men who had been with him in the kitchen trailed across the small front porch. Ernest, young, dogged workers in the cause. Their faces were grim. She knew they were headed for the Kensington Mill and trouble.

Janet rose to her feet.

"Mama, would you watch Wendy if I go along with Kevin? She's playing in the backyard next door." She gestured towards the rundown Connelly house, where chickens ran loose about the grounds and a hound dog dozed on the porch. "I won't be gone more than an hour." Her heart pounded as she visualized the confrontation ahead. This was the first time that Kevin would be responsible for taking workers out of a local mill even though he had participated in strikes in other areas.

"Janet, you shouldn't be there," her mother protested.

"I have to be there, Mama. Will you stay with Wendy?" She pleaded with her mother.

Ellen sighed.

"I'll stay with her."

Janet and the men piled into a decrepit truck – Janet and Kevin in the cab, the men in the back – for the drive to the Kensington Mill.

With an exhilaration Janet struggled to mirror, Kevin briefed her on the plans. They would arrive just before the workers took their lunch break. Six workers inside the mill had been talking strike to the other workers during the morning. An incident was to be staged that would set off a complaint of harassment. While the workers sat out in the sun eating their lunch, Kevin would convince them they should not return for the rest of their shift. Their wages had been cut by ten percent.

They were hurting. There would be days when their lunch bags would be empty. When their families would be hungry. Now was the time to strike.

The truck pulled up about fifty yards from the large, square red-brick edifice of the mill, silent now at the lunch hour. The workers were streaming out of the doors. Their faces revealed the rage that had been escalating in them since the wage cut was announced over a week ago. Some were already drawing chunks of cornbread from brown-paper bags.

The men in the back of the truck jumped down to circulate among the workers. A few stared curiously at the new arrivals. A young girl of about fourteen spied Janet and walked over to peer at her, simultaneously eating a cold sweet potato.

"Stay in the cab," Kevin ordered Janet and climbed out and up on to the back of the truck.

"Are you satisfied with what you find in your lunch bags today?" Kevin cried out in messianic zeal, and Janet saw the hordes of workers stiffen to attention as one. "Are you going to allow the mill owners to take the food out of your mouths?" Kevin's gaze swung about the gathering crowd. "Power is yours with a union! Alone you're nobody. Banded together you have a voice!"

"We join the union, we're gonna git fired," a gaunt-faced man said. "What's the union gonna do about that?"

"What unions have done in other industries!" Kevin shot back. "We'll bring the owners to heel. They need you. You're the lifeblood of the mills. Without the workers they are nothing. Don't go back to finish your shift. Let the owners know they're fighting a union. Strike, strike, strike!" Kevin entoned, and a cry of agreement welled up in the crowd. The workers – men, women, and children – pressed forward to hear Kevin speak. They felt his honesty, his determination to improve their lot, Janet told herself.

Suddenly there was movement in the crowd. None of the workers had noticed the approach of burly thugs. Clubs were wielded among workers who carried only lunch bags. A woman wailed in anguish. Fighting broke out.

"Stop it!" Kevin yelled. "These are unarmed people! Put down those clubs!"

"Shut up, you damn Bolshevik!" a male voice screamed. "Go back where you come from. We don't want the likes of you here. Go back to Russia!"

A shot over-rode the outcry of the workers. Janet screamed and jumped from the cab of the truck. Kevin lay on the ground. Blood oozed from a bullet-hole in his groin.

"Kevin! Oh, my God!" Janet dropped to her knees beside him. "Somebody call an ambulance!" The nightmare she had suffered on countless nights had come to pass. "Call Grady Hospital – ask for Dr Victor Hampton – tell him what's happened."

Victor and Josh would save Kevin.

"Don't let him die. Please God, don't let him die."

Thirteen

Liz sat with Janet in the waiting area of the surgical floor at Grady Hospital while a team of doctors, including Victor and Josh, fought to save Kevin's life. Day had slipped into evening and still they sat with no word as to Kevin's condition. A night-time quiet enveloped the hospital floor, interrupted only by moans of pain somewhere in the rear. Electric fans did little to relieve the humid heat that gripped the city.

"We've been here for hours," Liz said gently. "Why don't we go to the cafeteria for a sandwich and coffee?"

"No," Janet said. "Somebody might come out with word. I have to be here." Her mother was with Wendy – in bed by now and probably wondering, Liz thought with anguish, why Mama and Papa were not home.

"He's going to be all right," Liz said yet again, trying for an optimism she didn't feel. *Please God, let him be all right.* "He's young and strong – he'll pull through this."

Close to midnight Caroline and Eric joined the vigil.

"We stopped by your house," Caroline told Janet. "I promised your mother I'd call as soon as there's word. Wendy's sleeping."

"Poor baby," Janet whispered. "She doesn't know what's happening."

"There's Josh!" Eric's voice was electric. "Coming from surgery."

Janet and Liz leapt to their feet. Good news, Liz told herself. Josh was smiling. He strode to Janet.

"He's going to live," he said.

"Oh, thank God! I kept telling myself God wouldn't let him die. Not when he wants to do so much good in this world."

"He'll have a long, rough ride ahead," Josh warned them, his eyes taking in the others now. "A lengthy stay in the hospital, then months of convalescence." He hesitated, seeming in inner debate. "He's suffered some spinal injury. We won't know for a while how extensive this is."

Josh had been sent out to give the report, Liz realized, because Vic knew how close he was to Janet.

"He's alive," Janet whispered. "He's alive!"

"You won't be able to see him until the morning, and then just for a few minutes. Go home now and get some rest. There's a long road ahead."

For days Janet haunted the hospital waiting to spend a few minutes with Kevin. His condition was critical but stable. Still, Janet was terrified of a relapse. Her mother and Liz took turns staying with her at the hospital. Ellen had moved into the house to care for Wendy and to offer reassurances that "Papa will be home soon."

Caroline made it clear that Janet was not to worry about hospital bills.

"You're like family. You and Kevin and Wendy. It'll be a long-term loan," Caroline told Janet. "When it's convenient, you can repay me if you like."

At the end of the second week of Kevin's hospitalization Liz made a point of cornering Josh after a family dinner.

"You're not telling Janet everything about Kevin's condition," she accused.

"I told her there was spinal damage," he pointed out uncomfortably.

"But she's too distraught to explore that. What does it mean?"

Josh's face was drained of color. "He'll spend the rest of his life in a wheelchair. Both legs are paralyzed. But, knowing

Kevin," he said defensively, "he'll continue to fight for a union for the mill workers."

For now, Liz thought, Mama was able to blot that role out of her mind. Kevin was Janet's husband and Ellen's son-in-law. The Hampton family must be helpful.

The Republican Party held their convention in Chicago in mid-June. President Hoover was renominated on the first ballot. Later in the month the Democratic National Convention was held in Chicago, as well. On July 1st Franklin Roosevelt was nominated as president. To the nation's surprise Roosevelt flew to Chicago from the governor's mansion in Albany, New York, to accept. To the cheers of his party he said, "I pledge you, I pledge myself to a New Deal for the American people."

"Roosevelt will win for sure," Eric predicted on his return from the Democratic Convention. "Of course, most people are disenchanted with both parties, but Roosevelt holds out a ray of hope."

Through the long hot summer Kevin remained in the hospital. Janet was unnerved by the size of the bills. The union's funds were low – she could expect no help from that area. She knew how Kevin would fret once he realized that Caroline and Eric Hampton were paying for his medical care.

Josh and Victor were wonderful, she thought with recurrent gratitude. She knew their distress that they couldn't do more for Kevin. She had felt Josh's anxiety the morning he told her that Kevin would be wheelchair-bound for the rest of his life. "Except for that, he'll recover and live a normal life." How could it be a normal life when a man who was destined to fly was incapable of movement?

Late in September Janet received a phone call from a union official in New York. He explained that they would not forget what Kevin had done for the cause.

"And he'll do more," the union official said with a show of optimism. "As soon as he's physically able, we want Kevin to take over running the office we plan on opening down in Columbus. We're not abandoning him," the union leader stressed.

"Why must we move to Columbus?" Kevin railed when she relayed the news. "And why couldn't he tell me this himself?"

"He'll be writing to you in a few days," Janet comforted. "As soon as Vic says it's all right for you to travel, we'll move to Columbus." She didn't want to think about the separation from her mother, Liz, and all those close to her in Atlanta. "You'll set up an office there. I'll be your assistant. We'll be working together, Kevin." She strived for lightness. "Like always."

"What about the money situation?" he demanded.

"We're all right. The union will pay us almost as much as they have all along, and living is cheaper in Columbus. Liz is going to drive me down there and help me find a place for us to live as soon as Vic and Josh feel you're ready to leave the hospital. With all the mills down there, it'll be prime territory for you."

"What about the creep who shot me?" Kevin demanded. "He's still running free?"

"The police haven't been able to catch him," Janet admitted.

"They don't want to catch him! They think he did this city a favor."

"Kevin, no." Janet was startled by this reaction.

"Down here every union organizer is a damned Bolshevik – that's what they think. And you want to know something? The Bolsheviks have the right idea – they want to take care of their people."

For months now she'd worried about Kevin's changing political thoughts. This was the finest country in the world. Didn't he realize that? It was just that he was so compassionate, she told herself. He saw the way the mill workers lived, and it pained him. Not just the mill workers these days. All kinds of people. Hoover kept saying things would get better, but that wasn't happening.

* * *

Early in October Victor reported to Liz that he was discharging Kevin from the hospital in a few days.

"It's not going to be easy." He shifted nervously in his favorite chair in the Adams living room. "Janet will need someone to help with his care."

Liz discarded her crossword puzzle. "Did you talk to her?" Another expense – when Kevin's income was so small.

"I will tomorrow – when I tell Kevin he'll be going home shortly. Talk to Mary Lou. She may know a strong colored teenager who'll be glad for the job."

"I'll talk to her in the morning," Liz promised.

Victor was so wonderful with other people. Why couldn't he understand *her* needs? She loved him – the way Janet loved Kevin. And she was sure Victor loved her. But that wasn't enough to make a marriage work. He had no comprehension of her needs as a woman. How could he ask her to give him another child after what she'd been through? Yet she felt guilty at denying him and denying her mother another grandchild. This was what made their marriage a shambles. Each time he reached for her in bed, she thought, "He's praying I'll become pregnant."

In the morning Liz conferred with Mary Lou, who had a vast knowledge about colored folks in their area of Atlanta. Mary Lou gave her names and addresses. She waited until she knew Janet and Kevin had been briefed on his imminent discharge before driving over to the Mitchell house to talk to Janet about a helper for Kevin.

"Isn't it wonderful?" Janet glowed. "Vic said Kevin can come home day after tomorrow. In a couple of weeks he can be back at work. I was scared that time would never come."

"You're going to need help," Janet began.

"That's what Vic said." Janet's smile was shaky now. "He was very thorough in telling me what to expect. But I think I can manage on my own."

"You can't." Liz was firm. "Kevin weighs a hundred and

fifty pounds, and you weigh – what? A hundred and five? I've talked to Mary Lou. She gave me the name of a teenager who's dying for a job, and—"

"We can't afford that, Liz!"

"Talk with those union people – explain that Kevin is going to need help. And they need Kevin," Liz pointed out. "All this boy will expect is board and room and a dollar a week spending money. And Kevin will feel better in knowing he's not physically dependent on you."

"I'll talk to them," Janet agreed after a moment. But her eyes betrayed her anxiety. "Liz, I don't know how I would have survived these last weeks without you and your parents. And Vic and Josh," she added tenderly.

"We'll drive over to Columbus in a week or so," Liz said. "We'll find a little house for the four of you, and office space for Kevin. We won't have any trouble finding something." Her smile was reassuring. In these days – with money so tight, businesses failing – vacancies were available all over.

A week later, with Kevin out of bed and in a wheelchair for several hours a day, Liz drove with Janet to Columbus. It was a beautiful, balmy morning. Late flowers in bloom along the road as they drove.

But the country, Liz thought painfully, was not in beautiful condition. People were so scared. But Papa said fear was being replaced by rage and resentment that so many had so little. Victor said the one hope was that a new administration would be voted into office in November.

"I talk to people," Papa had said somberly. "I fear that democracy is on trial. We have to prove that it works."

Mussolini had established his Fascist government in Italy. Adolf Hitler was seizing power in Germany. In Russia liberty had been sacrificed for a meager security. And there were those in this country who believed the Russians had made the right choice.

"Columbus is a beautiful town." Liz smiled in approval as

they approached their destination. "And less than a three-hour drive from Atlanta." But Janet had no car, no prospects of acquiring one. To Janet it must seem a painful distance from home. "Mama says there're several big cotton mills right across the river in Alabama, in addition to the ones in Columbus. Kevin will have a large field of operation."

"He's so upset at the prospect of being tied down to an office." Janet was silent for a moment. "He's always been out there leading the action."

"He's always been a leader," Liz said with an effort at optimism. "He'll build a real organization in Columbus."

"Vic told me that Kevin and I can have almost a normal marriage." Liz knew Janet had worried about this. "He was clear about that. We – just have to make some adjustments."

"You and Kevin will work that out," Liz predicted. They shared the kind of passion that she had shared with Victor in those early years. That was precious. Would it ever be that way with Victor and her again?

They drove into town, parked on Broad Street, which was divided by an island of grass and trees that lent an air of elegance to the area. They picked up a copy of the *Columbus Enquirer* to look for rental ads. Now Janet became firm.

"We can't pay more than ten dollars a month," she said flatly. "No use looking at anything else."

Liz was repelled by the tiny, drab house that Janet agreed to rent. But Janet was being practical. The union paid low wages. Still, Kevin had a job, despite his condition, at a time when millions of able-bodied men were out of work. Would a new president be able to pull them out of this devastating Depression?

Within a week Janet, Kevin and Wendy were settled in the paint-hungry, white-frame house in Columbus. Office space – minuscule, Kevin said, yet suitable – had been rented. Wendy would go to a school close to the house. And husky fifteen-year-old Zeke was joyous at being part of the family.

Preparing to depart after her first visit, Liz felt almost overpowering misgivings at leaving Janet in a strange town. But it was absurd, she told herself – Janet would manage.

"I'll drive your mother down a couple of times a month," Liz promised Janet. "And I'll be here so often you'll think I've moved to Columbus."

"There's a wonderful library here in town," Janet reported, walking Liz out to her car. Reading was her big escape. "This marvelous granite building set atop a huge flight of stairs and right beside the Chattahoochee. And the librarians seem so nice."

"I'll call you when I get home." Liz forced a smile. "I'll call you every day."

In a way, Mama was relieved that Janet and Kevin had moved away from Atlanta, Liz forced herself to acknowledge. Kevin represented what Mama hated most – the unions. She always said the same thing, over and over again: "We're good to our workers. Why do they need a union?"

Fourteen

All through the long hot summer the entire Hampton clan had campaigned for Franklin Roosevelt, and they continued this activity into the autumn. Liz was grateful to be involved, and pleased that the Democratic candidates promised to fight for "the forgotten man".

On November 8, 1932 Franklin Delano Roosevelt was elected President of the United States in a Democratic landslide. Roosevelt had carried forty-two out of the forty-eight states. Liz and Victor listened to the returns on the radio at Hampton House along with Caroline, Sophie and Maureen. Josh was on duty at the hospital. Eric and Andrew were at Democratic headquarters in Atlanta. It was 12.17 a.m. when Hoover at last conceded, but everyone gathered before the radio at Hampton House had been confident of a Democratic victory.

"It'll be March the fourth before Roosevelt takes office," Victor said with a glow of optimism, "but once he's at the helm we'll see some action."

"And in 1940," Caroline said softly, "we'll bring out that bottle of Dom Perignon that I put aside a dozen years ago for the day that a Hampton is elected president."

"Because you're sure that Roosevelt will be elected for a second term," Victor joshed. "And after that it'll be a Hampton's turn."

While the country waited for the new president to take office, Americans saw unemployment soar even higher. Farmers were fighting foreclosures on mortgages in shocking numbers. Homes were being foreclosed at the rate of 1,000 per day. And with the arrival of the new year, banks across the country were failing. On February 15, 1933 an attempt was made to assassinate Roosevelt when he was driving through Miami with the mayor of Chicago. Mayor Anton Cermak was killed. But Roosevelt's calm in the course of the attempted assassination was heartening to the people of this country. They took it as a sign that he would be the leader strong enough to save the despairing nation.

At the approach of March 4, 1933 Liz was ambivalent about going with her father and mother to the Inauguration.

"Come with us," Caroline insisted. "It'll be kind of a dress rehearsal for 1941," she said, radiating a glow of anticipation.

"Go with them," Victor prodded. "A change of scenery will do you good."

Victor was perplexed, Liz understood, that she remained passive in their lovemaking. She knew Victor loved her and she loved him. But love was not enough to make a solid marriage.

Liz left with her mother for Washington D.C. the day before the Inauguration. Her father met them at Union Station.

"The city vibrates with fresh hope," Eric told them, though as yet this was not reflected beyond Washington. "Roosevelt will pull us out of the Depression."

Inauguration day was cold and clammy, the sky a dismal gray. Liz and Caroline drew the collars of their coats about their throats as they waited in their seats on the reviewing stand for the outgoing President and the President-elect to arrive. Over 100,000 people waited in the forty acres before the Capitol's East Wing. The marine band played "Hail to the Chief" as the President-elect walked up the red carpet, leaning on the arm of his son James. Chief Justice Charles Evans Hughes prepared to administer the oath of office. As the Capitol clocks struck twelve noon, Franklin Delano Roosevelt became the thirty-second president.

Tears filled Liz's eyes as she listened to the new President's speech, carried across the nation via radio. Long after he spoke she heard in her mind the stirring words that she suspected gave fresh hope to troubled Americans across the country: "Let me first assert my firm belief that the only thing we have to fear is fear itself."

Both Liz and Caroline were enthralled when the announcement came through on the eve of the Inauguration that the new President had appointed a woman, Frances Perkins, to be Secretary of Labor.

"The first time in the history of this country," Caroline effervesced, "that a woman has been appointed to a cabinet post!"

"Some people claim you're the first woman to head up a cotton mill," Liz reminded, her face aglow with pride, though there had been times through the years that she'd resented the mill's demands on her mother. And she felt woefully inadequate in her mother's shadow.

The next day – Sunday – President Roosevelt called a special session of Congress and proclaimed a national bank holiday of unspecified length to combat the wholesale closings of banks across the country. On March 12 – the following Sunday – he broadcast a "fireside chat" over national radio and announced that the banks would reopen the next day. The President assured the nation that banks were safe now – there would be no more bank failures. And so convincing was he that when the banks reopened on Monday morning they transacted more deposits than withdrawals.

In less than two weeks the new President had lifted the morale of most Americans. There was a new hope in the air. In the months ahead farmers were gratified that the government was proposing price supports for their products. The government was to refinance farm mortgages, stopping the frightening farm foreclosures. A Civilian Conservation Corps was to be formed, to hire 300,000 boys to work on land clearance, national park improvements, and similar tasks, and that number was to soar. A Home Owners' Loan Act was passed to provide financing for homeowners.

Still, millions remained unemployed. On November 15, 1933

the Civil Works administration was set into motion, scheduled to provide employment for four million people.

"It's a start," Eric said. He was home from Washington for Thanksgiving week. "But many millions more are desperate for work. Millions of Americans are going to bed hungry at night."

"The mill provided turkeys for every one of our workers," Caroline said with an air of guilt. But that was one day in a long line of days when food on their tables was meager.

Liz missed Janet's presence in her life. Adrienne had returned to Paris and wrote her frothy letters at intervals. With Maureen, Liz became involved in more volunteer work, though she fretted at the absurd pettiness that too often arose. True, many women worked hard to be helpful, she acknowledged, but for too many this was a game, to be played at personal whim.

She was sympathetic when Maureen confided her anxieties about Andy.

"I worry about him," Maureen confessed. "I can't seem to control him anymore. I worry about the friends he makes."

Though only in his early teens, Andy appeared years older. He was devious, charming, and even Andrew admitted he was badly spoiled.

At one of the monthly Saturday evening dinners at Hampton House early in the new year Andy unnerved Liz by his sensuous brushing up against her at moments when they couldn't be observed. She was shaken by the glint in his eyes when they met hers. He was fourteen years old! Maureen had good reason to be worried about him.

Liz realized that Maureen was unaware of this covert by-play and was fearful of wounding her by bringing it to her attention. Ignore the young idiot, Liz decided. If he saw no reaction, he'd abandon his behavior.

She became uneasy when Andy began to cultivate Francis – years his senior chronologically but still a child in his capabilities. Up till now she'd been annoyed that Andy treated Francis with a certain arrogance. Mama, too, resented this.

The family made a point of protecting Francis from disastrous social encounters. Despite all of Victor's work with him through the years – and they were grateful for the improvement in his condition – Francis's limitations were always of concern to them. Francis was warm, likeable, eager to please – and much loved by his parents and siblings.

Liz feared that Andy was fostering an unhealthy friendship with Francis. Should she discuss this with Victor? Would he believe she was making something out of nothing? She recoiled from appearing stupid – or a troublemaker – in Victor's eyes. Should she warn Mama that Andy could be a bad influence on Francis? She discussed this with Janet on her next trip to Columbus.

"Watch for signs that could mean trouble," Janet advised. "You're so anxious about Francis's welfare you might be over-reacting."

"You're probably right." But she was unconvinced. Enough of this, she told herself. "Are things any better for you and Kevin?" Janet had confided her frustration that Kevin rejected any efforts at lovemaking – though Janet said Victor had told him in frank terms that they could make accommodations, have a close to normal relationship.

Janet flinched. "Last night he suggested I divorce him. Of course, I laughed that off. He hates being tied down to a desk – he says he's making no headway with the mills here. The two organizers sent down to work with him have no real spark, he complains. The union refuses to allow him to go out and speak because he's in a wheelchair. They claim it would just remind workers of what might happen to them if they tried to join a union."

"Kevin will change with time." Liz tried to comfort her, not believing this. Kevin remained a bitter, angry man. "The three of you are coming to stay with us over the Easter holidays," she reminded her. "Your mother's so looking forward to that."

"I miss being home," Janet confessed. "I can't believe this is all I have to look forward to for the rest of my life." She hesitated. "I don't know Kevin any more. It's as though I'm sharing space with a stranger. Wendy feels it, too. I see it in her eyes."

"Something good will come," Liz said forcefully. "Hold on to that thought."

On the phone with Liz, Maureen confided her growing frustration over Andy's behavior at school.

"I don't know what to do next. I had a call this morning from that fancy private school of his. The principal's threatening to expel him if he doesn't stop talking back to his teachers. He said Andy's wrecking discipline." She paused for a moment. "And I think it was out of line for him to imply that Andy's too bold the way he treats Miss Leslie." A young, very pretty teacher, Liz recalled. "I know Andrew will be upset about that."

"I realize how you feel about having Vic work with Andy," Liz began cautiously. To Maureen, to have Victor take on Andy as a patient labeled him a "disturbed child", and Maureen couldn't accept this. "But maybe if Vic and Andy had a few talks –"

"Andy's just spoilt," Maureen said defensively. "He's not disturbed. And I keep telling Andrew – it's our fault."

"Maureen, it's not your fault," Liz protested. Did everybody in this family carry a truckload of guilt? "Andy needs guidance beyond what you and Andrew can provide. He –"

"My, you're beginning to talk just like Vic." Maureen strived for a lighter note. "But then you worked with him in the clinic when you first got married. I guess some of it rubbed off on you." She paused at sounds in the foyer. "Liz, Andy just got home. I better talk to him."

Andy slumped across the bed in his upstairs corner bedroom, his face etched with rage. It was mean of Mama to yell at him that way, making him stay up here until Papa came home and they sat down to dinner. All at once his face brightened. Boy, Miss Leslie sure got sore when he brushed up against her when she sent him to the blackboard. She knew it wasn't no accident. How did she feel when he did that?

In sudden resolution he rose from bed, crossed to his door, locked it. With a smug smile he went to a window, lifted it open, lowered himself to the trellis that was fixed to the side of the house – bereft of roses this time of year – and began to climb down. Francis had been home from his dumb job for three days with a bad cold. Francis would sure like some company, wouldn't he?

At Hampton House he was polite, almost deferential, when Mattie came to the door. Nobody else was home at this hour.

"My mama told me to come over and visit with Francis for a while," he told Mattie. "He must be tired of lying up there in his room all alone."

"He's almost over his cold," Mattie told him with a smile. "You jes' go on upstairs and visit with him. But don't get too close, you hear? Your mama won't want you to catch his cold."

"I won't." Andy's answering smile was guileless.

He bolted up the stairs and to Francis's room, knocked.

"Come in." Francis looked surprised, Andy thought, to see him, probably remembering how he got teased most times. "I thought you were Mattie –" He seemed ambivalent, "I mean, bringing me some hot tea with honey or maybe some bread pudding."

"I figured you'd be kind of bored being stuck at home with a cold and all."

"Yeah –" Francis was relaxing now.

Francis was lots older than he was, Andy thought. Even though he wasn't bright, he must know some things. About girls, and what you did with them. Did Francis have the kind of dreams he had? Did he do *that* under the covers, even though some fellas said if you did it too often it would fall off?

"Hey, why don't we get out of here?" Andy switched on the charm. "Go for a walk in the woods?"

Francis looked scared. “I couldn’t do that. Mama said I had to stay in the house till my cold goes away.”

“She won’t have to know.” Andy turned on his twenty-two-carat charm. “Mattie won’t hear us go out if we’re quiet. It’ll be good for your cold to get some fresh air. Come on, Francis –”

“I don’t know –” Francis was torn between obedience and adventure.

“It’ll be all right. I’ll go down first to make sure Mattie’s in the back somewhere. You be right behind me. But put on a warm coat,” he ordered. “It’ll be cold outside.” Andy crossed to the walk-in closet, reached for a coat and tossed it to Francis. “Put it on, Francis.”

“If Mama gets mad, you’ll tell her you told me to go with you?” But Francis was pulling on the jacket.

“I’ll tell her. Now let’s get moving.”

Out in the brisk cold of the afternoon they headed for the woods that separated Hampton House from the mill village. Squirrels scampered about among the trees. A pair of scrawny dogs frisked just ahead.

“Don’t you two start fightin’,” a young feminine voice exhorted the dogs.

“That’s Betsy Mae McRae,” Francis told Andy. “Her folks work in the mill.”

A delicately pretty fourteen-year-old in a worn coat and tattered gloves came into view.

“You know her?” Andy was taken aback. Mama always said Francis lived such a sheltered life, just going to his stupid job each day and then coming home. Did Francis do *that* with her?

“She’s pretty,” Francis whispered shyly. “Are they your dogs, Betsy Mae?”

“They don’t belong to nobody.” Betsy Mae gazed at Andy with something akin to awe. “They just follow me around.”

All at once Andy understood. Betsy Mae didn’t go to school or work. She was like Francis – not “right”.

"You're real pretty," Andy told her with a show of admiration. "I'll bet you know lots of boys." He felt a rush of heat. "I'll bet you do things with them."

"I got four brothers," Betsy Mae said. "Sometimes they're real mean to me."

"I won't be mean to you," Andy said soothingly, moving close to her. "I like pretty girls. Be good to me and I'll bring you a candy bar tomorrow." He drew her to him with one hand, opened the top buttons of her coat.

"It's cold," she objected, but the promise of a candy bar seemed to be an enticement. "What kind of candy bar?"

"Any kind you want," he promised, his breathing heavy now. "And I'll make you warm." His free hand caressed the small budding breasts.

"Andy, I don't think you ought to do that." Francis was troubled, but Betsy Mae seemed mesmerized.

"Shut up, Francis," Andy ordered, thrusting his body against Betsy Mae's. "I'll bet you've done things with fellows, Betsy Mae."

"What kind of things?" Betsy Mae was simultaneously bewildered and uneasy.

"You know," he scolded. With a sudden movement he pulled her down to the ground, lay above her, reached to pull her dress above her waist.

"Don't do that," she wailed. "Stop it." Her voice rose to a shrill outcry as he guided himself between too-thin thighs.

"Andy, stop it!" Francis pleaded, not understanding but aware that Betsy Mae was frightened. "Stop it, Andy – somebody's coming!" he lied.

Andy leapt to his feet. "Let's get outta here!"

Andy pushed his way through the bushes that led back to Hampton House. Francis hesitated, reached to help Betsy Mae to her feet.

"Don't cry, Betsy Mae –" Francis was distraught at her tears.

She gazed up at Francis with the beguiling innocence of a

child half her age. “You’re nice. I like you. You wouldn’t hurt me.” She paused in thought. “I’d let you,” she said with the air of bestowing a gift. “You’re not mean like him.”

Torn by emotions he didn’t understand, sensing what Betsy Mae offered was wrong yet feeling strange new emotions, Francis struggled between fear and a disconcerting need to emulate Andy.

“Betsy Mae, you go on home,” he ordered. “I’m going home, too.” He darted towards the bushes, not looking back. Home was refuge.

Caroline left the car and walked up to the house. It was so good to come home from Washington, she thought with the usual flurry of anticipation. Eric would follow in a couple of days. They’d both remain in Atlanta until mid-January. This was always such a pleasant time of year at Hampton House.

Mattie came hurrying into the foyer to greet her.

“Ain’t it nice that you’ll be home for dinner tonight. I got your favorite dessert ready to go into the oven.”

“How’s Francis’s cold?” Caroline asked Mattie. She’d called him each night from Washington, of course.

“Oh, he’s doin’ fine, Miz Caroline,” Mattie told her. “Like you said, he stayed home from his job for the last three days. He’s stayed in his room most of the time, readin’ his books or listenin’ to his radio.”

“I’ll run right up and see him,” Caroline said, her face tender. Sometimes it bothered her that she spent three days of each week in Washington, but that was her duty as a senator’s wife. The mill was operating only four days a week and on one shift. Andrew and Sophie kept everything rolling in her absence.

The phone rang in the library. Mattie went to answer it. Caroline was halfway up the long, curving staircase when Mattie’s voice came to her.

“Miz Caroline, I think you best take this call! It’s from the po-lice station! They’re holdin’ Francis down there!”

Fifteen

"Let me read a little longer, Mama," Kathy wheedled. "Just a few more pages."

"No more," Liz decreed. "Time for you to go to sleep."

"I want to say goodnight to Papa." An imperious note in Kathy's light voice. "Then I'll go to sleep."

"We don't know when Papa will be home from the hospital," Liz reminded her. Too many evenings Kathy went to sleep without saying goodnight to her father. "Go to sleep, sugar."

"All right." A touch of martyr in Kathy's voice now. "But I need a kiss." An ingratiating smile lit her small face.

"That you can have." Her precious baby, Liz thought, bending to bestow a kiss. "Sweet dreams, my love."

She had just settled down in the sitting room with Pearl Buck's novel, *The Good Earth*, which had won a Pulitzer Prize, when the phone rang. She put aside the book and went to answer it.

"Hello –"

"Liz, I'm so upset –" Caroline was distraught. "Is Victor home yet? I tried the hospital – he wasn't there."

"He's not here, but then I never know when he'll show up. When did you get in town?"

"Just now. I'm half out of my mind!"

"What's happened?" Alarm soared in Liz. Mama was always so in control.

"I just received a phone call from the police. They're holding Francis. Mattie thought he was upstairs in his room. He must have climbed out a window and down that big oak outside. He could have had a terrible fall!"

"Why are the police holding him?" Only Francis could ever disrupt Mama's composure.

"They wouldn't say – just that I was to come down right away, that he's awfully upset." Caroline's voice cracked. "He's never done anything like this. I need Victor to go down there with me."

"Call Jim Russell," Liz said. "And I'll –" Liz paused, hearing sounds in the driveway. "Mama, a car just pulled up. It's probably Vic. Hold on."

Liz hurried into the foyer, gazed out the door. Victor was emerging from his car.

"Vic, Mama's on the phone. She needs to talk to you."

While Victor joined her in the foyer, Liz explained what was happening. With Papa in Washington, naturally Mama turned to Victor. He was always there for everyone in every crisis. Except for her.

Victor picked up the phone. "Caro, this has to be some stupid mistake. I'll drive over for you, and we'll go down there together. Liz will call Jim to join us. Francis isn't capable of any wrongdoing."

"He went out his bedroom window." Liz heard her mother's voice filter into the room. "He's never done anything like that."

"We'll handle this," Victor soothed. "I'll be there in five minutes." He put down the phone, turned to Liz. "Call Jim. If he's left the office already, try him at home. Tell him what's happening and—"

The phone rang, was a jarring intrusion. Liz reached for the receiver.

"Hello."

"Liz, it's me." Maureen's voice was shrill. "I just got the craziest phone call. The police are holding Andy! Andrew's up in Greensboro on mill business, and I don't know where to turn –"

"They're holding Francis, too." Liz's mind was in chaos. "Mama and Vic are on their way to the station house – meet them there. Meanwhile, I'll try to get hold of Jim Russell –" She hesitated. "They may need a lawyer."

Liz tracked down Jim Russell, explained the situation to him. He promised to head straight for the police station.

"What are those two crazy kids up to?" He grunted impatiently. "This has to be Andy's doing – Francis is incapable of anything bad."

Two hours later Victor arrived at the house.

"I drove your mother and Francis home," he told Liz. "Maureen took Andy home with her. For the moment everything's calm."

"I'll tell Mary Lou to serve dinner." But Liz was troubled. What did Victor mean?

Over dinner Victor explained that Jeb McRae, Betsy Mae's father, had gone to the police and accused Andy and Francis of attempted rape.

"Maybe Andy . . . never Francis. Anyhow, Jim was able to get both of them released into their mothers' custody. But unless Jim can squash the charges, they'll go on trial for attempted rape."

"Oh, my God." Liz felt the color drain from her face. "Mama must be devastated."

"For Francis's sake she's fighting to handle the situation. I spent an hour alone with Francis." Victor's face softened. "You know he trusts me. He swears he did nothing wrong. He's upset about Andy . . . there's no doubt that Andy did try to rape that poor little girl, but got scared away. I've never seen her at the mill clinic –" He sighed. "But then you know that many of the workers are distrustful of my efforts. They're scared, sick at heart about troubled kids, but they'll do nothing about it." Frustration edged his voice. "And Andrew and Maureen refuse to face facts."

"What did Jim say about a trial?"

"He's hoping to get Francis out of the indictment. As for

Andy – he'll try to have the case dismissed." Victor sighed. "I may be dragged in to testify that Andy is disturbed, that he needs professional help. Andrew and Maureen will hate me for that, but it might keep Andy out of reform school. It *might*," he emphasized. "Jim's going to arrange a meeting at Hampton House with Betsy Mae's father for first thing tomorrow morning."

"Will her father agree to that?" Liz was skeptical. "I mean – if it really happened . . ."

"He'll come." Victor's smile was wry. "He'll be afraid he'll lose the three days' work a week he has. He'll be scared he'll be thrown out of his house if he doesn't show up."

"Mama wouldn't let that happen!"

"We know that, but he's not sure. Jim will arrange a meeting for tomorrow morning." Victor was somber. "This isn't the kind of publicity the senator needs."

Liz lay sleepless much of the night. She was convinced that Francis had had no part in whatever happened in the woods with Betsy Mae. How awful for Maureen and Andrew if Andy was sent to reform school. Victor was trying to convince himself that Jeb McRae could be persuaded to withdraw the charges, even while he, too, was outraged at what happened to little Betsy Mae.

Victor left the house before seven each morning to make his rounds. Most mornings Liz stayed in bed another hour. Today she was up with Victor.

"Have coffee before you leave," she coaxed. Usually he'd pick up breakfast at the hospital later in the morning. This morning she needed the comfort of his presence.

"No time," he said. "Jim may call me from the hospital to sit in on the meeting with Jeb McRae. As part of the deal, he may suggest that I work with Betsy Mae. You know, try to bring her out of the state she's in, much like I was able to do with Francis."

"Mama must be so upset – and Francis."

"She won't be going in to the mill this morning in case Jim does set up that appointment with Jeb McRae. Go over and visit with her."

"I will," Liz promised.

She knew her mother rose at five thirty even when the mill was closed. She would have breakfast as usual with Kathy, and when Matthew drove Kathy to school, she'd go over and visit with Mama.

But over breakfast, while she made a pretense of listening to Kathy's chatter, Liz was developing a plot in her mind. Maybe for once in her life she could make a real contribution to this family. She could go over and talk to Betsy Mae's mother about how Francis and Betsy Mae were special people. How Victor could work with Betsy Mae the way he'd worked with Francis. Francis would live now to his greatest potential. Victor had given him that gift. Today the mill would be running. Jeb McRae would be there. His wife would be at home. With the working week shortened because of the bad times the women had been laid off. Only men worked the three days a week the mill was in operation.

She was impatient to launch this budding project. Could she convince Betsy Mae's mother to talk to her husband about withdrawing the charges? She must convince Mrs McRae that this was a situation involving three children with serious problems.

Her heart pounding, she left the house and walked towards the mill village. Approaching the rectangular, red-brick structure that was the mill, she flinched, as always, at the horrendous noise that emerged from behind the mill's multi-faceted opaque windows. None of the morning sunlight could penetrate those windows. She walked past the mill to the company store, went in to enquire about the location of the McRae house. She saw the curiosity in the clerk's eyes, but he was polite. She and Victor were liked by the workers. Now she moved on to the adjoining village. Rows of squalid, monotonously identical frame boxes, supported by stilts that dug into the red-clay earth. The whole area barren of trees, of any semblance of greenery.

She walked down the strip of dirt separating the rows of houses, counting them until she reached the one occupied by the McRae family. Gearing herself for her mission, she walked up the steps to the front porch, knocked on the door.

A shabbily dressed grey-haired woman, looking older than her years, like most of the mill workers, appeared at the door.

"Yes ma'am?" The woman's voice was wary – she recognized Liz and was instantly suspicious.

"I came to ask you about Betsy Mae," Liz asked with genuine solicitude. "How is she?"

"I guess she don't rightly know what was happenin' to her," Martha McRae conceded. "But her Papa and me, we know," she said with sudden hostility.

"It was a terrible experience," Liz said softly. "May I come in and talk with you for a few minutes?"

Martha McRae pulled the door wide. Liz walked into the tiny room that served as bedroom and sitting room. Betsy Mae sat at one end of a cot, dressing a bedraggled doll.

"Hello, Betsy Mae," Liz said with a warm smile.

Betsy Mae regarded her for a moment. "You're pretty."

"Thank you." Liz struggled for calm. How could Andy have violated this sweet child?

"Betsy Mae, you go out into the kitchen and have yourself a piece of that pumpkin pie I bin savin' for supper tonight," her mother ordered. "And close the door behind you."

Betsy Mae's face lighted. "Yes'um."

Martha McRae waited until they heard the kitchen door closed before she spoke.

"Miz Adams, I don't know why you come here, but my husband is real mad at them two boys. He wants to see justice for our little girl." But her eyes were apprehensive. She feared the repercussions that might ensue, Liz interpreted.

"I'm real mad at Andy," Liz emphasized. "Francis was not part of it –"

"Betsy Mae, she told me last night, when she stopped cryin', about what happened. She said Mist' Francis was real nice, but not that other one." Fresh rage soared in her.

"Mrs McRae, Francis, Andy and Betsy Mae have problems. Of course, my husband – Dr Adams – has brought Francis far beyond what he was a few years ago, and he'd like to do the same for Betsy Mae. Why haven't you ever brought her to the mill clinic to see him?" She managed an air of puzzled bewilderment.

"What God gives us, it's for us to accept." She was truculent, yet Liz sensed that this was an emotion borrowed from her husband.

"God put folks on earth to help one another. Like my husband Victor, who's done so much for Francis. He wanted to work with Andy, too, but Andy's parents refused. Now Maureen and Andrew will surely want Victor to help Andy. And he could help Betsy Mae, too. Maybe she won't be able to do everything you'd like, but as with Francis, she could have a much better life."

"That boy tried to rape my baby." Tears filled Martha's eyes. "He's got to pay for that."

"Andy has devils in him that must be defeated –" Liz sought for words that Martha McRae could accept. "He's going to work with my husband to conquer this. Mrs McRae, from all this horror, let some good come. Let Dr Adams work with Betsy Mae – and he'll work with Andy so that nothing like this will ever happen again. And I'm sure that my mother will be anxious to make amends to you and your husband. In the future," she said recklessly yet confident her mother would go along with this, "there'll be an additional ten percent in Mr McRae's pay envelope each week. As long as he wishes to work at the Hampton Mill, this will continue."

Martha McRae's eyes widened with awe. "Every week?" she pressed. "Even five years from now?"

"Every week," Liz promised, fighting her guilt that she was buying Andy's way out of reform school. But what good would be served if Andy was committed? "I swear this on my daughter's life."

"But Jeb will get in bad trouble," Martha stammered in sudden alarm. "He told the police what happened to Betsy Mae. They could throw him in jail!"

"No," Liz soothed. "Dr Adams will go to the police and explain that Betsy Mae is like Francis – not quite clear in the head. That she makes up things without understanding. Believe me, the police will accept this. My father, the senator, will come down from Washington to see this through, if necessary." She sensed that the Senator's influence would be enough. The whole matter would be dismissed.

"I'll be at the mill with Jeb's lunch pail at noon. I'll tell him," Martha said. "And I'll make him understand he's gotta let Betsy Mae go to the clinic."

Liz rushed to Hampton House. No need for a meeting with Jeb McRae. Let that be aborted. Martha McRae and she had settled the matter: Andy would not go to reform school. Her father would not have to carry the scandal of a rape charge against Francis. For once in her life, she thought with triumph, she'd come forward to do something useful.

Sixteen

Liz was grateful for the arrival of spring. It was the season she always loved. Flowers had become an obsession with her in the last couple of years – a distraction from her sense of uselessness, her constant anguish that a wall existed between Victor and her. Now she brought a bunch of daffodils into the dining room to grace the table tonight.

From the sitting room came the sound of laughter. Victor was talking with Kathy. He was in high spirits tonight, Liz thought. He'd been pleased that at last Andrew and Maureen had agreed that Andy must receive long-term treatment. And Andy was scared after that run-in with the police. He never missed a session with Victor.

Just today – for the first time – Victor had felt a breakthrough with Andy. "The toughest patient I've handled," he'd said. Francis was still bewildered by what had happened. But Victor was sure he'd overcome this.

When would she accept that fact that Victor's life revolved around his work with troubled children? Yet she was constantly haunted by the suspicion that there would be more time in his life for her if she agreed to have another child. But she couldn't expose herself to further hurt. What could be as painful in this world as losing a child?

Mary Lou came into the sitting room to announce she was ready to serve dinner. Victor and Kathy joined Liz at the dining table.

"I love daffodils," Kathy effervesced. "When we go down to see Wendy and her mama next week, can I take a bunch to them?" Kathy frowned for a moment. "They don't have any flowers at all."

"Janet had no time to put in bulbs last fall," Liz explained. No money that could be allotted to buying bulbs, she thought sadly.

She admired the way Janet contrived to adjust her life to deal with Kevin's affliction. For Adrienne survival depended upon what she liked to call "new adventures". Most people filled their lives with manufactured panaceas to see them through each day. Only a few had a special something that ruled their lives. Victor with his work with children, that gave him such satisfaction. Mama with the mill. Papa with his yearning to see peace in the world. He forever fought for legislation that would keep peace.

Her face softened as she remembered what he'd said when Congress was called upon to vote for the country to enter the war in April, 1917. "There'll be men in the House and in the Senate who'll vote against war. Men who respect their principles. I have no respect for myself." Against his principles he had voted for war because he felt it was futile to do otherwise, and it would have shattered his usefulness in the Senate. Sometimes she asked herself why Papa remained in politics, when his heart belonged with those who dedicated their lives to fighting for peace.

In October Liz received a card from Adrienne, who wrote that at last she would be coming back to Atlanta in a few weeks – but she was so unpredictable.

> You've probably noticed – my last tenant pulled out several months ago owing me three months' rent! Grandma remains in the cottage. Of course, she doesn't know if I'm at the house or not. The lawyer keeps things rolling, but he warns I must retrench even more. Oh, I do miss you, Liz! We used to have such fun together. What's happening to the world when it's so hard to have a little fun?

Adrienne left her compartment on the Atlanta-bound pullman on this unseasonably cold October evening and headed for the dining car. Already she felt reservations about having left Paris. But Mr Meyers, her grandfather's attorney and now hers as well, had been explicit. It was necessary for her to cut back on her expenses.

"You may not be fully aware of the state of the economy or the distressing drop in your grandmother's income and your own. You cannot continue your current lifestyle," he had told her.

The real-estate broker had been unable to find a tenant for her house, even with a substantial drop in the rent. When Tommy's father once again pleaded for part-time custody, she'd finally agreed. Six months with his father, six months with her. That was cutting expenses, wasn't it? And she was returning to Atlanta to live in the house, eliminating the cost of the Paris house. Oh, well, she comforted herself, these bad times couldn't go on for ever.

She was pleasingly conscious of the stares that greeted her appearance in the dining car – at near capacity at this hour. She made an art of capitalizing on every minute charm with which she was blessed. She was wearing a Chanel "sweater-inspired" dress in Schiaparelli's famous "shocking pink".

She was seated at the one remaining unoccupied table and inspected the menu with desultory interest. This would be a long, dull trip, she warned herself. But that suspicion evaporated when she glanced up from the menu into the eyes of the latest arrival in the dining car. He was young, handsome, with an air of being ready to challenge the world.

Her smile was a blatant invitation when he was seated at her table – after the obligatory request by the head waiter to do so in view of the lack of other available seating.

"I'm Adrienne Carstairs," she drawled. "Who're you?"

"Mitchell Logan." His eyes told her he was delighted with this encounter. "My friends call me Mitch."

"Where are you headed?"

"Atlanta." He seemed amused at this cross-examination. "And you?"

"Atlanta," she said with a glow of triumph. Maybe life wouldn't be too dull. Mitch Logan could eliminate that. "But you're not a Southerner," she said, half-accusingly. "Not the way you talk."

"I'm from New York." His eyes sought out her left hand. No wedding ring, she hadn't worn one since the day the divorce came through. *He'll never guess I'm thirty-two, he'll probably figure twenty-three or twenty-four. He can't be over twenty-five*. "I expect to be in Atlanta for six or eight months." Questions in his eyes now. Was she interested in being his playmate while he was in Atlanta?

"What'll you be doing for six or eight months in Atlanta?" she asked with candid curiosity. He was traveling pullman so he couldn't be broke. But his clothes were bargain-basement, she suspected. "Business or pleasure?"

"I'm going down to Atlanta on a research project," he explained. "I have a contract to write a book about the problems of cotton-mill owners – the advantages of operating in the South over New England."

"My best friend's mother is Caroline Hampton. She runs the Hampton Mill down in Atlanta." His face told her he was familiar with Caroline Hampton's occupation.

"I'd like to meet her. She's on my list of important people to interview." Adrienne felt his excitement at this possibility. "I've been warned it's tough to get through to her." Again, questions in his eyes. Could Adrienne provide a shortcut?

"I know she's turned down interviews with magazine writers," Adrienne conceded. "But I can talk to Liz – that's her daughter – if you like."

"I'd like that." His smile was dazzling.

They sparred over a lengthy dinner, though Adrienne was certain of their destination. She guessed he wasn't surprised when she invited him to her compartment. She knew he wouldn't be returning to his seat in the pullman, which would become a berth at the bedtime hour. Let the pullman porters wonder where Mitch Logan spent the night.

Liz knew that Adrienne was returning to Atlanta, though Adrienne had been vague about just when. Several days ago she became aware that domestic help, probably hired by Mr Meyers, was involved in heavy housecleaning. Rugs were being aired, windows washed, lines of laundry hung across the rear of Adrienne's house.

Adrienne had a way of disappearing for months, or years, then returning and expecting them to pick up their lives as though she'd never been away. Adrienne never changed, Liz thought with a twinge of impatience. *She* did. To Adrienne life was supposed to be "a gas" – one long, uninterrupted party. But even in Paris Adrienne must have seen how the world had been turned upside down. No doubt she was coming home, Liz realized in a flash of prescience, because her funds had diminished in these trying times.

As always, Liz came downstairs to have breakfast with Kathy, Victor long gone to the hospital by now.

"Darling, wear your new coat to school," she told Kathy while they began to eat the silken scrambled eggs and grits Mary Lou served in ample portions. "It's cold outside today. And finish your eggs," she said, "or you'll be hungry before lunch." How many children in Atlanta went without breakfast? she asked herself in recurrent anguish. How many children in towns and cities across the country?

"Will you pick me up for dancing class or Matthew?" Kathy asked.

"I'll pick you up," Liz promised. Aware that Kathy saw so little of her father – and hoping to compensate by her own presence.

Late in the morning Liz saw a taxi pull up before Adrienne's house. Her first instinct was to hurry over to welcome Adrienne home, as she'd done so often through the years. But this was aborted as Adrienne began to scream at the abashed driver, her voice carrying to Liz.

"Be careful, you jerk! That's Louis Vuitton luggage. It's very expensive!"

Now Adrienne focused on the man and woman emerging from the house to take charge of the sea of valises and the trunk, that the driver deposited in the driveway. It was the couple Liz had seen beating rugs, hanging out blankets to air – Adrienne's new domestic help. In earlier years Adrienne had hired and fired with startling regularity. But today domestic workers were terrified of losing their jobs, they'd put up even with Adrienne's tantrums, her sometimes absurd demands.

Why did she feel this sudden reluctance to go out to welcome Adrienne? Liz asked herself guiltily. Because, the answer leapt into her mind, she suspected that Adrienne still clung to her hedonistic philosophy. No doubt, Adrienne still lived in the world that F. Scott Fitzgerald drew so vividly in *The Great Gatsby*.

Times have changed. But Adrienne won't accept that.

In her occasional letters Adrienne had poured out her outrage that her income had been slashed, as though only she in the whole world was so affected. People in Paris were hurting, too. And how could Adrienne have allowed her ex-husband, after all these years, to have part-time custody of Tommy?

While she debated about when to call Adrienne, but call she must because Adrienne and she had been friends forever, the phone rang.

"I'll get it, Mary Lou," she said and picked up the receiver. "Hello –"

"Sugar, I'm back home," Adrienne bubbled. "Just exhausted from all the traveling – but I'm dying to see you and to hear all the dirt. Where can we go for lunch? Though after Paris, anything will seem so provincial."

"Come over here for lunch," Liz invited. Despite her earlier reluctance she was eager now to see Adrienne. So Adrienne was a feather-brain sometimes. Maybe that was her way of surviving. "Mary Lou is still the best cook in Atlanta after Mattie."

"Does she still make that marvelous coffee?" Before Liz could reply she continued. "Tell her to put a pot up this minute. I'll be right over, just as soon as I tell my new girl to unpack for me." She exuded a melodramatic sigh. "I was dying to buy some of the fantastic new clothes Chanel and Schiaparelli are showing, but I didn't dare. Mr Meyers warned me I'm practically destitute. But let me get off the phone and dash over there. I've got so much to tell you." But her letters, Liz recalled, were brief bits of froth.

Half an hour later Adrienne charged into the Adams' foyer, hugged Mary Lou effusively, then threw herself into Liz's arms.

"Oh, I did miss you, Liz. And how's my precious Kathy?"

"She's growing so fast, and she's so pretty and so bright." Liz glowed. "She's a big girl now. I can't believe she's going to be eleven! She and Tommy are only weeks apart, remember."

"Don't say that." Adrienne shuddered. "How can I explain a son who's almost eleven, when I expect men to believe I'm twenty-three?" She turned to Mary Lou, hovering close by with a broad smile. "Mary Lou, I know you've got something scrumptious just out of the oven –"

"Yes'um. Pecan pies." Mary Lou beamed. "I'll bring you a piece with yo' coffee."

"I stop by every once in a while to see your grandmother," Liz told Adrienne while they strolled into the sitting room. Before Adrienne left for Paris, her grandmother, senile now, had been settled in the guest cottage with housekeeper and nurse. "Though I doubt that she ever recognizes me."

"Grandma doesn't even know me, and I'm her only close living relative." Adrienne leaned forward with a conspiratorial smile. "Liz, I met the most gorgeous man on the train. Or actually, in the dining car. I tell you, it was fate. The only unoccupied place in the dining car was at my table. He's about twenty-five, and I'm sure he thinks I'm about the same age."

"Does he live in Atlanta?" As long as there was a handsome man around, Adrienne wouldn't be bored, Liz thought.

"He'll be living here for the next six or eight months."

"What does he do?"

"He's researching a book he's writing about the cotton mills in the South and in New England. And I promised I'd talk to you – my best friend – about setting up an interview with your mother."

"I don't know, Adrienne. Mama avoids that sort of thing."

"I'll bet if Margaret Mitchell asked for an interview, your mother wouldn't turn her down. Talk to her," Adrienne said. "He's going to call me as soon as he gets settled in. I promised to drive him around. You know – show him Atlanta." Laughter was in her eyes. "Among other things. How're you doing? What about your love life?"

"Adrienne, I'm a married woman." Liz managed an indulgent laugh. All those years ago she'd confided in Adrienne about that first encounter with Rick, but not the second, nor the brief affair with Larry Burke.

"You're a woman," Adrienne drawled. "Does Vic still spend most of his time wrapped up in his practice?"

"A lot of his time," Liz conceded and paused. "But I'm spending a lot of my time in volunteer work. You don't know how bad things are down here."

"Maybe Mitch has a friend."

"No!" Liz hadn't meant to sound so sharp.

"Do you know how many wives play on the side?" Adrienne challenged. "That's what keeps their marriages together."

Adrienne hadn't changed in the past ten years, Liz thought impatiently. To her life was meant to be an endless party. "Don't you realize how terrible conditions are for most people today? We're so lucky –"

"Lucky?" Adrienne scoffed. "When I have to leave Paris without buying one thing at the fashion shows? With Mr Meyers screaming at me to cut back on expenses?"

"Everybody's cutting back on expenses. For so many people

each day is a battle for survival. Children are digging into garbage cans for food! Families are—"

"Oh, don't be so depressing," Adrienne broke in. "And promise me you'll talk to your mother about giving Mitch an interview. This book he's researching will be important. And he's a great admirer of the way the Hampton Mill functions. He asked me all kinds of questions, but what do I know about a cotton mill? Except that it's horribly noisy."

"Is he on the side of those union organizers?" Liz was skeptical. "Mama hates every one of them." Mama was civil with Kevin only because of Janet and her mother.

"He's not taking sides," Adrienne said. "He says he wants to present all the facts – and let the readers decide. Liz, it means so much to me. Mitch is special." She offered her most beguiling, wistful smile.

"I'll talk to Mama," Liz capitulated. "But don't expect her to agree to an interview."

Seventeen

Liz debated over the best way to approach her mother on behalf of Adrienne's writer friend. Perhaps this evening, she decided while she dressed for a family dinner at Hampton House. Mama was always in a good mood when they all gathered at the house: Maureen, Andrew and Andy; she, Victor and Kathy; Josh, Francis and Aunt Sophie. She'd find a few moments alone with Mama.

When the phone rang, she suspected it was Victor with some crisis at the hospital that would keep him from dinner.

"Hello." There was resignation in her voice. Once a month they all gathered together for dinner. Why couldn't Victor arrange to be free?

"Liz, I'll be a little late." That self-conscious tone in his voice that presaged his report of being unavailable for an occasion. "I should be there by the time you all sit down to dinner."

"Try, Vic." A hint of annoyance crept into her voice.

"I will," he promised. "I have to run now."

Moments later the phone rang again. Liz picked it up. "Hello."

"Sugar, you're having the family dinner tonight, aren't you?" Adrienne effervesced.

"I'm just about to leave," Liz said. A phone conversation with Adrienne could go on for ever.

"I just wanted to tell you that Mitch tried to get through to your mother at the office. Some nasty woman wouldn't put him through." Ellen, Liz thought. She was very protective of Mama's time. "But he has an appointment with Todd Murdoch the first of next week." Caroline Hampton's arch enemy. "He needs to get your mother's side of the business. You know, for an all-round view."

"I'll talk to her. But she's tough."

"Mitch will be so disappointed with me if I can't help him with this," Adrienne said plaintively.

"I'll talk to Mama," Liz repeated. "But I really have to dash now."

Off the phone Liz re-ran in her mind the conversation with Adrienne. Of course, Adrienne was always so dramatic. But was she becoming emotionally involved with this man? So quickly? She had always vowed she'd never marry again unless she met an eighty-year-old billionaire who was mad about her.

The door flew open. Kathy darted inside. "Mama, can I take my new nightgown over to Andrea's house?"

"Yes, darling." Liz reached to pull Kathy close for a moment. "And how many times have I told you to knock before you come into a room?"

"I'm sorry." Kathy's exuberance was undiminished by this minor scolding. "But I'm so excited. This is the first time I've ever slept over at somebody's house."

"I'll come in and check that you've packed everything. In about five minutes – so you be ready. I'll drive you over on my way to Grandma and Grandpa's."

By the time Liz arrived at Hampton House, the others were gathered in the sitting room. Andy wasn't here, she noted, and realized he was still being restricted to the house in the evenings. Victor said he was a tough patient but was determined to help him.

"Vic should be here soon," Liz said with a semblance of apology.

"I want to talk to him," Eric said. "About what he hears from his mother's family in Italy."

"They're not happy with Mussolini in power," Liz said wryly. "He's been trying to persuade them to leave the country while they can."

"Who's happy in Europe these days?" Josh challenged. "Mussolini is out to conquer the world with his Fascist party. Hitler's convinced enough Germans that he alone can save them from communism to get himself elected Chancellor. He, too, wants to dominate Europe. Between Fascism and Nazism the whole world faces danger. Can't you all smell war in the air?"

"Let the economy improve, and Mussolini and Hitler will be out on their asses," Eric said with rare vulgarity. "Both are reaping the benefits of shockingly high unemployment, hunger and desperation. Roosevelt has only just taken over – give the man a chance to bring this country back to prosperity. And that'll spread to Europe as well."

Liz sighed with relief when she heard a car pull up before the house; Victor had said he'd be here by the time they sat down for dinner. She felt less alone when he was with her – as though they had a real marriage.

Mattie appeared in the arched doorway that led into the sitting room.

"Miz Caroline, we's ready to serve dinner."

Not until they'd had their dessert – Mattie's superb New Orleans bread pudding with bourbon sauce – and were having coffee in the sitting room did Liz manage to get a few moments alone with her mother.

"Mama, Adrienne has this friend down from New York," Liz began casually. She wouldn't mention that Adrienne had picked him up on the train. "He's a writer. He's researching cotton mills in the South and up in New England, and she says he's dying to talk with you. But I gather Ellen brushed him off when he tried to make an appointment."

"That she should," Caroline approved. "My business is running a cotton mill, not wasting time on personal interviews." Her smile was a blend of irritation and indulgence.

"I gather it's a serious book," Liz went on. "Couldn't you give him a time limit?"

"We have endless problems in running our mills today. No

book is going to solve them. Tell Adrienne I'm just too busy to set aside time for such nonsense."

"He has an appointment with Todd Murdoch next week," Liz tried again.

"Well, bully for him," Caroline said drily. "Let Todd Murdoch spew out his weird conception of what the South needs to get out of this terrible downward spiral. Tell Adrienne I can't fit an interview into my schedule."

Adrienne gazed at Liz in abject desolation. "Why is your mother being so stubborn? Mitch will be terribly upset when I tell him I couldn't arrange a meeting."

"There're other mill owners in Atlanta," Liz reminded her.

"But your mother has such a great reputation," Adrienne protested. She paused, frowned in concentration. "You-all will be going to the Children's Relief Ball next Saturday?"

"Yes . . ." Liz's mind was following Adrienne's. "You mean to bring him there and try for an introduction?" She was doubtful that this would change her mother's mind.

"We'll be there, sugar," Adrienne drawled. "And Caroline Hampton is too much of a lady to be rude."

"We'll see." Adrienne was dragging this thing too far, and Liz was worried. "Oh, do you have tickets?"

"No problem to get them." Adrienne shrugged this off. "They'll sell as many tickets as they can – even they have to grease people to get them into the ballroom."

Liz was ambivalent about attending the Children's Relief Ball. It seemed crass to be attending such a lavish event in times of such want, she thought as she reached for the tiny lemon-yellow purse that matched her yellow silk evening gown designed by Hattie Carnegie. But this was a fundraiser. She was pleased that Victor would be with her, though he seemed exhausted. It was the long evening hours at the children's clinic, she thought tenderly – yet that was the work that was his passion.

"Papa said to tell you he's ready whenever you are." Kathy

paused in the doorway to the master bedroom. "Mama, you look so pretty!"

"Thank you, Kathy." She smiled lovingly at her daughter. How lovely to be thought pretty by your daughter.

"I wish I could go," Kathy said mournfully.

"In a few years you will be going with us," Liz assured her. Oh, the years sped past so fast! "But tonight Mary Lou will let you listen to the radio until eleven o'clock. That'll be fun, won't it?"

"I suppose."

"I have to run now, darling." Liz reached to kiss her daughter. "Be good."

By the time Liz and Victor arrived at the ballroom the party was in full swing. Almost immediately Liz spied her mother and father across the floor. She and Victor hurried to join them.

"Oh, this is going to be a huge success," Eric said with satisfaction. "God knows, every cent will go to a good cause."

"Mama, I love that dress," Liz said.

"It's six years old." Caroline smiled with satisfaction. "Remember when we were wearing those short evening gowns? I had Miss Alsobrook add this flounce – and now it's the latest in 1933 fashions."

"Liz!" Adrienne called and hurried to join the small group. "I was beginning to wonder if you'd decided not to come." Adrienne smiled beguilingly at Caroline and Eric. "You're looking beautiful, Mrs Hampton."

"Thank you, Adrienne."

"Oh, may I introduce my escort –" Adrienne reached to draw the tall, dark-haired man who hovered beside her into the group. "This is Mitch Logan from New York. He's a writer."

"How nice to meet you, Mr Logan," Caroline said politely, but Liz knew she was furious. "Eric, I really must talk with Alicia Madison about the ticket sales."

"My mother's on the ticket committee," Liz explained self-consciously to Mitch Logan. "She's anxious to know how much the ball will bring in."

"I'm sure it's a huge success." Mitch Logan's eyes belied his smile. "Adrienne, shall we dance?"

"I don't like that man," Victor said when he and Liz were alone. "But then Adrienne has a way of being involved with unscrupulous characters."

Liz was relieved that in the following days Adrienne dropped the business of Mitch's interviewing her mother. Thanksgiving was close at hand. Liz was caught up in the preparations for the family dinner to be held this year in the Adams' house because the reception rooms at Hampton Court were being painted. Liz suspected this was a job manufactured by her mother to provide Thanksgiving funds for laid-off mill employees.

She was upset that Janet and her small family would not be at the Thanksgiving table this year, though she had offered to have Matthew drive them from Columbus and back again.

"Kevin doesn't feel up to all that traveling. Wendy and I had been so looking forward to it," Janet had said on the phone.

Liz knew, too, that Josh would be disappointed. His eyes had lit up when she'd told him that Janet had as usual been invited to be with them for Thanksgiving. Mama kept pushing eligible Atlanta girls at him, but Josh rejected her efforts. Like Victor, he buried himself in his work.

She'd debated about inviting Adrienne for Thanksgiving, but realized Adrienne wouldn't really fit in with the family gathering. She was relieved when Adrienne announced that she would have Thanksgiving dinner at home with Mitch as her sole guest.

"I'll send dinner down to Grandma and her nurse," Adrienne said lightly. "Of course, Grandma won't have the foggiest notion about Thanksgiving."

Adrienne pouted because Mitch seemed so involved in his research.

"Maybe he's punishing me for not getting him an interview with Caroline," she said. When Adrienne was feeling defiant, she abandoned the more formal Mrs Hampton for Caroline. "But he isn't always too busy," she conceded. "He has a toothbrush in my bathroom and a supply of fresh underpants in my dresser."

"Adrienne, how much do you know about him?" Liz probed while they had a late breakfast in Liz's sunlit breakfast room.

"Enough." Adrienne dismissed this airily. "He's written several articles for magazines about conditions in the cotton mills both down here and in New England. He's got a college degree from some school in New York, and now he has this book contract."

"What about his family?" Liz persisted. Victor's comment about Mitch Logan lingered in her mind. Victor was such a good judge of character. Was Adrienne building up trouble for herself?

"Sugar, I'm not sleeping with his family." Adrienne laughed. "And I'm not thinking of marrying him. You know my requirements for a husband. Meanwhile, I play. And Mitch is so good-looking."

"I have to be out of here in about twenty minutes," Liz warned her. "It's my day to give four hours to the used clothing store."

She'd tried to persuade Adrienne to become involved in volunteer work, but Adrienne had shrugged this off with a shudder.

"Liz, it would be so depressing. And dull."

After her stint at the used clothing store, Liz drove home. She made a point of being there each day when Kathy came home from school. She ought to be so grateful, she chastised herself. None of the family had any real financial worries. She had her precious daughter.

Again, she asked herself how Adrienne had allowed Tommy to spend months with his father. He was due home tomorrow, she recalled. Adrienne had already arranged for his admission into Kathy's school. Matthew was to drive both children to school each morning and bring them home each afternoon.

At the house Mary Lou told her that Janet had called right after she'd left this morning.

"She say it ain't nothin' important, Miz Liz. She jes' called to see how you wuz doin'."

"Thanks, Mary Lou." But she knew that when Janet made a long-distance call it wasn't for nothing. Not the way Janet watched every cent.

Liz went up to her bedroom to call Janet.

"How are you, honey?" she asked with solicitude when Janet picked up.

"All right," Janet said and hesitated. "No, I'm not all right – I'm worried about Kevin. He's so depressed. I thought maybe if Vic could talk to him –"

"I'll have Vic call him tonight," Liz promised.

They discussed the local news. On impulse, Liz asked Janet if she knew anything about Mitch Logan.

"He's interviewing mill owners here in town. Not Mama," Liz said, chuckling. "You know Mama – she wants no part of mill publicity. I just wondered . . ." Her voice trailed off.

"I don't know anything about him," Janet said. "But I'll ask around." Liz understood – Janet meant to ask around among Kevin's cotton mill associates.

"I worry about Adrienne," Liz explained. "She's seeing a lot of this Mitch character."

"Adrienne's a big girl now." Janet had never been a fan of Adrienne's. "But I'll see what I can dig up."

A week later Janet phoned Liz.

"Liz, I have some information about Mitch Logan," she began.

"Let me call you right back," Liz said and hung up. She always did this to save Janet paying for the long-distance call.

Moments later Janet's phone rang.

"I asked around about Logan," Janet said. "He's a union

organizer, with a new union that Kevin says is prone to violence. I suspect they'll do anything it takes to bring their union, rather than Kevin's or the Textile Workers Union, into the Georgia cotton mills."

"That's why he's so anxious to talk to Mama!" Liz was furious. He was using Adrienne to get to Mama. "I'll call Mama and I'll call Adrienne. Thanks, Janet."

Adrienne listened with an air of bravado to Liz's report about Mitch Logan's real identity.

"How does Kevin know this?" she asked Liz. "You know most folks think Kevin is off the wall."

"This came from union headquarters," Liz pointed out.

"Are you going to tell your mother?" Adrienne exuded hostility.

"I have already. I had to."

"Maybe it's true, maybe it isn't—"

"Are you going to keep on seeing him?" Liz sounded anxious.

"Sugar, what Mitch does with his business doesn't bother me. As long as he's fun, I'll play."

"You're asking for trouble," Liz warned her.

"I love trouble. It's exciting. But I don't plan to marry him, if that's what's worrying you. You know me," Adrienne said flippantly, "I'm just out for a good time."

Adrienne put the receiver down and immediately called Mitch. She waited impatiently for him to pick up the phone in his furnished apartment in a dilapidated section of Atlanta.

"Yes." Mitch was terse.

"Sugar, you've blown your cover," she said sweetly.

"What are you talking about?" But a note of wariness lurked beneath his air of amusement.

"I was just on the phone with Liz Adams. She said the word is out that you're a union organizer trying to push your union into our cotton mills."

"OK," he said after a moment. "So I needed a cover.

Does this bother you? I mean, that I'm not researching a book?"

"Honey, you know what bothers me. It's not seeing you as often as I like."

"What about tonight?"

"What about right now?" she countered.

"I'm waiting for phone calls. Business calls, but I can be all yours after six."

"Be here," she ordered, "or I'll have a team of bloodhounds out to track you down."

Eighteen

Christmas, 1934 was cheerless for many Americans. Over ten million people were unemployed; the national average income was slightly over half its 1929 level. The communist party chief – a party expanding in numbers as the Depression continued – ridiculed Roosevelt's "New Deal" as the same as Hitler's program in Germany.

At family dinners at Hampton House the conversation was dominated by diatribes against Father Coughlin and Huey Long. Father Coughlin, the "radio priest", was a virulent anti-Semite who hated capitalism. He maintained that Alexander Hamilton's real name was Levine and predicted that in a hundred years Washington would be Washingtonski. He appealed to the poor and frightened. Millions listened to his weekly radio program. Huey Long, the Governor of Louisiana, believed in dictatorial powers. He'd managed to annihilate free government in the state and had built up a storm-trooper style of political terrorism.

Liz was pleased that Tommy was back in Atlanta – though she worried at moments that Tommy might see more than he should. Mitch Logan was always underfoot.

Kathy was delighted to have Tommy back home. They'd grown up together and were almost like brother and sister. They even battled like brother and sister, Liz thought indulgently.

Early in March Liz was startled to read an item in the *Atlanta Constitution* about Rick Pulaski. He was negotiating to buy land on which he meant to build a residential community. There was much public interest in the project. "Pulaski will bring much needed jobs into the city," the newspaper reported.

Liz tried to thrust aside unease. She remembered in sharp detail those last moments in Miami when Victor arrived after the hurricane. Victor had been so grateful to Rick. She remembered what she'd said: "I would have been killed if Rick hadn't pulled me from the car seconds before a telephone pole smashed it. It hit right where I'd been sitting." Victor hadn't thought to ask what she was doing in a car with Rick. And she remembered Victor's words to Rick: "Any time you come to visit Atlanta, please consider our house as yours."

Rick was part of the past. There was no space in their lives for him now.

She tried to convince herself that Victor would not notice the item in the *Constitution* about Rick's presence in Atlanta. He was all wrapped up in his work – he cared nothing about real-estate developments. She prayed that Adrienne would remain unaware that Rick was here in Atlanta.

Early in May Liz prepared to make one of her regular visits to Janet down in Columbus. She knew Janet was trying to find a job – at a time when there were no jobs. She knew, too, that Kevin was upset about this. He expected Janet to be with him at the office in the hours when Wendy was in school.

Victor had been candid, she remembered unhappily. "I've tried to talk with Kevin, but I can't get through to him. I guess I do better with kids," he'd said.

The evening before the scheduled trip to Columbus, she plotted her usual routine. She'd load a basket with fruit and vegetables, pretending they came from Hampton House gardens. And she'd add the two pies and cookies Mary Lou, who was sympathetic to this subterfuge, had baked. "Mary Lou said I couldn't go down to visit you without bringing something from her," she would say.

As so often happened, she and Kathy sat down to dinner alone. Victor was making a house call to a troubled mill village teenager. After dinner she and Kathy settled themselves on the verandah because this was a stifling hot evening. Aware of their presence, Tommy darted over to play with her.

"Tommy, it's too hot to run," Liz scolded him affectionately.

She knew that Adrienne was off somewhere with Mitch. At the proper time Adrienne's current housekeeper would summon Tommy home and see him through the bedtime routine. But tonight the two thirteen-year-olds seemed querulous as they played endless rounds of checkers. Twice she had to intervene in their quarreling. It was the heat, she decided, the first really hot spell of the season.

Tomorrow was a school day – one of the last before school would close. Despite the heat bed time was not to be postponed, though Kathy and Tommy both protested when Adrienne's housekeeper crossed the wide lawn between the two houses and ordered him home.

"It's time for both of you to go to bed." Liz backed up the housekeeper. "You can play again tomorrow."

With Kathy in bed Liz sat in a chair by a window in the master bedroom to read. Not a breath of air, she thought. And the electric fans, scattered through the house, did little more than circulate hot air. The only comfortable places in the city on nights like this were in the air-conditioned movie houses. One day, Victor insisted, private homes would be air-conditioned.

Close to eleven o'clock Liz heard a car pull up before the house. Victor, she thought, and went downstairs to sit with him over his belated dinner. Mary Lou was accustomed to these after-hours meals. Liz brought out a plate of cold chicken, beautifully ripe sliced tomatoes and cucumbers, a bowl of fruit salad, and a pitcher of iced tea.

"You look tired," she sympathized.

"Beat," he admitted and sighed. "What kills me is that I could get some really good results with this boy if I could spend more time with him. But I'm tied up with my practice and the hospital so many hours every day."

"You need to be twins," she said gently.

While Victor talked about the patient he'd seen this evening – just needing someone to listen without responding – Liz worried yet again about Rick's sudden appearance here in Atlanta. She'd want to die if Victor found out about Rick and her. Tonight, she thought, she'd welcome Victor if he wanted to make love. Rick's presence in Atlanta had made her aware of how much she wished that Victor and she could restore their marriage to what it had been in the early years. She lived on a lonely isle and it was devastating.

The moment Victor stretched out in bed, he was asleep. Liz lay wide awake – her mind and body too aroused for slumber. This could have been the night of sweet reconciliation.

She started at the sound of the phone. Victor hadn't even heard it, she thought, and reached for the receiver. Expecting a call from the hospital.

"Liz, Tommy's so sick!" Adrienne sounded terrified. "I know he's running a high temperature. Tell Vic he has to come over right away!"

"Calm down, Adrienne!" Why must she always be so dramatic? But Liz was shaking Victor into wakefulness. "I'll put Vic on in a minute. Tell him Tommy's symptoms –"

Liz stood by while Victor talked with Adrienne. At intervals he interrupted her high-pitched report, audible even to Liz.

"It sounds as though Tommy's coming down with chicken pox. It's been floating around in the school system. I'm coming over for a look at him, but it's just a common childhood disease – though normally it hits younger kids. Tommy will be uncomfortable for a few days, but it's not serious. Oh, try to keep him from scratching those little red spots. That could cause scarring."

"Oh, how awful," Adrienne moaned. "He's such a handsome child."

"Adrienne, stop being hysterical. Tommy will be fine. I'll be over in a few minutes," he repeated. He put down the phone and felt about on the carpet for his slippers.

"I hadn't heard about chicken pox in the schools," Liz said uneasily while Victor reached for his robe.

"There's been a few cases reported. As I told Adrienne, it's rarely serious."

"Kathy's been playing with Tommy. They're in the same class at school." All at once Liz was anxious. "Do you think she'll come down with it, too?"

"Very likely, but it's nothing to worry about." He headed for the door. "If she does, make sure she doesn't scratch."

Liz glanced at the clock on the night table. It was past one o'clock. She ought to try to get back to sleep. Adrienne would keep Victor over there for ever. Even when Tommy had a cold, Adrienne behaved as though it was a possibly fatal illness.

Liz lay back against her pillows willing herself to sleep, but guessing this would be futile. A few minutes later she left the bed, crossed to a window to stare out into the night. Tommy's bedroom was brilliantly lighted.

Poor baby, he missed his father. Those few months with Neil had created a bond he'd never truly felt with his mother. It was always the children who suffered the most in divorce.

With a sudden need to reassure herself that Kathy was all right, she left the bedroom and crossed the hall to her daughter's room. As always, the door was open because Kathy felt more secure that way. The night light was on. A fan whirred softly from on top of a chest of drawers.

Liz stiffened as she approached the door. Kathy was mumbling in her sleep. Liz hurried inside. Kathy had kicked off the sheet. Her nightgown was rolled up above her waist. She was threshing about in semi-wakefulness. Liz felt her forehead; she was running a temperature. Even in the faint illumination provided by the night light Liz could see the small red eruptions that were the indications of chicken pox. The trip to Columbus would have to be postponed.

"Adrienne, calm down," Victor ordered as she began to sob. "So

Tommy has the chicken pox – it isn't fatal. A hundred to one Kathy'll be coming down with it, too."

"Neil will blame me for it. He wanted Tommy to stay with him until the end of the school year. He'll say I'm a bad mother – he'll go to court to try for full custody!"

"That won't happen," he soothed. "Just calm down—"

"Oh Vic, you're so sweet." All at once her arms were about his neck. "If Neil tries to take me to court, will you testify that I'm a good mother?"

"Of course, but that won't happen."

"I hope Liz realizes what a treasure she has in you," Adrienne whispered, her sobbing abandoned. "I should have such luck . . ."

Could she bring Victor into her bed? Liz wouldn't have to know. On and off through the years she'd told herself he'd be a great lover – with the right woman.

"Mama –" Awake now, Kathy reached out with one hand. Her tone was querulous. "I'm so hot. And I itch. I itch real bad –"

"Darling, you mustn't scratch," Liz said tenderly. "I think you and Tommy are both coming down with chicken pox."

"Sally at school is out with it. Miss Thomas told us so."

"Papa will get a lotion from the drugstore that'll make it stop itching," Liz promised. "But you mustn't scratch."

"Open the window more," Kathy ordered. "It's so hot in here."

"I'll do that right now," Liz soothed, and headed for the window.

"And then I want a drink of water –"

Liz paused at the window as she opened it. She stared at the view into Tommy's bedroom. The brilliant illumination had been muted, but there was enough light for her to see. Victor and Adrienne were standing close together, with Adrienne's arms about Victor's shoulders. *When did this happen?* How long had it been going on? Liz asked herself in sick dismay.

"Mama, I want a glass of water," Kathy nagged. "I want it right now."

Liz pretended to be asleep when Victor slid into their bed again. Despite the heat, Liz was cold with shock. Her whole world seemed to be crashing down about her as she realized that Victor was her unacknowledged strength. In a corner of her mind she had always known that Victor was her rock of Gibraltar, but not any longer.

She should be furious with Adrienne – next to Janet, her oldest best friend, but her rage focused on Victor. How stupid to feel guilty about Rick!

Still, she knew that Adrienne was now forever out of her life.

Nineteen

Liz smothered a series of yawns as she tiptoed from Kathy's bedroom at close to ten next morning. Poor baby, so uncomfortable in the early stage of chicken pox. But the pink lotion seemed to be controlling the itching. Liz doubted that she could get back to sleep, not with that tableau of Adrienne and Victor locked in an embrace etched on her brain.

The phone rang as she walked into her own room, and she reached for the receiver.

"Hello?"

"How's the most beautiful flower of the South these days?" Rick's voice was a startling intrusion. With the Atlanta newspapers full of reports of the "Pulaski Development", she'd told herself he was too wrapped up in his new project to try to resume their relationship. "I've been thinking of you constantly since the moment I hit town."

"What a waste of time," Liz said coolly. He assumed she knew of his arrival. His name was constantly in the Atlanta newspapers.

"I'm busy as hell but dying to see you. Pick a time and I'll be there."

"It's over, Rick." Last night's defiance had evaporated. Yet the image of Adrienne with her arms about Victor mocked her. "I won't be seeing you."

"Pity. We're great together."

"Good luck on your project." She put down the phone, startled to discover she was trembling. Rick brought back frightening memories: the hurricane, her terror that the children and Patience had been killed.

Despite her shock, her agony, at seeing Victor and Adrienne together, she recoiled from putting her marriage in further jeopardy. She clung to crumbs now – knowing that without Victor her life would be destroyed. Scared to death what tomorrow might bring.

Everything that's happening is my fault. Retribution for my affair with Rick. How did I manage to mess up my life this way?

Adrienne sprawled across the four-poster bed in one of the black chiffon nighties she'd brought back from Paris and listened to Mitch rail against Caroline Hampton. He was still furious that she had treated him like dirt at the Children's Relief Ball. He churned with frustration that he was making no real progress with the mill workers. Adrienne exuded sympathy.

"Mitch, she was rotten to you," Adrienne agreed when he at last paused for breath. "But you don't need her." She nuzzled against him in sultry invitation.

"I do need her," Mitch admitted. "I need to get inside her brain, to know how she thinks. She's one of the most influential women in the whole industry – perhaps the most influential. Damn it, Adrienne, she must have a vulnerable spot somewhere. I need to find that spot and use it." He gazed into Adrienne's eyes as though determined to find an answer. "Talk to me about Caroline Hampton," he ordered. "Tell me all about her."

Adrienne recalled the old stories about how Caroline had come to Atlanta from London to present herself to her grandfather, General Josiah Hampton. She took Mitch through the years to Caroline's marriage to Eric Hampton, a distant cousin.

"Eric Hampton had been married before," Adrienne recalled.

"Back up." All at once Mitch was alert. "Tell me about his first wife."

"Oh, before she married Eric Hampton she was Tina

Kendrick. The Kendricks were Old South, but they had lost most of their money by the time Tina was born. Marrying Eric was a triumph for Tina. You know, all that Hampton money. And then –" Adrienne paused for dramatic emphasis – "Tina killed her mill-foreman lover in a fit of jealousy and ran off to Paris with her brother Chad."

"What happened to her in Paris?" The atmosphere was suddenly electric.

"She died in a fire just a few months after she left Atlanta."

"How do you know?"

"Oh, it was all over town. My grandmother told me."

"Suppose she didn't die in that fire?" Mitch drawled. "Suppose that was a story to make the police close the murder case?"

"Well, she did," Adrienne insisted. "Her mother left town because she just couldn't face all the talk."

"I know the odds are that she did die in that fire, but suppose she didn't?" Mitch's voice was hypnotic. "Suppose she's still alive?"

"Oh my God!" Adrienne's eyes widened as she considered this. "Then Eric and Caroline Hampton would be living in sin! Liz and Josh would be illegitimate!"

"Like I said, the odds are against it, but it's sure as hell worth investigating. The senator's political career would be finished if he was exposed as a bigamist."

Adrienne considered this. It was a heady prospect. "Like you said, the odds are against it." Her smile was dazzling. "What are you going to do?"

"I'm going to pursue it," he said calmly. "First of all, you said Tina's mother had left Atlanta. Where is she living?"

"I don't know –" Adrienne waited for Mitch to continue.

"Does she have any other family here in town?"

"Her sister Elaine. She went to school with my mother." All at once her mind was charging ahead. She'd concoct a story about Elaine's mother going to school with her grandmother and use a pretend class reunion as a way in. *Everybody knows Elaine Kendrick isn't all there anymore – she won't ask questions.* "I could go to Elaine and dig out her mother's whereabouts," Adrienne offered.

Mitch snapped his fingers. "Do it. When I have the address, wherever it may be, I'll call on Tina's mother and give her a story about running into Tina in Paris."

"Right." Adrienne nodded. Wow! What a shocker if Mitch's hunch was right.

"When will you talk to Elaine? I've wasted too much time already."

"Tomorrow morning." Adrienne purred.

"If Eric Hampton's first wife is alive, Caroline Hampton will dance to my music." Mitch's eyes glittered with satisfaction. "But hey, let's don't waste any more of this night." His eyes swept over Adrienne's provocative figure, on inviting display beneath the black chiffon nightgown. "It's play time."

"Well, let's play, sugar."

Adrienne enjoyed a leisurely breakfast with Mitch on the small gallery off her bedroom. After breakfast, at Mitch's insistence, she left the house to make an impromptu call on Elaine Kendrick. As always, all the drapes across the front of the small dilapidated colonial house were drawn tight. Elaine had long been a recluse, living, folks said, on the income from a house she rented out in a poorer part of town. She didn't even have someone to come in and clean, Adrienne recalled.

She walked up the steps, across the verandah, to the door and rang the bell. Moments later she heard footsteps coming down the hall. Adrienne summoned what she called "the sugar won't melt in my mouth" smile.

The door opened. Elaine Kendrick stared at Adrienne with the wariness that had been part of her life since her sister's scandal had shocked Atlanta society.

"Miss Elaine, I hope you won't mind my popping in this way. I'm Adrienne Carstairs – I was Adrienne Hollister. I'm helping out with a class reunion at the Madison School and—"

"I didn't go to Madison." Elaine frowned in annoyance.

"I know," Adrienne said soothingly. "My grandmother and your mother went there – in the days when it was the best private school in the county. We want to send your mother an invitation to attend and—"

"My mother won't be attending," Elaine broke in coldly. "She moved away years ago."

"I know." Adrienne managed a delicate smile. "But the committee would like to send her a souvenir program. So if I could have an address to send it to?" She contrived to be both beseeching and beguiling.

"My mother is living in Dallas, Texas." All at once Elaine seemed amused. "You can find her address in the Dallas, Texas phone book. If your committee cares to bother."

Adrienne started as the door was closed in her face. Never mind, she thought with satisfaction. Mitch would know how to track down Tina's mother.

Is Tina still alive? Wouldn't a smart man like Eric Hampton have made sure his first wife was dead before he married again? Or was it like Mitch said? The police wanted to close the murder case.

Did Eric ever see a death certificate?

As Mitch's train pulled into the Dallas railroad station, he felt a surge of anticipation. Within the next forty-eight hours he stood to push his stock high with the union, he congratulated himself. Some sixth sense told him he was right about Eric Hampton's first wife. She was alive and well, and he'd have Caroline Hampton in a corner. She wouldn't be able to refuse to let his union come into the mill.

Wishing the union bigwigs were not so tough about expense accounts, he headed for a taxi to take him to the hotel favored by traveling salesmen which meant the tab would be low. His first objective was to locate a telephone book and find Olivia Kendrick's address.

Alone in his room at the hotel, he reached for the local

telephone directory. All at once he was perspiring, though this was an exceptionally pleasant day for Texas in May.

Suppose I'm wrong? Suppose I wasted all this time and money on the word of a nutty broad?

He flipped through the pages, paused with a grunt of satisfaction. Olivia Kendrick was listed in the directory. He reached for a pencil, scribbled down the address. He wouldn't call; he'd just show up.

Without bothering to unpack he left his hotel room and sought out Olivia Kendrick's house. It was in a shabby section of Dallas, but that was what he had expected. He stood before the hungry-for-paint cottage, noted that the flower pots that lined the sagging porch showed loving care.

Gearing himself for the charade he was about to perform, he walked up the four steps, crossed the porch and rang the doorbell. The screen door had been patched. From inside the house came the sound of a phonograph record. Olivia Kendrick liked opera.

"Yessuh?" A tall, amply built colored woman came to the door.

"I'd like to see Mrs Kendrick," he said with a deferential air, contriving a hint of a Southern accent. "I've just come back from Paris. I promised her daughter that if I was in Dallas, on business, as I'd planned, I'd stop by and tell her mother she sent her love."

Tina Kendrick's alive – this old woman knows that!

"Please come in to the sittin' room." Mrs Kendrick's maid said, glowing. "I'll tell Miz Kendrick you's here."

He sat in a white wicker chair that once, he suspected, had been porch furniture. The two chairs and table graced with a vase of artificial flowers comprised the room's furniture. The drapes that blocked the strong summer sunlight were faded as though from too many washings.

He stood up with a smile as a small woman with an erect, almost regal, bearing came into the room. She was unnaturally pale, her eyes exuding alarm.

"Mrs Kendrick, my name is Mitchell Logan. As I told your maid, I've just returned from Paris. I met your daughter there at the Opera. We—"

"My daughter Elaine lives in Atlanta," she spat the words at him, defying him to claim anything else.

"I don't know Atlanta," he lied. "It was your daughter Tina that I met in Paris. We both happened to attend a performance of—"

"My daughter Tina is dead. She died in Paris in a fire." Olivia Kendrick interrupted in rage. "Leave my house. I have nothing to say to you!" She spun round and stalked from the room.

Swearing to himself Mitch went out of the house. Why was the old woman lying? She *was* lying. The maid knew the truth! He walked down the steps, his thoughts chaotic. Where the hell did he go from here?

"Mist' Logan!" A breathless feminine voice stopped him. He turned to face Olivia Kendrick's maid. Tears were streaming down her face. "Please, suh, I need to talk to you." She paused a moment. "Will you be goin' back to Paris?"

"Yes, I will." Her attitude seemed to hope for that, he interpreted.

"Miz Tina – she alive. I wuz her maid when I wuz fourteen. I went with her when she married Mist' Eric. Her mama scared to tell you." She pulled an envelope from a pocket of her dress, held it up for him to see. "Heah's her last letter, jes' three weeks ago." Mitch made a mental note of the return address. "Iffen you see Miz Tina again, you tell her Lucinda is takin' good care of her mama. And her mama loves her very much. She keeps all her letters in a pretty pink box covered with seashells."

Twenty

There was an exultant spring in Mitch's step as he walked away from Olivia Kendrick's house. He'd known this was a long shot – but he'd hit the jackpot. He'd have Caroline Hampton eating out of his hand. What else could she do?

At the hotel he put through a call to Adrienne, willing her to be home.

"Miz Carstairs' residence," the housekeeper said, as coached by Adrienne.

"This is Mr Logan. I'd like to speak to Miss Adrienne, please."

"Yessuh, jes' one minute please."

Moments later Adrienne's voice came to him. "You're in Dallas?"

"I'm in Dallas. I've been here less than three hours – and guess what? Tina Hampton is very much alive and living in Paris!"

"Her mother admitted it?" Disbelief blended with malicious pleasure in Adrienne's voice.

"No. But I scared her shitless." Mitch chuckled. "Don't forget, Tina was wanted for murder. I don't think there's a statute of limitations in murder cases. But," he drawled, "her maid – who used to be Tina's maid – was so touched when I said I'd seen Tina in Paris that she came running after me. She told me Tina's alive and that she writes to her mother regularly."

"Oh, wow! Queen Caroline is going to tumble right off her throne."

"By the way, when is Caroline in Atlanta and when is she in Washington? Does she have a definite schedule?"

"She's a very systematic lady. According to Liz, she's in their Washington D.C. house on Monday, Tuesday and Wednesday – the rest of the week she's in Atlanta."

"This is Wednesday, so she'll be in Atlanta tomorrow."

"Right, she takes the train from Washington tonight. She'll be here tomorrow morning. What are you going to do now?" Adrienne demanded avidly.

"I'm drafting a telegram," he told her. "Tomorrow I'll go in search of the Western Union office here in Dallas. Caroline Hampton is about to receive the shock of her life. She's living with a bigamist. She's the mother of three illegitimate children." He paused. "You don't say a word about this to anybody, Adrienne. That would ruin everything."

"Not a word," she vowed.

As was customary Caroline went directly to the mill from the train. Matthew would take her luggage to Hampton House. Ellen greeted her with a cup of coffee, the way she'd done all those years ago when she was first Caroline's secretary.

"How's Washington?" Ellen asked affectionately.

"It's never been my favorite town." Caroline's smile was wry. "But then you know that."

"There's rumor of an imminent strike over at the Murdoch mill," Ellen reported, "but I suspect it's just talk. The workers are scared to death at the prospect of losing jobs. Striking won't help that."

"How're Janet and Wendy?" Caroline asked, realizing that she had not included Kevin in the question, but whenever the mention of a strike in the mills came up, she was reminded of Kevin's occupation.

"They're getting by." Ellen's eyes were somber. "Most people are feeling the pinch these days. I know they say in Washington that this year is better than last, but don't try to explain that to all the people out of work."

"It's not just the working class who're hurting," Caroline said. "There are so many small business people who've lost out, salesmen without jobs, stenographers and secretaries. How are they supposed to survive?"

"I thought with all of President Roosevelt's 'bright young people' pouring into Washington we'd have some answers." Ellen sounded wistful. "But we hear weird reports like Henry Ford saying that the boys and young men riding the freight trains around the country are getting 'the best education in the world', and some big wheel at Sears, Roebuck insists that relief should be no more than a 'bare subsistence allowance'. Let him try to live on the three dollars a week families on relief receive!"

"Miss Caroline, this just arrived for you." The office boy handed over a Western Union envelope.

"Thanks, Ralph."

Caroline ripped open the envelope. The sender was Mitchell Logan. Her heart began to pound. Liz's warning about his union activities tickertaped across her brain.

> YOUR PREDECESSOR IS ALIVE IN PARIS. COULD CAUSE GREAT EMBARRASSMENT. WE NEED TO TALK. WILL PHONE ON RETURN TO ATLANTA.

Caroline's face was ashen. "Oh, my God!"

"Caro, what is it?"

"Read this –" Caroline handed the sheaf of yellow paper to Ellen.

Ellen was bewildered. "I don't understand –"

"He's talking about Tina. He's trying to blackmail me. To make me bring his union into the mill."

"He's bluffing. We all know Tina's dead!"

"We thought we knew that." Caroline fought for calm. How could this be happening? "Eric had filed for divorce, but then he dropped the suit because we were told that Tina had died in that fire –"

"Who told you she'd died?" Ellen pressed her.

"The Kendricks' family attorney. He told Eric there was no need to proceed with the divorce because Tina was dead. He said that her brother Chad had cabled the news to her parents. I remember it as though it was yesterday. We were all so shocked. Why would Chad lie about that?" But before Ellen could reply, Caroline came up with the answer. "He did that because Tina was wanted for murder. By saying she was dead, he knew the case would be marked closed. That's what the family wanted."

"There was an item in the *Constitution*," Ellen said, "announcing her death."

"The Kendricks stood by in silence while Eric and I were married," Caroline raged. "If what the man says is true –" Now her mind charged into action. "Call Eric's office in Washington, Ellen. He'll be tied up now in the Senate. Leave word for him to phone me as soon as possible." She hesitated. "Say that everybody's well." He'd be so anxious – but this had to be dealt with quickly.

Caroline repeated the contents of the telegram only to Sophie. No need to upset the children just yet. She knew Ellen would say nothing to anyone else. It was unlikely, she warned herself, that she'd hear from Eric until this evening. He was so conscientious about attending every session of the Senate.

As usual she ate lunch from a tray in her office. Ellen and Sophie joined her. The three women were shaken by what lay ahead.

"Caro, it could be just a ploy to frighten you into letting this man unionize the mill. He knows if you go ahead with unionizing, half the battle for the entire state will be won."

"But how can I let this man disrupt the mill? Of all the unions that have tried to get through to our workers, his is the one most prone to violence. We know how ugly – how deadly – these situations can become!" Caroline closed her eyes in anguish for a moment. "But how can I expose the family to what this monster threatens? How can I allow Eric's career to be destroyed?"

The day dragged by. Caroline debated about whether to remain at the mill to await Eric's call or to go home early and wait for it there. While she considered this, Eric phoned.

"Caro, what's up?" Despite his calm tones, his anxiety showed through.

"Eric, I don't want to talk about this over the phone. Everybody's all right," she assured him, "but there's a problem that needs immediate discussion."

"I can still make tonight's train to Atlanta," he said with the same calm he had displayed in every crisis through the years.

"I'll be at Terminal Station tomorrow with the car," Caroline said with an air of relief.

"Whatever it is, Caro," Eric said softly, "we'll see it through together."

Somehow, she would survive the intervening hours, Caroline told herself. Logan probably wouldn't call until the day after tomorrow. It was a long trip from Dallas to Atlanta. She and Eric would face him together. But she knew she faced a sleepless night.

Can Tina be alive?

Caroline was at Terminal Station forty minutes before Eric's train was due to arrive. She'd slept little in the course of the night. She tried to tell herself this was all an absurd nightmare. *No way could Tina be alive.*

At last Eric's train was announced. She hurried from the waiting room to greet him. She stood impatiently among the clusters of people meeting the train. Passengers began to disembark. The atmosphere became convivial. She grew anxious that Eric didn't appear. Had he missed the train? And then she saw him emerging from the pullman. Encased in relief, she darted forward to greet him, to be gathered into his warm, reassuring embrace.

In the car – fighting for calm – she told him about the telegram from Mitchell Logan. The words etched on her brain. "Liz, told me. The man's a union organizer."

"Who hopes to blackmail you into letting his union into the mill." Eric's face tightened in rage.

"I should be hearing from him tomorrow. I know about his union. The worst of the lot. It's supposed to be communist-backed." Her words were tumbling over one another in her rush to brief Eric. "I know his story sounds insane, but Eric, could it possibly be true?" Her eyes pleaded for denial.

"We'll meet with him. I think he's trying to scare the hell out of you. We can play that game, too."

"We never saw a death certificate," Caroline reminded him.

"Hell, her brother wrote that she'd died! What else did we need to know?"

"I'm not going in to the mill today. In this state I couldn't make a rational decision." Her laugh was shaky. "Sophie and Andrew can handle the situation."

"You need a day off." Even when the mill was officially closed, she went in to her office. "You know what we're going to do? After one of Mattie's superb breakfasts –" he paused, his eyes tender – "I'm sure you didn't have breakfast this morning –" She shook her head in agreement. "We're going into town and visit a travel agency. Pick up some brochures, ask some questions. When this nightmare is over, we're taking ourselves on a real vacation. We haven't done that in years. There's always been some crisis at the mill or some major problem in the Senate each time we planned a vacation."

"You may have to go to Paris," she pointed out. "To track down the truth on this business."

He abandoned his attempt at lightheartedness. "My mind tells me there's no truth in this, but we have to be prepared for whatever this man Logan throws at us. If I have to go to Paris, so be it."

"We won't see him at the mill," Caroline said with a touch of defiance. "I don't want our workers to see him coming in there. We'll see him at the house. But damn it, Eric!" Her hands tightened on the wheel. "How dare he come up with a story like this!"

* * *

Late in the afternoon Caroline received a call from Mitchell Logan.

"I've just returned to Atlanta," he said after introducing himself. "I suggest we meet tomorrow morning. I can be at the mill by eight."

"Not at the mill," she said coldly. "At Hampton House. My husband and I will expect you at nine." Let him see that she was in charge. Let him understand that she regarded Eric as her husband – despite his allegations. "Do you know the address?"

"I'll find Hampton House." He was terse. "I'll be there at nine."

Off the phone Caroline struggled for composure. This was insane. Yet her mind warned her that Logan could be right. They should have demanded a copy of Tina's death certificate before Eric called off the divorce proceedings.

"Should we tell Liz and Josh what's happening?"

"No need at this point," Eric said after a moment. "Why upset them?" But his eyes told Caroline that he was nervous about the meeting tomorrow morning with Mitchell Logan.

"I know the time will come when I'll have to allow a union into the mill. I've been fighting with myself to accept this. I've always prided myself on doing good by our workers. Perhaps it hasn't been enough."

"In these times, Caro, they're grateful for whatever work you can provide," Eric said gently.

"When are these bad times going to end?" Caroline asked. "How much longer can people endure such hardships?"

At nine exactly Mattie ushered Mitchell Logan into the library at Hampton House. Caroline and Eric stood side by side, as though announcing their unity, while the union organizer strode into the room.

"Mr Logan, please sit down," Eric told him.

"Thank you." Logan sat in a comfortable armchair, radiating

confidence. How arrogant he is, Caroline thought. He waited while Caroline and Eric sat on the sofa opposite before proceeding. "I see no point in wasting time on small talk." He allowed himself a faint smile. "I have definite knowledge that Tina Hampton is very much alive. She writes regularly from Paris to her mother in Dallas. You may recall her maid, Lucinda." His eyes moved from Caroline to Eric. "Lucinda cares for her mother now. Lucinda showed me a letter that arrived just three weeks ago."

"The letter could be a fraud," Eric said.

Logan's smile combined amusement with condescension. "Tina lives in Paris under the name of Tina Kendrick." He reached into a pocket of his jacket, pulled out a sheet of paper. "Here's her address. This means, Senator, that you are a bigamist." His eyes challenged Eric to deny this. "Now under certain circumstances I will agree to forget I ever received this information."

"Surely you don't expect us to accept your word, Mr Logan." Eric's tone was scurrilous. "We're familiar with the steps the unions will take in their desperation to infiltrate the Southern textile mills."

"Have a private detective check it out – or go to Paris, see for yourself. I'm sure you wouldn't want this matter to become public knowledge."

"I'll go to Paris." Eric gazed at him with contempt. "I don't believe this monstrous story." Yet Caroline sensed an alarmed ambivalence in him.

"I'll give you two weeks." Logan's smile was infuriating to Caroline. "After that we sit down to negotiate – or every newspaper in Georgia and in Washington D.C.," he emphasized, "will know that the Senator is living in a bigamous relationship and has fathered three illegitimate children."

"Two weeks is not very long," Eric shot back.

"Ships make it to Cherbourg in five days." A supercilious note in Logan's voice now. He knew he'd put them on the defensive, Caroline thought in silent rage.

"You're forgetting the train trip to New York," Eric pointed out. "We're talking about fourteen days of travel time alone."

"I'm not sure my husband should undertake what's probably an unnecessary trip."

"Sixteen days," Logan sparred. "I've given you Tina Hampton's address in Paris. In a matter of hours after your ship docks at Cherbourg you'll come face to face with your wife, Senator." He shot a triumphant glance at Caroline.

Caroline exchanged a loaded glance with Eric. They both knew they must discover the truth.

"I'll leave for New York tonight," Eric said after a pregnant moment. "I'll be back in sixteen days, with proof that Tina died years ago in a fire in Paris, as her brother Chad informed us. And if you pursue this insanity, we'll take you to court for libel."

But what if Tina is alive?

Twenty-One

"Liz and Josh must be told," Caroline said, and Eric nodded.

"Tell them to come for dinner tonight. Victor, too. Just say that there's a matter of importance that must be discussed."

"We'll give Jason and Daisy the evening off," Caroline decided. "Mattie can serve dinner." She allowed herself a faint smile. "There's little that happens in this house that slips past Mattie."

She sensed the uneasy curiosity in Josh and then in Liz when she explained the reason for her call. But they understood they must wait until she and Eric chose to speak. They knew that only a matter of urgency would bring their father from Washington at this time. Francis, who was oblivious of the anxious undercurrents, was delighted his father was home, and asked no questions.

After dinner Caroline contrived to send Francis on a trumped-up errand.

"It's important you deliver this envelope to Mr Russell personally," she told him. Jim Russell had been alerted to expect it. Eric had discussed the situation with him at length. He, too, was disturbed by the possible ramifications.

Not until the others gathered in the library for coffee did Eric explain his presence in town. Caroline felt their shock as they listened.

"I leave for New York in the morning. The following night I'll sail for Paris aboard the *Ile de France*."

"Mitch Logan's bluffing." Liz was outraged. "He didn't expect you to try to establish the truth!"

"I don't want his despicable union in our mill. He's scum." Caroline exuded contempt. In a corner of her mind she remembered that Liz yearned to see all textile workers represented by a union. Did Josh feel that way, too? "But if –" She paused, fighting for composure. "If what Logan claims is true – and we don't know that it is – then he has us over the proverbial barrel."

"Mama, you can't let him into the mill!" Liz protested. "A decent union, yes, but not Mitch Logan's."

"I can't expose your father to the kind of scandal he threatens." All at once Caroline felt drained of strength. "I can't expose you and Josh to that."

"Mama, let's not assume there's truth in this," Josh said gently and turned to his father. "You're going to Paris. You'll learn the truth. Then you and Mama make decisions."

Caroline called Terminal Station, arranged Eric's train reservations for the following day. Despite the late hour Eric phoned the necessary Washington official at his home and arranged for him to issue an almost-instant passport – to be delivered to him by courier when his Atlanta to New York train made its Washington D.C. stop. In the morning – before his train was to depart – he secured a reservation for a first-class cabin aboard the luxurious *Ile de France*. He was relieved that a reservation was available. It always amazed him that in such horrendous times there were those who continued to live as though this was still the Roaring Twenties.

On the long train trip to New York Eric searched his mind for answers to the problems that lay ahead. He vacillated in his thinking. At one moment he was convinced Logan was grandstanding, bluffing – no foundation in what he claimed. The next he worried that surely Logan knew they'd not accept his mere word. They'd demand proof of what he said.

He lay sleepless most of the night, awoke exhausted. How the hell were they to cope if Tina should be alive? Why would Chad have lied that way? The same mocking answer came up each time: the Kendrick family wanted the police file on Tina closed and the only way to do that was to claim she was dead. Chad had been dead for four years – there was no way to confront him now.

The following evening Eric was at the pier to board the *Ile de France*. His mind darted back through the years to his honeymoon with Tina. They'd sailed first to England, then to France. Onboard ship that first night he had been unnerved by the way Tina flirted with the ship's captain. But not until Paris had he discovered that she was unfaithful.

He closed his eyes for a moment, remembered the night he'd walked into their hotel suite at the Ritzn Paris to find Tina in bed with a Hungarian diplomat. They both thought he was at a party given by the American Ambassador. Tina had remained at the hotel saying she had a headache. He never touched Tina after that night.

This evening there was the usual air of festivity on the pier as passengers arrived to board the huge, black-funneled ship. There was a kind of magic about sailing on the *Ile de France*, he mused.

Feeling little of the gaiety that surrounded him, he was directed to his first-class cabin. He knew the days ahead would be fraught with tension – each night he'd toss sleeplessly, waiting for morning. He'd take most of his meals in his cabin rather than in the huge main dining room.

He remembered the lively description of the ship's accommodations provided by the travel agent who'd arranged his reservations. "There's a marvelous first-class lounge and a replica of a Parisian sidewalk café, even with the awnings you'd find there. And statues, bas-reliefs, paintings." But all he wished to discover was that Mitchell Logan was either a superb liar or misinformed.

The boat-train from Cherbourg brought him into Gare St Lazare in Paris. From there he took a taxi to the Hôtel Crillon. He registered and was escorted to an elegant Louis XV suite with a view of the place de la Concorde. The sitting room had a handsome, high, curving ceiling and a magnificent crystal chandelier. He paid momentary tribute to the charm of the suite.

First thing tomorrow morning, he promised himself, he would travel to the Left Bank address where Tina presumably lived. He would find her apartment, if, in truth, she was alive. His college French was rusty, but he would manage.

Again, sleep was elusive. The memory of Mitch Logan's confidence unnerved him at intervals. But a sharp con man would have that effect, he thought defiantly.

He remembered all those years ago how Chad had talked about the rebellious year he'd spent in Paris. On the Left Bank, favored by the young. But Chad had died four years ago. Tina would be on her own.

Just after dawn he fell into heavy sleep and awoke four hours later. He called room service for coffee and a croissant. Thus fortified he prepared for the day. A glance out a window told him the city was encased in fog. He would take a taxi to his destination.

His heart was pounding when he emerged from the taxi on the narrow cobblestone street. A shabby area, he noted, unlike the section on the Left Bank favored by artists and writers and expatriates. Had Chad, too, lived here until his death? The Kendricks had little money. His widowed mother could not have supported Tina and Chad for long after their flight to Paris. How had they survived?

Here it was. The address he sought. He opened the street-level door of the tired, old building and walked into a dark, ill-smelling foyer. A woman was walking down the badly lit stairs. Marshaling his shaky French he asked if she knew in which flat Tina Kendrick lived – praying to be told there was no such tenant.

"At the top," the woman told him with an air of contempt.

"That scum, bringing –" She used a phrase he couldn't interpret but its meaning was clear. "Once this was a respectable house!" Eric felt a tightness in his throat. Oh, God, that man Logan was right! "But that Tina will be asleep," she warned.

He climbed the stairs to the attic flat, knocked. His mind in chaos. There was no response. He knocked again, with greater force – determined to awaken the woman inside who called herself Tina Kendrick. Clinging to the hope that this was some terrible mistake.

In heavily accented French the woman inside responded in colorful language. Tina's voice, Eric thought in disbelief. All these years later he recognized it.

The door swung wide. A woman stood there in a bedraggled, sheer black nightgown. For a moment he thought he was gazing at a stranger. She was fragilely thin, yet her face was bloated, her skin a chalky white. But she stared at him with Tina's eyes.

"Tina –" His voice was harsh with shock.

Half-awake, she squinted at him. "Oh my God, I don't believe it!" She broke into raucous laughter. "Eric!" All at once alarm darkened her eyes. "How did you find me?"

"Through Lucinda."

"What are you doing here? Mama wrote – oh, a long time ago – that you married Caroline after I went away. But you can't do that." She pulled him inside the room, closed the door behind him. A cunning smile lit her face. "You're still my husband," she said in triumph. "You can't have two wives." Her meaning was obvious.

"You're wanted for murder –" He'd have to play her game, he realized.

"Not in Paris." He sensed the wheels spinning in her mind. "Let's make a deal, Eric. I won't say a word about you still being my husband – that you're a bigamist. You just send me money every month and I won't say a word. And to seal our deal," she stipulated, giddily smug, "you go down and buy us a bottle of the best bourbon in the store. Go on, do it. Go, Eric."

In a daze Eric left the attic studio, went down into the street to search for a shop where he could buy a bottle of bourbon.

Tina's alive. How do I handle this?

Tina was afraid to come back to Atlanta. She knew she'd be tried for murder. He could send her a check each month – the way she'd said. *How can I file for divorce against a wife who's supposed to be dead?*

Struggling to clear his head, he found a shop where he could buy a bottle of bourbon, then headed back for the attic studio that was Tina's home. He'd make her understand that, yes, he would send her money each month. But what next? How could he and Caroline face the world knowing their lives were in shambles?

At her door he knocked. There was no response. He tried the knob. The door swung open. Tina lay asleep across the bed. He was aware of an odd, sickly sweet odor in the room.

He deposited the bottle on a table by the window and left. Tomorrow morning, when his head was clearer, he'd come back and talk with Tina. Instinct told him she would sleep for hours. And her evening, he told himself in disbelief, was spent at a profession he couldn't face giving a name.

For the next few hours he roamed about the streets of Paris. Seeing nothing, searching for answers that refused to come. At last he was conscious of hunger, returned to his hotel and ordered food to be sent up to his suite.

Exhausted from the hours of aimless walking, he fell into a disturbed, intermittent slumber. In waking moments he longed to talk with Caroline, but instinct told him he must not discuss the situation over the long-distance phone. Nobody, inadvertently or otherwise, most overhear what they had to say. Tomorrow evening he was scheduled to set sail for New York. All arranged to fit Mitchell Logan's time slot.

How was he to convince that conniving bastard Logan that Tina had died all those years ago? How was he to face the fact that Logan might go to the necessary lengths to prove him wrong?

* * *

Eric woke with a start. Never mind that Tina would probably sleep till afternoon, he told himself in a surge of impatience. He was going back to her flat, work out a payment schedule with her.

She'd be skeptical of monthly checks, he reasoned. Somehow, in the stretch of hours before he was to board the ship for his return trip to New York he must make arrangements with a French bank to hold funds to be distributed to Tina at monthly intervals. *But how are Caroline and I to deal with Mitchell Logan?*

He dressed in haste, left the hotel, found a taxi to take him to Tina's squalid Left Bank studio. Swearing at intervals because his French was so inadequate. But a bank would have an interpreter, he told himself. He could make the monetary arrangements for Tina in the course of an hour.

En route to Tina's flat, he gazed out the taxi window without seeing, vaguely aware that yesterday's fog had dissipated. Could he in some fashion convince Logan that Tina was not alive, that Lucinda's story was a fabrication? His mind was in too much of a muddle to think clearly, he chastised himself. Back in New York he'd sit down with Jim and figure out how he could contrive to divorce Tina without exposing the ugly truth.

He left the taxi at Tina's house, stood immobile for a moment at the curb. What was going on here? Police were interrogating a pair of overwrought women at the door. His French was not equal to translating what was being said in those volatile tones. Instinct told him to move on before becoming involved.

Then he spied the woman he'd met yesterday, who'd spoken with such contempt about Tina. On impulse he approached her again. In his poor French he asked what had happened in the house.

"Ah, it's you again –" This much he understood, nodded. "*Elle est mort.*"

"Tina Kendrick?" he gasped in shock.

"*Oui.*" She spat on the sidewalk.

"How?" He reeled in disbelief.

She burst into an elaborate explanation, while another woman joined them, nodding excitedly in agreement.

Eric struggled to follow her French. She was astonished that Tina had acquired the money to buy an expensive bottle of bourbon. The bourbon and the drugs she'd taken earlier had killed her, the woman announced with a melodramatic flair. She and other neighbors had overheard the police discuss this. All at once Eric remembered the odd odor in Tina's flat. Opium.

He left the scene, his mind in high gear. All within the course of the day he must contact the police, arrange for a decent burial for Tina. But Mitchell Logan must believe that Tina died thirty some years ago, or he and Caroline would be blackmailed for the rest of their lives.

With manufactured calm he contacted the police, provided funds for Tina's burial. He ignored their curious stares, the philosophical shrugs at his explanation that he was a "friend of the family" who happened to be in Paris at this time. Only when this was done did he call Caroline. He breathed a grateful sigh when she was at last on the line.

"Caro, no questions please." He was searching for words. "Meet me in New York City when I arrive. Plan to be there for at least three days. Make a reservation for us at the Plaza."

"Are you all right, Eric?" She allowed herself this one question.

"I'm all right," he assured her gently. "But we need to take care of some matters in New York. We'll work this out some way," he promised. "I'll come directly from the ship to the Plaza."

"I'll be waiting." He felt her tension, the questions that she longed to ask. But they could take no chances of being overheard in indiscreet conversation. "I love you, Caro."

"I love you, Eric."

"Tell Liz and Josh the problem will be worked out."

Could he bluff his way through this? Could he out-fox Mitchell Logan? He felt a tightening in his throat. So much depended upon how he handled the situation. The family's future hung in the air. *Can I handle this?*

Twenty-Two

At Pennsylvania Station in New York City Caroline climbed into a taxi, instructed the driver to take her to the Plaza. At intervals through the years she had spent brief visits here with Eric – on business for the mill or fulfilling Eric's political obligations. But today her mind was assaulted by questions with hurricane force.

Ever since Eric's transatlantic phone call she'd struggled with soaring frustration to read between the lines of what he'd said. She'd told Liz and Josh what was happening. Liz had offered to accompany her to New York, but she'd brushed this aside.

"No need to drag you up there. I'll manage on my own." Damn it, she ran a mill with hundreds of employees – surely she could handle this situation. "As soon as I have answers, I'll call you. It's futile to speculate."

Did Liz take this as a rejection, she asked herself in retrospect. How often words were misinterpreted! In truth, she never stopped worrying about Liz. She knew Liz wasn't happy, yet what could she do to change that? She was ever aware that since Debbie had died something was missing in Liz's marriage.

The taxi pulled up before the French Renaissance-style masterpiece that was the Plaza. When in New York, she and Eric always stayed here. Always they asked for a suite with a view of Central Park. This time she'd forgotten. But this wasn't a vacation. It was a traumatic occasion.

Eric had tried so hard to be reassuring, yet he hadn't come

out and said, "The problem is solved." What had happened in Paris that he couldn't discuss in a phone call?

Settled in her suite at the Plaza, she geared herself to await Eric's arrival. The reservation clerk must have remembered their earlier requests. Their suite looked down on the park.

At regular intervals her eyes strayed to her watch. Finally, churning with impatience, she phoned the shipping offices to inquire about the arrival time of Eric's ship.

"The ship has docked," a cordial voice informed her. "Passengers have been disembarking for the past twenty minutes."

Ten minutes later, as she paced about the small sitting room, she heard a tentative knock at the door. Eagerly she rushed to respond. Eric stood there with a tender smile. While the bellhop deposited his valise in the sitting room and waited politely at Eric's signal, he reached to embrace Caroline.

"There's much to tell," he said softly and paused to tip the bellhop.

"Thank you, sir." The smiling bellhop made a swift retreat.

"Oh, Eric, I've been so worried –" Caroline's eyes searched his.

With the door closed, Eric pulled her down on the sofa with him, began the report of his encounter with Tina.

"In a way I feel responsible for her death," he said somberly. "It was the mixture of drugs and alcohol that killed her."

"Not your fault," Caroline refuted. "She insisted you bring her the bottle of bourbon."

"I arranged for a copy of her death certificate to be sent to the house." His smile was wry. "Money can be most helpful. The certificate should be there by the time we arrive."

"Suppose it isn't?" With fresh anxiety she remembered Mitchell Logan's time slot.

"It'll be there."

"Why did you ask me to come to New York?" She was bewildered.

"Caro," he began lovingly, "will you do me the honor of becoming my legal wife?"

"You mean for us to be married here?"

"We can do that without the word hitting the Georgia headlines. We'll just be a man and woman of a certain age, who've decided to marry. A judge here in New York City – whom I've known for years and who'll understand the need for secrecy – will marry us."

"But what about Mitchell Logan?" Alarm soared to the surface again. "He'll still have the winning card."

"He may have lost it." Eric's face acquired the stubborn intensity she knew so well. What she called his "fighting mode". "We'll confront him in rage. He sent me on a crazy chase across the Atlantic with no validity. I'll wave the death certificate before him – with the date carefully changed. He'll be too shaken to demand a closer inspection. I'll warn him that he and his union will be sued for libel if he utters his ridiculous accusations to a living soul."

"Do we dare?" Caroline was ambivalent, but hope was already winning out.

"We dare," he insisted. "But let's pray there's no slip-up on receiving the death certificate." Unexpectedly he chuckled. "I paved the way with lavish greenery of the most respected kind."

Liz waited in the parking area of the hospital for Victor to join her. Mama and Papa had arrived on the morning's train from New York. Mama had said, "If Victor can get away, bring him to the house with you." She'd waited anxiously to hear from them in New York, but there'd been no word. Victor had insisted she not call them at their hotel. "Don't push them, Liz – give them room."

Ah, Victor was coming. In her impatience she leaned forward to open the door on the passenger side for him.

"Mama said if you were all tied up, it was OK," she told him with an air of apology.

"If your mother called, it's important." His smile was meant to be reassuring, yet she suspected that Victor too was uneasy.

At the house Mattie told them to go into the library.

"Miz Caroline and Mist' Eric are waitin' for you there." Mattie's face was solemn. "And Mist' Josh said he'd be right down."

After the initial warm greeting, Liz searched her mother's face, then her father's. Despite their air of calm, Liz was conscious of a disturbing tension.

Josh strode into the library moments later. "I had to take a call from a patient. How was your trip?" He was trying so hard to be casual, Liz thought.

"Eventful." Eric's smile was wry.

"You have to know what's happened," Caroline said. "Eric, explain everything to them."

In an aura of unreality they listened to a detailed report of the events in Paris. Then they were told about the marriage ceremony in the judge's study in New York. This was like a bad dream, Liz thought, struggling to assimilate everything her father had said.

"I've called Mitchell Logan," Caroline picked up. "I told him to be here at four this afternoon."

"Suppose this creep doesn't buy what you tell him?" Josh was somber. "What's the next step?"

"We'll have to face that when – *if*," Eric emphasized, "it happens. Right now let's take one step at a time."

"Most of the workers don't want a union," Caroline said defensively. "And we'll do nothing to fight Logan's efforts – unless he resorts to violence. We won't have our workers victimized."

"The violence comes from belligerent employers fighting the unions," Victor reminded her. "That won't happen at the Hampton Mill."

"A renegade union will scare workers into joining," Caroline shot back. "That'll be Logan's tactics – and he wants to be sure the mill won't threaten firings if they join. Logan's demanding union recognition before he resorts to tough measures to force workers to join up. He's sharp."

"If you can't out-bluff this man," Victor warned, "he can blackmail you for the rest of your lives."

"Then it's up to me to give an Academy Award performance," Eric said with grim determination. "Pray for me." His eyes swept the other four. "All of you."

At exactly four o'clock Mattie ushered Mitchell Logan into the library at Hampton House. Caroline contrived to appear serene as they exchanged casual greetings. Eric seemed almost arrogant, she thought nervously. Don't let him overplay his hand.

"You were misinformed," Eric told Logan. "There was no Tina Hampton at the address you gave me. I—"

"She could have moved." Logan bristled. "I saw the letter with that return address. Three weeks ago she was alive in Paris. I—"

"As I said, you were misinformed," Eric broke in with an air of barely contained rage, "but I pursued the matter. Tina Kendrick died thirty-six years ago. I have a copy of her death certificate." Which had arrived just four hours ago, Caroline thought with gratitude. "How dare you send me chasing across the Atlantic on the strength of what a deluded maid tells you! Lucinda knows that Mrs Kendrick believes Tina is still alive so she has a reason to go on living. She lied to you." Now Eric reached into his jacket, withdrew a copy of Tina's death certificate. "The French government says otherwise!" He thrust the official paper before Logan – too rattled to demand closer scrutiny. "If word of this fairy tale ever emerges anywhere in this world, you and your union will face a million-dollar libel suit. Tell that to your superiors!"

"Now if you'll excuse us, Mr Logan, we have more important matters to handle," Caroline said coldly. "Good day."

For weeks, it seemed to Caroline, she walked around in a daze. Fearful of repercussions. Liz told her via Adrienne that Mitchell Logan was now in fierce combat with Todd Murdoch. Logan was throwing all his efforts into unionizing the workers at

Murdoch's mill. Caroline was betting this would never happen. For the Hamptons the madness with Mitchell Logan was over. The family could breathe freely again.

At intervals Caroline told herself she must consider the possibility of a decent union coming into the mill. Josh's words after the confrontation with Logan lingered in her mind: "Mama, if you accept the union, the other mills will go along. There'll be no violence. And the workers need a union – a decent union, not Mitch Logan's – to fight for them. Other mills don't treat their workers with respect, the way you do."

But Andrew and Sophie persuaded her to hold back on any such decision. Senator Wagner of Massachusetts and Congressman William P. Connery Jr of the same state had introduced legislation that would create a National Labor Relations Board.

"It'll guarantee the right of workers to bargain as a group with managements via unions that are chosen in government-supervised elections," Andrew pointed out. "The Board will define unfair labor practices."

"Let's face it," Sophie added. "This damnable Depression will never end until workers earn enough to buy what the country produces."

"You're saying we should increase wages?" Caroline was startled.

"We pay better than any mill in the country," Sophie reminded her, "and we're showing a minuscule profit."

Caroline debated for a moment. "Andrew, go over our records, see how much profit we show. That amount must go to increase wages. So for a time we'll operate without a profit. We'll survive."

Liz worried about Janet and her family. Secretly Janet had talked about trying for a job with the Works Progress Administration, which was supposed to provide three and a half million jobs. But Liz knew that Janet would not be eligible even to apply. Kevin had a job. The family had an income.

The WPA was for destitute families with no employed member.

With late summer heat invading Atlanta, Liz decided to go to Columbus to visit with Janet for a couple of days. Not that it would be any cooler in Columbus, but the heat was a good excuse.

"Janet's house is right by the river – if there's any breeze, they get it." School was out. Kathy would love to spend time with Wendy. And she herself was restless. As always. Early next week she and Kathy would drive to Columbus.

Perspiration glistening on her forehead, Janet ironed a shirt for Kevin.

"I don't know why you have to iron a clean shirt for me to wear to the office in this heat," Kevin grumbled. "Ten minutes after I put it on it'll be stained with sweat."

"You have to look decent in the office," Janet insisted.

"In the closet-sized office where I'm getting nothing accomplished," he taunted. "How long do you think the union's going to keep paying my wages when I'm getting nowhere with any of the mills? The workers are scared of their shadows, afraid they'll lose the little work they're getting. What chance have I got with them?"

Kevin had been especially bitter these past few weeks because he'd discovered she'd been applying again for jobs around town – though the prospect of her finding one was nil. But if she could land a job, they'd be so much more comfortable. She'd given up trying to work at one of the five-and-tens in town. When they hired, it was always some young girl. The one Saturday she was able to fill in for somebody, she'd spent the dollar she'd earned on a shirt for Kevin as a Father's Day present from Wendy and herself.

It broke Kevin's heart that she could even think about going out to work; it meant he couldn't provide for his family. Didn't he understand that times were changing? Women went out to work these awful days – when they were lucky enough to find jobs.

"Mist' Kevin –" Zeke, ever cheerful, came into the kitchen with a fan in tow. "I'm carryin' this to the office again. It helped a little yesterday."

"Nothing helps in this God-forsaken heat. But OK, bring it along."

Wendy burst into the kitchen with an anticipatory smile. "Mama, when do you think they'll be here?"

"Not for hours, sugar. They have to drive all the way from Atlanta." It bothered her that Liz and Kathy had to stay at a hotel for the two days they'd be here, but where could she put them up here? She hated their house, but the rent was only ten dollars a month. Their house in Atlanta had been modest, but this one was little better than a mill-town shack. Always reeking of kerosene from the cooking stove. Two tiny bedrooms – one that Kevin shared with Zeke and the other for Wendy and herself – plus the kitchen and the tiny sitting room.

Janet handed Kevin the shirt. "Here –"

Kevin pulled on the shirt. "All right, Zeke, let's get moving. Wendy, give your old man a goodbye kiss."

Kevin was grumpy much of the time, but he loved them, Janet told herself. Victor had tried so hard to talk him into a better mood. She could hear Victor's voice now: "Kevin, the legs are just to move you around. It's the mind that counts. Your mind is in tiptop shape." She suspected Kevin was relieved that it was necessary to share his bedroom with Zeke. Kevin had lost his legs. She had lost her husband.

With Kevin and Zeke out of the house and en route to the office, Janet focused on what to serve for lunch. It should be a party for the four of them, she thought in a burst of rebellion. Liz and Kathy hadn't been here for three months. More often Liz just drove down to pick up Wendy and her and drove them back to Atlanta to visit with Mama.

"Can I wear my new dress today?" Wendy wheedled,

bringing Janet back to the moment. New to Wendy, Janet's mind mocked. Kathy was a couple of inches taller than Wendy at the moment – an acceptable excuse for Wendy to inherit Kathy's dresses. Thank God Wendy liked that. "We won't play out in the dirt –"

Janet forced a smile. "Of course, sugar." It upset her that Wendy, young as she was, had to deal with family financial problems. "Go change now."

"What will we have for lunch? Will you bake a pie?"

"Oh, not in this heat." Janet shuddered. "We'll have ice cream," she promised and Wendy's face brightened.

"Chocolate?" Wendy pushed. "Kathy loves chocolate."

"Chocolate. Now scoot. And make sure your nails are clean."

Janet dug out her purse. This time of the month money was short. She always made a point of buying staples – like spaghetti and rice – when Kevin received his check from the New York office each month.

She opened her purse, frowned at the lack of bills in the side pocket. The change compartment offered only a couple of dimes and several pennies. All right, she thought, time to make another trip to Mr Johnson's jewelry store. Mr Johnson was always willing to buy something that was silver, though what he offered was shockingly small.

She went into the sitting room, inspected the contents of the small mahogany chest that had been her mother and stepfather's wedding gift. Here was stored what Janet, with an effort at humor, described as the "family assets". Wedding gifts, anniversary and birthday presents from the days before the stock crash that had moved her mother from comfortable, middle-class living to the desperate poverty that inflicted so many these days.

The chest of silver cutlery had gone – all of it; the exquisite Waterford crystal was gone. Janet hunted through the remains of what she called "the loot". With a tender smile she pulled out the silver cup and matching feeding dish that Caroline and Eric

Hampton had given her when Wendy was born. That would bring enough to buy ice cream and a chicken for lunch today.

"Wendy," Janet called. "Let's go see Mr Johnson at the jewelry store."

She always made this sound like a small adventure. But did Wendy see it that way? It was hard to know what went on inside kids' heads.

Twenty-Three

Right on schedule Liz drove into the pretty city of Columbus, rich with summer greenery, flowers in riotous bloom. They headed for the Ralston Hotel where she and Kathy would stay for their two nights in town. Janet lived just a few blocks away, in the heart of town. With the car parked they walked into the elegant, red-brick structure, registered, and were escorted to their room.

"We'll unpack later," Liz told Kathy. She was always grateful that Kathy never questioned the shabby lifestyle of her best friend.

They drove over to the dilapidated white clapboard house, were greeted joyously by Janet and Wendy. Liz was relieved that Kevin was at his office. Often she was conscious of a covert hostility in him. Janet and Wendy made a charming ceremony of inspecting the contents of the basket Liz had brought from Atlanta.

"Lunch will be ready in about twenty minutes," Janet said, striving for a festive air. "Wendy, take Kathy next door and show her the new kittens."

"How's Kevin?" Liz asked gently when they were alone.

"So bitter, so angry," Janet said. "Tell Vic how grateful I am for his talks with Kevin, but nobody can get through to Kevin these days."

"There has to be some way to reach him." Liz seemed to hesitate. "Janet, do you suppose he'd agree to see a psychiatrist? Vic has contacts."

"Kevin would never go to a psychiatrist. But thanks for trying."

The day sped past. At dinner Liz was conscious of the tension between Janet and Kevin. He was even impatient with Wendy.

"Is your mother going to recognize Mitch Logan's union?" he asked Liz while they lingered over tall, frosted glasses of ice tea.

Liz was startled. "No. Why should she?"

"The word around town is that Murdoch may be going with him. He's bad medicine." Kevin grunted in contempt.

"It's probably just rumor." Liz shrugged. "My mother doesn't think Murdoch will accept Logan's union. I don't know much about the business, of course." Kevin was seething, she surmised, because he thought Mama might be willing to work with someone other than himself.

"The day's coming when every mill in the country will be unionized," Kevin predicted. "How else will workers ever get a living wage?"

"Oh, did I tell you about Margaret Marsh?" Liz determinedly diverted the conversation into less hostile topics.

"What about Margaret?" Janet asked.

"You know that novel she's been working on for ever? Ten years, I guess. Well, she's sold it. It's going to be published! It'll be brought out under her single name – Margaret Mitchell."

Earlier than she'd anticipated, she and Kathy prepared to leave for the hotel. "This heat is so awful. It just makes everybody sleepy."

But far into the night – because sleep was elusive in the steamy weather – Liz thought about Janet and Kevin. Should she talk to Mama about considering Kevin's union – if Mama decided to go along with allowing a union into the mill? If Kevin could deliver the Hampton Mill, he'd be in the bosses' good graces. It would make life so much easier for Kevin and Janet. They could move back to Atlanta.

Mama knew the day was coming when she'd have to accept a union. Still, Kevin hadn't been able to organize much support from the workers.

* * *

Janet emerged from the bedroom she shared with Wendy. She was still wrapped in an aura of well-being because of Liz's presence today. His wheelchair as close to an open window as possible, though only a hot breeze came into the sitting room, Kevin stared out into the night.

"Wendy's fast asleep," Janet reported. "All tired out from the fun of being with Kathy for two days."

"So Lady Bountiful can go home feeling smug," Kevin drawled.

Janet tensed, trying to ignore Kevin's inference. This was not the first time he'd made snide remarks about Liz and her family. "Zeke says it's a good night for fishing. We'll have fried fish for supper tomorrow for sure."

"I don't want you to encourage Liz to come slumming down here," he ordered, his face taut.

"She isn't slumming, Kevin." She hadn't meant to sound antagonistic. She kept telling herself to avoid these encounters. "Liz and I have been best friends since kindergarten."

"She and her bloody family. They think they're so high and mighty living off the blood and sweat of their workers at the mill!" His voice was scathing.

"You know Caroline Hampton runs one of the best mills in the country," Janet shot back. "She pays more. She keeps the mill houses in decent condition. Her company store gives credit when families are strapped."

"If she'd let a union in, you can be damn sure she'd have to pay more. If I could go to the workers and make them believe she wouldn't fire them for joining a union, I'd make some headway." This was his familiar litany: "The workers are scared shitless to join a union. They're sure they'll be kicked out on their asses if they do!"

"In these terrible times all workers are afraid of their shadows," Janet said tiredly. It wasn't just working-class folks who were hurting. The professional people – teachers, doctors, lawyers – were fighting for survival.

"In other industries the unions are making headway!" He leaned forward, a vein pounding in his forehead. "Russia's got the right idea. Fight for the people in the street and to hell with the bosses!"

"Roosevelt's working hard to make things better. Look at the WPA, the Social Security Act."

"Small potatoes," he scoffed. "I tell you, the day has to come when communism takes over. And—"

"Kevin, don't talk like that!" she broke in, "we live in the best country in the world!"

"Bullshit. How do you think we're living?" he taunted. "How do you think the union keeps paying me for doing practically nothing? The money comes from Russia."

Janet stared at him in shock. She felt sick. At intervals she'd been suspicious of the union's backing. Now it was out in the open. "I don't want to hear anymore. I'm going to bed, Kevin. Goodnight."

Twenty-Four

Liz was relieved that the summer heat was on the wane in early October. It was so enervating, she thought as she changed into a fresh cotton frock for the family dinner that evening at Hampton House. Or was it just that she allowed small irritations to escalate out of boredom with her way of life? She felt instantly guilty at such thoughts. Considering the state of the world today she ought to be grateful that her family was so comfortable.

She worried constantly about Janet. Inadvertently Janet had let it slip that Kevin's salary had been cut by the union. How were they managing? Liz frequently asked herself. Janet was too proud to accept loans. Even Janet's mother found it difficult to persuade Janet to accept what little financial help she could manage.

"All I can do is invent holiday gift occasions," Ellen had confided in a candid moment. "Sometimes I think they'd be better off on Relief. But no," she corrected herself, "both Janet and Kevin are too proud for that." Everybody knew of families who went hungry on many nights because they couldn't bring themselves to accept Relief.

When the phone rang, Liz knew before she picked up that it would be Victor to say he would be late for dinner or couldn't be there at all. When he knew Papa was in town for a long weekend, he ought to try to be there.

"I'll be a little late," Victor said. "Don't let Mattie hold up dinner for me."

"All right, Vic." Couldn't he ever make dinner on time? "I'll tell Mattie to serve when dinner's ready."

She and Kathy arrived almost simultaneously with Andrew and Maureen. They explained that Andy was having dinner at a friend's house and would be sleeping over. Maureen held up crossed fingers. Liz understood; the sleepover was a "first". But Andy was more stable now and Andrew and Maureen were grateful to Victor for that.

Minutes later Josh arrived. "I wasn't sure I'd get away," he said, grinning. "There always seem to be some emergencies on weekend nights."

"Vic's still at the hospital." Liz refrained from sarcasm because Kathy was present.

"When did you see Janet last?" Josh asked with an effort at casualness.

"Oh, just this past Monday," Liz told him. "She's all right. Kevin's depressed . . ."

"He's had a rotten time," Caroline reminded her. Her mother always felt guilty that she had refused to discuss business with Kevin, Liz thought sympathetically. "Still, he does have a job. In these days that's something to be grateful for."

"You want to play checkers?" Kathy asked with a quick smile when Francis joined them in the sitting room.

"Yeah." His face brightened.

"You won't be playing for long," Caroline said. "Mattie said she'd be serving dinner in a few minutes."

"We'll play more later, Francis," Kathy told him. Young as she was, Liz thought tenderly, she understood that Francis needed special care.

By the time they gathered about the dinner table a chilly breeze drifted into the house. Jason lowered the windows. Liz frowned when her father and Josh abandoned casual conversation for a volatile discussion about the ugly situation in Spain.

"Look, the revolt again in Asturias is having repercussions all over Spain," Josh said heatedly. "There's street fighting in Barcelona and—"

"What's Asturias?" Francis asked, eager to share in the conversation.

"It's a province in Spain," Eric explained.

"Sorry to be late –" Victor came into the dining room with an apologetic smile and took his place at the table.

"Better late than never," Caroline said with a loving smile.

"We're talking about the fighting in Spain," Josh said. "The death rate's soaring. And there are rumors that reprisals will be made all over Spain."

"How many changes in government in the last year?" Victor grimaced. "Six or seven?"

"This is not dinner-table conversation," Caroline objected. "Let's settle on something more pleasant."

"Andrew and I saw *Mutiny on the Bounty* last night," Maureen contributed. "It was marvelous. Do try to see it while it's in town."

"I loved Bette Davis in *Dangerous*. I just may go see it a second time," Sophie confessed.

"The great escape of the thirties," Andrew said humorously, "the movie houses."

After dinner, while the men launched into more heated conversation about the troubles in Europe and Kathy and Francis played checkers, the women discussed local volunteer projects.

"Oh, I think the Techwood project is doing great," Maureen said enthusiastically. "I mean, the way they're clearing away hundreds of those awful old shanties and are replacing them with decent housing. Of course –" her smile was wry – "that's only a drop in the bucket to what's needed."

"I've been thinking about refurbishing the houses in the mill village," Caroline told the other women. "It would supply some much needed jobs."

"You can't afford that with the state of business these days," Sophie objected. "We're barely breaking even – though the three of us have cut back our salaries to not much more than the workers' pay."

"But we're not suffering." Caroline was grim. "The way so many people in this country are suffering."

In the midst of farewells Liz found herself in a brief, private exchange with her mother.

"I'm thinking about the union situation," Caroline confided to Liz. "I know you and Josh both feel it's time we made a deal with a union we feel is decent."

"Are you considering Kevin's union?" Liz's face lighted. "Oh, that would be such a boost for Kevin."

"I'll think about it." Caroline hedged. "But don't say anything yet to Janet."

Caroline sat at her desk in the office and contemplated the repercussions of allowing a union to come into the Hampton Mill. Not a conniving manipulator like Mitchell Logan. He was hungry for power, for all the money he could skim from union dues.

From what Janet and Ellen said, she was convinced that Kevin was sincere about wanting to improve the working conditions of textile workers. The Hampton Mill operated under good conditions, she told herself. No children under fourteen were ever hired. Their workers received the top pay in the textile industry – allowing a union in wouldn't create havoc for them. It would, however, lead the way to push unions into other textile mills where working conditions were horrendous. Where men and women worked a sixty-six hour week for nine dollars and fourteen-year-old children – sometimes even younger – worked in dangerous, unsanitary conditions for five dollars a week. Where they lived in constant fear of being thrown out of their jobs and their mill-owned houses. Maybe Liz and Josh were right. Maybe the time had come for the Hampton Mill to lead the way.

Caroline waited impatiently for Ellen to arrive. She would talk to her about setting up a meeting with Kevin. Ellen would be pleased, she thought. Ellen was so concerned about Kevin's future.

Ellen knocked sharply on the door in order to be heard over the clamor of the machines and walked into Caroline's office with the usual cup of coffee.

"It's a beautiful day outside," she said with a teasing smile. She knew Caroline had been at her desk since six, when the whistle blew for the workers to arrive for the day shift. "Do you still get up so early when you're in Washington?"

"Eric is at his desk at seven. I have breakfast with him at six," Caroline told her. "You live the good life," she joshed, "not showing up at the office until eight."

"How was dinner last night?" Ellen asked. As always, she'd been invited but had been involved in some church benefit.

"The usual. Much talk about politics, the rough state of the world. But I've been doing some thinking, Ellen –" Caroline took a swig of coffee then put down her cup – "about the union situation. When I consider it with a clear head, I know we have little to fear. Of course, I wouldn't want a rabble-rouser like Mitchell Logan heading a union that we had to deal with," she conceded. "But with Kevin it would be a different situation." She paused because Ellen seemed all at once upset. "What about Kevin's union?"

"Before you make a move," Ellen said after a moment's hesitation, "talk to Janet. Listen to what she has to say about that."

"All right, I'll call her."

"No, don't do that." Ellen frowned in thought. "Liz is driving down to Columbus on Friday afternoon to bring Janet and Wendy up here to stay with me for the weekend. Talk to her then."

"All right." Was Janet leaving Kevin after all this time? Caroline asked herself. She knew from what Ellen let slip at unwary moments that Kevin had become very difficult. But that wasn't like Janet. "I'll wait to discuss it with Janet when she's here in town."

On Saturday morning Caroline drove over to Ellen's modest

little house. She sat down with Ellen and Janet in the kitchen for coffee and casual conversation.

"Janet, Caroline needs to talk with you," Ellen said gently. "She's thinking about giving approval to a union to come into the mill."

"I want no part of Mitchell Logan and his union," Caroline said. "I've been considering Kevin's union. Even though he's down in Columbus now, I'm sure he could make the necessary arrangements if I decide to go ahead." She paused, her mind in high gear. *Why does Janet seem suddenly distraught?* "I thought that might be a morale booster for Kevin –"

Janet exchanged a loaded glance with her mother. What was Ellen afraid to tell her? Caroline asked herself.

"I don't think you'll want to do that," Janet said with an effort. "Kevin's changed so much since his accident. Much of the time he's like a stranger to me. He's come out and admitted what I've been suspecting for many months. His union is backed by communists. Funds for the operation come from Russia." Janet took a deep breath. "I had to tell you the truth. I can't let you walk into that situation without knowing the truth."

"Thank you, Janet." Caroline's voice was tender. "I know what an effort it was for you to tell me. I'll hold up on the union business for now. I'll have to do some serious checking before I make a move."

How awful it would be for Eric, Caroline thought, if word circulated that the Hampton Mill was dealing with a communist-backed union. Everyone said that communist party membership was soaring. How awful for Janet, she commiserated, to be tied to a man whose ideology had moved so far from her own.

She knew that for a long time she'd be haunted by Janet's words: "Kevin's changed so much since his accident. Much of the time he's like a stranger to me."

On the occasions when the Hampton clan met, conversation in these troubled times was heated. There was concerted distaste among thinking Americans for the sinister activities of Father Coughlin, whose radio show drew 80,000 letters a week. Father Coughlin was strongly controversial, what with his hatred of Jews, his denouncing of the American Federation of Labor, his blatant advocation of the assassination of President Roosevelt.

Eric was pleased that Secretary of the Interior Harold Ickes had desegregated the Interior Building cafeteria; that he, along with Eleanor Roosevelt and Frances Perkins, was championing Negro causes. Relief projects were building schools for Negroes. The all-Negro Howard University was given a three million dollar grant by the government.

"It's not a lot," Eric conceded, "but it's a beginning."

In Germany in the past year Hitler had passed the Nuremberg Laws, which deprived all Jews of German citizenship, property rights and legal protection. Already a handful of German Jewish refugees had arrived in Atlanta. Italy had seized Ethiopia, was devoting major efforts to building up its military strength. And Spain was the scene of great repression – a keg of dynamite poised to explode.

Liz was disappointed that once again Janet had declined an invitation to Thanksgiving dinner at Hampton Court because Kevin "doesn't feel up to all that traveling".

"Janet told me that Kevin went down to Albany and Bainbridge with one of the big wheels from the New York office. If he can drive down there, why can't he come to Atlanta when he knows how much it means to Janet?" Liz demanded indignantly.

"There's nothing we can do about it." Caroline sighed. "Ellen's not going down there for Thanksgiving, she's coming to us. She was blunt. Kevin made her feel like an intruder because she's working at the mill. We're the enemy."

"Maybe they'll come for Christmas." Liz forced a smile.

She'd thought once that Janet had the perfect marriage. She'd thought the same about herself in those early years. Adrienne's marriage had been destined to fail from the start. Mama and Papa had a solid marriage. So did Maureen and Andrew. What was wrong with her generation that their marriages fell apart?

Twenty-Five

The mid-December cold seeped into the house. Janet paused in her dishwashing to button up her sweater. Only the newer houses in Columbus provided steam heat. Others depended upon fireplaces or stoves to combat the winter weather. Janet turned to Kevin, hunched over the cards on the kitchen table. Why did it annoy her that he spent every evening playing solitaire?

"Would you like a warmer sweater?"

"I'd like my legs back," he drawled. "And why is Wendy listening to the radio? What about her homework?"

"She did it already. Why don't we go into the sitting room? I'll light the fire."

"You go." Kevin focused on the cards.

In the dank, cold sitting room Janet tossed kindling and chunks of wood into the fireplace grate, and thrust folded up newspaper beneath it to encourage the wood to ignite. For a few moments she relished the sudden burst of heat, though it failed to reach beyond two or three feet.

The phone rang. Janet picked up the receiver.

"Is it as cold down there as it is in Atlanta?" Liz's voice came to her.

"It's real cold," Janet confirmed, "and the weather man promises more of the same."

"What's the chances of you all coming up for Christmas? It'd be wonderful if you could stay for a few days. We'll go to Hampton Court for Christmas dinner, as usual."

"I'll have to talk to Kevin." She and Wendy would love to

go up there for Christmas, she thought wistfully. And Mama would be so pleased.

"Talk to him now," Liz encouraged. "I'll call you back in about an hour. All right?"

"Perfect." Janet tried to sound cheerful. She glanced up to see Kevin wheeling himself into the sitting room. "Talk to you later –" She put down the phone and braced herself to discuss the invitation with Kevin.

"Who was that?" Kevin asked, almost surly.

"Liz. She's invited us to stay with her and Vic for a few days at Christmas."

"You go with Wendy." His eyes were hostile when they met hers. "It's about time we disconnected the phone. One less bill to worry about every month."

"You need the phone." Janet strove for a casual tone. Kevin resented her closeness to Liz. "You know how the New York office sometimes calls you in the evening. They expect you to have a phone." The phone was her lifeline to sanity.

"Make some coffee. Wendy, turn down the radio. We're not deaf." It wasn't too loud, Janet thought, but Kevin needed a whipping post.

Janet went into the kitchen. Kevin returned to his unfinished game of solitaire. When the coffee was ready, she poured a cup, took it to Kevin.

"You know, Kevin, it might do you good to get away from the house for a couple of days," she began tentatively. "The New York office could—"

"Oh, stop it!" he yelled. "You're always whining!" He leaned forward, smacked her across the face with such force that she staggered.

Steadying herself at a corner of the table, Janet was suddenly aware that Wendy hovered in the doorway.

"Sugar . . ." she began, but Wendy had wheeled about and fled from the room.

Wendy had seen Kevin hit her. She felt sick at this realization. And something snapped in her head.

"Yes, Wendy and I will go to stay with Liz over the Christmas holidays," she told Kevin. Zeke would be here to take care of him.

"You're going to walk to Atlanta?" he taunted.

"Mama sent me money to buy Christmas presents," she told him. "It'll pay our bus fare both ways."

Later, lying sleepless in the bed she shared with Wendy, Janet tried to excuse Kevin's hitting her. He was so upset these days he didn't know what he was doing. Nothing was going right for him. But she couldn't erase from her mind the knowledge that Wendy had seen Kevin hit her.

In the following days Janet was conscious of Kevin's hostility, his contempt towards her. She was impatient for the time to leave for Atlanta. But she and Wendy would spend Christmas Eve with Kevin – for what it might mean to him. They would take the first bus out on Christmas morning.

Kevin mocked the whole idea of Christmas. "Religion's a fairy tale for stupid weak people." The communist line had routed out reason in him, Janet thought tiredly. She knew that Zeke, whose family was devoutly religious, was disturbed by Kevin's attitude. He'd hoped to be able to go home for Christmas, but Kevin rejected this. He could go home the following weekend, Kevin decreed.

Three days before Christmas Zeke went out and cut down a small pine tree. Janet decorated it with cranberries and popcorn. There was no money for gifts. Wendy painted pictures to give as presents. Janet baked cookies and wrapped them in colorful Christmas paper. Zeke, she knew, was involved in some small wood project, to be offered on Christmas Eve. And all the while Janet made a point of keeping a physical distance from Kevin. She realized that she was afraid of him.

Kevin spent most of Christmas Eve in the kitchen, where he focused on playing solitaire. He ignored the small gifts that were offered to him. Janet and Zeke struggled to make it a festive occasion for Wendy. Zeke reported that he'd been invited for Christmas dinner at the home of a colored family to whom he was distantly related.

"I'll jes' be gone for maybe two hours," Zeke told Janet.

"You stay as long as you like," Janet told him. "Just leave sandwiches in the ice-box for Mr Kevin and a pot of coffee on the stove."

In the morning Kevin pretended to be asleep when Janet and Wendy left to walk to the bus station. Zeke insisted on carrying their suitcase to the station and saw them off. Christmas shouldn't be like this, Janet thought, fighting feelings of guilt that she and Wendy were leaving Kevin alone with Zeke. But then, she consoled herself, he'd said that Christmas meant nothing to him.

At the bus terminal in Atlanta they were met by Liz and Kathy. All at once the holiday seemed real. Wendy glowed, Janet thought with pleasure. Poor darling, life was not easy for her.

"Your mother's at the house," Liz told Janet. "She's teaching Mary Lou to make the banana pancakes you always love."

It was so wonderful to be here, Janet thought as she and Wendy were greeted at the house. This was reality – the house in Columbus was a nightmare.

"The pancakes are wonderful, Mary Lou," Janet said when they were eating. "But we'd better not stuff because we have to save room for Christmas dinner."

At shortly before two o'clock, Victor ordered everyone into the car for the twenty-five-minute drive to Hampton Court. There they were welcomed with a holiday spirit that Janet relished. For these few days, she promised herself, she wouldn't think about Kevin.

"Come see the tree." Josh took Wendy and Kathy by the hand, led them into the spacious sitting room graced with a huge, beautifully decorated Christmas tree. Josh was wonderful with children, Janet thought with gratitude. Wendy adored him. "And I think Santa Claus left some packages for you two."

He grinned, knowing both were well past the age to believe in Santa Claus.

Gradually Janet began to relax. For a while she could forget the problems that plagued her at home. Here she felt part of the family. Mama had always said that Caroline Hampton was the sister she'd never had.

Only for a brief interval did the holiday mood give way to somber conversation. Reflecting on Christmas in other countries, Josh talked about the severe government repression in Spain.

"The Fascists are determined to rule," he said with exasperation. "They've disregarded the liberal legislation that was passed. Now new elections are scheduled to come up in February, but they'll be a farce. The landowners and the clergy reap all the benefits."

"The world should learn to live in peace." Eric's face was etched with pain. "I remember the June thirty-seven years ago, when I went down to Cuba as a foreign correspondent with Teddy Roosevelt's Rough Riders. But in twenty-four hours I was a soldier with a carbine in my hand. I remember the heat and the rain, but mostly I remember the dead and dying on every side. That's when I knew I'd go into politics." He paused. "I know, politics was the way to fulfill the General's dream, but that dream became important to me that day in Cuba. If four senators in Washington had voted against our fighting in Cuba, no American soldier would have died there. We were pushed into the war because some American newspapers decided that it should happen!"

"You were wounded at San Juan Hill," Caroline remembered tenderly. "It was a frightening time for us."

"It's a frightening time for those in Spain," Victor said. "Civil war is breathing down their necks."

"Enough of this," Caroline ordered. "This is Christmas Day."

Jason appeared to summon them to the sumptuous feast Annie Mae had prepared. It was so good, Janet thought, to spend a special holiday like Christmas with those she cherished. Mama was so happy that she and Wendy had contrived to be here. Here was a true Christmas spirit – so lacking in their dreary house in Columbus. In a corner of her mind she hoped wistfully that Zeke, too, would enjoy his holiday dinner.

Annie Mae and Jason brought endless platters of food to the table. Now the conversation was convivial. Everyone determined, Janet thought, to enjoy the holiday despite the state of the world. They lingered long at the table, debated which of Annie Mae's festive pies to choose.

"We'll have coffee in the sitting room," Eric decreed. "After that magnificent meal we need to spread ourselves out. Hot chocolate for Kathy and Wendy," he said with a flourish, and then gently, "and for Francis, too."

While Josh was relating an amusing story about a little girl patient who was on the mend – almost a Christmas miracle – the phone rang. Nobody moved to reply. Jason or Annie Mae would pick it up. Moments later Annie Mae came into the sitting room with a genial smile, picked up the phone.

"Hampton residence," she bubbled. Then all at once her face contorted in alarm. "Now Zeke, you talk slow so I can understand –"

Janet leapt to her feet. The others exchanged anxious glances.

"Zeke, you stop cryin', you hear? Tell me what happened –"

"Let me talk to him." Janet took the phone from Annie Mae. "Zeke, what's happened?"

"Mist' Kevin – he taken bad. I called for an ambulance, they took him to the hospital. Miz Janet, that bottle of pills he keeps handy, you know, the ones to stop his pain. That bottle was on the floor – empty. It was almost full when I went off to have my dinner. The doctor on the ambulance – he say Mist' Kevin in a coma."

"I'll be home as fast as I can," Janet gasped. "Stay by the phone in case the hospital calls." She turned to the others, struggled for composure. Her voice hoarse as she explained what had happened.

"I'll drive you to Columbus," Josh said. "Let Wendy stay here with Kathy –"

"Shall I go with you?" Ellen was unnerved.

"No, stay with Wendy," Janet urged.

"I'll get the car out of the garage," Josh said. "Janet, you'll need your coat."

"I'll bring down a coat for you, Josh –" Caroline was on her feet.

Within minutes Janet and Josh were in the car and leaving Hampton Court behind.

"Are you warm enough?" Josh asked solicitously while he coaxed the heater to life.

"I'm fine," Janet managed. What had happened to push Kevin over the edge? she asked herself. *I should not have left him alone on Christmas Day. I should have been there for him.*

The holiday spirit had evaporated. Those left in the Hampton Court sitting room were somber. Ellen and Liz tried to divert Wendy, but she sat on the corner of the sofa, the Christmas gifts forgotten as she stared into space. Strangely reproachful, Liz thought.

"He's going to be all right," Liz tried to comfort Wendy. "The doctors at the hospital will take care of him."

"He hit Mama. Hard," Wendy blurted out. "She almost fell. I don't like him anymore!"

Liz felt sick with shock. She knew Kevin had become difficult, but she'd never suspected physical violence. Her eyes turned to Victor. But he was already trying to reach out to Wendy.

"You know, Wendy, how rough life has been for your father since the shooting," Victor said gently. "Sometimes people do things without thinking. He—"

"He hadn't oughta hit Mama," Wendy broke in. "He's a mean man."

"You know, Wendy," Liz tried for diversion. "I was thinking that maybe your grandmother and I could take you and Kathy to the movies tomorrow. I know you both love Shirley Temple, and her new picture's playing there."

"I want to go home," Wendy said plaintively. "I want to be with Mama."

"We'll talk about that tomorrow," Liz soothed.

"Let's go up to my room," Kathy said to her. "I'll show you my new party dress."

Josh drove faster than normal because he knew Janet was anxious.

"I shouldn't have left him alone." Janet reproached herself for the dozenth time. "For all his blustering against religious holidays, I should have understood he didn't mean it."

"Janet, he meant it." Josh forced himself to be realistic. "A lot of folks who suffer turn against everything they grew up believing in."

"You're right." She capitulated. "He's not the Kevin I knew in those early days. All he cared about then was seeing life made easier for working people. But he's become so bitter, so angry." She shuddered. "And now this."

"We'll go straight to the hospital. Zeke did the right thing in calling for help."

The doctors would fight to save Kevin, but what would he be like if they did? Josh dreaded the prospect of Janet's being tied to a husband who might be brain-damaged. A vegetable. Since they were teenagers, he'd been in love with her. He'd known even then there'd be nobody else for him. And then, straight out of college, Janet had married Kevin.

At the hospital Josh talked with Kevin's doctors.

"He's still in a coma," the doctor in charge told Josh. "We don't know if he'll come out of it. The next twenty-four hours are critical."

Josh sat with Janet through the evening. Instinct warning him that Kevin's chances were slight.

"You don't have to stay with me, Josh," Janet told him just past midnight. "You've been wonderful."

She looked up, fearfully, as Kevin's doctor approached them.

"Nothing's going to happen for the next dozen hours or so," he said gently. "Go home and get some rest."

At Josh's insistence she allowed him to drive her home. They found Zeke, inconsolable, sitting by the phone in anticipation of a call from the hospital.

"We don't know yet," Janet told Zeke in response to his poignant gaze.

"It wouldn'a happened if I stayed," he whispered. "I did wrong, Miz Janet."

"No, you didn't do wrong," Janet said with unexpected firmness. "Neither of us did wrong."

"I found a letter on the floor by his chair. I don't read too good, but I think it came from the union."

"Get it for me, Zeke," she said with sudden urgency and turned to Josh. "Kevin didn't say anything about a letter from the union."

Zeke returned with the letter, gave it to Janet. Josh read over her shoulder. The union had fired him, was closing down the Columbus office. They were abandoning their efforts throughout the whole state.

"Kevin said nothing about the letter –" Her eyes swept over the brief message yet again.

"That was why he did it," Josh said gently. "Not because you weren't here. Not because you left him, Zeke. He couldn't face failure as an organizer."

The phone rang. Both Janet and Zeke froze in fear. Josh reached to pick up the phone.

"Hello –"

"Dr Joshua Hampton?" a feminine voice asked.

"Yes?" His hand tightened on the phone. He'd given instructions to be called here if there was any change in Kevin's condition.

"I'm sorry. Mr Michaels never emerged from the coma. He died a few minutes ago."

Twenty-Six

Josh realized that Janet knew Kevin was dead even before he put down the phone. She sat immobile, in shock. Tears rolled unheeded down Zeke's face.

"I'll have to make arrangements," Janet said after a moment, fighting for composure. "Kevin had no family except Wendy and me –"

"I'll take care of everything," Josh told her. And then because Zeke appeared so distraught, he amended that. "Zeke and I will handle what has to be done. Perhaps you'd like to go back to Atlanta until the funeral?"

"Yes," she whispered, and Josh fought against an impulse to take her into his arms to comfort her.

"We'll drive back this afternoon," Josh said, going over in his mind details that must be handled immediately. "I'll drive you back down for the funeral."

"You're so good to us." Janet forced a smile. "The brother I never had."

"You're family." But his feelings were not those of a brother. Janet was the only woman he'd ever loved. "Zeke, make Miss Janet a cup of tea. We'll leave Columbus about three o'clock."

The next few days were chaotic. All the family had returned to Atlanta. Despite his heavy work schedule Josh handled all the arrangements for Kevin's funeral. It was diplomatically explained to Janet that she was not to worry about the cost.

On the day Kevin was to be buried, Atlanta was deluged by

sleet and snow. Already tree branches were becoming weighed down with ice. The wind shrieked through the trees.

Josh was to drive Janet, Wendy, Ellen and Zeke to Columbus. Caroline and Eric would drive with Liz and Victor and Kathy. Emerging from Hampton Court, Josh was anxious about arriving at Columbus in time for the services at the funeral home.

"The roads are going to be a mess," he called to his father and mother, walking down the steps of the house to the second car in the driveway.

"According to the radio news the storm's hitting mostly to the north," Eric told him. "Hopefully we'll drive out of the storm."

Traffic was light this morning. Roads were icy. Utility company linemen were in evidence, trying to restore service in areas where it had been interrupted. What a rotten day for Kevin's funeral, Josh thought.

Approaching Ellen's house Josh saw Zeke shoveling a path through the snow that had been falling since dawn.

"You stay in the car, Mist' Josh," Zeke called. "No need for you to come out in this wet."

In drab funeral black Janet and Ellen hurried to the car. Zeke insisted on carrying Wendy. "She light as a feather." The weather offered a safe topic of conversation, Josh realized in relief. Midway on the long drive, Zeke revealed that the parcel he'd carried from the house contained a thermos of coffee and a second of hot chocolate plus a collection of cups. Josh pulled off the road so that Zeke could pour without burning himself.

With the roads clear for the second half of the trip, both cars arrived on schedule. A handful of people, neighbors, Janet explained in a taut whisper – nobody from the union – attended the services with them. Only the Atlanta contingent went on to the cemetery on this gray, dank early afternoon.

The return trip was grueling once they were at the midway point. The roads ahead were treacherous, ice-encrusted. They arrived to find Atlanta almost immobile. The trolleys had ceased to run. Electric power and phone services were out. Josh was anxious about the situation at the hospital. At Caroline's orders both cars were to head for Hampton Court. Caroline knew that Jason would have been shoveling the driveway. Mattie would be standing by with food.

The ice storm, the worst that had hit Atlanta since 1905, continued for forty-eight hours. Atlanta seemed isolated from the rest of the world. Josh and Victor had managed to make their way to the hospital, would sleep there until the storm was over.

Ellen insisted that Janet and Wendy move into what she humorously called "my dollhouse". It consisted of a sitting room, bedroom, and kitchen.

"We'll manage." She was determinedly cheerful.

As soon as the weather permitted, Josh promised to help Janet with moving whatever she planned to bring from the house in Columbus. He said he would try to arrange a job for Zeke at the hospital. For now Zeke would share Jason's room in the servants' wing of the house.

Shortly after New Year Josh drove Janet down to Columbus to pack. She arranged to have the phone disconnected, settled the bill, sold the furniture to a local used-furniture dealer, and gave notice to her landlord. Josh sensed she would be relieved when she could say her final goodbye.

"I don't know how I would have managed without you, Josh," she told him as they drove away from the drab little house for the last time. "I wish I could make you understand how grateful I am."

Janet knew that her mother's small salary would be strained to the limit with two more mouths to feed. She sought desperately to find a job with no more success than she'd encountered in Columbus. She had a degree in education, which she'd never used, but this was hardly the time to expect to find a teaching job.

It was Josh, on one of those evenings when he dropped by

to see if "you three women need a man to fix something around the house", who suggested she start a small child-care group for working mothers.

"Not every mother has a family to take on this care. And you have your teaching degree – that's the perfect qualification," he said optimistically.

"Where will I find interested parents?" Janet was ambivalent. "I don't think it'll work. There're so many colored girls who're anxious for work. They expect so little –"

"You'll be offering something more," Josh argued. "You're a teacher – you can handle three or four three- or four-year-olds."

"But how do I find parents who'll want this kind of service?" Janet exchanged a doubtful glance with her mother.

"I know two nurses at the hospital who're frantic for such help. And they probably know others. Shall I have them call you?"

"Do it, Janet," Ellen urged her. "Josh, that's a wonderful idea!"

To Janet's amazement early in February she found four mothers who needed her services. The husband of one had bolted when their daughter was an infant. The other three were nurses who were having a problem finding care within their families. Two were divorced, with ex-husbands reluctant or unable to provide child support so it was necessary for them to go out to work. The husband of the fourth woman was recuperating very slowly from an accident.

"Women go out to work these days," Liz said with an air of defiance that Janet had heard from her in the past.

"A lot of us have to," Janet pointed out.

"Victor – and Mama and Papa – would think I was taking a job away from somebody who needed it if I tried for one," Liz sighed. "So I stay with my volunteer work. And Vic works himself to death." She was pensive for a moment. "When we were young—"

"Liz, we're not old," Janet broke in. "We're only going to be thirty-five this year."

"When we were younger," Liz amended with a wry smile, "I thought the two of us had perfect marriages."

"Kevin became a total stranger. I suppose I shouldn't say that –"

"You can say it to me. Vic hasn't changed – except that he works such horrendous hours. Sometimes I think he does that to get away from me. But things happen," she said with painful intensity. "You know how it is with us. Even now, each time Vic reaches for me in bed, I think, 'He's hoping I'll get pregnant.' He can't understand that to even think about having another baby makes me sick at heart. Janet, I couldn't bear to lose another baby."

"You have Kathy – and that's a blessing," Janet said softly. "And I have Wendy. They make life worth living."

Janet was startled when she realized how much a part of her life Josh had become. Early in the spring he'd called to ask her if she'd like to go to a concert featuring music by Sigmund Romberg and Jerome Kern – two of her favorite composers. She'd hesitated because it was soon after Kevin's death, but Josh had persuaded her to go with him.

Then there'd been several movies he was sure she would enjoy.

And now today – June 30th – he'd taken time from the hospital and his practice to go over to the Davison-Paxon book department, where Margaret Mitchell was signing copies of her novel, *Gone with the Wind*, to buy a copy for her.

She was alone at the house when he arrived. Ellen and Wendy had pretended they were going to see another Shirley Temple movie, but she knew her mother and daughter were going shopping for a birthday present for her.

"I hope I'm not intruding at a bad time," Josh said self-consciousnessly.

"Of course not," she reassured him. Josh had always been special to her. In a corner of her mind she'd suspected for a long time that he harbored romantic feelings for her. She'd always pushed these thoughts away, but now she'd become conscious of reciprocal feelings. *How can I feel this way with Kevin dead only six months?*

"Liz happened to mention that tomorrow's your birthday," he explained. "And I know that you and Liz went to school with Margaret Mitchell."

"I'm thrilled to have a copy." Her smile was tender. "You're so good to me, Josh." She waited expectantly. Would he say more?

"You'll be at the Friday evening dinner at Hampton Court?" His eyes said what he couldn't seem to bring himself to voice.

"Oh sure. I look forward to that." Her eyes said she'd welcome romantic pursuit. It wouldn't be wrong, she thought defiantly. She'd had no marriage since the day that bullet hit Kevin.

"See you Friday evening," he said with an awkward smile. "And happy birthday."

Much of the talk at the dinner table on Friday evening revolved around Margaret Mitchell's just published book.

"That was an interesting article about Margaret and the book in last week's *Constitution*," Liz recalled. "Of course, we all knew she'd been working on a book for the last ten years, but she never thought about having it published. And here it'll be the Book-of-the-Month Club selection for July."

"How did all this happen?" Caroline asked.

"Oh, Margaret was bringing a group of Georgia writers to be interviewed by this man from the Macmillan Company – a publishing house," Liz explained. "He was looking for a Southern novel. And then he learned that Margaret herself had just finished a novel about the Old South. He asked to see it, and she gave him sixty large manila envelopes."

"It's a long book – and fascinating." Janet sent a warm glance in Josh's direction. "I'll give it to you as soon as I've finished reading it, Liz."

Not until those at the dinner table deserted it for the sitting room, with Kathy and Wendy preparing to take turns playing checkers with Francis, did the conversation take a serious tone.

"I worry about what's happening in Germany." Eric was somber. "What Hitler's doing in the Rhineland could lead to another world war."

"And he's getting too close to Mussolini," Victor pointed out. "That spells trouble."

"What scares me," Josh said with muted intensity, "is the violence in Spain since February. Sure, the people voted for a republic, but look at the way the Nationalists are fighting it. Innocent people are dragged out of their homes and murdered. It's the familiar story – the bankers, landlords and clergy, plus the army, though not the air force, against the democratically elected government supported by the workers and the peasants."

"I hate to say it," Victor said, "because I know what it means, but now's the time when the world should step in to stop Fascism from taking over Europe."

On July 17th the military in Spain revolted against the government and the country was engulfed in civil war. Six days later Josh received a phone call from his medical-school buddy Tim Reiss, on staff at a New York City hospital.

"I'm taking four months' leave from the hospital," Tim told him with a note of urgency in his voice. "You know what's happening in Spain?"

"I know." Josh was grim. The newspapers and newsreels were painfully graphic.

"A few doctors in this country are getting together to go over there. It's not an organized effort – not yet," Tim explained. "A surgical resident here – an Italian-American – has family in Italy who just managed to escape before Mussolini slapped them in prison. His cousin who's a doctor fled to Spain to try to help set up a mobile hospital. They've been in contact. Come with us, Josh."

Josh hesitated. "I don't know if I can get leave –"

"Try," Tim urged. "Innocent civilians – women and children along with men – are dying for lack of medical care!"

"How do we know the reports coming through are true?" Josh remembered his father's contempt for the reporting of the Hearst newspapers during the Spanish-American War.

"I read the *New York Times*," Tim shot back. "They report what they see. We were trained to save lives, Josh. We can give four months to those civilians in Spain."

"When is your group going over? Can we get into Spain?" Weren't Americans being alerted to stay out of the country?

"Everything has been worked out," Tim assured him. "We realize that any minute American travel there will be banned. We're going to Paris – ostensibly to attend a medical convention there. Loyalists will meet us with full instructions. You have your passport?"

"It's expired," Josh said. The summer of their second year at medical school he and Tim had roamed through England and France. "I'll have to get it renewed, that'll take time –"

"Your father's a senator." Tim was impatient now. "He'll know how to rush through a passport for you."

"When do I have to be in New York?" Josh suddenly knew that with or without leave from the hospital he was going to Spain with Tim. This was a crusade against Fascism. How could he not help?

"We sail in eight days on the *Normandie*."

"How did you get reservations this time of year?" Josh asked in astonishment.

Tim chuckled. "Where have you been the last few years? The country's in a Depression. How many people are vacationing in Europe? Be in New York the day before we sail. Let me know when your train arrives in Pennsylvania Station. I'll meet you."

Off the phone Josh tried to gear himself to go downstairs and tell his parents that he was going to Spain. They would be upset, but they would understand.

And no more playing the awkward, shy suitor, he admonished himself. Tomorrow he must talk to Janet. He couldn't go off to a war without telling her he'd loved her for years. That when he came back – if he came back, he conceded realistically – he hoped she would marry him.

Twenty-Seven

The late July evening was sultry, uncomfortable in the way that valley towns along the ever muddy Chattahoochee in Georgia are uncomfortable. In truth, much of the country was suffering from an unusually hot summer, with temperatures soaring above 100 degrees. The continuing drought brought forth a prediction from the Secretary of Agriculture that another two million people would have to go on relief during the coming winter. The fan that sat on the ice-box in Ellen's small kitchen did little to alleviate the heat. At intervals Ellen swatted at an unwary mosquito.

"Can I have some more lemonade?" Wendy asked plaintively while they lingered over supper. In this weather nobody felt like moving.

"Sure, darling." Janet went to pour lemonade for the three of them.

"There's a seven o'clock showing at the movie theater," Ellen said when Janet returned with three glasses of lemonade. "It's a Shirley Temple picture. Why don't we all go? The air-conditioning will be so nice."

"Can we, Mama?" Wendy's face glowed. "I love Shirley Temple."

"You two go," Janet urged. At twenty-five cents admission for adults and ten cents for children under twelve they allowed themselves this luxury only two or three times a month. At fourteen and petite Wendy could pass for "almost twelve". "I've got some hand-washing to do." They gave out one bundle a week to Ellen's long-time washerwoman. What couldn't fit into that bundle Janet or Ellen did by hand.

"Can't it wait?" Ellen scolded.

"Not if Wendy's to have clean socks and underwear for tomorrow." Janet chuckled. "I'll listen to *Amos 'n' Andy*."

"You and thirty million other Americans," Ellen was already rising from the table, "including President Roosevelt."

Janet had finished the washing and was listening to Kate Smith's radio program when she heard the doorbell. She went to respond, surprised, but pleased, to see Josh waiting there.

"Hot enough for you?" he teased.

"Isn't it awful?" She swung the screen door wide. "Come in quick before the mosquitos rush in."

"Is this a bad time?" All at once he seemed uneasy.

"No." Her smile was warm. "Let me get you a glass of lemonade."

"That'll be good."

Josh was smiling, but his eyes were so somber, Janet thought as he trailed behind her into the kitchen. What was bothering him? She opened the door to the ice-box, brought out the pitcher of lemonade.

"Shall we sit here in the kitchen? Or we could take the fan into the sitting room."

"Let's stay here." He took a glass from her, sat at the table. He frowned in thought for a moment. "I guess there's no point in beating around the bush." He smiled wryly. "I wanted you to know I'm taking four months' leave from the hospital to go to Spain with a group of doctors."

"But that's dangerous!" Her heart began to pound. "There's civil war there –"

"The Loyalists are fighting for democracy, and the casualties are high. Civilians are being hurt. They need doctors desperately." His eyes were full of questions.

"Josh, I don't want anything to happen to you," she whispered.

"I have to go, but when I come back, I'd like to think you'd consider marrying me."

"Oh, Josh –" The tenderness in her voice was an unvocalized "yes".

"I've been in love with you for such a long time, Jannie –" Not since she was a little girl had she heard that diminutive.

"I'm not sure it'd be right. I mean, so soon . . ." Josh understood what she was trying to say, didn't he?

"It's been a long time," he corrected. His eyes were an eloquent plea.

"I'd like that so much." All at once her face was radiant. "But let's not tell anyone just yet. Not till you're back home."

"We won't tell anybody," he agreed.

"When will you leave?" *Why does he have to go? I'll be so scared.*

"A week from tomorrow." He reached out a hand to cover hers.

"So soon?" Her eyes betrayed her alarm.

"But there'll be all the years ahead," he promised, rising to his feet. Instantly she was on her feet, eager for the touch of him.

She closed her eyes as his arms brought her to him and his mouth reached for hers. Emotions she had thought had died sprang alive in her.

"Mama and Wendy have gone to the movies," she whispered when, with an air of reluctance, he lifted his mouth from hers. Her message clear.

"Janet, I love you," he murmured. "This is the most wonderful moment of my life."

Hand in hand they walked into the small bedroom that she shared with her mother and Wendy. They clung together for a few moments, savoring the joy that welled in them. She felt so young, so loved, she thought joyously while he helped her out of her clothes.

"You're lovely –" His eyes swept over her while he stripped – "I used to dream of this moment."

"Then let's not waste time." She managed a shaky laugh, feeling like a brazen young girl.

She felt the slight sag of the mattress beneath her, and then the weight of him above her. She rejoiced that he was so passionate. Their hands in mutual searching, as though in recompense for all the time they were denied this.

She cried out softly, tightened her arms about him. She'd never felt so alive, she thought in glorious abandon. A whole new world lay ahead for them.

But in six days Josh was going to leave for Spain. How would she survive if he didn't come back to her?

It seemed to Janet that six days had never passed so quickly, and yet they seemed so full. At every free moment she and Josh contrived to be together. To make love, when they managed to be alone, with an abandon that was new and exciting.

Yet every moment she lived in dread of what he would encounter in Barcelona or Madrid or wherever Josh might find himself in Spain. Knowing he would be in constant danger.

The night before he was to leave for New York they walked along the river – caught up in poignant farewell. Pausing at intervals to embrace in the privacy of the starless night.

"I'll write to you every chance I get," Josh promised. "I doubt I'll be able to receive mail in the middle of a civil war, but I'll manage somehow to sneak letters out to you."

No one guessed that they had sworn an eternal love. That they would marry when Josh returned. And a small taunting voice mocked her: will he return? Reports of the casualties were terrifying.

In the master bedroom at Hampton Court on the night before Josh was to leave for Spain, Eric stared out into the darkness through the parted drapes. He remembered Cuba all those years ago. He'd hoped the world would see no more wars. But then there had been the World War, and now Italy and Germany and Spain were threatening to push the world into more turmoil.

"Eric, come to bed." Caroline's voice was deep with love and compassion.

"Caro, I hate what's happening in Europe." He turned to face her, his eyes showing his inner anguish. "And I know what I must do with the rest of my life. I'm not going to run for re-election for the Senate. I know –" He raised a hand as though to silence her. "I'm letting the General down. But I want to devote the rest of my life to fighting for peace. We'll say nothing to the others just yet." His eyes were pleading for understanding. "They'll know in good time."

"You've given enough of your life for the General's dream," Caroline told him. "It's time to live your own. I think he'd understand that."

Josh was touched that his mother and father insisted on seeing him off on the morning train bound for New York. Both so fearful yet determined to hide this.

"You'll be traveling in style," his father said with an air of amusement. "I've heard that the *Normandie* is even more impressive than the *Ile de France*."

The three waited in the limestone and marble Union Depot for the train to arrive. To mask her anxiety his mother chattered about the beauty of the Depot, completed just six years ago. She and Papa understood why he had to go, Josh comforted himself. Spain was the place where Fascism must be stopped. Still, Mama was determined to make this seem just an ordinary trip overseas. But he knew his parents would spend many sleepless nights in the four months ahead. And how could he truthfully say that he'd be back in four months? Who knew how long this war would last?

Then his train chugged into the station. He kissed his mother, embraced his father, and boarded the pullman with the single valise he had allowed himself. He hadn't needed Tim to tell him that they must travel lightly.

The trip seemed endless. Josh passed the time in reading the pile of magazines provided by his mother. General Franco had already set up a Fascist government at Burgos. While the rest of the world appeared to agree not to intervene, many were sure that in time Germany and Italy would support Franco.

The following day Josh arrived in New York, was met by Tim.

"You've got your passport?" Tim asked immediately.

"Got it."

"We sail tomorrow night on the *Normandie*," Tim said, prodding Josh towards an exit where taxis would be waiting. He glanced at Josh's small valise with approval. "Smart. We'll be carrying a load of medical supplies. Thank God, we're well-financed."

Boarding the *Normandie* the following evening, Josh was impressed by its elegance. Over 80,000 tons and 1,029 feet long, he thought, recalling the information in the brochure Tim had picked up. But this wasn't a pleasure trip. He and Tim were headed for a war zone. Their objective: to save lives.

Tim had explained that their group of six to nine doctors and seven nurses was to make a point of appearing to travel alone or in pairs. "To avoid any suspicion that we're volunteers headed for Spain." At Le Havre they would take a train to Paris, register at a small hotel. Twenty-four hours later they'd board a train to the French border town of Hendaye.

The trip across the Atlantic was uneventful except for the tension of maintaining the necessary appearance of being en route to a medical convention. They registered at the hotel where reservations had been made for them. Here they were met by a pair of Loyalists sent to escort them the rest of the distance into Spain. The following day they boarded the train to take them to Hendaye.

"Just yesterday the French government closed the border to all military traffic," the younger of their escorts, probably no more than twenty, Josh gauged, told them. "We'll be met in Hendaye on the French border by two ambulances that'll carry us and the equipment over one of the passes of the Pyrenees. Luckily it's not winter." He grinned. "That would be rough."

Lucky, too, Josh thought, that both Tim and he had college Spanish to see them through.

The two Loyalists briefed the group of Americans when they gathered together in Hendaye. The atmosphere was charged. Josh sensed that the French here were sympathetic, closed their eyes to what was now clearly a cluster of American volunteers prepared to fight for the Loyalist cause.

A few hours later they entered a village that had been the scene of recent, bitter street fighting. The Nationalists had burned houses, small shops, the local school and then departed. Not wasting a moment the American doctors and nurses set up their tiny mobile hospital. The injured lined up for care.

"Hey, we're not exactly Bellevue Emergency," Tim said with a wry grin to Josh while they labored over an injured small boy, "but we're supplying a needed service.

Janet was relieved three weeks later when a letter arrived from Josh.

> Dear Janet
>
> I hope this reaches you. It's being taken out of Spain by a foreign correspondent who has been slightly injured and is going home for treatment. We're kept busy every waking moment. It's heartbreaking to see how innocent lives are being disrupted. Men, women, and children being killed because they're in the wrong place at the wrong time. We hear unnerving rumors about atrocities, but we focus only on caring for those who need our help.

Each night she re-read Josh's letter. She'd debated about sharing it with Liz and Victor and Liz's parents but that would reveal her new closeness with Josh. Guilt lingered in her. Then she learned that Caroline and Eric had also received a brief letter.

"He didn't say much," Liz reported. "Just that he's well and occupied with caring for the injured twenty hours a day."

* * *

The group of American doctors and nurses moved from village to village trying to avoid the actual fighting. Sickened by the destruction everywhere. The shocking atrocities repeated.

News seeped through to them. On September 6th Great Britain had finally set up a Non-Intervention Committee. Every European country except for Switzerland had agreed not to take sides – but it soon became obvious that Germany, Italy and Portugal were not keeping their word. On October 17th the Soviet Union repudiated the agreement and, by the end of the month, was sending planes, pilots and tanks to aid the Loyalists.

Word came through that International Brigades were being formed in Europe and the United States to fight on the side of the Loyalists against Fascism. On November 8th the first International Brigade arrived. But Josh was shaken by the knowledge that the Loyalists behaved as badly as the Nationalists. *What the hell are we doing here?*

Janet waited hopefully for more letters from Josh, but none arrived. She tried to tell herself he was too busy to write, that it was impossible to get mail out of a country in the midst of anarchy. And she was fighting a constant tiredness.

On a particularly hot night Janet and her mother sat in rockers on the front porch. Ellen engrossed in a book, Janet fanning herself. Like Kathy, Wendy was attending an evening birthday party, an unusual event at their age. Birthday parties were usually afternoon affairs.

Janet glanced up to see Liz's Packard approaching.

"This is such a scorcher," Liz said, emerging from the car. "Why don't you two come with me to see the new Bette Davis movie? It'll be air-conditioned," she said with a blissful smile. "I've arranged for Jason to pick the girls up when the party's over."

"You go, Janet," Ellen urged and chuckled. "It's finally my

turn to read *Gone with the Wind* and nobody's tearing me away from this book."

"I may fall asleep, I'm so tired all the time," Janet warned her, "but I can't resist air-conditioning."

Sitting beside Liz in the car, Janet forced herself to voice the question that had been darting in and out of her mind for days now.

"Have your parents heard anything from Josh?" She tried to sound casual.

"Nothing since that first letter. But Papa says that's to be expected. Josh is probably too busy to write, and if he did, it'd be hard to get a letter out considering he's in the middle of a civil war."

"I'm sure he's OK." Was she imagining that Liz suspected something serious between Josh and her? There was a special glint in Liz's eyes when they talked about Josh that told her this.

"Josh comes over to people as so disciplined, so in control," Liz said lovingly, "but inside he's so intense."

"He felt he had to go to Spain," Janet said, "the same way that in early years Kevin felt he had to fight to help mill workers to a better way of life. But somewhere along the road Kevin lost his way." Janet stifled a yawn. "I can't seem to get enough sleep."

"How's the work going with the little ones?" Liz asked.

"Oh, they're so sweet. A handful sometimes," Janet admitted. "It's wonderful that Josh thought about my doing something like this, and then finding the children for me. I felt so lost –" She yawned again.

"If I didn't know better," Liz said with gentle laughter, "I'd think you were pregnant."

"Remember how we used to make jokes about it when we were both pregnant at the same time?" But all at once Janet froze. Her mind in high alert. *What's the date? I'm late! Three weeks late. That never happens.* "Oh, my God –" The words were wrenched from her.

"What's the matter?" Liz's hands tightened on the wheel.

"I think I *am* pregnant," Janet whispered.

Twenty-Eight

Liz pulled over to the side of the road. She gazed at Janet in disbelief. "You think *what*?"

"I'm three weeks late. I fall asleep in the middle of the day. It's a miracle I stay awake with the kids. I know it sounds crazy –"

"It's not another immaculate conception," Liz said softly, her eyes searching Janet's. "*Could* you be pregnant? Is it Josh?" Liz asked in sudden comprehension.

"Yes." Janet's face was luminous. "Before he left for Spain, we knew we were in love. I didn't want to tell the family just yet. I've felt guilty because it was so soon after Kevin died."

"Janet, your marriage was dead for years."

"We didn't think – we were careless." With Liz she could be honest. "I guess we figured at our age – at my age," she corrected because Josh was two years younger than she, "that nothing would happen."

"Janet, when will you realize that you're still a young woman?" Liz shook her head in mock dismay. But Janet's pregnancy evoked painful memories of the time she was pregnant with Debbie. She'd been so happy – Victor had been so happy. They hadn't known then what pain awaited them, that they would lose their precious baby.

"I can't stay here in Atlanta." Panic was closing in on Janet. "I don't know quite how I'm going to manage. I can work for a while. Oh, Liz. Everybody's going to be so shocked."

"We'll forget the movie," Liz said briskly. "We'll go and talk to Mama. Mama will know how to handle this." She hesitated. "Jannie, you're sure?"

"I'm sure."

Janet's radiance was a stab in the heart to Liz. Despite the threat of panic, she thought, Janet welcomed this child. And in the months ahead Victor would look at Janet with such wistfulness.

Liz was relieved that her father was back in Washington now the summer recess was over. Since her stroke Sophie made a point of retiring shortly after dinner. Her mother would be alone.

"Mama will be in the library," Liz said as she and Janet walked into the house. "She'll be going over mill accounts, or reading."

Caroline greeted them warmly, yet Liz sensed her curiosity at their unexpected appearance at the house.

"I'll ask Mattie to bring us ice tea," Caroline began. "And—"

"No, Mama," Liz stopped her. "We have something to tell you."

With synthetic calm Liz explained the situation to her mother, with an occasional addition from a clearly anxious Janet. She was aware of a blend of shock and elation in her mother. For so long Mama had been trying to marry Josh off. And Mama loved Janet.

"It's very simple," Caroline summed up. "I'll talk to your mother in the morning, Janet. We'll send in a note to the *Journal* and the *Constitution* announcing the marriage. And of course," she added with a hint of indulgent laughter, "the baby will be premature."

"But how can we?" Janet stammered. "Suppose – suppose Josh has changed his mind?"

"Not a chance," Liz insisted. "After waiting all these years for you? In another two or three months I'll give a baby shower for you. With the family obviously behind you nobody will ask questions. And in a couple of months," she said with a silent prayer, "Josh will be home from Spain."

"I pray for that every night," Janet said.

Liz's phone rang endlessly on the morning that the society pages of the *Constitution* carried the belated announcement of Josh and Janet's marriage. This would take place secretly in the future, Liz reminded herself. Probably in New York, like her parents' remarriage after Tina's death. But she'd anticipated a rash of phone calls this morning and was prepared to deal with them.

"Oh, I should have known something like this was coming," one Atlantan, who'd gone to school with Liz and Janet, effervesced. "I saw them together at a concert and then later at a movie, and just the way they looked at each other said they were in love. And when will Josh come home from that awful war?"

"We don't know for sure. He took four months' leave from the hospital – I doubt that he'll come home before that's over."

She'd always felt close to Janet, Liz acknowledged – but now there was a special bond between them. As the weeks passed and Janet's pregnancy became visible, Liz was haunted by the tenderness she read in Victor's eyes when he looked at Janet. He was thinking, "Why isn't Liz pregnant?" He couldn't understand – and was troubled – by her cold response when he made love to her. *He thinks I've stopped loving him. But I couldn't bear going through again what I went through when we lost Debbie.*

In the weeks ahead Liz made a habit of stopping by to help Janet with the four little girls who were in her care on weekdays. On this late October afternoon, with autumn at last finally in full bloom, Liz and Janet relaxed over coffee in the kitchen while the little girls napped.

"I can't believe Thanksgiving is barely a month away." Janet sighed. "And I'm popping out of my clothes already."

"You're barely showing." Liz chuckled affectionately. In a way, she thought, she was sharing Janet's pregnancy. During both of her pregnancies she and Victor had been so happy. And Victor would be so happy, her mind taunted, if she was pregnant again. *No, don't think about that.* She forced herself back to the moment. "You'll soon need somebody to replace you with the girls. It'll be too much for you to care for them." Mama had invited Janet and Wendy to move into Hampton House, but Janet was not quite at ease with that.

"I've been talking with a reliable woman," Janet said. "She's desperate to earn money. I'm sure she can take over." She paused for a moment. "Has your mother heard again from Josh?" Each of them had by now received two brief letters. "I know it's difficult for him to write," Janet said quickly, "and difficult to get letters out of the country."

"I would have told you if she had," Liz chided. But she knew how frustrating it was for Janet not to be able to write to Josh. No way for her to tell him she was pregnant. He'd written in that first letter that "we're on the move – to whatever town or village where civilians need medical care."

"His leave is up the first of December," Janet reminded Liz. "I'm scared he'll stay longer. When he sees a need –"

"Others are rushing to help the Loyalists." The newspapers told of brigades forming all over Europe and in America. Democracy was at stake. That was a call to arms. "He'll come home soon."

"I want him here when the baby's born. I want to know he hasn't changed his mind about us."

"He hasn't changed his mind, and he'll be here," Liz soothed. "The hospital and his patients are important to him. He felt that for four months he could be covered but he'll want to come back and take on his responsibilities here."

In what seemed to be a never-ending downpour Josh and Tim staggered from the town's improvised hospital to the shack that was their shelter for the four or five hours in each twenty-four that they took off for sleep.

"Thank God for the Russian doctors who arrived yesterday," Tim said, dropping on to the rumpled cot that had been his bed since they arrived here a week ago. The town had been pillaged by workers and peasants, who killed and maimed without discrimination. "But it would be nice if they spoke more English."

"They speak enough," Josh said tersely. "Tim, what the hell are we doing here?"

"Playing doctor." Tim sank back against the flabby pillow. "Saving lives." He paused, sighed. "Sometimes."

"You know what I mean," Josh accused. "Look what we're seeing! Sure, the Nationalists are responsible for unspeakable atrocities, but are the Loyalists any different? Murdering nuns and priests." He flinched in recall. "Innocent people, who've done nothing wrong in their lives. Remember that woman who died a couple of hours ago. A crucifix shoved down her throat, because she had two sons who were Jesuit priests."

"They're out for revenge." But Tim seemed uneasy.

"What do you want to bet that people back home are only hearing about the brutality of the Nationalists?"

"We don't know what they're reading back home. We haven't seen an American newspaper in over three months."

"We're suckers," Josh blurted out. "This isn't a war for democracy. It's a war between communism and fascism. Russia against Italy and Germany. We're suckers."

They started at a brisk knock on the door.

"Yeah?" Tim called.

The door swung wide and the officer in charge of the doctors came into the one-room shack. "More doctors just arrived," he said in his shaky English. These doctors were scheduled to relieve the current group. "Three from America, five from France. The Americans say if you want to leave, you can catch a ride on a plane taking off at dawn."

"Fly?" Tim grimaced. "Across the Atlantic?"

"We'll be leaving a week ahead of schedule." Josh hesitated. "But we might just be able to be home for Thanksgiving."

"Yeah," Tim jeered. "If we make it across the Atlantic."

"I'll take a chance," Josh said. "Where's the airfield? How do we get there?"

Liz drove Janet, Ellen and Wendy to Hampton Court on Thanksgiving morning. They'd have breakfast there. Victor had left before six in response to an emergency call from the hospital. "But I'll be at Hampton Court in time for Thanksgiving dinner," he promised. This was to be an all-day gathering of the family. Mama needed this, Liz thought compassionately, with Josh off in the midst of a civil war.

Annie Mae served them breakfast. After they'd eaten, Kathy and Wendy joined Francis in the sitting room. Each of the girls would take turns playing checkers with Francis. Caroline and Eric left with Ellen for the Thanksgiving morning service at the small country church. Liz and Janet settled themselves in the library.

"Oh, I forgot to tell you the latest news about Adrienne," Liz said. She and Adrienne encountered each other at intervals, of course, and the family had attended her grandmother's funeral eight months ago. But the long friendship had been disrupted.

"You mean besides the fancy shower she's planning for me next week?" An impish smile crossed Janet's face. Liz and she both realized the shower was Adrienne's effort to make peace with Liz.

"Adrienne's getting married again. To her ex-husband. She says she wants Tommy to have a father. I gather that at fourteen he's more than Adrienne can handle."

"She's probably decided the eighty-year-old millionaire she figured on marrying will never appear," Janet drawled. A wistful glint appeared in her eyes now. "I wish we'd hear something from Josh. I know you keep reminding me he's not part of the actual fighting, but he's right there where it's all happening. Even if he doesn't have a gun in his hand."

"He went to Spain for four months," Liz pointed out gently. "He's due home early next month."

"But he was so intense about the need to be there," Janet worried. "He might disregard the end of this leave if he feels so strongly about helping the Loyalists."

"We'll hear soon that he's coming home," Liz predicted, striving for optimism. "Once he's out of Spain and in France, he'll have no trouble getting a reservation on a ship bound for New York. Not at this time of year. Sugar, we'll all celebrate Christmas together."

With a mutual compulsion to hear about the war in Spain, first Liz then Janet fiddled with the radio in search of a news program.

"Nothing," Janet finally conceded, and they settled for a program of classical music on Station WSB.

Sophie came down to join them. She brought with her a yellow crocheted sacque she'd made for Janet's baby.

"It seems like yesterday that Caroline was pregnant for the first time, and I crocheted for the baby she was carrying. That was with you, Liz, then there was Josh, then Francis. And when you were pregnant, Liz, I crocheted for Kathy. And now for Josh and Janet's little one."

"It's beautiful," Janet said, "like a little bit of sunlight."

They heard a car pull up before the house.

"Mama and Papa and Aunt Ellen back from church," Liz said. "I'll ring for Jason to bring us coffee."

"We can't disturb Annie Mae on Thanksgiving morning," Sophie said, chuckling.

A few minutes later, after pausing to greet the two girls and Francis in the sitting room, Eric walked with Caroline and Ellen into the library.

"We should have a fire going," Eric said and crossed to the fireplace to move logs from the box at the side to the grate.

"Papa's the champion fire-maker in the family," Liz jested,

knowing he enjoyed the small ceremony of coaxing the pile-up of birch logs into a cozy blaze.

"It's quite cold outside," Ellen remarked. "I started a fire in the coal stove when I got up this morning. My other sleepy-heads hadn't got up yet."

While the others sipped at their coffee and watched the logs begin to crackle in the fireplace, they heard another car pull up before the house.

"Vic," Liz guessed, pleased that this time he would not arrive when the rest of them were already at the table.

"There are tantalizing aromas coming down the hall from the kitchen," Victor announced with an anticipatory grin. "I was smart – I just had coffee and toast for breakfast."

"Have more coffee," Caroline urged and reached to pour a cup for him. "It's a good two hours before we sit down for dinner." She radiated affection. "It's good you could get over early."

"This is a special Thanksgiving." Victor bowed towards Janet. "We'll soon be inviting a new Hampton in the world."

"Not too soon, I hope." Janet's smile was wry.

Liz stared into her coffee cup wihtout seeing. Would Victor never drop this obsession about their having another child? He was forty-six years old. But not too old, her mind traitorously taunted.

"Grandma –" Kathy burst into the room. "Is Annie Mae making a pecan pie? She knows I don't like pumpkin."

"There'll be pecan pie," Caroline promised.

"Is dinner soon?" Kathy was wistful.

"It'll be a while yet," Caroline conceded. "Go back and play checkers. We'll call you when dinner's ready."

Restless, Liz drained her coffee cup, crossed to gaze out a window. A taxi was drawing up before the house. Who'd be coming here today in a taxi? She waited for the passenger to emerge.

"Janet!" she exclaimed joyously. "It's Josh! He's home!"

Twenty-Nine

Liz rushed into the foyer with Janet close behind. The atmosphere electric. The others were on their feet, yet refrained from coming forward to welcome Josh. This was Janet and Josh's special moment. Liz pulled the door wide as Josh bounded up the stairs and across the veranda.

"Josh, how wonderful!" Liz rushed into his arms for a moment, then stepped back, feeling herself an intruder, while his eyes clung to Janet.

"You're home safe," Janet whispered, going to him. "I prayed for that every single night –"

Josh gazed at Janet with a mixture of incredulity and joy. His eyes dwelling on her extended midsection. "Jannie?"

"Our baby, Josh. Our son or daughter."

Unable to delay her welcome any longer Caroline dashed into the foyer. "Oh, Josh, what a wonderful Thanksgiving Day gift!" Tears in her eyes as she embraced him.

Now the others joined them in the foyer. The house reverberated with convivial spirits. And all the while Josh clasped Janet's hand in one of his.

"Mist' Josh?" Annie Mae's voice filtered down the hallway. "Now ain't this the perfect Thanksgiving!"

Caught up in the spirit of the day the family gathered in the library to await Annie Mae's summons to the dinner table. They listened with somber attention to Josh's assessment of the war in Spain.

"For most of us it was a crusade to save democracy," Josh said. "And we were right to answer that call. But democracy has no role in what's happening in Spain today." His face tightened in rejection and rage. "It's a battle between communism and fascism."

"I'm fearful of what lies ahead," Eric said after a moment. "With Hitler and Mussolini on the loose, and now Franco, the whole world is in danger. But I know, for me, the most urgent battle is for peace." He paused, took a deep breath and shared a glance with Caroline. "That's why I've decided not to run for re-election at the end of my term in the Senate." A ghost of a smile crossed his face in recognition of the sounds of shock from the others. "Nor will I be able to fulfill the General's dream of a Hampton in the White House. But I feel he'd understand."

Liz sat in silence amidst the flurry of questions the others hurled at her father. There was a new serenity about him, she marveled. At long last he was at peace with himself.

Liz didn't hear the lively conversation ricocheting about her. Her mind was making startling assessments. Victor wasn't at peace with himself. That accounted for his frenetic work schedule. He was trying to live two lives. He'd been blessed with a wonderful gift – he looked into the minds of troubled children and knew how to help them. But through the years there was less and less time to devote to what was truly important to him.

Like Papa throwing himself into politics when he wanted so desperately to focus on the fight for peace. But Papa and Mama knew how to deal with this. She and Victor had allowed themselves to be thrown off course. Her fault! She had always been so insecure, tormented through the years by her sense of worthlessness when her father, her mother, her husband were successful in their fields.

She'd been so wrapped up in her own grief when Debbie died that she had forgotten that Victor was hurting, too. When Victor needed her, she had pushed him away. When he wanted to make love, she saw this only as his desire to see her pregnant again.

Why had Victor allowed himself to be derailed from what was meant to be his life's work? Why hadn't she been there to prod him in the right direction? Why had she allowed that awful wall to develop between them? *How am I to tear it down?*

As was customary on Thanksgiving at Hampton Court, the family remained together for a late light supper. And as on other years, Kathy and Wendy wheedled second pieces of pecan pie from Annie Mae. In his usual fashion Eric reminisced about earlier Thanksgivings when the General was alive.

"Perhaps another member of the family will fulfill the General's dream." Sophie's gaze settled lovingly on Janet. "Josh knows what he wants to do with his life, and Francis would hate politics," she said diplomatically. "I don't think the country is ready yet for a woman president –" she aimed an apologetic smile at Kathy – "but perhaps Janet and Josh will provide us with a candidate."

"Hear, hear!" Victor chortled.

Shortly after supper they prepared to leave. The atmosphere mellow. But Liz's smile as she kissed her father and mother goodnight hid the inner anxiety that had haunted her since the moment her father said he was bowing out of politics. Was it too late to save her marriage?

Liz and Victor drove home in companionable silence. What was he thinking? Surely he understood how important it was for Papa to follow his private obsession. Did Victor realize what that could mean for him?

In their bedroom Liz and Victor prepared for bed. Though the steam heat was sufficient against the chill of the night, Victor busied himself at the fireplace grate. He knew how she liked to fall asleep with logs crackling in the fireplace.

"This was such a fine Thanksgiving," she said, crossing to stand behind him at the fireplace. "I mean with Josh coming home that way, and Papa telling us he was leaving the Senate to fight for peace –" She paused, searching her mind for the right words to help Victor make a similar decision.

"He's always fought for legislation that would lead to world peace," Victor reminded her. "But that isn't enough. He needs to give all of himself."

For a few moments Victor concentrated on thrusting kindling wood between the logs, then struck a match and touched it to the newspaper that laced the logs.

"That's beautiful," Liz said when flames shot up with brilliant color. "There's something so peaceful, so relaxing about burning logs." Now, she ordered herself. Talk to Victor now. "I'm so happy Papa decided to leave the Senate." Her heart began to pound. "He'll find such satisfaction, doing what's important to him." Don't spoil this. "Vic," she said, seemingly on impulse, "why don't you follow in Papa's footsteps. Do what's important to you. Turn your practice over to Josh and other doctors at the hospital. Set up a full-time clinic for troubled children."

Victor was startled, but she saw the yearning in his eyes. "Liz, how can I do that?"

"You owe it to yourself – to us, to concentrate on what gives you the most satisfaction. You're wonderful with kids. Everybody at the hospital says that. It's a gift that shouldn't be ignored. You can bring such happiness to people."

"It's impractical." He squinted in thought. "Most of those cases can't afford to pay for care. I have responsibilities – a family to support."

"We can cut back in so many ways," she insisted. This was a period when most people were forced to cut back to survive. "We can manage without two new cars every year. All the expensive gifts you give Kathy and me – they're lovely but unnecessary." She paused, searching for convincing words. "And I can come in to help you at the clinic – the way I did before Kathy was born. We were so happy in those days. I felt as though I was giving something to the world. I wasn't a parasite."

"Can we go back, Liz?" His eyes settled on her with a hungry glow.

"We can," she said urgently. "Vic, I've never stopped loving you –"

"There were times I was sure I'd lost you." He reached to pull her close.

"I've been so envious of Janet these last months," she whispered. "I want us to have another child."

"Liz, you're sure?"

"I've never been more sure of anything in my life. Debbie will always be part of us." She struggled for total honesty. "I thought I couldn't bear to carry another child and perhaps face another loss. Each time you reached for me in the night, I thought you meant only to make me pregnant again. I wouldn't let myself believe you came to me with love."

"I'll always love you, Liz," he murmured, caressing her hair as they swayed together. "Nothing can ever change that."

"Let's never go off-course again. Promise me, Vic."

"I promise."

After so many empty years, she exulted, she felt gloriously alive. Together Victor and she would build a whole new world for themselves. The security, the sense of worth, that she'd fought for all these years was hers.